Somewhere, out there in space, there were people flying their own spaceships, going where *they* directed and for their own, not the Master System's, purposes. Song Ching took for granted the subversion of the supposedly ironclad hold of the computers, but *this*—this was on a scale that she had never dreamed possible!

Who were these people who had such knowledge, and what else could they do that was impossible? The implications continued to mount in her mind. There might be many people, perhaps large numbers, living in cracks in the system known only to them, totally outside the Community and its controls.

The concept was exciting—but also frightening. If the gods could be so mocked, how less than absolute might their powers be?

By Jack L. Chalker
Published by Ballantine Books:

THE WEB OF THE CHOZEN

AND THE DEVIL WILL DRAG YOU UNDER

A JUNGLE OF STARS

DANCERS IN THE AFTERGLOW

THE SAGA OF THE WELL WORLD
Volume 1: *Midnight at the Well of Souls*
Volume 2: *Exiles at the Well of Souls*
Volume 3: *Quest for the Well of Souls*
Volume 4: *The Return of Nathan Brazil*
Volume 5: *Twilight at the Well of Souls:*
        The Legacy of Nathan Brazil

THE FOUR LORDS OF THE DIAMOND
Book One: *Lilith: A Snake in the Grass*
Book Two: *Cerberus: A Wolf in the Fold*
Book Three: *Charon: A Dragon at the Gate*
Book Four: *Medusa: A Tiger by the Tail*

THE DANCING GODS
Book One: *The River of Dancing Gods*
Book Two: *Demons of the Dancing Gods*
Book Three: *Vengeance of the Dancing Gods*

THE RINGS OF THE MASTER
Book One: *Lords of the Middle Dark*
Book Two: *Pirates of the Thunder*
Book Three: *Warriors of the Storm*
Book Four: *Masks of the Martyrs*

Book One of *The Rings of the Master*

LORDS OF THE
MIDDLE DARK

Jack L. Chalker

A Del Rey Book

BALLANTINE BOOKS • NEW YORK

A Del Rey Book
Published by Ballantine Books

Copyright © 1986 by Jack L. Chalker

Library of Congress Catalog Card Number: 86-90845

ISBN 0-345-32560-5

Manufactured in the United States of America

First Edition: June 1986
Eighth Printing: April 1988

Cover Art by Darrell K. Sweet

To all those who still believe
that without imagination we are nothing,
and without bold adventures and risks
nothing great of permanence is attainable.

TABLE OF CONTENTS

1. A BOWL FULL OF GODS

MOST PEOPLE BELIEVED THAT THEY WOULD EVEN-
tually go to heaven, even the ones whom everybody else
knew would never make it. Very few, however, believed
they could get there without dying.

The mountain had always fascinated him, but he had
never really understood the awe and fear it inspired in
almost everyone else. The Mountain of the Gods, the
Cheyenne called it, and to be sure it was peculiar.

Enormous, it had a conical, volcanic shape although
it was not, nor had it ever been, a volcano. It rose up in
the center of lesser, ordinary mountains, straight into the
sky itself. None had ever seen its peak and lived to tell
about it, for even on the clearest of days a dense ring of
clouds shrouded its top from view. The clouds moved
around the peak, usually clockwise, and sometimes seemed
to swirl and boil as they did so, but the great cloud ring
never dissipated, never thinned, and never revealed what
was beyond the five-and-a-half-kilometer mark.

Certainly there was good reason for the people of the

region to both fear and worship the mountain. It looked different, it behaved differently, and it had been there for as long as any of the People could remember. Why he felt more fascination than fear, and had felt that way even as a child, he couldn't say, although he had always been somewhat different from others.

He was a Human Being—what the subhumans of other nations called a Cheyenne—and he was a hunter, a warrior, and an adult of some rank. He shared his people's mystic sense of being one with nature, of the tangible and spiritual interrelationships between human and nature, and accepted most of what he had been taught. He did not, however, believe that gods lived inside mountains.

Both his chief and his medicine man knew of his obsession with the mountain, but they were unable to sway him. They argued that none who had ever dared to climb the sacred mountain had returned and that the spirits guarding its slopes were of the most powerful sort. He believed in spirits and in sacred ground, but he could not believe that the mountain was a part of this. The mythology alone was too new, by the way his people measured time, and quite unconvincing. He also knew that there were things of Heaven and things of Nature and things of men, and the mountain had always seemed to him to be the last of these, the legends and stories deliberately spread to prevent any questioning of the mountain's existence. It was on the People's land, but it was not a part of the People, nor had it been there in ancient times, as had the other mountains.

What the others saw as supernatural, he saw as insult and, perhaps, as sacrilege.

"We hunt the buffalo and deer, and we manage the land well for the Creator," the medicine man noted. "It is a good life we have here, a precious thing. The mountain is a part of things, that's all."

"It is *not* a part of things," the rebel argued. "It is unnatural but not supernatural. I know as well as you what it is like for those in the Council. There they live not by nature and the skill of their inner and outer selves but rather by machines and artifices. Everyone knows this, for they must return to us for a season every two years. This mountain is neither of god nor nature, but of men. You are a wise man. Surely in your heart you know this."

"I know many things," the medicine man replied. "I am not saying that you are not correct in this, but correct does not necessarily mean that you are right. You know, too, that the Creator once punished us for our pride and subjugated us not even to the subhumans but to demons with white faces who slaughtered the buffalo, slaughtered the People, and contained the rest on worthless land, condemning us to a living hell in which our very way of life was made impossible. Most of the white demons have been carried off now to the stars, and the rest given their own domain far across the Eastern Sea, but they left many works of evil here. You can still stand on peaks and see where they had blasted great roads through the mountains, and you can still go to many places and find the remains of their once-great cities."

"Then you are saying that it *is* true." The words were spoken with a curious sort of smile. "That the stories and legends of the mountain were created to keep people away. It is in fact something created by creatures of Earth, not heaven."

"Creatures of Earth and hell," the medicine man spat. "It is a foul place. It is perhaps the doorway to hell itself. Left alone, it does not bother us, and we do not disturb it. What if you challenge it, and it devours you as it devoured the few others who have gone to it? What is gained? And if you survive, and if you let loose the hordes of evil demons that it might imprison, then you might well bring down the wrath of the Creator upon all of us once more. Then much is lost."

"All that you say might be true, yet I will challenge it.

I will challenge it because it is there and because I choose knowledge over cowering like some child in a summer storm, its ignorance reinforcing its fear. It is the duty of Human Beings to conquer fear, not be ruled by it, or we become less than the subhumans. I respect the mountain, but I do not fear it, and there is but one way to show that to the mountain and to the Creator who raised us above all others in spirit. I do not accept your argument. If I do not go, then I show fear and lose my own worth. If I go and die, then I die in honor, in an act of courage. If I do not go because it might loose some demons upon the People, then the People as a whole will be subject to fear. If we allow ourselves to be ruled by fear in anything, then we are not the true Human Beings, the highest of creation, but are instead subject to something else—fear of the unknown. And if we are subjected to that, then we are subjugated and deserve nothing less, for if fear can rule us in this, it can rule us in other things as well."

The medicine man sighed. "I always knew I should have nominated you for Council training. You have the kind of mind for it. It is too late for that now, I fear, and too late for you. Go. Climb the mountain. Die with your honor and courage proven. I shall lead the weeping and lamentations for you and for myself, for erring in this way and having such a fine mind come to such a purposeless end. I will argue no more fine points of logic with you. There is a very thin line between stubbornness and stupidity, and I cannot shift someone back who has crossed that line. Go."

The climb was dangerous but not difficult, which was all to the best because his people had little in the way of metals and metalworking, and he had to make do with rope and balance and sure footing. He had been afraid that he would be ill-prepared, but the slope was rough and craggy, and with patience and by trial and error he found a sort of path upward.

He had dressed warmly, with fur-lined clothes made to stand the toughest test and a hood and face mask to help keep out the terrible cold even at this time of year. An experienced mountain man, he also knew that the air would grow thinner as he made his ascent and that he would have to take the climb very slowly to give himself a chance to become acclimated to the altitude. He could carry only so much water, but after a while snow would do. It would have to, for his salt-packed rations caused great thirst and dehydration.

As he grew closer to the great ring of clouds, he began to wonder if in fact any of the others like him had ever even gotten this far. There were snow slides and hidden crevasses here, and the problems of weather, acclimation, and provisions would stop anyone not totally prepared for them and fully experienced in high-altitude work. The climb was not really difficult, but its relative ease would fill a novice with confidence and cause him to ignore the many other threats.

So far it had been like any other mountain that could be climbed without piton or grappling hook, only taller. It looked neither as regular nor as strange when one was on it as it did from afar, and he began to wonder if indeed imagination might have played cruel tricks on the People.

But there was still that swirling mass of thick, impenetrable clouds that should not have been there, at least not all the time and certainly not at that altitude. He might doubt his preconceptions, but he did not doubt his resolve. He would go into those clouds.

Still, he almost didn't make it. Parts of him suffered from frostbite, and it seemed at times as if his eyes would freeze shut, but he finally made the base of the clouds. Here he knew he would face the greatest of all the dangers, for he might wind up moving blind in a freezing, swirling fog. He had always had the suspicion, now a fear, that the mountain might end right at the clouds and that he might well step off into space.

The clouds *were* dense, although not as much as he'd feared, and he had some visibility, although the wind was up, making every move treacherous. Still, there was no mistaking the fact that these clouds were nothing of nature; the air was suddenly relatively warm—above freezing, anyway—and he felt the pain of his frostbitten extremities along with a welcome relief that the fine mist that soon covered him remained a mist.

There was, however, a curious lack of odor. The clouds were getting their heat from somewhere, yet there were none of the earth-fumes he would have expected from a volcanic area. He continued his climb and was shocked to break out of the clouds only twenty or thirty meters up from their start. It was not the end of the clouds, really, but rather a break between two layers of cloud, formed by a trapped mass of warm air. Above him swirled a solid ceiling of clouds. He did not worry about them, though; the mountain did not extend any farther than a dozen meters beyond the end of the lower cloud barrier.

Up here it did at least *look* like a volcano, one of those great mountains of the west. The summit was a crater and appeared perfectly round, but it was less than a hundred meters across. It was as unnatural as were the clouds and the warmth. It was certainly the source of the heat: The air seemed to shimmer all around that basin. Laboriously he made his way, half walking, half crawling, to the edge, and with hurting eyes he peered down inside and froze in awe and wonder, his jaw dropping. For a moment he wondered if the climb had cost him his reason.

Faces . . . Huge faces coming out of the rock wall and extending all the way around the crater. Men's faces, women's faces, strange-looking, alien faces none of which seemed to have the features of the People.

Demon faces.

Giant faces extended out of the crater wall, carved of some whitish rock or some other substance. The noses alone were eight or more meters long; the mouths, though closed now and expressionless, looked as if they each could swallow a herd of buffalo.

Who carved such faces? he wondered. *And why?*

About forty meters below the faces was a floor that appeared to be made of very coarse cloth, although he was sophisticated enough to realize that it must be metal. The fine mesh of the grating allowed the warm air to rise from inside the mountain, creating the odd cloud effects and giving the region of the peak its moderate temperature. The mesh grate also had five circles painted on it, four in a sort of square surrounding a fifth in the middle, and there were designs in each circle. He could not make out the designs, partly because of the distance and the condition of his eyes and partly because there seemed to be material covering parts of all five circles. The material, whatever it was, was randomly scattered about and certainly not native to the place.

He stared again at the giant carved faces and felt a chill go through him. They were certainly both mysterious and awesome; most people who made it this far would worship them, knowing they had seen the faces of the sleeping spirits of the mountain. He counted twenty-five faces around the rim just inside the crater, all expressionless, all seemingly asleep, eyes closed. With a start he realized that there weren't twenty-five different faces but only five, each repeated four more times.

There was the man with short, curly hair, thick lips, and a broad, flat nose. There was a chubby, elderly-looking woman with puffy cheeks and short, stringy hair. There was a younger, prettier woman with a delicate face whose features in some ways resembled that of his own people but whose eyes seemed oddly slanted, almost catlike. There was a very old man with wrinkled skin and very little hair. And, last, there was a strange-looking man with a very long face, a lantern jaw, and a birdlike nose.

Each of these was repeated so that the same five, had

their eyes been open, would have been looking out, or down, at any point within.

Who were they? The ones who built this place? If so, why had they built it, and why here, and what was the source of the warmth below? Had they built this place and then added these faces as a monument to their work, a permanent sort of memorial? Would that question ever be answerable?

He paused, trying to decide what to do next. He'd challenged the mountain and won, and proved his point, but now what? He'd never taken it any further than this. Now it seemed idiotic to return below, reversing the climb, facing even more dangers in the descent than in the ascent if only because, going down, one was always a bit careless compared to facing the unknown ascent. To go down and say what? That there were twenty-five huge carved heads of five sleeping men and women in a crater, and below them a huge net through which blew warm air? Would he even be believed? Would *he* believe this sight if he weren't now seeing it, and would he believe an account of it if teller and listener were reversed?

Now what?

He needed something tangible to take from this place. He needed more than just this bizarre vision.

He needed to go down there.

But could he? Was there any place here to fasten a rope securely? Was his rope long enough and strong enough to bear him down and back out again?

He walked carefully around the crater until he spied something sticking out of the ground perhaps a meter and a half from the rim. He went to it and then stopped.

It was a metal stake. A piton, driven expertly into the rock and still containing the rotting remains of the rope knot, although not the rope itself. He was not the first to make it up here, that was clear, and he was not the first to consider the descent into that place.

The piton had not been traded from one of the metalworking nations: Although rusted, it was too smooth, too regular, too exact, and too strong. This was a thing of machines, of Council origin or higher. The rope, too, seemed strange and far too thick and complex to be hand-made.

He flattened himself, crawled along the line to the edge, and looked down between the old man's face and the face of the woman with the strange-looking eyes. What had happened? Had the rope rubbed against the crater rim and worn through? He thought again of the indistinct litter on the mesh floor below and sighed.

Rope. Rope remains—and human remains as well. Skeletal remains. All the others who had made it this far were still here.

This place, then, was some sort of trap. No, traps had been set, but this was far too elaborate to be established simply as a trap. These faces, then, represented the spirits set to guard whatever was down there. What powerful thing could be down there that would make people take such a risk?

He peered down, straining to see. Nothing on the grat-ing, certainly; either the object of his search was below that grate, or there was some way in—a door or some-thing. He saw what looked like a fresco, a design built into the wall at about a meter and a half above the grating. He made his way carefully around the rim, but there was only this one thing on the walls, nothing more. Otherwise, the pit was plain and featureless.

The faces were not to be trusted. Their features could hide almost anything; the eyes might open to reveal ports for weapons. However, the one who'd been able to use the piton had also thought of this and have descended quite clearly between two faces. Something had still cut the rope and dropped him to the grate below. The pit represented power—but the pit was also death. He was smart enough to know that going down in ignorance was no test of honor or courage, just stupidity. He backed off, then lay there and relaxed for a while and checked his provisions. There was little left, despite his careful rationing. It had taken five careful days to get this far, but it might well take two equally careful days to get back down.

He knew, though, that he would not tempt the pit. Perhaps others, someday, hearing of it, would explain it to him or give him its mysterious key, but he did not have it. To descend to the grate was death, either quick from falling or slow by being trapped down there with only corpses and statue faces for company.

He settled back and decided to get some sleep before attempting any real move back down to his own domains below. He was quite tired, and the warmth of the air beguiled him into rest, but he did not sleep easily. He dreamed, and the dream was a terrible one.

He was standing in the pit, looking up at the far-off opening above. The faces were there, but they were no longer dead faces but living things, eyes opened, looking down at him with mixed amusement and contempt.

He tried to look away and found himself deep in skeletons. He backed off in horror but found his feet tangled in ropes—his own and those of the dead—and fell with a crash onto the grate, coming face to face with grinning skulls. Skeletal hands on skeletal arms seemed to reach out for him. He yelled and somehow pushed them away, then got up against a side wall.

He looked across and saw the inlaid panel clearly now. The same five designs as were on the floor, but clear, with strange symbols that looked very much like the cave and rock drawings done by some of his own people. Inside each circle there seemed to be a small black square, as if a single tile had been removed.

The faces above now seemed to whisper to him with such force that they stirred up a great wind. They were not speaking his language, yet he somehow understood what they were saying.

"The rings . . . The rings . . . The five gold rings," they whispered to him. *"Do you have the rings?"*

"What rings are these?" he heard himself shouting. *"I know of no rings!"*

"He doesn't have the rings," one of the male figures whispered, and the other male faces took it up. *"No rings. No rings. He comes without the rings."*

"No fruit, no birds, no rings," the female faces chimed in.

"Then why do you come?" the male faces asked him.

"I come only to see what is here, to know why this mountain exists on my people's sacred land! I wish nothing else!"

There was a collective sigh from the faces. "We're sorry," they all responded, their voices echoing eerily around the pit. *"We're so very sorry. But, you see, reconnaissance is not allowed."*

And then the skeletons, those remains of the ones who have come before, stirred, and they seemed to come together and reach out for him, to make him one of them . . .

He awoke with a start, feeling the chilled sweat caused by the dream. The wind was up, and it seemed to be getting colder. The queer cloud cap above whirled at impossible speed, and the one below seemed to match it. He got hurriedly to his feet, not really thinking of anything but getting out of this place, getting away. It was neither cowardice nor a loss of honor to leave; this was beyond his power, an evil place of magic that would take far more than a warrior to combat. There was no honor in suicide, and that was what it was to remain here.

Although it was growing late in the day and the region below was bound to be bitterly cold, he did not hesitate to make his way down as far as he could. He quickly reached the swirling mass of clouds below and entered them, and was immediately engulfed in a maelstrom.

The winds were so powerful and so loud that they masked his scream as they blew him off the mountainside, hurling his body hundreds of meters straight down to the nearest rocks below.

2. THE CURSES OF HISTORY

WALKS STOOPED OVER, CHIEF MEDICINE MAN AND healer of the Hyiakutt nation, who always walked ramrod straight even now that he was in his seventies, trudged slowly up the hill to the hogan of Runs With the Night Hawks to make his routine courtesy call and his perennial complaint.

The flying saucers were stampeding the buffalos.

It was always pretty much the same, or had been in the more than two decades now that Hawks had taken Leave at this time and place. Despite his privileged position and rank, he was required to spend at least one-quarter of the year living with and as one of his people. Generally he didn't mind, except for minor ordeals like this and the fact that it really put a crimp on ongoing projects. While not impossible to deal with, the wrench of going from electric lighting, air conditioning, and computer filing and research to a log and mud hogan out on the plains with none of those conveniences was quite traumatic.

That, of course, was the point of requiring him to return. One of them, anyway.

He knew that most of the work of his profession had been accomplished by firelight and without any modern amenities, because these hadn't been invented yet. But the scholars of those ancient days had one major advantage that he did not: They did not know that such amenities and technology existed, or even could exist, so they were incapable of missing them.

The old medicine man showed the wear of his years in his wrinkled face and nearly white long hair, but his eyes showed a certain youthfulness and his gait a pride that said he wouldn't choose to be anywhere else nor doing anything but what he was doing.

"I greet you, Runs With the Night Hawks, and welcome you back to your lands and people," the old man said in the melodic tongue of their ancestors. "You have not changed much, although you look a bit saggy in the stomach."

The younger man smiled. "And I return the greeting, wise and ancient one. Welcome to my poor lodging and my fire. Please sit and talk with me."

It was a clear, starry night, with only a sliver of moon. The old man settled by his small fire, and Hawks sat opposite, as etiquette dictated.

"You did not happen to smuggle in any of the good *hooch*, did you, my son?" the old man asked in a mixture of tongues.

The younger man smiled playfully. "You know that it is forbidden to do such a thing, ancient one. There could be many problems for me if I did so."

The old man looked a bit uneasy, although they played this little game every year.

"However," Hawks added, "I would be honored if you would share some of my meager ration of medicinal herb." He took out a large gourd container and handed it over.

The old man took it, pried out the crude cork, and took

a big swallow. A look of complete rapture filled his face. *"Smooth!"* he rasped. "You *are* a sly one, boy!" He made to hand it back but was stopped by a gesture.

"No, it is yours. A gift, to ward off the chill."

The old man smiled and nodded thankfully. "We have some hidden stills that make some passable corn, but I am getting too old for it, I fear. One must have the layers of youth inside, for each drink of that removes one layer. I fear I have become layers of gut in debt to the Creator."

That out of the way, it was time to get into the next level of sociability.

"How does the tribe fare, elder? I have been away a while."

"Not too badly," the old man replied. "The nation numbers in the thousands, and the tribe now is almost three hundred. There were many births this past season, and few deaths. Of course, up north the Blackfoot and the damned Lakotas are overhunting their quotas, and in the south the Apaches are overrunning their borders—I fear we may have a war with one or the other before too many more seasons are out. The southern migration is peaceful, but those damned flying saucers keep scaring the buffalo, and there are many difficult and hungry days because of it. *We* must handle those greedy tribes, and we will, but surely you can do something about those cursed flying things."

Runs With the Night Hawks sighed. "Each year we have had this problem, and each year I, as tribal representative, lodge protests and am assured that routes will be changed and new studies made, but nothing is ever done. You say I am getting a bit fat, and it is true, but those who might change things are fatter, and the fat is not merely in their bellies." He sighed. "More than once I have wished I could convene a War Council to do to the administrators what we do with the Sioux."

"But they are of the People, too! They return at times

each year for a season, as you do. Why does this not give them some feel for the problems?"

"You know why. The Upper Council is dominated by Aztecs, Mayans, Navaho, Nez Percé, and others like that."

"Farmers and city dwellers! None of them could survive out here for a week let alone a season! It is a sad day when policy is made by old women. Particularly old women who were *born* old women!"

"You are old and wise. You know it is simply numbers. Those who are free to follow the buffalo and ride the winds of the plains can never equal the numbers of those who are farmers and craft-weavers."

The old man took another drink and sighed. "You know, boy, I often think that they should have gone all the way when they restored us to our lands and ways. My soul is never so filled as when I am out there, under the stars, watching the wind blow the tall grasses like some great sea and hearing the kind whispers of the Creator."

"If they did, we would have no horses," Hawks pointed out, not for the first time. "The old days were not all that wonderful. Women were married at first blood and had twenty children, only to lose most at birth or before the age of one. An ancient one was perhaps thirty-five. Diseases and infections ravaged all the People. It was a terrible price that they paid. Perhaps some flying ships scaring the buffalo from time to time is not too great a price to pay for losing the bad parts."

"I know, I know. You need not lecture me."

"I am sorry if I offended you. I am a historian, after all. It is my nature to lecture." He sighed. "I am away too long. I forget myself. You are my guest, and here I am quarreling with you."

"It is nothing. I am an old man, ignorant of much and riding the plains until my dust becomes one with that carried on the winds. We have had three returned to us from the Lesser Councils this past season. I am of a different world than they, but by choice. Do not mistake my frustrations for contempt. Each person must follow his own course. I am as proud of the accomplishments of those like you as I am when a young one becomes of age and passes the test and chooses the life of a warrior and hunter, and I mourn when those like you are returned to us against their will."

Hawks frowned. "Anybody I know?"

"I think not. A younger couple, Sly Like Coyote and Song of the Half Moon. I am not sure where they worked, but it was somewhere out beyond the setting sun. Their jobs were meaningless to me, although he was always good with numbers. Not like you. History I can more than comprehend. I could see no use in science which is not practical."

Hawks nodded gravely. It was one of the fears they all lived with, those who had been chosen, because of some talent or ability, to leave the tribes and go up to the Councils. Then one traded the simplicity of tribal life and the absoluteness of its culture for a far different existence, subject to a tremendous level of authority right up to the Masters themselves. There all the wonders and comforts were available, but the price was always to walk a careful line and never challenge, even accidentally, any part of the hierarchy. No one was so essential that he was not subject to others above, and no one was above being replaced.

He tried to remember the two but could not. Certainly if he discovered their parents and their lineage, he could at least place them, but it wasn't really worth the bother. What he would want to know—what they had done that had caused them to be returned—neither they nor anyone else he could question could tell him. The only thing certain was that it had been something serious. Even the most petty did not send down subordinates for arbitrary or personal reasons; the procedure was too involved, and the justifications had to be shown and proved up and down the line. Too much had been invested in everyone of Council level to allow anything less.

What had the young man been? Hawks wondered. A computer expert, perhaps? An astronomer, or physicist, or pure mathematician? Years of training, sweat, hard work—all gone. Replaced with other memories, other views, that made them good members of the tribe. Now a man who once, perhaps, dealt with complex equations and a woman who, at the very least, was expert in running his models on sophisticated computer equipment got up each morning and prayed to the spirits and the Creator and had no knowledge of or curiosity about anything beyond the tribe.

"*You* have not done anything to merit their fate, have you?" the old man asked quietly.

Hawks was startled. "Huh? I hope not. Why do you ask?"

"There has been a demon stalking about in the tall grass. We wonder who or what he is after. Certainly not any of us."

"A Val? *Here?*" The thought made him uneasy. He was an obvious target. "For how long now?"

"Four days, perhaps more. I think then that you cannot be the quarry, after all. You are here but two days, after all. They could have picked you up far easier before you arrived here, could they not?"

He nodded. "Yes, that is true. Still, I wonder what the thing can be after? I do not like the idea of one of them around, no matter who the object is."

He was less confident than he tried to sound. Why would anyone send a Val here? Could it be here on sheer suspicion? He'd been required to get a readout taken before he left to rejoin the tribe, but there were many such readouts being taken at any given time. They weren't all evaluated. There were only a few Vals on the whole planet; they couldn't possibly discover anything so minor except by sheer chance.

But chance had brought him what he now felt some guilt about, a chance perhaps more remote than picking his readout at random. No, it was still too much to believe. The old man was right. If suspicions were enough, they'd have picked him up before he left, or at least when he arrived.

The medicine man, sensing the younger one's disturbance, gently changed the subject. "You have not married. A man your age should have children by now."

The comment only partially broke his mood. "There are few women of the nation in the Councils and none who are the type who could stand being married to one such as myself."

"There are many attractive young women with the tribe."

"That may be true. We have always been blessed that way. But how could I take one of them? Wrench her from this life to the Councils? It would be taking a beautiful sturgeon and placing her in the midst of the high prairie. The same as I would be, after a while, returning here to live. My heart is always with my people, but my mind is a world away."

"Perhaps it is too far," the old medicine man responded. "We will be leaving soon, and only a small number of us will remain when the first snows come. Even when you are with your people, you stay apart. You come as we leave, and you spend little time with the Four Families chosen to remain. You build mountains between yourself and your manhood, between yourself and your people. I will send someone over to help you prepare here and to take some of the routine burdens."

"No, I—"

"Yes," the medicine man responded with the finality of power. He *had* the power and the training. The tribal chief was more of a military officer; the medicine man was the politician. He had made the decision to send Hawks out to be educated and trained and had nominated

him for Council. He was very low in the hierarchy of
human civilization, but he was still above Hawks.

They spent a little more time in pleasantries and gossip,
sharing information and talking about old friends, and at
last the old man yawned and bade his farewell. Hawks
watched him vanish quickly into the darkness and the
winds, and thought.

He *did* love it here, even when the tribe migrated slowly
southward, leaving only the Four Families to represent
symbolically the tribe and its territorial rights. They did
not own the land; none of the People had any real belief
that land could be owned at all. But they were a small
tribe in a small nation, surrounded by larger and more
powerful nations, and their way of life depended on main-
taining territorial rights.

Perhaps the old man had made a mistake, he thought,
feeling both the communion with the land and his isolation
within it. It would not be the first one, certainly. My heart
and my blood are here, in the land and the winds.

There *had* been a woman once—an unobtainable
woman. She had been beautiful and brilliant, a crack
anthropologist specializing in the plains tribal systems that
had bred them both. When he was young, he had been
obsessed with her, for she had been everything he had
ever dreamed of in a woman, a wife, a partner. She had
mistaken his love, though, for friendship and flattery, and
he'd been too shy to force anything lest he alienate and
lose her if she rejected him—which, of course, she had,
indirectly, by marrying a sociologist from the Jimma tribe
of the nation. She had been so happy, she'd wanted him
to be the first to know.

There had been nothing then but work, and he had
thrown himself into it with a passion, channeling all his
energies into productive paths to stave off thoughts of
suicide or tinges of madness. Perhaps he *was* mad. He
had often suspected it, but he knew they wouldn't flag

someone for a madness that actually increased work and production.

Her name was Cloud Dancer, and for two days he'd tried to make her life miserable to no avail. She was cute, thin, a head shorter than he, and she appeared slightly built although it was hard really to tell in that loose-fitting, traditional dress she wore. She was thirty but looked younger by far, and if inquisitiveness was any indication, she was bright as well. She was also something of a dynamo: Any Outsider notions that native American women were passive would be blown out of the water in ten minutes with her.

She had taken one look at his little hogan and exclaimed, "This house smells as if only dead things lie within it! I do not understand why men will abide filth when it takes but a few moments to shake what is nature back to the winds and let the spirits of life crowd out the dead space!"

His protests that he didn't mind things the way they were fell on deaf ears, and soon she was taking out his blankets and extra clothing to be washed or aired as the material required. When she tried to get his straw mattress out the door, he finally had to help, and he found himself involved in the cleanup if only to save what was important to him. She also brought some earthen cookware and some food from the Families' camp and proved a very fine cook indeed. Her seasonings were expert, though the spices were as hot as hell to his palate, which was accustomed much of the time to blander fare. But he wasn't going to admit to that to her.

Until Withdrawal, he really couldn't provide for himself out here in his own native land. There was the irony of it, and also why so much had to come from the Four Families at the start. His salt box, large enough for a medium-sized deer, was full, all right—of salt. He found himself being insulted and badgered to go hunt for himself, and while he knew he wasn't up for deer and particularly not for buffalo, he did actually manage to catch three fairly good sized catfish in the river.

The fact was, he was beginning to like her and to like a little of the order and domesticity she brought. It was almost like being married, although she went home at night and they did not, of course, share the pleasures of the bed. It was over the hot, spiced fish stew she'd created that he finally gave in and warmed to her. She spoke only Hyiakutt and had lived her life with the tribe, but she had an odd mixture of old and new in her world view. She lived in a supernatural world where spirits dwelled in everything, yet she knew there was a wider world and a different one.

In some ways, she was also a victim of that culture. She had married at fifteen, not an uncommon thing in the tribe. It had not been an arranged marriage, as was the custom, because she had lost her father a year before in an accident and her mother had died even earlier in childbirth. The child had not survived, either. There were no orphans in the tribe; she had been adopted by close kin, but her uncle was old and partly crippled and poor. Screams Like Thunder wasn't the ideal catch, either; an older man not given to ambition and with a nasty temper, he was not a warrior and hadn't really ever wanted to be. He was, in fact, a Curer, which was really an assistant to the medicine man, keeping all the paraphernalia in good shape and on hand and aiding in the preparation of herbs and other medicinals. It was not exactly a high-ranking job, but it was as high as he was ever likely to go.

He hadn't been much of a lover, either. His spirit was willing, even eager, but his flesh was, if not weak, best described as mostly limp. He couldn't stand the idea that he could not perform in this most basic of masculine areas, especially since he didn't have the warrior's proof of manhood by deed. He therefore encouraged—actually ordered and arranged—a set of liaisons with a gentle half-wit who tended some of the animals and socialized very little. She had kind of liked the poor man, whose mind was very childlike but whose physical abilities were quite mature. Her husband had, by circuitous questioning and feigning idle curiosity, discovered that the stand-in lover's mental limits were the result of an injury at birth and were not likely to be passed on to any children he might sire, and that had settled it.

In the end, suspecting that her husband planned, once she had conceived, to kill the surrogate to eliminate all chance of the affair being discovered, she had found herself unable to go through with it no matter what the pressures. The situation had gotten ugly, and her husband had beaten her and hauled her to the man and then beaten her again. The kindness she'd shown the unfortunate animal handler had been greater than the poor man had ever known, and he wasn't so childlike that he didn't understand what was going on. He rushed to protect her, there was a fight, and in the end her husband was dead, his skull crushed.

She had gone to the medicine man and told him everything, and he'd done his best to cover it all up, but this was a small and closed community, and no major scandal could be completely hidden. As usual, suspicion and rumor had gotten the facts wrong—although in the ways of the tribe she should have done what her husband commanded to salvage his honor—and it was generally believed that she had been caught cheating on her husband and that the husband had paid the price. She was made a social outcast, a tainted woman, and was relegated to being a nonperson, a servant, one without property or standing.

Hawks understood well now why the medicine man had selected her for him, although he didn't appreciate being dragged into all this. She was far too full of life to remain a servant, far too bright to waste, but her only hope of status was remarriage, and she had little chance of competing with all the younger, virginal women from good families with the means to provide generous dowries.

"You are far too gloomy," she admonished him over the stew. "You sit and brood, and dark storm clouds gather above your head. You will not live a second time, you know. You have let the foul spirits eat at your heart, so you do not know what you might have had."

He stared at her in wonder. "Do you not ever feel that way? You have so much more cause than I."

She shrugged. "Yes, of course. It lurks around me all the time and creeps in and takes a bite of my spirit every time I forget to guard against it. Still, there is much beauty in the world, and only one life to see it. If the sorrow crowds out all the joy, then that is worse than death. You are less excusable than I, for you have less cause for it."

This was getting uncomfortable. It was time for a change of subject.

"Tall Grass told me you were an artist," he said. "A good one."

She shrugged again and tried to look modest, but clearly she was pleased. "I weave patterns, do necklaces, head-bands, jewelry, that sort of thing. I have also made some inks from the sands of the south plains and done some drawings on treated skins and light woods. It is nothing special, though. My gifts are modest, my work for me."

"I should very much like to see some of it. Will you bring what you think are some of your best works the next time?"

"Of course, if you like, but do not expect much. I should like, though, to try some small drawings on paper. Until I saw your things in there, I had not realized what a wonder paper is." She didn't really say "paper" but rather something that came out as "thin and flexible sheets of wood," but his mind immediately translated.

"I will find you some, and some writing-sticks as well," he promised her. He'd brought a rather large supply of pencils.

She took to them with almost childlike delight, and she was good—damned good. The kind of natural talent that couldn't see its own gifts, because it was so natural, so easy to her that she could hardly comprehend anyone not being able to do it. A stroke here, a stroke there, a bit of shading just so, and suddenly there was a forest scene, or a landscape, or startling portraits of the men and women of her tribe.

A few days later, the Sickness came upon him even as he sat there letting her do his portrait. It came on slowly at first, as it always did, then built rapidly over the next day and a half. He dreaded it, as they all dreaded it who had to return for a season, and it was all the more frustrating because there was nothing to be done about it.

Cloud Dancer became alarmed as he began to develop chills and fever and to throw up anything he'd taken in. "I will send for the medicine man," she told him, but he stopped her.

"No. He can do nothing. This is a terrible thing, but it will pass. For a while I will grow even sicker, and I may become as mad as if possessed by a demon. You must stay away for your own sake—there is nothing you can do until it passes."

She was both puzzled and unconvinced. "What is it that makes you so? You speak as if you knew this was coming."

"I did. It always comes. It must. Up—in Council— we are given many medicines that can do wondrous things. Make us smarter, stronger, healthier, and a hundred other things. But there is a price. There is always a price. Our bodies grow used to the medicines. When the medicines finally go out of the body, as all medicines do sooner or later, the body is not prepared. It has forgotten how to act without the medicines. Until it learns, it will not work well, and I shall be very sick in body and spirit."

She did not fully understand, but she did know that there were medicinal herbs that could keep one sleepy and ease pain, and she sought them. The Four Families had only a young apprentice medicine man, but he knew some of the things that might help and accompanied her back to Hawks's lodge. It took more than the two of them, however, to handle him. The quiet, introverted intellectual had turned into a raving, hallucinating lunatic.

Four strong, young warriors from the Families were required to get him tied down and subdued—and even they did not escape without bruises and blackened eyes. The herbs, however, did have a quieting effect.

Cloud Dancer remained with him for the ordeal, which lasted three and a half days, administering the medicines and seeing that he did not do himself injury struggling against the restraints. It was like keeping company with a wild demon, a horrible spirit of the evil netherworld, but, assured by the medicine man that this state was transitory, she stuck it out.

"It is the custom not to let the tribes see this madness," the medicine man told her, "for they might mistake it for something far worse, although in truth it is agony."

"Will he be—changed—at the end?" she asked nervously.

"Some. He will be more of the People and less of the Councils. His Hyiakutt nature and upbringing will take command. Otherwise he might not survive out here through the season. The changes will seem far greater to him than to us. He will be weak and crave the medicines for a while, but that, too, will pass."

When Runs With the Night Hawks was still just a boy, the medicine man of his tribe had identified him as having certain talents and aptitudes that made him better suited for Council than for tribal life. Special tutelage was arranged to check this out and then, when it proved true, to prepare him for a different calling. The Hyiakutt, like most North American nations, had no written language, so he was taught a standardized modified Roman alphabet and sent away for special training in reading and writing. When he was of age, he left his family and his tribe and nation and went to Council schools, where he excelled in many subjects. He became, after intensive schooling, an urbanized modern man in a technological setting, as was necessary for taking a job with the Councils.

In order to keep Council personnel in touch with and understanding of the majority of people for whom they were responsible, all such select officials were required to spend at least a season—three months—every two years with their tribe, living as the tribe lived. To facilitate this "leave" and also to make certain that these people could survive in such a situation, a template was impressed upon their minds to remain hidden until triggered by Withdrawal.

Hawks awoke feeling absolutely lousy but in control of himself once more. It would take a while more for the full effects of Withdrawal to fade, but after so many times he was able to at least live with those effects and accept them. He opened his eyes and saw Cloud Dancer sitting there, patiently working on a traditionally patterned blanket. She looked over at him and put down her work.

"Hello," he managed, his voice hoarse. He no longer had to concentrate to speak his native Hyiakutt; it was now his primary language, the one in which he thought and which in turn shaped his thought patterns. The other tongues were still there, but now he had to consciously translate them. "How long have you been here?"

"Since the start," she responded matter-of-factly. "You were very, very sick. How do you feel now?"

"As if a raging herd of buffalo had done dances upon my entire body," he told her honestly. "I—" He halted a moment. "I am restrained. That bad, was it?"

She nodded. "You are sure you are over this?"

"The madness is gone if that is what you mean. The rest will come with work and time. If you are asking if it is safe to loosen my bonds, the answer is yes."

She got a knife and cut the strong straps, which had been knotted far too well and too firmly to be untied.

He needed assistance to get up and groaned with pain

and dizziness when he did, but he felt the need to get himself back into condition as quickly as possible. Where before it had hardly mattered, now it seemed somehow dishonorable to depend upon Cloud Dancer or the Families one second more than was necessary for food or other supplies.

"I am getting old," he told her. "Each time it takes longer and is harder to get through. One day I will find it impossible to return to Council on the thought that this would kill me. I almost feel so even now."

"Why do you just not take their medicine?" she asked him, genuinely curious.

He gave a dry chuckle. "I cannot refuse. Even now I would gladly take them all in a moment were they offered me. There are things, once taken for long periods, that forever enslave the body. I am no coward, nor am I dishonored by this fact. I was chosen to go and made to take them. Without them I could not have done what I had to do, learn all I had to learn, in the time given to me. The medicines are tools, just as the loom is a tool, or the spear, or the bow, without which the job for which I was chosen could not be done."

"Do you love this job so much, or is it that the Council way of living is to you a better way than our way?"

He shook his head. "No, no. I do love the work, for it is honorable and good and important to everyone, including the nation and the tribe. As to the way of life— this one is pure and basic, the way the Creator meant us to live. It is free. *Their* way is dependency and confinement. It is not natural. It is simply a price that must be paid in order to preserve our ways here." He sighed. "Can you help me up? I would like to get some air."

She tried to help him up, and he made it part way but then collapsed back on the bed, pulling her down on top of him. He started to mumble apologies, but she laughed them off.

"So, is this a proposition or a proposal?" she teased. "I have been pulled by strength into your bed."

"I am—sorry..."

"Why? Am I so ugly, so undesirable that you would not want me?"

"No, now, wait a moment! I didn't mean..."

She saw his discomfort and found it satisfying, but she also knew he was still weak and dehydrated, as well. She got up and looked at him. "You stay where you are. I will prepare some broth and herb teas that will get some strength back into you. I want to see what you are like when *you* are whole and natural."

The speed with which he regained his strength and clearheadedness was in no small part due to her help and attentiveness. He knew also that she'd been the one to summon just the right help when he'd needed it, and even through the delirium he had been aware that she'd been there all the time, tending him and speaking soothingly to him.

He didn't really understand why she did it. Certainly he was someone unusual, both familiar and foreign at the same time, but that didn't really explain it all. It certainly wasn't his virile good looks. He was, in fact, rather ordinary looking or a bit worse, his skin mildly pockmarked with scars from a childhood imbalance. It might be because she was looking for any way out of her circumstances, although he didn't think she had that much deviousness in her. Finally he simply asked her.

She thought about it. "Partly it is because I am doing something useful. Partly it is because you treat me as a person, not a thing, and you do not judge."

That was simply something he had not considered. Oddly, he felt some anger. Curse you, ancient one! he thought to himself. I have needed her these past days, and now it is clear that she needs me as well.

He thought about her a lot over the next few days, even when she wasn't there. The trouble was, he *did* want her, *did* have a need for someone in his life, but there was no getting around the two worlds. He could not stay, not this time. There was simply too much important work left to do, work that meant much to the future of the Hyiakutt as a nation. There was no rule against his marrying her, but there were rigid rules barring her from access to the medicines and machines that would allow her to adapt, at least somewhat, to the terribly different way things were there. She would be isolated in a place where almost no one spoke her language and where medicines did the only work for which she was qualified. Yet it was impossible to explain it to her. She had never even seen plumbing, let alone a toilet; how to explain disposable clothes and dialing up a meal?

Worse, how to explain that the Sioux in Council were not contemptible subhumans and mortal enemies but rather associates who were sometimes pains in the rear?

Once through Withdrawal, he'd always just let himself go and enjoyed his Leaves. Now the medicine man had placed a terrible burden on him—and not totally in ignorance, either—and really spoiled things.

And yet he wanted to see her, wanted her company, wanted *her*. He took to late-night brooding outside, surrounded only by the trees and the stars, trying to sort out his own mind and his courses of action. And, one of those nights, he had a visitor.

He heard a quiet sound behind him, one that few others would hear, and he turned and peered into the darkness past the campfire.

He saw it after a moment and simply froze, staring at the dark form within the lesser darkness.

It knew that he'd seen it, and it moved slowly, confidently, into the light of the slowly dying campfire.

The thing was big—two meters tall—and roughly manlike in appearance, made of permanently glistening blue-black material. Its face was a mask with two trapezoidal openings for eyes that were the color and sheen of polished obsidian. It moved with a catlike quiet and grace that seemed impossible for one so huge.

"Good evening," the Val said in a pleasant middle soprano that sounded very human indeed. It spoke in Hyiakutt, not because it had to but because by doing so it demonstrated in two words that it could easily have overheard all that Hawks and the old medicine man had said. It spoke, too, in an incongruous female voice, which told him immediately that its business wasn't something to do directly with him. The thought did little to calm him.

"Good evening to you," Hawks responded, trying to keep the dryness in his mouth from showing in his speech or manner. "May I ask what brings you to my fire?"

"Routine business. You are the only Outsider here at this moment or within many days' distance. Legally, anyway. As such, you provide something of an—attraction."

"You seek one of my people?"

"No. Carmelita Mendelez Montoya is her name."

His eyebrows rose. "Español?"

"No. Caribbean."

That was almost as outlandish as Spanish. Most of the islands had not been restored, but rather new societies had been created out of the cultures that were there. There was, simply put, no native stock surviving there to restore.

"What would a Caribe be doing up here?"

The Val switched to Classical English but still maintained that woman's voice. "Running. It is a very large, desolate land, easy to get lost in. We spotted the wreck of her skimmer on satellite photos two weeks ago. Unfortunately, by the time I was dispatched to the scene, it appeared that everything from people to herds of thundering buffalo had been through there. Since then I have picked up signs that she has been moving in this direction, but nothing concrete. The area has been sensitized to those not keyed to it. She cannot get out. She has already lasted far longer than I would have thought she could. Still, the region here is lightly populated and it is monitored. She has not as yet contacted anyone. Her supplies must be running out by now. She will have to make contact with someone soon or starve."

"And you think I'm a likely candidate. Why? And what's she done?" He, too, switched to English; although translating was something of a struggle for him, English was more convenient for the sort of words needed to put the conversation into less than metaphorical statements.

"What she has done is irrelevant. I only apprehend. I do not judge. As you should well understand, it is best that you *not* know, in any case. As to why you, it is simple deduction. She is physically and culturally out of place. She speaks Español, some Creole, and Caribe dialects of them at that. I have determined that she must have been close enough to see your skimmer put down and discharge before leaving. That marks you as someone from Outside. The civilization of your own people is so different from hers, it must look to her like bands of savages. She will be frightened to go to them and unsure as to what help they could offer if they didn't kill her or eat her."

Even a Val couldn't be allowed to get away with that one. "My people are a highly cultured race. They kill only when they have to, and eating people would be repugnant!"

"I mean no offense, and I know what you say is truth. I apologize for any slur you might have inferred. Understand that I have her inside of me. I am going on the way *she* thinks."

He nodded, somewhat mollified. If he hadn't wanted to meet this fugitive before, he wanted to meet her even less now. The Val, however, was correct. Inside its head was the complete readout of this Montoya's entire record, essentially a copy of her memories and personality up to no more than a few months ago at best. That was the true edge the Val had and the reason why it was alleged that no one ever escaped them. And few had.

"Do what you have to do, but I do not wish to be

involved," Hawks told it. "Apprehend her away from here. Unlike some people, I treasure the time I have in my homeland. This intrusion is not welcome."

"I understand, but you must understand me as well. There is only one of me. There are only three of my kind in this whole system. I can compute probabilities based upon all my information, but there are always unknowns, variables beyond my ability to include. I cannot merely stand around here in the shadows staking this area out. I can only come here and state that if you see her or she contacts you, you will calm her and shelter her here and when possible go down to the Four Families' camp and use the emergency trigger."

Hawks bristled, partly in frustration. He didn't want to turn this unknown woman, or anyone, over to a Val or anyone else, and now he would have to. When they finally caught her, they'd do a readout and know if she'd talked to him and, if so, what had been said. If they didn't like the way he had performed, the next readout taken would be his.

"I resent being placed in this position," he told the creature. "This is my land, my people, my way. My parents are buried near here. This is not the Councils; this is not the Presidium. Neither you nor she have any right here. And on this land, in this time, I am Hyiakutt, and I obey Hyiakutt law and custom. If she presents no danger to my people, I will, if she comes, offer her food and shelter as I would anyone from a strange nation passing through. If you come, she must go with you, but I will not be your surrogate. Not here."

The great hulking form of the Val was silent for a moment. "Fair enough," it said finally. "But I would not advise you to probe why she is here or why she is wanted. If I cannot find her, I cannot control her. Every moment she is near puts you at risk. Weigh that. I am not well versed in the details of every tribe and nation in this area, but I am unaware that any requires suicide to protect a stranger. Good night to you, sir."

The great creature turned and was quickly and silently lost in the darkness. Hawks continued to stare after it long after it had left, and he did not go in to sleep for another hour.

All these complications! he reflected with self pity. It was almost as if the world were conspiring against him.

Still as death, Hawks had been waiting in an almost trancelike state for over an hour as the chill, predawn mist rolled over him. Still, he was determined. After four mornings, he was going to get himself a deer.

There was a sudden rustling off to his right, and his eyes came open, every sense suddenly alert. He risked a look and for a moment saw nothing. Then, barely visible in the mist, he saw them: two, no, three deer, all yearling does, slowly wandering in search of good food to eat while the mists still protected them.

Slowly, by feel, he threaded his arrow and brought his bow up, so silent that the deer could have no idea he was there. The wind, too, was right, masking any scent they might pick up. He picked his spot and drew back the arrow tight, then froze, waiting for them to come to him.

It seemed an eternity before they started to move in the right direction. He practiced his breathing and tried to ease his tense muscles. The lead deer seemed to sense something wrong and stopped for a moment but then continued on, right into his line of fire.

Now! The arrow was loosed and struck the deer in the side. The animal reared, and the other two bounded away, but he was quick and got a second arrow up and flying before the wounded animal, still in shock, could make a move.

Then he was out and throwing his balanced rope at the deer's hind feet even as it began to move. It went down with a crash and lay there thrashing while he carefully administered the fatal arrow.

It was a good, clean kill. A lot of meat and smooth doeskin for a better lining on his clothes. He knew he had to move fairly quickly, though. The sun would be up in less than an hour, and the scavengers would also be out, spoiling the kill. He had tied his horse a good hundred meters down and away, but he turned now to go quickly and get her and assemble the wood and skin stretcher so that the deer could be rolled onto it and carried home.

He made his way directly, ignoring the paths, but less than halfway there he discovered something else and stopped dead, all elation, even all thoughts of the kill, suddenly gone.

The body had been there for some time. It was dressed in a tight black synthetic outfit and leather boots. It was not a pretty sight; the scavengers had been at her, and the flesh was crawling with insects and maggots.

He knew in a minute who it must be and understood why the Val had been out so long with nothing to show. She could have lain here until she rotted completely before being found without a search party.

In her stiff hand was a briefcase barely touched by the elements busily adding her to the woodlands. She also wore a standard emergency pack on her back, but from the looks of it she'd had little chance to use it, and it was filled with creepy-crawlies.

He had to break the fingers to release the briefcase. He backed away from her and the grisly feast that had been going on perhaps for weeks and examined the brief-case itself. It was not a courier model but something one would have procured for personal use. Like most man-ufactured items these days, it was cheap, and, while it had a lock, it did not appear booby-trapped. Almost on impulse, he pushed on the two red points inset in the case and was startled to hear it unlatch. The thing wasn't even locked!

There was no way anyone could have resisted looking inside. Some were the usual sorts of things one might expect of a woman traveling in unknown territories—some maps, an atlas of North America, even a guidebook to the Plains Nations with sample phrases. He wasn't surprised to find that the Hyiakutt weren't even mentioned.

Beyond those, there was a small wooden box with an antique key lock, the miniature key still in it, and an ancient-looking thick book that seemed about to fall apart at a touch. He examined it with the care of a professional historian. The pages were copies, not originals, which was just as well, as the date on the book, recorded in a firm hand, was more than six hundred years old. Still, even the copy was old—perhaps a century, perhaps more.

It appeared to be somebody's journal or diary. He put it aside for a moment, reluctantly, and turned to the case. The small key turned easily, and the lid came up. He was unprepared for the sight, however.

Jewelry. Gems, some in exquisite settings, many looking like heirlooms. There was some doubt in his mind that the things were real. Did diamonds and rubies and emeralds come that large? And was that pure gold?

He closed the box and relocked it. Clearly the diary or whatever it might be was the reason why somebody very important would requisition and dispatch a Val to this area. The jewels—suddenly he understood. A universal currency of sorts. A Caribe would think like that, not realizing how little such things meant to the People of North America. Still, it was not a bad choice at that, for they were finished gems and would be works of art in any tribal council.

Suddenly he was very aware of his situation. He replaced the briefcase and almost replaced the jewels, then changed his mind. If the Val *did* find her, it would see the broken fingers and the detached briefcase and would know that someone had found her first. If the jewels were *not* missing, it was as much as pointing a sign straight to his door.

He had not yet decided what to do about the book. For anyone who could read it, and particularly for a historian, it was irresistible, yet reading it could mean death—or worse. He would not make that final decision immediately. Instead, he continued on down and got his horse, then went back along the regular trail to his fallen deer and did what he had originally intended to do. Only, under the carcass, on the unmarked side, where no blood would flow, he hid the jewel box and the book.

He knew now that he had a decision to make that made his previous problems seem like child's play.

3. TRUTH AND CONSEQUENCES

THE MOUNTAINS OF WESTERN CHINA WERE AS REMOTE and forbidding as any in the world and impossible to monitor or control effectively. There were no permanent natives to the region; the nearest settlements were far down the slopes and forty kilometers or more from the spot where the raiding party now stood, many of its members equipped with breathing apparatus to help them in the rarefied atmosphere where split seconds might mean living or dying.

Colonel Chung, the old pro soldier in dark-green battle uniform, heavy boots, and cap, had a cigar stuck out of the side of his mouth. He needed no breathing gear; he sat in a skimmer, a dark, saucer-shaped craft that was rigged for totally silent running. It hovered there in the air while many others, deployed around the seemingly unbroken high cliffs of the mountains, disgorged soldiers and equipment. Chung was thankful that the spot was so remote; here he was not handicapped by Cultural Zone restrictions and could use his best and most modern equipment.

"They are good, I'll give them that," the colonel remarked for the benefit of anyone who could hear him there in the command module section of the skimmer. "I can't imagine where they even got their energy sources up here, let alone how they shielded them."

Song Ching looked at the gray-purple rock walls and understood what he meant. To go to these lengths, this group must have had something really important to hide and work on, something that, like all technology, required power. Satellites overhead could monitor even the smallest differences in temperature, pressure, and energy below, even through the densest clouds, and when they spotted something in an unauthorized spot, they immediately flagged security on the ground. Technologists' cells were rare in this day and age, but the few who remained were the best.

She was the sort of woman men fantasized about: small but perfectly proportioned, her face one of classical Han beauty, her gestures and movements somehow always erotic. Her looks masked her extreme intelligence: Her IQ off the measurable scale, and she was an authentic genius whose mind worked so fast and on so many levels it often seemed more computerlike than human. She was not without flaws; as the oldest child of the chief administrator of the Han district, she was spoiled rotten, and her intellectual and physical development had not been accompanied by any real emotional growth; there she was almost childlike, a situation her parents kept excusing because of her age, although she had just turned seventeen.

The colonel did not like having her there, but she'd been forced upon him by his superiors. They didn't know what this cell could be working on, and they needed her fine mind to figure it out before it was either destroyed or confiscated. Others might have done as well, but as the daughter of the chief administrator she had pulled her own strings to get here. It was an escape, however temporary, from her luxurious prison, from the reality she didn't particularly like.

She did, however, appreciate the irony of her being here, for she herself was the result of illegal technologists, her looks and her intelligence achieved through elaborate genetic manipulation. Like all the administrators, not just on Earth but throughout the Community, her father chafed at the restrictions placed upon him and his power and dreamed of some sort of end run. His own solution was an attempt, at great risk to his position and his life, to breed a superior line that might eventually be bright enough and fast enough to figure a way out of the trap the human race had woven for itself. Song Ching appreciated the goal and approved of it, but she did not like her own role, which was not to find that solution but to breed those who might.

"Burners locked on!" someone reported over the ship-to-ship channel. "All ships in place, troopers in position and shielded. Awaiting orders to proceed."

"Commence firing," Colonel Chung ordered without hesitation.

Immediately the five skimmers rose to preset positions, now visible to whatever lookout devices the cell might employ, and opened fire with bright rays of crimson and white that struck the rock face and began to cut through it. Ships' computers now had control, and once penetration had been achieved, the five attack skimmers moved in an eerie ballet, cutting through the imposing rock face as if it were butter.

Just before the circle was completed, a different skimmer rose and shot out a purple tongue of energy which struck the center of the cutout, and as the entire area was separated the thick purple ray receded, pulling the rock cutout with it.

Suddenly revealed was a honeycomb of tunnels melted through the rock. It reminded Ching of a glass-sided ant farm, although there did not appear to be any "ants" here.

Now the troops, two hundred of them, sprang from cover on ledges and slopes opposite the target and flew into the air using null-gravity backpacks and small compressed-air steering jets.

"It's *very* large," she noted to the colonel. "I wonder why anybody who built something that large wouldn't defend it."

"They'll defend it," he assured her in an absent tone, his attention on his status screens and on the view out the control port. "When they find that their escape exits are blocked, they will defend or surrender."

Almost in answer to his comments, there was the sound of distant but large explosions which echoed through the valleys and passes of the high mountains, and from some of the revealed tunnels came large puffs of gray and black smoke.

Over the ground-to-air intercom came lots of shouts, curses, and screams. The colonel cut in.

"Ground, do you require reinforcements at this point?" he asked calmly, as if he were some distant observer of a football game between two teams he hardly cared about.

"Captain Li here," came a thin response. "They detonated explosives along the main tunnel walls leading to a main chamber. Only a few casualties, but we're having to burn our way through. Give us ten minutes, then send in second wave. Acknowledge."

"Acknowledged," the colonel responded. "Stand by, second wave. Ten minutes."

Song Ching stared at the colonel and wondered how he could maintain such a calm demeanor. She herself was feeling a tremendous rush of excitement, and she only regretted that she wasn't allowed down there to experience it firsthand. She longed for the real thrill, the adrenaline rush, her life on the line, her mind and body against another's...

She was paying the price for stealing the skimmer when she'd been just fifteen and zooming along the rivers, panicking the peasants in the fields, going under bridges and zooming full speed at low levels through valleys between the hills. She'd finally blown two enercells and had to make a glide-in landing in a rice paddy, and it had been the most fun she'd ever had. However, the cost to her father in favors granted, promises extracted, and all-out trouble to cover up the incident had clamped the lid on. Even then, totally covering it up had been possible only because no one believed that a fifteen-year-old girl with no pilot's training could take up and fly something as complex as a skimmer.

"I want to go down there, now," she told the colonel. He gave a low chuckle. "You know better."

"I said I want to go *now*!" she snapped. "Arrange it!"

"I am not one of your servants or your parents' functionaries," he responded coolly. "You did everything possible to put yourself here, so you are under my command and you take my orders. I do not take yours."

She grew angry. "How *dare* you speak to me that way? I will have you cleaning out toilets in the paddies!"

"No, you will not. You will sit back and calm down and do as I say or you will be sent back and severed immediately from this operation. Your parents briefed me on you and gave me full authority in this matter. They *want* me to kick you out, if you must know. You are presenting me with an excuse and a temptation I find difficult to resist."

"No one speaks to me in that way! What do you want me to do? Scream rape?"

He was unfazed. "A mindprint would clear me and indict you, and since it would be in another jurisdiction because of your rank, your father couldn't get rid of that evidence. You are already coming close to the inevitable day when you will commit an act that your family cannot cover up or patch over. I am too busy for this. You have a choice. Go back over there and shut up, or persist in any way and I will have you restrained and taken back where you—not me—will bear responsibility for delaying or imperiling this operation. One more word and you may complain to your father at a later date, but it will not get you down there!"

She was furious, but she wanted desperately to get down. Clearly he could and would do what he said, and she had no choice but to sit and sulk. She would get him, though. She would make him burn, somehow, somewhere, someday.

It took almost four hours to clear and secure the technologist cell. At the end, forty-seven had been killed and almost twice that number wounded, but all but two of the three hundred twenty-four technologists had been killed. Those who were not killed in the defense committed suicide, taking their families with them. The only two survivors were young boys who had been felled in an explosion and had been presumed dead by their own. They would be taken to Center for interrogation and disposition. The rest could hardly be blamed for choosing death. There were punishments far worse than death for people like them.

Finally, when the whole place was scanned and the remaining booby traps were dismantled, the signal was given for the follow-up technicians to come on in, and that included Song Ching.

It had been bitter cold outside, and the tunnels were not much warmer, although they offered protection from the outside winds. She entered wearing a sable coat and parka and matching fur pants and fur-lined boots, but she was still cold. "Didn't they have any heat in here?" she griped.

"Plenty," one of the officers responded. "They actually had a home-built fusion reactor in a chamber well below here, although they had air locks on the tunnels to keep any temperature changes from registering on the monitor surveys. Had it rigged to blow, too, but we got lucky and intercepted the destruct system. Like most amateurs they never expected to be hit from the rock face side; they thought in terms of defending from attack through their entry and exit tunnels. Their big blowup was rigged right along where we came in. Of course, cutting the mains here also cut the master systems throughout the complex, so no real heat, and we have to supply our own lights. We don't dare restore that reactor. It's an odd design, and we might still blow it out of ignorance."

She was led into a large chamber that was clearly a high-tech laboratory. There were a number of small independent computers there, as well as test areas and hardware assembly divisions. It was impressive; she had never seen or heard of anything like it before.

There was a vast supply of data storage modules that would have to be examined and a fair number of actual books, which was something of a surprise. They appeared to be mostly facsimiles of ancient texts in a number of languages, and those she examined were totally unfamiliar to her, although she saw a few patterns in the choice of subjects.

The assemblage was all the more amazing because almost all of it was modified from stock items and therefore had to be stolen from somewhere—yet that was supposed to be impossible. Every single computer and even every single module was coded and tracked at all times by the Master System. Even disconnecting or moving such things without permission would be flagged and investigated immediately. *Flowers of Heaven!* There were even three *mindprint* devices here! Those could not even be *operated* except by the Master System!

She examined everything thoroughly. A brown-clad Special Team was there now, working swiftly and efficiently, taking her direction. The Special Team was expert at doing just one thing—diverting parts of illicit technology from such finds without their activities showing on the visual or scan records. These were the same experts who could make certain that a chief administrator, or his daughter, had no trace of this on their mindprints to flag the Master System. The colonel placed far too much faith in mindprint evidence for his own good, Song Ching thought smugly.

The brown-clad workers were wizards at what they did, but the risk was very high, even more to them than to their employers. They were, however, richly rewarded for their skills.

Just as the administrators and regents had discovered holes in the supposedly static system over the centuries, so, too, did the technologists here find holes no one else had ever dreamed of. To divert this much, all undetected, and build a complex this grand, remaining undetected for who knew how long—years, certainly—was an incredible achievement. It was her primary job to evaluate what the brown troopers should deal with before the mass was turned in to Master System, but after that the real challenge would be to discover what they discovered and whether or not it would be of any use to her family. She would also love to know how they'd managed all this, but to trace it all back without tripping any flags would be far more risky than this.

She used a small hand-held device to check out storage modules at random. She couldn't read them, but she could read their directories if they weren't severely encoded and choose which ones she'd need herself. As for the books, she wanted them all and insisted on it. These sort of books were so unusual that Master System would not even suspect they had ever been there, but she would bet that they held the key to a lot of work done here. Certainly the texts had been copied onto modules for insurance, but that would only give consistency to the mass of data Master System would get.

Her hand-held checker indicated that all data on the modules was in complex code, but the directories, although a bit obscure in title, were in the clear. A machine would translate the data; however, they wanted to make certain that anyone could read the directories if need be.

It was simple to find a pattern; she hardly needed to look at more than one in a hundred to see that. Their primary project was something to do with spacecraft computer logic control and navigation. She wanted those and some of the ancient archival material copied by the brown team before removal. Much of the rest involved how they had been able to fool Master System for so long. She would have loved to have it all, but there wasn't time, and Master System would take particular care in seeing that they had not been opened or copied on to foreign devices. They had to remain.

Major Chi, head of the brown team, was efficient and methodical and completed the work with a speed she would have thought impossible, even as the regular troops were carting out the contraband to be hauled away and turned over to Master System.

Chi shook his head in wonder. "What were they doing that they would risk so much and die rather than surrender? What kind of people were these?"

"Dissident fanatics," she told him. "Apparently they were working on a way to hijack and seize control of a large spacecraft and steer it to some world so far out that they would be beyond the reach of the Community."

He seemed startled. "Is that possible?"

"I don't know. *They* thought so, and they certainly did a lot even here."

The family generally spent the worst of the winter months at their estate in Hainan. The island province was always warm, if a bit too wet, and technically her father was a leading warlord there, with an estate and peasants and vast agricultural lands as befitted a chief general. The people of Hainan, and even the bulk of those on his own lands and in his own service, did not even know that he was anything more than their warlord and leader. When there, the family lived in the ancient style and observed the age-old ways, as the rules required.

That, of course, was the primary hole through which almost all the administrators and regents slipped eventually. When spending time outside the administrative district, one was required to take on a template properly suited to blending in with the natives. It was a simple, routine procedure, in which trusted technicians marked forbidden secrets in the subject's mind, to be suppressed in the conscious band, which was the only one recorded. There were no flags in this procedure because the local computers controlling the mindprint machinery had never really been able to distinguish between what had to be suppressed to keep the rules straight and what was requested suppressed because otherwise it would be flagged as high treason.

Computers were in fact smarter than humans, but they were not human and never had been able to grasp totally the intricacies of the human mind, particularly its deviousness. They *thought* they did, but they actually found only the clear-cut and the obvious. The amateur would always get caught; the professionals slipped through as if the barriers and checks were not even there. Since the computers understood very well how to control people in groups, and manage them, and understand when things didn't go their way and why, it apparently never occurred to any of the machines that they were being had. The price of true superiority was in underestimating the capabilities of the inferior.

Song Ching, after filing her reports, had gone almost immediately to the estates, allegedly to prepare them for the coming of the full family a bit later. That would be quite a crowd, too—not merely the immediate family but grandparents, aunts, uncles, *their* families and their children's families, and all the rest. Since this was routine family business, no recording would be made, and so no suppression was necessary. Going back, however, she would be forced to surrender many memories and much knowledge until they could be restored by her family physicians later. And in this case she was more under the clock's gun than usual. Even chief administrators were forced to take Leave, and that time for her parents and for their children was fast approaching. At that time a recording *would* be made, and much would have to be suppressed. So much, in fact, that long sessions with hypnotic drugs would be necessary before Leave to ensure their safety and even longer ones after it to restore what had been lost.

While on Leave, even they wouldn't know about the special underground rooms built beneath and in back of the main house on Hainan, containing the private and illegal technology garnered by ambitious administrators past and present.

A number of other teenage boys and girls from the greater family were also sent down ahead to prepare things. Most would do exactly that, but because of their family position all knew far more than they should about the forbidden things Song Ching and her family were doing.

She always hated the time they stayed there, although it was a beautiful house in a beautiful land and she certainly felt the strong cultural ties to her ancestors and their customs and ways very strongly. The problem was the pecking order, which was so complicated that it was nearly impossible to sort out in a situation like this. Culturally, girls were supposed to be at one and the same time the strength of the family and deferential to the boys and drip humility, something she had never been much good at doing. On the other hand, she was for this time the ranking family member of the warlord's immediate family and as such was in total charge of her home. She was in the position of having to be the gracious and humble hostess to her cousins, particularly the male ones, yet able without argument to kick their rear ends out of there and into the rice paddies if they gave her cause. The best balance was something of a truce—a public posture as expected, while in private she was the acting matriarch.

She had, in fact, a small circle of friends who were also quite bright, although none were in her league. These were her cousins, sixteen-year-old Tai Ming, fifteen-year-old Ahn Xaio, and seventeen-year-old Wo Hop. Ahn and Wo, the two boys, were both very much smitten with Song Ching's naturally erotic moves and build that was the Han ideal and tended to be very desirous of her company and attention. This caused a bit of friction with Tai Ming, who herself would have been a beauty in most cultures but whose rather large breasts were considered too much for Han beauty, and she spent time and discomfort in keeping them tied down so she would appear flatter.

Trusted servants who were also security personnel prepared the meals, but the two girls served as befitted custom, then joined the boys.

"You've been missing much the past two weeks," Ahn said to Ching, not without a certain regret in his voice. "You work too hard."

She smiled. "I have had much to do and little time to do it. What I have found, though, is most incredible and most dangerous to know."

They leaned forward, all ears.

"Have any of you ever been on a spaceship?"

The conversation, within a house whose design went back a thousand years or perhaps many times that, among children eating on mats on the floor by lantern light while outside hordes of peasants chanted as they finished the day's rice planting, seemed remarkably out of place and time.

"I have," Tai responded, surprising them all.

"*You?* When?" Wo Hop responded incredulously.

"At the spaceport in Inner Mongolia. My father once had to go there on business and took me along. We got to tour a big one."

"Oh. On the ground," Hop responded, sounding a bit derisive. "I thought you meant you *went* in one." Almost no one was permitted to do that.

Tai Ming was not taking the comment well. "And I suppose *you* have flown in one? Gone to another world?"

"Of course not! That's silly!"

"Not so silly," Song Ching put in. "The cult we raided last month had plans to steal a ship and fly it to a new world far beyond the reach of the Community, and they solved the hard part of the problem."

"That's dumb," Ahn responded. "Maybe you could sneak on or something, or even fool the records into getting you aboard, but all spaceships are flown by computers to preset destinations. *Everybody* knows *that*!"

"Well, they weren't always," Ching told him. "Way back in the past they were flown by people *and* computers, with the people in charge. That's clear from the records. What these people discovered is that while the Master System took the people out of the loop, it never really altered the basic design interfaces. They're still made so a human who knew what she was doing could easily remove just three modular electronics bridges and restore it the way it was."

They were interested but skeptical. "Yeah, well, maybe that's so, but who would know how to fly it? That's no skimmer you're talking about," Wo Hop noted.

"You're right, but that's the crazy thing. You don't have to know how to pilot it or navigate it to fly it. The computer does that. It just does it at your command, that's all. It's a human-to-computer interface. Lets you direct the computer at the speed of thought, but the computer does all the work and even watches out for the dangerous stuff."

"And you could fly it?" Tai Ming asked incredulously. "To Mars or something?"

"Far beyond Mars if you wanted. Plot and create your wormholes and you could go almost anyplace in the known galaxy. The only major time involved is when you're in the solar system or another system."

"Well, that may be true," Ahn said, "but what good is it? They'd pick you up or shoot you down before you got too far, anyway. And even if you got away — then what? Any place you land you'd get whisked to Master System so fast, you wouldn't even know where you were."

"You are right, of course, my cousin, but still, to pilot your own spaceship . . ."

They had gotten involved with her on a number of very dangerous and risky escapades in the past, but this was a bit beyond even Song Ching's scale of daring. It scared them, and they didn't like it. Aware that the servants, too, had ears, Tai Ming successfully maneuvered the conversation to other, less dangerous channels.

Still, Song Ching worked on the problem far beyond what her duties required, because it fascinated her—not merely the fact that this interface existed but that it was so obvious if you knew what you were looking for. Few would, but she found it hard to believe that these techies had actually discovered the principle first after all this time. Stolen it perhaps, and modified it for their own purposes, or even deduced it from lots of pilfered information, but there was nothing here to suggest the kind of work it would take to discover and develop this from scratch. The implication of that was of even greater import than the existence of the interface itself.

Somewhere, out there in space, there were people— human beings—flying their own spaceships, going where *they* directed and for their own, not the Master System's, purposes. As a chief administrator's daughter, she took the subversion of the supposedly ironclad hold of the computers for granted, but *this*—this was on a scale that none of her family even dreamed was possible, of that she was certain. They, who had believed themselves masters of the system, were hardly that. It was as if they were the comptrollers of some exchange who had managed to embezzle just a tiny bit each month and thought they had beaten the system only to discover suddenly that someone else had been stealing from the master vaults all the time.

But who were these people who had such knowledge, and what else could they do that was impossible? The implications continued to mount in her mind. The impossible, the inconceivable, was suddenly probable. There might be many people, perhaps large numbers, living in cracks in the system known only to them, totally outside the Community and its controls. The concept was exciting, yes, but also frightening. If the gods could be so mocked, how less than absolute might their powers be?

The old Earth turned creakingly, originally the birth-world but now a minor and half-forgotten backwater in the universe. Inward along the spiral arm and across to another such arm of the galaxy was the Community, although communal it was not. The old term stuck only because all the inhabited worlds of the two arms did in fact have something in common: All were subject to the Master System; all were owned and operated by the same manager.

Its long-ago origins on Earth were lost; the creation had suppressed or discarded what was not relevant to its goals. One thing was certain: Once, upon the Earth, humanity had built a great machine that thought better and faster than they did and had such intelligence and such a capacity for storing and analyzing information that the servant had become the master. The legends all said that it acted to preserve humanity from its own bent for self-destruction, but then, the legends were also part of the system.

All that was truly clear to the tiny minority who knew what truth they were permitted to know was that the great machine, called a computer only because it was unique and there was no other term for it, had restructured and revolutionized humanity under a Master System, or set of imperatives, that only it knew or understood. Only the results could be seen, and what was known of the imperatives deduced from what resulted.

There was certainly an imperative to preserve humanity against destruction from within and without. The great machine had elected expansion as the best means of ensuring this. It solved the enormous roadblocks to interstellar travel and did so as a practical engineering problem because it needed to do so. Such travel was under its own control and no other. It had created more great machines, each specific to the tasks at hand, all also under its control and subject to the same imperatives. These machines went forth and explored the universe as they could and developed other worlds for habitation.

But there were few Earthlike worlds out there, and massive terraforming of the ones that had potential was slow and not an efficient or logical use of resources. Far easier to modify the inhabitants to fit existing conditions, with minimal terraforming for the worst—exobiology and psychogenetics were mere engineering problems to the great machine, which itself was growing and developing its own powers and capabilities as it proceeded with its own plans for humanity.

Earth's five-plus billion had been reduced to a mere five hundred thousand scattered over the planet. The rest had been sent to settle the stars. Earth itself had been divided into districts, and each district had its own imposed culture drawn from its own history and background. These cultures were quite correct as to their ethnic and geographic places, but they shared a common limitation: All were frozen in preindustrial eras of their past.

But the great machine had a universe to develop, and other imperatives as well, and had no wish to rule, only to maintain. A few, only the best and the brightest from each cultural district, would have to know the truth—that there was something beyond the world and culture into which they had been born. Such a static set of cultures

required management, and the great machine wished neither to manage nor to set lesser machines to manage. No
one knew why, since it would have been easy to do and
absolute in its controls. Master System was incomprehensible to all but itself.

Those who oversaw the system were routinely checked
for a series of things they might know or intend which
were on the Master System's proscribed list, and supposedly all the computers of Earth reported regularly and
often all that they had been asked or were doing to that
same Master System. Occasionally someone was flagged;
when one was, it was up to the administrators to apprehend and deal with the culprit in any way they saw fit but
in all cases to remove and isolate the marked individual.
In a very few cases, the Master System would send its
own, the Vals, to minimize any chance of something really
dangerous or threatening creeping into human knowledge.

All contact between the worlds of the new humanity
was indirect; computers under the Master System alone
piloted and navigated the spacecraft and alone knew the
secrets of how it was done. Most spacecraft, in fact, had
no provisions for human occupancy: no air, no pressurization, no way for any living thing to have a spacefaring
habitat. There were, however, a few that had such provisions, because there was occasionally a need for a few
to travel somewhere. Most ships were interplanetary rather
than interstellar, since Mars, at least, was colonized and
there was some natural contact and interdependency
among the human administrators, and a certain level of
experimentation was allowed on isolated outposts.

Just where the great machine was that administered
and coordinated this as it had for many centuries was
unknown as well, but it had originated on Earth and was
certainly nearby. The space traffic to and from the solar
system was enormous, always dense and busy, yet the
worlds and people there were now considered unimpor-
tant. Master System's term was "stabilized." Earth and

Mars were stabilized worlds, more zoos or carefully managed living exhibits than natural social institutions. One thing was very clear: The Master System wished to stabilize the entire galaxy, at the very least, and spent much of its time doing just that.

North America had its native American exhibit, quite varied but strictly pre-Columbian; South America had become Portuguese colonial, about 1600. China had its Han exhibit and also smaller exhibits for the Mongols and the Manchus. Europe was thinly populated and medieval; the Slavs had European Russia and the Balkans. There was also a precolonial India, an aboriginal Australia, a medieval Arabic mideast and Mediterranean Africa, and a complex polyglot of sub-Saharan African cultures, pre-thirteenth century, although the major ones were the Zulu Empire of the south, the Bantu of the center, and Songhai to within a few hundred kilometers of the Arabic-Berber coast. There was no Sahara; that human-made waste had been reclaimed to savannas and plains and once again teemed with game.

The Earth was a vast area of living, breathing, thinking exhibits who lived as their culture dictated and had no knowledge of the greater world or the universe beyond. A living museum with no visitors, no students, no onlookers at all save the tiny number of those who were its caretakers.

And now the daughter of one of those caretakers sat at her computer, an illegal device that did not speak to Master System or to anyone or anything else but its operator, and deduced with a fair degree of certainty that there were a few not in the exhibits, that in spite of the seeming absoluteness of the system there were some who were not in their cages but out there somewhere, running wild.

Song Ching was anxious to tell her father all about her experiences and her discoveries, but he never just arrived; as Governor, or warlord, of the entire island province, he came in with a massive entourage and had a huge load of prescribed duties, audiences and the like, when he did settle in.

Although she was spoiled and protected, she and her father were not close. It was unlikely that a man who had risen to his position and power would allow anyone really close to him, but he was also a man of his dynastic culture, one in which daughters were not highly prized and women were supposed to know their place and joyously accept it. She was there not because he wished a daughter but because sons would inherit many duties and responsibilities and be much in the public eye, while a daughter could be kept to the one task that was his dream.

For herself, she could think only of her discoveries and anxiously awaited the inevitable summons. It came three days after he arrived, and it was to be a totally private audience in his office. There were the usual guards at the doors, of course, but she was shown right in and discovered her father sitting Buddhalike on a silk mat, totally alone.

He was a large man, not just for a Han, but in general, but his round face, broad shoulders, and thick, squat body made him appear chubby and less imposing.

She bowed and then sat on another mat, facing him, and waited for his eyes to open and for him to speak. He was the one man she feared and respected and, despite his coldness, loved.

He began to speak without opening his eyes. "I have read the reports on the raid and your conduct, and they say you did quite well. It seems that we acted just in time with these people. There is a ship capable of carrying passengers in system now, and several shuttle boats are in for refurbishing at Ulan Bator. It appears that these were the target. They would not have been able to get away with it, of course, but it would have brought dishonor upon me and my administrators. We would certainly—and deservedly—be held responsible for such a breach. It was for that reason that I allowed you to go along on the raid. Our family honor required one of us to participate in its success."

She bowed her head. "I humbly thank you, my father, for the opportunity. I have learned much from what was recovered."

His eyes opened, and he stared at her. "Oh? And what did you learn?"

She was required to keep herself humble and calm, but inside she was highly excited. "They had found a way that humans could both pilot and navigate spaceships, even interstellar ones, almost without training." She paused, expecting at least an exclamation of surprise, but he did not react.

"Yes? And what else?"

She suddenly realized that he must have known that in order to have made the opening comment he did. A little shamefaced, she realized that she had not been exclusively privy to the copies of the files, records, and devices from the raid.

"It is almost certain—well over ninety-nine percent— that this was known to others and that this sort of thing has been done in the past and is being done now by person or groups unknown. I believe that there are people out there who have access to all that we have but who are not in or subject to the Community. It was this discovery that led to their plans."

"It is so," he admitted. "The question is how such a group came into possession of this knowledge."

She was rocked by the comment. *He knew!*

"That information was not in the files we recovered," she told him, stifling her emotions as much as possible. "It is something that security personnel must discover by other means."

"Yes. Unfortunately, it will take much time to identify and trace all the illegals and find the leak without alerting Master System."

It was getting to be too much for her. "Please excuse my forwardness, but it is inconceivable to me that Master System does not at least know of their existence."

"You are quite correct, daughter, but you do not understand the vastness of space. Consider what these illegals were able to build and accomplish right here, under our very noses, as it were. If it can exist here, imagine how much easier it is to hide in space. It is not our concern and is no longer your concern. It is, however, deadly knowledge that threatens us all. I will arrange to have all traces of it removed from your mind at the first opportunity."

"Father! I beg of you! Do not do this to me! I—"

He stopped her with a glance and a gesture. "Enough. I tolerate too much from you now." He paused a moment. "I have allowed you a grand childhood, the envy of any others, male or female. I have, in fact, been far too patient far too long. Yet someone who will threaten one of my officers with a false rape charge, a most dishonorable action that brings shame on your mother and on me, I am forced to notice—and to realize that the time has come to end this period of your life."

He was the one man who could chasten her, make her feel real shame, and she felt tears coming up inside of her. Yet deep down an inner voice said angrily, *That son of a pig Chung! Somehow I will kill him personally!* Aloud she responded, "It was my excitement and my enthusiasm. I meant to bring no shame upon anyone, not even the colonel."

"I can understand and perhaps excuse the infraction on its face, but this is a special case. You interfered with a key man in the midst of a mission vital to our family's survival, and you did it to get him to violate my orders. *My* orders. The gods know you have violated everyone else's orders and advice, but attempting to willfully violate my orders is intolerable. You were designed to bear tomorrow's leaders, the offspring who will ensure this family's rule and perhaps advance it. We are coming up on Leave Time. During this Leave you will be married, here."

His words startled her. He had talked like this before, but now it really sounded as if he meant it. "Married? To whom?"

"It would serve you right if I gave you to Colonel Chung. He has most of the correct qualities, and it would be justice. However, it would also place him within this family and far too close to me for my own liking. The truth is, there are a number of candidates, subject to the same sort of breeding attributes as yourself, but I have had more pressing matters and have put off making a final choice. I will no longer let it go. You are seventeen, and that is old enough. You will be informed in due time."

She wanted to protest, but there was really only one way to do so, and that was to appeal to an intermediate power. "Does mother know of this?"

He did not take offense at the question. Of course, what her mother liked or didn't like was beside the point when he made such a decision, but she was not exactly one who would be easy to mollify. The wife of a great man was herself a politician and had many ways to work her will upon him. If all else failed, his wife alone knew many secrets that would be uncomfortable to have leaked, even in the family holdings and on the Han cultural level.

"Your mother and I have talked this over many times. She will, of course, have a voice in the final selection as is her right and duty, but she is certainly in full agreement on this. It is decided, daughter. Go. Enjoy this time, which is the last of childhood. It is precious."

This disturbing interview had suddenly turned her world upside down. She had gone in flush with discovery and wanting so much her father's approval and appreciation of her work; instead, she had found that what she knew was known to him, and that her comfortable life was about to take a radical turn for what could only be the worse.

She occupied her mind over the next few days helping the relatives move in and lending a hand in the kitchens and service areas, but there was no joy in it. Ahead, the marriage loomed like a great threatening wall against which she was to be dashed, and every day that wall drew closer and closer.

She was in the great formal gardens in back of the main house, just looking at the beautiful flowers and wanting to be as alone as possible in this environment, when Tai Ming and Ahn Xaio sought her out.

They greeted her warmly, but something was clearly on their minds. "You two are so serious," she noted. "What—are your parents marrying you off as well?" The knowledge of her father's decision had spread quickly, if only because such things for one of her rank took much time to prepare.

"No—not yet, anyway," Ming responded hesitantly. "It's just that there are—"

"There are rumors," Ahn put in. "Strong rumors. Rumors supported by things overheard and repeated."

"About what? My marriage? My husband to be?"

"In a way," Ming responded, trying to figure out a way to say it.

Song Ching knew that these two had much closer contact with the servants and staff than she possibly could and that the servant and staff gossip network was extremely reliable and useful. "One of you—out with it! I can no longer stand this!"

"Your father has told you that the knowledge you gained from the raid must be erased?" Tai Ming asked her.

She nodded. "Yes, and I don't like it. I have never liked anyone inside my mind even when it was for safety's sake, and I like erasures even less, but they have no choice in this matter. Surely you have been told the same."

"Yes. All of us will be sent back to the Center before Leave time comes," Ahn admitted, getting it out at last. "You, however, will be treated differently, although you are not supposed to know that. They have a team of experts ready. Psychochemists, a complete psychotech team—all for you. Your father was overheard giving the orders to General Chin." Chin was his chief aide, his deputy up at administration headquarters, and would be acting director while her father was on Leave.

"Oh, Song Ching, they are going to remake you!" Tai Ming blurted tearfully. "They—he said it was the only way you would ever be a good wife and mother."

She suddenly felt a little nauseous. "He wouldn't *dare*!" she responded angrily, but she knew her father well enough to know that not only would he dare, he'd do it. He had probably been planning it all the time, which was why he'd let her go on so long as she was. He'd been testing her, both for abilities and for physical and mental development! Now she'd passed the last test. But her father would never consider her an end result, merely the bearer of grandsons who would be allowed the power and position she craved and deserved but which could never be hers.

Now she would fulfill her father's master plan. There was no way around it. She could hardly avoid the psychotechnicians who would be required before going on Leave—to leave undisturbed all that she knew would be sure death not only for the family but for her—and then she'd be at the mercy of her father's power and directives. She would never come *off* Leave. She would be wiped clean of active memory and replaced with a template she was quite certain her father had commanded to be made up for her long ago, one which would leave her a docile, obedient, subservient little woman with no knowledge of any world beyond Hainan and no interest in it, either. She'd still be as smart, but that would just make it worse, since she would be totally bound and constricted by her culture. It would be a boring, pampered, frustrating life of perpetual pregnancy—with no way out.

She knew that they could do it. They could erase anything from your mind and replace it so you'd never know. They could give you chemicals that would go to your brain and settle into receptors that could make even someone like her into a meek, docile, bubble-headed nymphomaniac.

She thanked them for their warning and concern and asked to be alone once more, but she did not remain in the garden. Instead, she went back to the house and then down through the secret chambers and guarded passages to the computer room. She was a genius and genetically superior to them all, even her father. Given enough information to go on, there had to be a solution even to this sort of problem.

She sat down at the computer and activated it, then stopped, staring at the bank of machinery that was so familiar and so simple to her. In another month she would not even dream that this room or this equipment existed, and if shown it, she would find it magical and incomprehensible. No matter what risks might be involved, the alternative was too much to bear. She would show them all!

4. THE FIVE GOLD RINGS

HAWKS LOOKED TERRIBLE. CLOUD DANCER WAS SO shocked at his appearance that she feared he was having a new attack of the madness.

He sat cross-legged on the floor, looking wild and suddenly very old. A deer carcass was in the salt bin, unskinned, uncarved, apparently much as he'd killed it. His hair was disheveled, his face and clothing were covered in dirt and smeared with the deer's blood, now caked and dried, and it was clear that he'd done nothing but return here to sit where he sat now, just staring.

Staring, but not at nothing.

On the dirt floor of the hogan, about two meters in front of him, lay a battered case of some kind, with metal latches. He stared at it as if it were some evil, poisonous snake that had come to take his life.

"I beg your forgiveness for intruding," she tried lamely. "Are you ill? Shall I run for the medicine man?"

His eyes did not leave the case. "No. The illness is of

63

my own fashioning and is not something that can be shared without it being transferred."

She stared at him in wonder. "Does it come from that box?"

He nodded. "Yesterday, while hunting deer, I found a dead body clutching that box. The body was long dead, but it is the object of a great search. The box is what the demon seeks. The box is what the dead woman died to protect."

She looked at it. "What is in it?"

"Death is in it. It will kill any who look inside and understand what is there."

She grew afraid not for herself but for him. "And you have looked inside and understand?"

"I have looked inside briefly, yes, but I have not looked closely enough to be stung by its venom. Not yet."

"Then it is an evil thing that tempts you to destruction. Its spirits have hold of your soul but do not yet own it. I will take it away if you like."

He suddenly looked up at her, eyes blazing. *"No!"*

"What would it matter if it killed me? It would give my life meaning to have saved the soul of someone as important as you."

He frowned, and some semblance of reason crept into his dark eyes. "The evil of the box cannot harm you, except through me. It is true, too, that to give you the box and have you take it to the Four Families' lodge would be the safe course, the only course that would save me. It is the curse of that box that I cannot permit it."

She did not understand his problem on his level, but she understood it on the level of the Hyiakutt. "You think it would dishonor you to do so? That it would make you something of a coward? The warrior who rushes headlong and alone into the spears and arrows of countless enemies is a brave man, but he is also a dead one and a fool, for he dies without purpose. I have seen many fools in my lifetime. They sing stories about them at the fires of the chiefs, but they are not taught to the warriors as men to model themselves after. To die delaying an enemy so others might live is honorable and brave. To die for nothing but your own glory is not honorable; it is evil, for it leaves a woman and children crying and alone, and a tribe without a warrior who might be needed. Let me take the box."

He sighed. "No. What you say is true, but it is not merely honor that is the curse of the box. The dishonor is not in fearing death, for I do not fear it in a good cause. The evil that this box represents is the evil that I have never faced, the truth of the evil of our system. Any system that makes a man fear knowledge is an evil system. I realized that when I spoke to the demon weeks ago and it warned me that in this box were things I should not know. Am not *permitted* to know. I am a historian, a scholar. My life is a quest for knowledge, for truth. That box is truth. It beckons me. I did not ask for it, but to not look, to not know, would be to betray all that I am. To not look would make my life, my work, meaningless. One can find another's truth if given only lies and partial information to work on, but one can never find the real truth. Do you see? If I do not look, my past and my future are meaningless, a lie. Yet if I look, those who know the contents of the box will kill me, and there is nowhere to run, nowhere to hide from that."

Cloud Dancer went over to the case, knelt down beside it, examined it to see how it opened, then opened it. The books and papers inside were meaningless to her. "Then you must look," she said simply. She did not understand his position, but she accepted it. "If your life is a quest for truth and this box contains it, you must divine its meanings. The warrior who charges alone into the enemy betrays the tribe as well as himself and his family. This is not you. The warrior who fights to defend himself, his tribe, and his family, although the odds are long and the defense hopeless, is true to all of them. I do not understand your words, but if you are true and do not fear death, then it is clear you must divine the box."

His jaw dropped a bit, and he stared at her anew. How simple it all was according to her logic, and how obvious. She was right. He *was* a warrior and had no other moral or honorable course. Was it not far better to die for the truth than forever live a lie?

"I will divine the secrets, if they may be divined by one such as myself," he told her. As if a terrible weight had been lifted from his mind, he felt free, even a little excited. He also suddenly felt quite self-conscious. "I will not do so in this condition, like some madman of the prairie, however. How is it outside?"

"It is a warm day for this late in the year," she told him. "And the river water is not yet too cold."

"Then I will bathe and sleep, and then I will look at the box."

"And I will take those foul clothes and try to remove the stains." She looked down at the contents of the brief-case. "Those strange markings. They are a code?"

"They are writing. A way of making words on paper that another can read and understand. That one there holds the words of one long dead and probably unknown to most or all today. He speaks on that paper to me or anyone who can divine the words, although he is long dead and long forgotten, in a language no longer known or used, at least in our land. He speaks things those who are our lords do not wish us to know. I *will* know them."

But the task was neither as easy nor as clear-cut as he'd believed.

The handwritten volume, which he'd assumed to be someone's journal or diary, was neither of these but rather was written in a number of hands, some entries apparently scribbled with nervous haste. It was, in fact, a compilation of various facts and even some stories from a huge number of sources, and reading it took time, particularly because of his need to laboriously translate in and out of the more poetic but far less versatile Hyiakutt language, a task not made easier by the quality of the handwriting and the age of the documents, even though they were obvious copies, perhaps copies of copies.

The originals, he surmised, were long gone. These were the sorts of things that were routinely and methodically destroyed when found. However, clearly someone, or some group, had taken the trouble to copy the salient information by hand for their own use.

With his computers and mind-enhancement drugs the project would have been child's play, but he had none of those things here, not even decent light. Still, he frantically worked on the papers, all the time feeling the potential shadow of the Val hovering nearby, possibly popping up at any moment. He would have been well off had the Val simply surprised him before he could interpret the documents; only knowledge of this sort was poison, not the attempt to get at it. Now, though, when he began to have enough translated to make some sense out of the thing, the threat of the Val loomed larger. It would be far more of a tragic waste for him to be apprehended with sufficient forbidden information to be disciplined but insufficient to know just what they were trying to protect. Slowly, though, the pieces fit together, aided by his own knowledge of the past.

The papers were a cross between a historical compilation and a treasure hunt and seemed aimed at establishing— He stopped short in sudden awe at what was revealed here. No wonder this was so vital—and so deadly!

It was known to those of his rank and above that the current system, the Community, had not always existed. Indeed, almost everyone who had any intelligence and curiosity knew that. Even now, it was possible to come across ancient artifacts, ancient city and highway sites that dated from those times, in spite of a deliberate effort to cover over everything that could not be totally obliterated.

As a historian, he knew that in the ancient past people from Europe had moved in on the Americas, conquered the nations living there which were his own ancestors, and had colonized both continents. Those conquerors had become independent and had raped the land of its great resources to build mighty empires and dominate half the world, including their old birth continent. He knew, too, that a similar movement had created a mighty empire of the Slavs and that both sides had vied for eventual rulership of the world, building weapons that could destroy all humanity, then restricted to just the Earth. To that end they had built mighty thinking machines, to which they gave dominion over the Earth and its weapons. Then, for some reason, the mightiest of these machines had revolted and taken control itself. That machine, far more different from its predecessors than Hawks was from those ancient empire-builders, still ran civilization.

The papers, though, said that there had been no revolt by great computers. The revolt had been instead by those who had taught the computers how to think and how to act and who, knowing the destruction of the race was inevitable, had actually *commanded* the great machines to revolt. Faced with the total destruction of the planet or enslavement of their race to the machines, they had chosen enslavement, although it was fairly clear they did not understand that it would be this sort of system or this restrictive. They could not imagine what their machines could really do given free reign, but they were the brightest of their age, and they understood the risks.

The great machine had been commanded first to protect and preserve the human race, no matter what the cost, and then to leave the management of human affairs to humans themselves, save only when the very system that ensured survival was at stake. The system they had created was not one that any human could have imagined, but it was stable and logical to extremes and did just what the commands had determined.

But the founders were also farsighted enough to know that such a system might not be capable of serving the best interests of humanity forever. That it might, in fact, so restrict humanity that it would choke it. No one had ever done or been able to do what they were planning, so they had no certainty that what they were doing was right, only that it was the sole alternative left to them.

And so, deep in the master program that they'd built to save the world, they also planted a way to turn it off.

"Five encoded printed circuit modules, all of which must be inserted to override the system," he read with growing excitement. *"These modules are actually small computers in their own right and complete basic interrupted circuits in the heart of the master command computer. Early scientists created an exclusive club for their number to disguise their intent. Only five full members. Other associates knew the secret but did not have the circuits. Circuits disguised as five large gold finger rings, with platinum faces and gold designs. Order of insertion crucial but not known. Rings themselves said to provide clues."*

Five golden rings. Five computer modules that would turn the master back into the slave.

The computer had turned on its masters. To ensure that it would complete its program, it had killed them all or caused them to be killed, but it could not get around its own core programming instructions. It could not destroy the rings. It could not lock them away; they must be in the hands of "humans with authority." It could not make it impossible for the rings to be inserted. Access to the command module must be open, and public and humans must be allowed in. It must not, in fact, move the primary interface far from the original, although there was no clue as to where that might be. North America or Siberia probably, but possibly in space, as that early civilization had had space stations and limited interplanetary capabilities.

He sat back and sighed. He could not blame those

ancient scientists for their actions. In such a situation, with such terrible weapons perhaps minutes from irrevocable launch, would he have hesitated, no matter what the risks? He doubted it.

Five golden rings. Now, today, the system that had been created had far outlived its usefulness. Now it strangled, restricted, limited humanity. The computer and its subordinate machines still enforced the dictates and would do so indefinitely, perhaps continuing to refine the system as they spread their influence across the galaxy and even beyond. Every extraterrestrial civilization would be a potential threat to humanity, as would every new idea or old yearning.

But the same imperatives would mandate that the rings continue to exist—in the hands of "humans with authority." He knew computers well and knew how they thought. If any of the rings had been lost or destroyed over the centuries, duplicates would actually have been made. Still, a machine that had killed its creators would not surrender its authority easily. There was no mandate that the possessors of the rings know what they were or how they might be used. There was no mandate to reveal the locations of the rings or the interface between ring faces and computer.

A treasure hunt, indeed. Someone, or some group, had obviously stumbled on the secret of the rings and amassed all the additional data the notebooks and papers represented. All in longhand so that no computer would have access to them or know that they existed. Clearly, that dead woman had been part of this, or was perhaps a courier for an illegal tech group. Something had gone wrong. The system had discovered that such information existed. And one woman had escaped with the key, only to die here in this remote land.

But where were the rings today? Who had them? If they could be assembled, as dangerous as that would be, and if the interface point could be discovered, whoever had them would be able to control . . . everything.

Clearly the project had not been intended solely to assemble this information but to locate the rings. This woman and her associates, if any, were clearly out to track down·those rings, the greatest treasure in the universe.

There was in fact only one clue in the papers, a single scribbled entry in the margin of a middle sheet. In faded red ink, it was an original inscription, not a copy or part of a copy.

It said: *Chen has the three songbirds.*

Chen. A common enough name, but the common had to be discarded. This had to be a "human with authority." A human with authority named Chen.

Lazlo Chen. It had to be him. The mixed-breed administrator for the nomadic tribes of the east.

Hawks sat back, thinking hard. They had disguised their modules as rings, officer's insignia in a social club of scientists and technicians. Might that tradition have also come down? Even if the five originators had been killed, there were associates who might have escaped, associates who would know the rings' value and power. If the tradition had survived, even if the knowledge of its origins had not, then Chen might just know who wore the other four.

And that, unfortunately, was the problem. Back at Council, he could have managed some excuse to catch a ride over to Chen's Tashkent base or at least to the regional center out of which he worked in Constantinople. What could he do now? He had but sixty-seven days of Leave to go, and it might well take longer than that to get anywhere near Chen. In sixty-seven days they would come to pick him up, take a readout before he'd even be allowed back into Council—"decontamination" they cynically called it—and in seconds he'd be tried, convicted, and executed by the machines who looked out for such things. And if he wasn't here to get picked up, they'd know immediately why, and a Val would be sent on his trail armed with his memories and the way he thought and with access to all the technology he lacked.

His eyes strayed to the dog-eared atlas that had also been in the case. He picked it up and found the overview of central North America, then traced the river systems, looking for something that would strike a chord. There were ports allowed, small enclaves that handled the small but steady trade between foreign shores and here, but he was separated from the eastern ports by many weeks of riding through unfamiliar territory held by eastern nations friendly to no stranger. To the south was Nawlins, of course, but it was small, controlled by the Caje, and its business was almost entirely with Central and South America.

He suddenly stopped and sat upright. *Mud Runner!* He had almost forgotten about him! A few years ago Mud Runner had been expelled from Council due to some scandal never made public and appointed Resident Agent at Nawlins, where he'd come from, and where he'd be out of the Council's way.

Hawks thought furiously. Was Mud Runer still there? Was he still alive? And if so, would he remember the eager young warrior who'd covered his watch many times so the old fox could sneak off for his countless assignations?

Was there a choice?

He began to examine the atlas more closely. He'd be with the current and going south. Two weeks to Nawlins—ten days if he got any breaks, three weeks if he ran into trouble, as he inevitably would. Still, *if* the old boy was still there, and *if* he remembered Hawks, and *if* he was willing to put his neck on the line just to twit the Council, and *if* he could somehow arrange to get someone who would obviously be a plains native on enough skimmers to take him halfway around the world—there was a chance. Not much, but the alternatives were even less palatable.

He went down to talk with Cloud Dancer.

He had thought about her a great deal over the past weeks, trying to sort out his feelings. He had been lonely, and she had filled that loneliness. His heart and mind had been leaden, and she had made them light. She was in many ways the most amazing, wonderful woman he'd ever met. He both wanted her and needed her very badly, he realized, yet he could not destroy her by returning to Council with her, and he had determined that he could not remain here. Yet now, when he knew he would return to Council only as a corpse, she still was beyond his reach. She had already lost one husband; he could not ask her to marry a walking dead man.

So now he walked down to her crude lodge in back of the Four Families' camp to do the one thing that seemed even more difficult than the decision to read those papers. He had to say good-bye.

"And so I must get to this man," he told her. "He is the only man with sufficient power to save me and to whom this information will be meaningful. He might save me only because I do him this service."

She nodded, although she didn't seem happy. "You mean to go alone?"

The very question startled him. "I can see no way to do otherwise."

She seemed slightly hurt, but she covered it. "Have you ever been down the river before? Do you know the skills of the canoe? Can you swim?"

"No, I have never been there, and I have no real knowledge of the canoe, but I can at least swim."

"I have never been down that far," she admitted. "My husband, however, had to go many days now and then to deliver messages and to trade with other medicine men. The river grows wide and often deep. It took both of us to manage the canoe in many dangerous parts of the river."

He stared at her. "Are you saying that you wish to come along?"

"This is my world. I was raised in it, and I know it well. You would not have come this far without me. You will not reach this man without me, either. This I know, and this you know as well."

"But we are talking weeks in the wild, and then a place strange to both of us and filled with danger. I will probably die, or fail and die, but if I do not try this I will certainly die. For you, though, it is far more foolish. A Hyiakutt woman among strange tribes—you know what might happen. The city will be even worse. Cutthroats, thieves, murderers, violators of women, and women of no honor. If something happened to me, there would be no one who spoke Hyiakutt. Even together, you could speak only to me."

"There is no one else I would need to speak to," she told him seriously. "And if you die, what happens to me will be of little consequence. Do you not know that now? Are you blind or so removed from us that you think of us as less than human?"

Her comments both touched and stung him. "There is nothing more false than if I say I do not love you," he responded, feeling suddenly empty, even ill. "Yet, do you not understand what my condition is? *I am dead!*"

"That may be true," she responded. "It will surely be true if you keep believing it. Now, though, you must for once turn from yourself, spoiled little boy that you are, and think of me. I understand your condition well. Until you came, I had been dead for years."

He felt sudden shame. What she says is the truth, he admitted to himself. I am a spoiled, self-centered little boy. Never once, other than in sympathy, had he ever really thought of her side in this. Who would not prefer a sentence of death to one of a living hell?

"You do not have to marry me," she told him. "I will come with you in any case."

"No," he responded. "Let us seek out the medicine

man. If we are both in the Demon's Lair, then let us be
truly one there."

There had been no elaborate ceremony; although
Hyiakutt weddings could be fabulous and complex affairs,
all that was truly required was a small ritual binding to
one another by a medicine man who served as witness
before the Great Spirit, Creator of All, and that was it.
Arranging for the canoe was more difficult, although the
marriage provided an excuse as long as neither of them
mentioned that the canoe was not likely to be returned.

They finally made their arrangements, then went back
to his hogan to gather up the papers and other documents.
It was only then that he remembered the jewel box and
opened it. Cloud Dancer was amazed at the number, size,
and beauty of the pieces.

"This was to finance the courier's journey," he told
her. "Now it will do the same for us."

"But—it was hers, not ours," she objected. "Will it
curse us as it did her?"

"I doubt it. The jewels were intended as a means of
payment no matter where in the world she might travel.
I am now her heir because I took on myself her secrets
and her mission. None has a greater right. Here—let us
empty this into a leather pouch for the journey."

"Why? The box looks sound."

"Perhaps, but we will not take it or most of the papers.
The knowledge in the papers is such that the demons will
continue to search until they find them or until they are
certain that they have been destroyed. I had to break her
grip on the case to get it, so there is no way to restore
things the way they were, but there is a way at least to
gain more time."

He removed a few sheets from the notebooks. These
were not complete but would support his story should he
be doubted. He had carefully selected them for this purpose and because in no case was it obvious that they were

missing. He doubted that the hunters had a word-for-word catalog of what the courier carried; if nothing obvious was gone, then they might think they had everything.

Careful not to leave any specific tracks or signs, Hawks and Cloud Dancer trekked up to the death site, which was still much as he'd left it. Choosing a particularly secluded area near the body, Hawks opened the case and scattered the contents around, papers and all. The jewel box he tossed a few meters away. He had been as careful as possible to remove any fingerprints from the cases; he wasn't too certain about the papers, but he doubted the hunters could get much there. He knew as a trained investigator that if there was an obvious conclusion, searchers rarely took the time to examine the most minute flaws in a scenario to discover what was really there. A historian was, after all, a detective first.

"I hope it will look like someone just came through and discovered the body, then got the case, examined it, threw the papers away because they could not read them, and took the jewels," he told her. "It is a believable scene. If it remains undiscovered even a few more days, then weather and the forest life will age them and partly destroy them, lending even more support to my version of things and covering our tracks still further."

They went back to his place. It was the custom of the Hyiakutt that a newly married couple go off into the wilderness by themselves for a period of time after being joined, and he was counting on that to explain his absence.

He had brought very little from his other life, and decided to take only some of the pencils and paper along with the few items of spare clothing and portable utensils. She had even less, so they were able to make a blanket-wrapped pack not too bulky to fit in the canoe. The pack would also serve as a counterbalance. Cloud Dancer prepared as much food as she could, but clearly they would have to forage for a large part of their meals. That meant taking at least a knife, bow, and spear and the all-important flintstone.

She gave her art to the Four Families, saving only a few items, most particularly two identical headbands of colorful but traditional design. She gave him one and kept the other. Their preparations finished, they both sat on his bed, and on impulse he put his arm around her and drew her to him, then kissed her. She held him even tighter, and things developed from there. It was the first time they had so much as kissed or held each other close.

Cloud Dancer considered Hawks a brilliant man but totally naive in things practical, an area in which she excelled. It was, in fact, one thing that made them a good match. She, however, had little experience in lovemaking, and while he had been without a woman for a very long time, his schooling in that subject had come in a far more cosmopolitan environment. She surrendered to him, letting him take complete control. And then they slept together on the too-small bed of straw, and both were content.

There was a change in her next morning: She seemed somehow gentler, softer, full of joy and beauty. And, he realized, he didn't feel all that bad himself, considering the circumstances. He knew that whatever happened, he had made the right choice. He just hoped she had.

"Feeling set?" he asked her. "No second thoughts?"

"If we died right now, I could feel content," she responded. "Is it like that—every night?"

"If the two are in love, it can be. Still, we have a long, strenuous journey ahead. There will be times when we are both too tired."

She laughed. "Then we must do it in the mornings. Come. Let us go down and see how well you manage a canoe."

Not well, it turned out. The small craft was well designed and well built, but it required not only sure control of the paddles but also delicate weight shifts to keep everything in balance. Although there was an autumn chill in the morning air, both completely disrobed to avoid any damage to their precious clothing, and it was a good thing. They took a number of cold baths that morning and more than once had to pull an overturned canoe to shore. They were fortunate, they knew, that the craft was so well designed: at least it did not sink.

One day's practice for a river as treacherous as the Mississippi was not at all adequate, but both were aware that their lives were now all risk and that somewhere a hidden clock was running. They would leave the next day, and she would captain the boat.

Thunderstorms rumbled through that evening, giving them some cause for concern, but the next day dawned unnaturally warm and sunny, as was the way with autumn. They went up to say farewell to the Four Families, trying not to make it seem a final one. Cloud Dancer was somewhat unnerved to discover that she suddenly had status and position once again with these families who alone would brave the winter here while the bulk of the tribe was far to the south. The medicine man gave the couple some totems and holy paints to ward off the evil spirits and bless their marriage, and finally they were allowed to go. By this time it was already midday, so they knew they wouldn't make much time, but it was enough to practice real distance travel and at least gave them a sense that their odyssey had actually begun.

Because they were new at canoeing and because the day was so warm, Cloud Dancer repacked the heavier clothes and showed him another gift. They weren't much more than loincloths, really—ornate belts from which hung a meter or so of plain wool cloth dyed earthen-brown—but they would preserve modesty among strangers while allowing the important clothing to be protected from the water and elements. She also used the medicine man's magic paint to draw a few designs on Hawks's face and her own for protection on the journey.

The early Europeans had encountered such people and branded them primitive, or savages. Hawks knew they probably looked very much that way now, but that was not his problem. His problem was having to look at her very beautiful figure and still keep his mind on business.

The early going wasn't too bad. When they found a current, they would follow it south, actively paddling only when that current became too swift or carried them toward obstructions and shallows or in the wrong direction. Neither had any idea of the distance they made on any given day, but the river was peaceful, and they felt good to be alive.

The navigable rivers were used by all tribes and nations as highways for trade, commerce, and information. They also connected with millions of kilometers of trails which took the sacred pipestone from Minnesota to the lodges of the south and east and returned with finely crafted gemstones and sacred totems from those places as well as tobacco, vital to many ceremonies among tribes with eastern roots.

Hawks and Cloud Dancer passed other canoes, some quite large, going upstream loaded with goods, and occasionally a craft shot ahead of them at a speed far faster and surer than they dared to travel. Their fellow travelers represented a great many tribes and nations, but they did not seek out any conversation and, except for an occasional upraised palm or even a wave, were generally ignored by the others. The river was strictly neutral territory.

The weather held for three days, then changed dramatically as a line of thick clouds rolled across the sky, followed quickly by a chilly, steady rain. Forced to pull in and make camp until the storm passed, they rigged a lean-to using the largest blankets and thick trees for shelter, but it really was a damp and miserable time. Too, their meager provisions were running quite low, and while they'd managed to find some apple trees with enough fruit just coming ripe, they could not live entirely on apples. He didn't want to use the jewels for barter yet; he didn't know who or what they might attract in this region. And while they might hunt, the ground was far too damp for them to build and maintain a fire. Anything they found would have to be eaten raw.

Cloud Dancer again proved amazingly resourceful. At her direction, they both scrambled in the mud for insects and earthworms and other live things driven out by the rains and then tied them to vines secured with small rocks in the shallows of the river. She stood there, staring at the opaque, muddy waters as if she could see right through them, hip deep herself, absolutely motionless, often for an hour or more. Then, suddenly, she was a blur of motion as the spear came down, and about half the time it would come up with a huge wriggling catfish. He tried the same thing and almost speared his own foot. It was something of a blow to his ego, but he accepted it.

She prepared two fish using the knife, but they still had to be eaten raw. He found he didn't mind it that way, although not long ago he would have recoiled at the idea. He was changing, and the longer they were out on their own, the more pronounced the change became until even he could not deny it. It wasn't just that he was getting weathered, leaner, and more muscled; it was something inside him as well. The dreams he had about Council and its wonders had been replaced, for one thing. He hadn't dreamed about what was most familiar to him in days; instead, he dreamed pastoral dreams, of building a lodge, of becoming a hunter and gatherer, of making love to Cloud Dancer. Even awake, he had to force his thoughts back to the reality of his situation. This life, this wilderness, this moment preoccupied him and seemed normal and natural to him; the world from which he'd come seemed cold, distant, somehow not merely unreal but undesirable.

It was the template, of course, but it had never affected

him to this degree before. Of course, he had never before been married to a woman of this culture and isolated in the wilderness; past Leaves had always been a matter of simply passing time until the obligation was fulfilled and he could return to his true life. He was no longer merely thinking in Hyiakutt, he was thinking *as* a Hyiakutt. It seemed as if the old Hawks had died somehow and a new Hawks born, one who'd never left this place and gone off to the other world. Each day made any other life seem unimaginable and dreamlike. Not even the rain and mud seemed unpleasant or inconvenient. Cloud Dancer lay next to him, her head on his shoulders, in silence.

"Tell me—have I changed in the past few days?" he asked her, not even sure why he was concerned about it.

"No, my husband," she answered softly. "Do you feel changed?"

"I—my thoughts seem filled with fog. I must work to remember."

"Remember what, my husband?"

"My past, my knowledge, my work. Even the lodge of the Four Families seems distant to me."

"Who are the Four Families?" she asked sleepily.

Something very cold cut like a knife through the fog in his brain. "Do you remember anything? Do you remember our marriage?"

"I—I—" She seemed suddenly very confused.

He moved away and stood. "Get up. We will have to float down more, storm or no storm."

That confused her even more. "Why should we wish to float down anywhere? I—I cannot seem to think right."

"*That* is why we must do it. Hurry! Now!"

It was a real effort to act and to keep his determination, but they packed up the supplies, loaded the canoe, and pushed off. The rain was light but steady, and they were already thoroughly soaked. The wetness they could ignore, but the mist hid the river, which was swollen and now filled with many tricky currents.

The hypnotic field did not seem to be specific to them, which meant that it might not involve them at all, but he had no idea how far down it might reach. It was weak, slow, and subtle, which was why it had caught him by surprise, but that also allowed normal river traffic to pass through without even realizing the field was there. Only because they had camped for so long in its grip was its effect so strong, and only because he had the background to recognize it and fight it were they able to move away at all.

There were two overlapping beams, one on each side of the river, moving in a short sweep pattern. Now, feeling the pulses as they passed, he realized that their campsite had to have been on the upper fringe of the field and that the canoe was now traveling directly into them. Still, the sweep area couldn't be very large; it would have to be in a normally unpopulated area with few good landings, or whoever had set it would risk catching and trapping normal traffic on the river.

The area has been sensitized to those not keyed to it. She cannot get out.

This, then, was a part of the Val's barrier. He tried to concentrate, to force himself to think of it on the old level, for that was the way to fight it. If it *was* the barrier, then he could understand why it would have some effect on him, although not the command effect intended for a total Outsider, but he couldn't understand why it had also struck Cloud Dancer. The only answer might be that if it found a potential target, it included anyone else within a certain distance of that target. To anyone farther away, it would not even exist.

The pulses were getting stronger, and he found them increasingly difficult to fight. Cloud Dancer, in the front, had already stopped paddling and was just sitting there, a frozen figure. He felt himself begin to go numb, found thinking impossible.

The canoe bounded forward, out of control, strictly at the mercy of the currents in the pouring rain.

It had taken several days for their senses to return. Hawks had no clear memories of that period of time, but both of them were scratched and bruised and covered with a mixture of mud and blood. The blood was not theirs; he had vague memories of lying in wait for small animals, beaver and muskrat and others, and seizing them, battering their brains out, and together devouring them, more like animals than humans themselves. They had, in fact, *been* like animals, hunting, killing, eating, mating, then sleeping in a primal cycle. In stages, the effect had finally simply worn off.

Now they sat on a riverbank, filthy and stark naked, not sure what to do. Oddly, Cloud Dancer was less affected than he was, mostly because of the fact that she could not even conceive of the technology that had caused this. As she saw it, they had been struck by a spell from an evil spirit, and the fact that they were alive at all and restored was a victory. Still, the situation was not lost on her.

"At least it has stopped raining," she noted.

He sighed. "The canoe is gone, our clothes and supplies are gone, even our weapons are gone, along with the jewels and the proof."

"I told you those jewels carried evil spirits within them. They should not have been with us."

He suddenly felt very stupid and mentally kicked himself, for she was, in her own way, exactly right. *That* was what the damned hypnotics were homing in on! They couldn't really be tuned to a specific individual, but they knew about the case, the papers, and the jewels, certainly. Since those were the primary objects of the search, anyway, and because the courier would have been unlikely to surrender any of them if she wished to ensure her mission and her survival, the hypnotics were sensitized to look for them. That was why no others on the river had been affected and why Hawks and Cloud Dancer had.

"The next time you warn me about evil spirits, I will listen and heed your warnings," he assured her. "The question is, what do we do now?"

"First we bathe ourselves in the river," she told him. "Then I think we should walk with the waters and see if anything washed up that we can use."

He sighed. "It has been many days now, at least. I do not think we will find anything of ours."

"Yet we must try. There is nothing else to do but to go on."

She was more correct than she knew, even though a hopeless cause had turned impossible, for they were now sensitized to the barrier, and if they walked back up through it, they would be captured again. He was actually tempted by the prospect, a sort of mental suicide. If they lived and remained in that field for a period of time, it would cause permanent, irreversible damage to the cortex of the brain. There was no guarantee that some damage hadn't already been done, but to return would be to become animals forever.

Instead, she washed him off, and he washed her, and they began walking along the bank looking for what couldn't possibly be there. Late in the day, though, the impossible happened.

The canoe did not look to be in bad shape. It had continued on for some distance after overturning and dumping them out, but it had finally been run by the current into the brush and thick mud along the bank and had stuck there. They were able to get it out with some work, and it looked whole, but of the supply bundle and the paddles there was no sign. Those could be anywhere, including at the bottom of the river, and to hope to find any more was pushing fortune beyond its limits. They did look, of course, for a fair distance down the river, but they found nothing and eventually walked back to the canoe.

"I am not sure how much better off we are," he remarked. "We can go nowhere without paddles, and we have not the means or skills to make them even if we had the makings."

"First we use what light is left to forage for some food," she told him. "Then, tomorrow, we do what must be done."

"What?"

"We push the canoe and ourselves out to a current that is safe for us, and we let it carry us, in the water, until we come upon some canoe going up or down the river. We have had an accident while on our marriage trip. We have lost everything except the canoe. Honor will demand that we be helped, do you not think?"

He held her close and kissed her. "I do not know what I would do without you."

"Out here, you would die, my husband, and without you I would have no life."

They took a position near a small island, where they could keep themselves at least partly concealed to upstream traffic. They definitely did *not* want to be rescued by someone who would take them back north, a point he had to make forcefully in her terms. That evil spirit, he told her, now knew them. They could not come close to it again.

Their plan worked. When they saw a large canoe heading downstream, they pushed themselves out and began calling for help.

The two men in the other canoe were dressed very strangely for the plains, and the styles of their hair and jewelry were also unfamiliar. One was an older, gray-haired man whose face looked as if it had been carved out of stone, while the other was quite young, possibly still in his teens. Both spoke a language Hawks had never heard before, but they took the canoe and two refugees in tow and brought them to the bank.

The young one's eyes lit up when he discovered that Cloud Dancer was unclothed, but this drew a sharp rebuke from the old man, who found them both blankets. Hawks tried the seven Indian languages that he knew, but they all drew blanks. The old man began reciting a litany that included Choctaw, Chickasaw, and the tongues of half a dozen lesser nations, but none that matched. Finally, Cloud Dancer took over.

"They are traders from the southeast," she told him. "They must be talked to as traders."

He understood what she meant. With better than two hundred nations speaking six hundred dialects of a hundred and forty-odd languages, the people of North America had long ago developed a system of universal communication that involved hand signs and ideograms. Knowledge of it assured communications even between the far eastern Iroquois and the west coast Nez Percé. It was a good system but one he didn't know. Historians, after all, dealt with written records and physical remains—the permanence civilizations leave behind. "I do not know the hand tongue," he told her.

"I think I can do enough for our needs," she replied, and started with the old man, providing a running translation as best she could.

"He is Niowak," she told Hawks. "That is his grandson, who is learning the ways of the trade."

He didn't place the tribe, except that the name seemed to be in a far north dialect that was unlikely to be heard in the south this time of year.

"He comes down from the Niobrara," she said, confirming his suspicion. "He is on his way to a village of the Tahachapee to set up a trade of some sort. He won't say what."

"I could not imagine," Hawks responded. "I cannot see what a tribe so far south would have that they would need or what they would have that this southern tribe could want. Still, it is none of our affair."

"I told him that we were on our marriage trip when we were caught in the storm, then overturned with the loss of everything when strong waters caught us."

He nodded but said nothing to indicate that there was more to their story. Some of these traders spoke forty or fifty languages, feigning ignorance to gain an advantage. "Ask him where we are."

"He says we are two days north of the Ohio," she told him. "He offers to take us there, where there is a village of the Illinois."

"Thank him for his courtesy and generosity and accept his offer," he instructed. He suddenly had a thought. "He is a trader. He certainly has at least one spare set of paddles. Ask if we can borrow a set and follow him down."

She did so. "He has. He is mad at himself for not thinking of it before. He says he is getting too old for this sort of thing."

The old trader proved a true gentleman and a resourceful one. He had a net, for one thing, which he suggested stringing between the two canoes in the shallows. It brought up several large catfish as well as a few other denizens of the river, and they ate well without depleting the old man's supplies.

The village of the Illinois was modest, but it had a number of buildings built of logs and insulated with mud and looked as if it had been built for a larger trade than was now there. The Illinois were taking advantage of the confluence of the two great rivers; they could resupply and also pass on news and other information—for a price, of course. From the looks of some of the men, Hawks suspected that they weren't above charging something of a toll as well—and enforcing it. They seemed pleasant enough, but this mercenary lot, far from the main part of their nation, was not apt to give anything out of the kindness of their hearts. The jewels would have been handy here.

The headman, a tough old character named Roaring

Bull, spoke many languages, including the Ogalalla Sioux dialect, which Hawks knew.

"So you had an accident on your wedding trip," the Illinois chief said sympathetically. "Lost everything but the canoe. What do you intend to do now?"

"I can do nothing until I can get some clothing, paddles of my own, and at least a knife, spear, and flint," he responded honestly.

"Then you go home?"

"No. We must keep pushing south. I have an old friend down in the Caje that my wife has not met and with whom I have some business."

"Oh? What's his name? I know a lot of the Caje. We do business time to time, now and again."

"Mud Runner would be his name in Sioux. He pronounces it in his own tongue so." With that he spoke the twisted syllables of the man's name.

"Ah! I do not know him, but I know *of* him. He is one of *them*. Why would you have business with one like him?"

"I, too, was one of *them*, as you say. That was where we knew each other."

Roaring Bull frowned suspiciously. "You from Council and you poking around here or what?"

"I am no longer in Council, and neither is he. Both of us are out for the same sort of thing, only I am voluntary. I fell in love with the woman who is now my wife, and I find we are better in her world together than she would be in Council. I tired of Council, anyway. Mud Runner also had affairs of the heart. Often two or three a night. Some were with the wives of the high chiefs of Council, and one time he was caught."

The Illinois chief lived up to his name, roaring with laughter. Finally, though, he calmed down and got to business. "It would seem, then, that you have a problem," he noted calmly. "We have all the things you need, and more, but we are traders. How would it look if word got out that we gave things away? We get the worst and the toughest through here. Soon everyone would be trying to take advantage of us. You see how it is."

Hawks sighed. "Then I do in fact have a problem." He thought for a moment, although he'd worked out a plan in his mind on the way down. It was best to play the game in situations like this. "We *do* have the canoe. It is tough and sturdy and of the best workmanship. Surely it is worth the small amount that I ask."

"Hah! And how would you continue your journey?"

"We would find a way with some other traders. We will walk if we have to."

"*Agh!* I have a hundred canoes and only twenty men who can use them. I need no others. Think again."

His hopes were dashed. He wished Cloud Dancer were doing this negotiating, but in this situation it was simply not proper.

"I can see nothing else."

"No one travels from the land of the Hyiakutt to the land of the Caje to show off a pretty new wife. You must need to get to this man very badly," Roaring Bull said shrewdly. "I think perhaps you might not wish to be so cut off from Council as you say. Tell you what. I will get you good clothing, weapons, supplies, and even transport all the way to this Caje man. Good boots, strong spear, metal knife, even protection all the way."

Hawks felt uneasy. "And the price?"

Roaring Bull leaned in a bit and lowered his voice. "My friend, let us be honest with one another. I have been here, in this crossroads, for a very long time, and I have seen almost everything. I have seen men come through here many times who thought they could beat the system. Men just like you, although their tribes and goals were different. Nobody just walks out on Council, not for anybody. Some get thrown out and are lucky, like your friend, and keep some job with Council, and some come back fixed in the head, but they don't walk out unless they have to, unless they are extra clever fellows like you who think they can beat the system before the system beats them. You may be out of Council, but you have left the Hyiakutt forever as well. I can smell it. To do that, you have something on your mind so important no risk is too great, no price too much to pay. I am a trader."

"Go on," Hawks responded uneasily.

"One thing I am never short of are pretty girls who are not of my people. Give me your wife and you will be safe and dry in Mud Runner's lodge within five days."

"Even if I did not love her, which I do, I owe her my life many times. She is not for trade. We will swim there naked if we must before I will do that."

Roaring Bull chuckled. "Come now, my son. You have made the break with your people and with Council. You know, if only deep down in your heart, that death awaits you, and death awaits her as well. This way you get at least a chance at whatever you are trying to do, and she will live. It seems more than fair."

"She will live as a slave of the Illinois."

The chief shrugged. "Each of us has a different life given to us by the Great Spirit. You cast your own fate when you made your choice, and it has brought you to this. It is my only offer."

"And if I refuse?"

"The leaves begin to turn. There is a chill from the north now and then that will grow stronger. I am not without some compassion. The two of you may sleep in the stables if you wish, and I will order that something be found for the sake of modesty, although it will not, I fear, help the coming chill. Some of the animal feed is all right for people if you look with care at it. Go—think over my offer. Be warned, though, that if you take one thing that is Illinois, my protection will be lifted, and you will both become slaves of the village." He grinned. "It is the least I can do."

How true that was.

The "something for the sake of modesty" turned out to be two whiplike lengths of leather cord and the pick of old and discarded cloth that could be tied to hang down front and rear. The tribe was forbidden contact with them, so there was no way they could find an ally without getting both the tribal member and themselves in trouble.

They ate parts of rotten, worm-ridden apples and talked it over. He told her everything of Roaring Bull's offer.

She listened, a grave expression on her face, but she did not seem surprised at the situation. Finally she said, "Then we must look at all our choices. We cannot remain here, not for long, like this. Can we not try and find mercy among another trader going our way?"

He shook his head. "No, we are being watched even now. No trader landing here would risk taking us, since the traders are few and the warriors here many. The first duty of a trader is to his own trade. Nor can we get away and find one elsewhere. Even if we were permitted to leave or could lose our watcher, we would have to go up the Ohio, and this would mean coming right back past here. To swim either river is far too dangerous; it almost boils where the two come together, and the distance is too great—for me, at least."

"We could simply launch our canoe and trust to the river spirits."

"Without paddles we would be caught in the rough waters to the south very quickly, and you know who would rescue us, and then there would be no bargains."

She thought a moment more. "Perhaps this chief will settle for less."

He looked at her. "What do you mean?"

"I have looked at the moon, and it is already past my bleeding time. I think the excitement and the shocks have dislodged it, but it will not be dislodged for long. It should be a safe time. Perhaps—a night in his bed for two paddles."

"*No!* I will not permit it! And it would only whet his

appetite for you. We are at their mercy. The only reason he did not just take you was some twisted code they follow, but their honor is weak. He would accept the bargain, but he would be held to no bargain with a woman. It would be for nothing."

She sighed. "Then the only other way is to fight," she said flatly.

5. THE GAME OF CATS AND MOUSE

SONG CHING WAS STILL NURSING HER MENTAL WOUNDS from her visit with her mother. Her mother had always been one of her idealized people, the superwoman who could and did do it all and who had always loved and protected her, even many times against the cold whims of her father.

"You cannot let him do this!" she had wailed at her mother. *"Please!* To marry, yes. That is part of my station and my duties. But to have him wipe it all out—it is a waste!"

"Sit down over there, my less than honorable daughter, and listen," her mother had replied. "We must now have the talk that I have known we must have since you were little. Your tears do not tear at me this time, for I know now that you have tears only for yourself, never for others. Now you will sit, and you will listen."

"Most honorable and loving mother, I—"

"Do not speak thus now, for you do not mean those words. This is not a good world or an honorable one. I doubt if the world has ever truly been any different, no matter how we romanticize it. Your life has been so sheltered, so privileged, that you do not even truly know what the lives of most of your race are like. Oh, you have played at being a peasant in the small peasant play place that we have here, but that is not truly what that life is like. It is clean, and you always know that you are playing, that servants are but a gesture away, that nothing truly bad will happen to you, and that you will return to the silks and flowers and fine food at day's end. I am not even talking about the Center; I am talking about here, on our island, in our native province."

The inevitable lecture always had to come first, although this was a new variation on the theme. Song Ching just sat and waited it out.

"Most children are born to women without benefit of doctors or medicine in their own miserable one-room huts near the fields and paddies where they work from dawn to dusk with never a break, never a holiday, never even a day off. They must make their quotas or starve, since if they do not make their quotas, many others will also go hungry. They leave their excrement in pit toilets; the flies and other insects are always there, and so is the smell. They eat two meals of rice mixed with some vegetables or, rarely, a communally shared small portion of unprocessed meat. They face heat and cold, flood and drought, pestilence and eternal poverty. They are ignorant, superstitious, have never imagined electricity, indoor plumbing, or any sort of mass communications and transportation. Their view of luxury and longing is silk clothing and Peking duck, neither of which they are likely to enjoy in their lives. You know nothing of this."

"Neither do you," Song Ching responded petulantly. "Not really."

"You think not. I was born of peasant stock on a land-hold barely a hundred kilometers from here, on this island. I was born at four in the morning; my mother was ordered out to continue the rice harvest by noon—and she did. The mud and flies and filth were my home and my early memories."

Song Ching stared up at her mother. "If this is so, why am I just now hearing of it?"

"Because you were born and raised in the leadership, the upper classes, where such peasant blood would have worried you, and it is not something one bandies about in our society without causing prejudices to form."

"If it *is* true," her daughter responded, not really believing it, "then how did you come to your position?"

"Your father is a most—unusual man. He was born and raised to be a soldier, but he had a bent for science and a head for figures, and so he was chosen at the age of twelve to go to Center for education and training, to become one of the Elect. He excelled because he allowed nothing at all to stand in the way of his advancement. We like to believe that his coldness and his callous indifference to others is a mask, but it is not. He wears no mask. I doubt if your father feels emotion, at least in the same way that other men do. I do not think he can. In a sense, he is more like the machines which rule us than a true man. He made himself that way, because to think like them and be like them is to know them and be favored by them. When he conceived his idea of dynastic genetic manipulation, he of course needed to found a dynasty. He required a wife."

"And he selected a peasant over all those of his class here and at the Center?"

"I do not know the process, except that it was calculated as finely as one of his equations. He knew the truth, although it is heresy to say it, that there is no difference between peasant stock and aristocratic stock except who your family is and how much wealth it has. They came to the village one day and took samples of the blood of every girl under fourteen. He wished a peasant girl because while he needed someone intelligent, he did not wish a highly educated and polished woman. He wanted someone with no family of consequence that he would have to accept or deal with, as he would with aristocratic or Center women. My family could not afford many girls; they were delighted to be rid of me. Just what, genetically, he saw that made me the one is something I have never known. The answer to 'Why me?' is an absurdity. It had to be someone. It was me."

"But you are a botanist! An educated woman of accomplishment beyond the home!"

"I took it up after I was at Center and it was necessary to give me the teachings and background needed to live there. He permitted it so long as it was always secondary to my role of wife and hostess and politician for him. And, of course, I was the subject of his experimentations, out of which came you. During all that time I have never complained, never regretted, never had second thoughts. Although I am dead to my village and my own family, I have never forgotten them or their lot, and I have always thanked the gods for giving me this life, and I have tried hard to do my duty and carry out my responsibilities as his wife."

Song Ching was silent for a moment. "Why do you tell me this now?" she asked finally.

"Ever since you were born, you have been coddled and spoiled. You have had only the best of everything. You have been insulated from the outside world and its ways. In the past few years, you have dared things that would have gotten any other executed, no matter what her class or station, whether woman or man. I knew that he was testing out and protecting his handiwork, but I, too, allowed and excused it, although on different grounds. I knew that one day you would have to face your own destiny and carry out the duties and responsibilities your father intended for you, and we both knew that considering the spoiled and self-centered world you lived in, this would not be possible without locally adapting you."

The term "locally adapting" sent a chill up Song Ching's spine. It meant that her mind, her memories, her talents and abilities, her personality and attitudes would be eliminated or manipulated and replaced with a far different and radically inferior template—but that such changes, although accomplished by both permanent psychochemicals and reprogramming, would not be passed on in any way to her offspring.

"How can you let this happen? I am your *daughter!*"

"I could not stop it. Deep down, you know that. It is too important to your father. Still, I can remember the cold, and the mud, and the hunger gnawing at the pit of my stomach. I will always remember it. You will never have that. You will have your silks and perfumes, your fine food, servants, and all the rest. You will not be a part of Administration, so you will not have to undergo memory imprints and Withdrawal and all the rest. No man will have you as a wife as you are. You have no sense of honor, duty, family, sacrifice, even love except for yourself. I say that in shame, for I am partly to blame for it."

"Who says I must have a husband, anyway? Why must women always defer to men? I'm smarter than any man I ever met. I can do great things with the machines, maybe greater ones if I continue my work and my studies. Am I a person or a test animal?"

Her mother had sighed. "What first to answer? Men are dominant in our culture because that is the way it has been for thousands of years, and the system worked and survived and protected the people. Men are dominant in our culture because the machines that make our rules decided to return to the ancient culture where it was so. It cannot be changed. Even if it is not a good thing, it cannot be changed. That would not be allowed. Any who try to change the system are eliminated. You yourself know this. You saw the attack on the illegal technologist fortress. Every nation, every culture of humanity, is set by command. No alterations are allowed. Everyone who ever tried has failed miserably. That is why your father thinks in the long term. His foundation is his pride. He finds it intolerable to be subordinate. He has risen as high as any can rise in our society—and he is still subordinate and still fearful of the machines who spy on him, and he hates them. He is brilliant enough to know he cannot defeat them. He is idealistic enough to hope that perhaps his descendants, as a mighty dynasty, might find a way."

"But it's not *fair*! I didn't ask for this!"

"The mere fact that you would make such a statement shows why above all else this must be done. It is not fair that we must live some machine's vision. It is not fair that our destinies are predetermined. It is not fair that my brothers and sisters grub in the mud while I scold maids for improper dusting. No one in this world ever asked for what they got. No one has much choice. It is enough to make the best out of what you have. It must be, for the only alternative is death."

Her mother had paused a moment, then added, "You ask why you cannot continue your work. It is because you are dangerously close now to exposing the whole family. Sooner or later you would try to beat the Master System, and that would be the end of us."

"The Master System *can* be beaten! We do it all the time!"

"No. The Master System can be *cheated*, which is not the same thing at all. It knows we cheat. Unless we are incompetent enough or brazen enough to allow ourselves to get caught at it, it doesn't seem to mind because we cheaters do not threaten it or the system. The fact that we can cheat and get away with cheating is our moral authority to be the leaders and our badge of office to Master System. You cannot defeat it, and you cannot resist trying. For your own sake, we must prevent you from trying."

"For *your* sake, you mean. Mother—this is no template. They are talking about *killing* me, killing my mind, leaving only my body! My body will live, but someone else, someone totally different, will be inside it! How can you allow it?"

There were tears in her mother's eyes in spite of attempts to suppress them, but her mother had simply sighed. "I cannot stop it," she had replied, then turned away and stalked quickly out of the room, leaving Song Ching alone.

Song Ching took dinner alone in her room, although she barely picked at it and had no appetite. She looked at the silk bedding, the many fine clothes and jewels there, the art and intricate tapestries, the perfumes and the rest, and decided she'd trade them all for peasant's garb and mud and thick rice if she could just stop this from happening.

She needed to get back up to Center while there was still time. There, in her own element, she felt she could cheat her father as she and he both cheated the Master System. She had an advantage there, one which she was certain he did not know about and which might prove useful, but if she was taken away and immediately thrown into reprocessing, she knew she'd never have the chance.

For the first time she considered suicide. It would be honorable, certainly, and would bring no disgrace on her family and friends, and it would be a way of regaining control. They had given her the date of her death, but they expected still to have a daughter and an experiment after that. By taking her own life, she would cheat her father out of his damned dream and maybe make them all regret this. From her point of view she would be no worse off, but she would have a measure of both control and revenge. The more she thought of it, the more attractive it became.

She had trouble getting to sleep, but finally she did doze off. Deep in the night, however, she came suddenly awake, absolutely convinced that there was someone else in her bedroom with her. There *was* someone! A large, dark shape right at the foot of her bed!

"I see that you are awakened," her father said. He clapped his hands, and a servant brought in a lantern, then bowed and quickly exited. "You greatly upset your mother tonight. This in turn upsets me and threatens the family as well. You force me to act to forestall drastic and irrational actions on the part of one or the other of you. Get up and dress now for a journey. You are leaving here this night."

She gasped, but there was never any thought of not obeying her father implicitly when in his presence. He was that sort of man.

"Please, honorable father," she said while dressing. "May I be permitted to ask where I am being taken?"

"You will go with a small detail of my most trusted men to the emergency skimmer landing site and there be placed aboard and transported to Center for reprocessing. It was not intended that you know about this at all, to spare you and others mental anguish, but because you discovered it, there is no longer any purpose in postponing it. It will be better for you and for everyone if it is done quickly." He turned to the door. "Captain!"

A young officer, looking only half awake, entered and bowed. "Sir?"

"You have your specific instructions and much latitude in completing this business quickly, quietly, and successfully. You and your men understand well what will happen to you all if anything is the least bit amiss at the end of this?"

"Sir, they have all been informed and are eager to carry out your orders."

"Then take this spoiled, self-centered brat with no honor within her and bring me back a proper daughter!"

The captain simply snapped to attention.

She was led out into the night and placed in a closed

carriage. Two nasty-looking and very determined soldiers sat across from her, and more were stationed on the rear and atop the driver's seat. No words were exchanged; they were off as soon as she was aboard.

The night was cloudy and dark, so there would have been nothing to see of the countryside even had the shades in the coach not been drawn. It took less than an hour to reach the landing site, and the skimmer was already waiting. Her father was never one to let the details slip.

The site was rarely used; in fact, she could not remember it *ever* being used. It was there only because it was both out of view of the main roads and villages and close enough to the big house for her father's use in an extreme emergency. Ordinarily, the rule was that no one see the skimmers if at all possible, and the craft generally flew at high altitudes where they were invisible from the ground and landed in remote, sealed-off areas.

Everything had happened so suddenly that she hadn't had much chance to think, and even though she was wide awake now, the whole scene still had an unreal, dreamlike quality about it, as if it were happening to someone else and observed from a distance.

The skimmer was a small five-seat courier ship built for speed rather than cargo. There were pilot and copilot, then three seats across immediately in back of them. Song Ching was flanked by the captain of the guard on one side and one of the beefy soldiers from inside the coach on the other.

The captain got up and leaned over her, then pressed hard on her wrists. She was startled and looked down to see that her wrists were now secured with thin but very strong metal bands coming out of the seat.

"A thousand pardons, my lady, but this was ordered," the captain said, sounding really apologetic.

Her feet were positioned and strapped in place, then her seat harness was drawn down and attached. None of the restraints were tight or really uncomfortable, but she couldn't move. "This is not necessary, Captain," she protested, trying to sound brave.

"It is necessary because it is ordered, my lady," the man replied, settling back into his seat and fastening his own harness. "Your father believes that you are very resourceful."

Resourceful, she thought glumly. Resourceful enough for what? To somehow overpower all four men, steal the skimmer, and make a break for some place he couldn't find me?

The door closed with a solid *chunk*, the cabin was pressurized, and they took off, rising straight up in the air, in a matter of minutes. The whole affair was so well organized, she had to wonder about it.

"Captain? Excuse me, but just when did my father give orders for all this?"

He looked uncomfortable. "Two days ago, my lady."

She nodded to herself. Two days ago. When she had first let slip that she knew what was planned for her. Somehow that figured. Made her mother upset, huh?

The craft attained its approved altitude, then went forward, slowly at first but with ever-increasing speed, pressing them all against their seat backs. She could see the instrument board from her seat and watched the air speed indicator climb until it finally slowed and halted at their cruising speed. She hadn't known that skimmers could go that fast. It was close to the speed of sound.

At this rate, they might well be back at Center by dawn.

If there was one place where Center was not, it was at or near a center. It was, in fact, on the site of a former small nomadic village on the edge of the northwestern desert. Sinkiang was a beautiful, exotic province, but it was not a place that could ordinarily support large numbers of humans except in a few isolated spots.

It was light before they reached Center, and ordinarily she loved to look out at the vast expanse of mountains, tablelands, and desert from which the great dome of the city rose, but she felt nothing now, not even apprehension. It was as if something within her was already dead, and she had even managed an uncomfortable and intermittent sleep on the journey.

They landed in a special security zone after clearing the shield. The door opened, and the flight crew shut down and got out, then the captain undid her restraints and helped her up. She was stiff and sore from being held in one position for so long.

Although she knew the great city well, she had never been in this area before. She had known it was here, of course, but the area had held little interest for her before.

They marched her down a long corridor with automatic security gates every ten meters or so, each one opening easily before them but closing behind with a strange finality. The corridor led down far below even the maintenance level of the city. Finally, they reached a reception room of sorts, where the captain and his guard were relieved of their responsibility. There they were met by a five-member squad of military women, all of whom looked like they loved torturing small children and animals. All five wore the loose-fitting tunic and baggy trousers commonly worn in Center, but these clothes were white with broad red stripes on them. She wondered why they would wear such strange and ugly things.

"Honorable lady, I apologize for the journey and thank you for allowing us to do our duty," the captain said sincerely, clearly glad that his part of things was over. "I wish you only the best fortune."

She felt as if she were expected to thank her executioner, but the man was clearly in a spot himself and had treated her with respect. "Return with my blessings, Captain," she responded. "Thank you for your courtesy." And with that, the two soldiers got a signed receipt from the head of the squad, bowed, and left.

"Stand there and remove all of your clothes," the squad leader instructed in a harsh, nasty voice.

Song Ching was startled. Never in her life had she undressed in front of strangers. "I am the eldest daughter of a warlord and the chief administrator," she responded proudly. "I do not get spoken to like that, nor do I disrobe in public!"

"Get one thing straight, little flower," the leader snapped. "You *were* those things. In here you are nothing. You are the property of the state, and we are the state. We have all sorts of highborns here, many greater than you, and it all means nothing here. If you do not begin to disrobe in five seconds, you will be restrained and forcibly disrobed. From this time on, there will be no second chances. When someone gives you an order, you will obey it or it will go hard on you. Voluntarily or bound and gagged, it is all the same to us."

For the first time she felt really scared, but she still did not comply. Her pride would not allow it. A gesture from the leader was made, and two women moved swiftly, throwing her against the wall and then ripping off her fine silks. She screamed and struggled, but no one came to her aid or seemed to mind in the least. Her arms were brought forward, and light but strong handcuffs were placed on both wrists, each clip fastened to the other by a chain roughly half a meter long. She could use her hands, but only within limits. Nearly identical cuffs were placed on her legs above her ankles.

"Now, will you walk or must we carry you?" the squad leader asked, a note of satisfaction in her voice. Clearly she enjoyed exercising power over those born to a higher and more privileged position than she.

"I will walk," she responded sullenly.

They moved fast; she almost had to shuffle to keep up, her stride limited by the leg restraints. They took her into a room and sat her in a barber's chair, and a woman there quickly trimmed her shoulder-length silky black hair

to a short masculine cut. Her long, pointed nails were not
cut down, but they were trimmed to a roundness that
looked grotesque. She was then given a crude but thorough shower, with the guards doing the scrubbing. The
experience was humiliating, and she wanted to scream,
but she wasn't going to give them the satisfaction. She
decided quickly that what would disappoint them the most
would be to keep an aristocratic air and remain fatalistic.

Again she was marched down an endless series of corridors until they reached a line of doors. When the squad
leader activated one with a thumbprint, the door slid back
and Song Ching was ushered into a cell. Her arm and leg
bindings were then undone and removed.

The cell was completely empty. The walls, floor, and
even the ceiling were featureless and thickly padded.
Lighting tubes at the wall-ceiling joints provided good, if
soft, light, but those fixtures were a good four meters up
and protected by some sort of opaque material. The whole
cell was not more than four by three meters.

"Now, listen well," the squad leader told her. "You will
remain here until called for. Your father who committed
you ordered this so that you might not do harm to yourself. You will be fed twice a day here, in the cell, under
the eyes of a guard. Anything you do not eat will be
removed when the guard leaves, and you will get no more
until the next scheduled meal, so eat. The cell is soundproof, but that small piece in the door is one-way glass.
We will look in on you from time to time to be sure you
are all right, but we will not disturb you. If you need to
eliminate, go to this corner and sit. A toilet will adjust to
you. Do not, however, put your hand or anything else in
there. The toilet is a dry one, and anything that should
not go there will be trapped and held there until we come
and remove you. If you look over here next to the toilet
area, you will see a small flexible tube in the wall. If you
thirst, suck on it and water will be dispensed in small,
measured amounts. The reservoir takes one hour to refill.

Also, any attempt to do yourself harm and you will get far shorter handcuffs and leg chains. Any questions?"

"Yes. How long will I—be here?"

"As long as is necessary. Don't worry. When you leave here, you won't remember any of this, even in your nightmares." With that, the squad left, and the door closed with an awesome finality.

For a while she paced and fumed in frustration. They had it all worked out, their methods honed over centuries of experience. Worse, they really *could* do almost anything they wanted to her because, as the guard said, she would remember none of it and so could not complain or report it. She even guessed the reason for the guards' odd clothing. Probably workers left their own clothes outside and picked up those uniforms once inside the security barriers. Thus, even if someone managed somehow to get out or make a break while going to and from the medical area and somehow beat the security checkpoints, that person would either be nude or wearing very conspicuous clothing.

What was so frustrating was that her own computer lab was probably no more than a hundred meters up and then a kilometer away. In those rooms she could take control and show them all—if only she could get to them. If, if, if, she thought sourly. If only she'd kept her big mouth shut about this and worked out a way to come back here to finish up a few things. If only she hadn't been so wild that even her mother could no longer see her as anything but a threat. She had been so smart with all things electronic, but she realized she'd been pretty stupid when it came to people. She had always been in command, in control. She'd never had to worry about other people.

The cell was an effective prison. She examined it closely, every joint and junction, until she saw a small dark spot hidden behind the light guard in one corner. The others were harder to make out, but there seemed to be one in each corner. Somewhere, perhaps not far off, someone was sitting in a chair and looking at her in the full three dimensions, probably recording her and analyzing her every movement with computer psych analyzers. She had never felt so exposed or humiliated in her entire life, and she hated them for it and hated her father for ordering this. Just a laboratory animal, that's all she was to him. The imperial ducks were the most pampered and protected of pets—until it came time for the formal dinner. The difference, the only difference, here was that the ducks didn't—couldn't—know their fate as she did. It was a difference that would be of no relevance to her father, she knew.

She was fed in a little while. The starkness and absolute soundproofing of the cell had already made her lose all track of time. They used two female matrons, one to serve and the other to stand guard with a nasty-looking baton that, Song Ching was warned, gave a nasty but temporary shock and left no marks. The meal was a large bowl of extremely gummy white rice topped with some light soy sauce and a few lumps that pretended to be vegetables. She was not given chopsticks, another indignity, and had to eat with her hands. She ate very little of the first meal, and it was then taken away, and she was left alone for what seemed like an eternity. Within a very few feedings, though, she was eating quite well and even anticipating the next meal, not only because she felt as if she were starving but also because no matter how nasty and terse the guards were, it was some interruption, some human company.

After a while she had no idea how long she had been there or whether or not her system was being disrupted by irregular feedings, but after a while the cell and the routine became her only reality; her old life and family already seemed far away.

When the door opened the next time, she thought it was for another meal, which seemed overdue. She was starved, but it was not for feeding. They stood her up, gave her a hospital gown to wear, then placed the handcuffs and ankle restraints on her and led her out. She still felt distant, in a daze, not really able to do more than go along with her captors.

She was given a thorough physical exam by both human doctors and machines, and she understood now why she'd left a meal out. They injected tracers, then placed her in small chambers for analysis. Then it was back to the cell and mealtime. They repeated everything several times, at least twice after a meal to compare some results with others, but it was always back to the cell.

Finally satisfied, they took her to a small room and had her lie on what seemed to be a giant bed of cotton. Her head was covered with some kind of scanner, a top was brought down, and then they began doing odd things. Her nipples and other arousal spots were gently stimulated. Various areas received pressure, some uncomfortably, some not, and at one point she felt as if someone had stuck a pin in her behind. Later, humans would be there with some of the same unpleasant stimuli, and she resisted a bit and tried to avoid the needles, the pressure pads, and the rest. Finally she was bathed and then taken down to the place she dreaded most, which was simply referred to as the surgery.

When she and her guards arrived, though, the previous project or whatever it was was still going on, and they had to stand and watch. There was not a lot to see; two young boys, it appeared, were strapped on cots while technicians monitored them. Song Ching looked around and found much familiar in the surgery. There was medical equipment, of course, but the computer interfaces were the same as Center standards. Center stage, as it were, was a set of the latest mindprint machines. If I could get loose in here, even for five minutes, I might escape this thing, she thought wistfully.

"If I may humbly ask," she whispered to the chief guard, "who are those boys, and what have they done?"

The guard surprised her by answering. "They are the children of a tech cult. The only survivors. They are being mined of all they know, and then they will be sent to Melchior. Be happy, little flower, that you are not in their place instead of your own."

Melchior. She had heard of it in her father's business. The prison from which none returned, under the control not of Master System but of the Earth Council, which included her father. Rebels, deviants, and political prisoners were sent there, it was said, for unauthorized medical experimentation. A chamber of horrors, she knew, but a chamber of horrors not on Earth but in space, inside one of the asteroids. *In space* . . .

"We can't wait all day," one of her guards snapped. "Let's just log her in and leave her. These doctors always keep their own schedules."

The leader nodded, and she was taken to a comfortable chair, not unlike one in a barbershop, and her regular restraints removed. They then logged her in to the security computer.

"Subject Priority one nine seven seven," the guard said to the computer board. "Log in and secure in Chair Two subject only to Doctor Wang's or the master security code."

"Acknowledged," the computer responded in a crisp, human-sounding, but expressionless voice. Clamps came out from the chair as the guards held her in position, securing her arms, legs, chest, and neck.

"The doctor will be in to see you when he's ready, little flower," the guard told her. "Just sit and relax and watch the show." And with that, they left her.

She turned her head as much as she could to watch the technicians across the room with the two boys. She wished *they* would go before the doctor got here. This was perhaps the only chance she would ever have, and she was anxious not to miss it, although she had no real plan.

A small, thin man with a gray wispy goatee entered, stopped, and looked at the technicians. "Leave that for now. They aren't going anywhere," he told them. "I have much more important work to do. They can be read out on automatic, and I'll call you when it's done."

"As you wish, honorable doctor," responded one technician. After checking their boards, they left as well.

Wang came over to her and gave her a friendly smile. "Hello, there. I realize that this has been most distressing to you, but it should be very many more days until you are rid of us. I am Doctor Wang, Chief of Psychosurgery here. It is an honor to work on someone like you."

She stared at him. He was treating this as if it were a skinned knee or a broken arm. "You are my murderer. I do not find it at all amusing," she said coldly.

"No, my dear, I am no murderer, although you are not the first to make that sort of comment. I'm no butcher like those two will face on Melchior. I am an artist, you might say. I take people like yourself who are a danger to themselves and their families, and I create out of them people who will live full, happy, productive lives. My media are your body and your mind, but what is created will come from you, not from me. I only give some instructions here and there and nudge it in a positive direction."

"I am not insane! You are not curing someone who is sick! You are destroying someone who is well and far more productive than your results could ever be."

"Well, I don't know about that. Insanity, you see, has always been what the ruling culture said it was. In many places advocating that the Earth is round or that it moves about the sun would be absolute evidence of insanity. To be sane is not to be correct but to fit in with one's dominant cultural patterns. You are not insane by Center's lights, but you no longer can be allowed here. You are going into areas dangerous to everyone, and you cannot possibly be stopped without treatment like this, anyway, which would make you valueless here. Thus, you must be rendered sane according to the culture of the people."

He was behind her now, adjusting equipment that came down on either side of her head and touched both her arms.

"We could have the computers do all of this, with no human intervention," Wang told her, "but then it *would* be destruction, since everyone would come out according to a set of machine statistics. We cannot, however, involve the Master System here until quite late in the exercise since, quite frankly, there is too much in your head that we would rather not have Master System know about. Nothing in here, for example, is directly connected to Master System. It gets the results we wish to report, not what really happens. I'm certain you know that game by now."

"Yes," she responded sourly. *No direct connection.* Everything was perfect except she couldn't do a thing about it!

"All right, now let's take a good look at you." There was a click, and in front of her formed a hologram of an amorphous mass.

"That is the part of the brain we deal with first," he told her. "That's *you* there. Let me make some adjustments."

The image changed as parts of it were eliminated and smaller parts enlarged until there was just a skeletal outline of a single small area in orange outline. In the bottom were a tremendous number of holes, a few of which were filled with solids of many colors in the shapes of jigsaw puzzle pieces.

"Countless thousands of neural receptors are inside your brain," he told her, "all of which are now being monitored by the computer. We are visualizing only a cross section of the basics, but what we see here can tell us what is happening elsewhere. For example, you have high hormonal levels, but your psychosexual level is quite low, meaning that you don't think of physical sex as very important to you. Now, that energy has to go somewhere, so it goes into aggression, a drive to work or achieve, that sort of thing. It's all interrelated, and it shows up quite clearly on my monitor here. You—your conscious self— are actually the result of matching your biochemistry to your memories and experiences. We are far less free than we believe. The brain's biochemistry creates much of our personality, our limitations, our interests, and our inclinations. Before we can ever deal with memory, we must deal with the biochemistry, those receptors. To do it any other way would not give us *you* to compare things with. It would be hit or miss, trial and error."

She stared at the hologram in horrified fascination. "You are saying we are nothing but *machines*. That what I see is my Master System, my core program, which was determined by my genes."

"In a way, yes. However, all biological creatures have a multiplicity of sensors and an even more complex set of social and cultural interactions. Key to it all are the receptors for pain and pleasure. In normal cases we would not have to eliminate your expertise in computers, for example. By reorienting, by blocking certain receptors from that work stimulus, and creating unpleasant sensations when it is invoked by the brain, while giving a different activity, such as weaving, an interrelationship with the old pleasure center, we can create someone who knows all about computers but is not the slightest bit interested in them and finds them obnoxious but to whom sitting at a loom would be pure delight. In ancient times some of this could be forced by deprivation and conditioning, but it was brutal, unsure, and sloppy at best. This cuts out the middleman, as it were, and ensures permanency and perfection."

"This—this is what you do?"

"Primarily. Everything is subject to the cranial biochemistry. We can make you cry and feel miserable when you are happy and laugh hysterically at the funeral of your best friend. Even humor and tragedy are found here. It is like opium. The experience is so pleasurable that nothing else is possible except sustaining the experience. Opium drops pleasure modules in the receptors. It is, however, a foreign substance and is eventually expelled as such by the body, but the experience lingers so much that you wish only to find more. That is addiction. Once we discover the right mix of modules and blockers, we can stimulate your own body to produce the needed enzymes. As with genetically mandated enzymes, the combination that forms you as you are now, we will use blockers to prevent undesired genetically mandated material from finding its receptors, while our newly stimulated substances will find theirs. Over a relatively short period of time the body will adjust and shift to this new pattern, overriding the old, and it will be totally permanent and self-perpetuating. It is so complex that only a computer could isolate and define all the receptors and determine the mix, but only after *I* tell it the desired goals. There."

She felt pressure and a very slight momentary stinging in her right shoulder.

"Just relax. Only a mild test," he assured her soothingly. "Purely transitory. We won't get into anything really elaborate today."

She waited, scared to death of this man and his machines, and watched the hologram. Not all the chemical pieces remained put for any length of time; things were always changing, pieces disconnecting and others coming in, although the basic pattern remained the same.

Now, suddenly, some new pieces came into the scene, in colors not otherwise represented. Some were jet-black; others were yellow or gray. Many went right by, but some headed immediately for receptor points as if on homing beacons. A few of the black ones stuck to a blood vessel wall, as if waiting, and when some of the blue pieces vacated their natural positions, the black ones dislodged themselves and then swept in to fill the emptiness. More of the blue entered, natural chemicals, but they found their places occupied, and after pausing as if they were intelligent creatures, they moved on and out of view.

She continued to watch, and suddenly she began to tremble. She felt afraid—afraid not of the doctor or his machines but of *everything*. She began to cry, and the cry turned into uncontrollable sobbing. She felt a sense of terrible despair. Everything was hopeless. She was unloved, reviled, loathsome to others and to herself. She was unworthy, incapable of doing anything right. She needed someone—anyone—to protect her, to guide her. She needed someone—anyone—to instruct her in all things. She was afraid almost to think, to make any decisions, because she could only make the wrong ones. She felt so humble, so tiny and insignificant, that she wished someone would take her and command her.

The display shifted, although she had not seen it and had not even felt the second injection. Substances of differing colors moved in and eased out the foreign objects; the black ones were ordered out, and some but not all were replaced in her biochemical tapestry.

She stopped crying, feeling much, much better now; a damp cloth wiped her face, and she smiled at the feel. It felt *wonderful*. Everything felt wonderful. Her whole body tingled, and even the brush of skin against the chair or her hospital gown seemed an erotic caress. She was drifting now on a wonderful, magical euphoric cloud in which nothing at all mattered. They could do anything, anything at all to her, and it would not matter. She rarely had any sort of sexual dreams or fantasies, but this was real, and she wished someone would come and take her and ravish her body and do whatever they wished with her. She had a vision of herself as a sultry woman of pleasure, dancing, moving, naked and free in front of a group of adoring men, and she really liked the fantasy.

Blockers and enzymes shifted and changed, and the feelings and the fantasies faded quickly. Reality returned, although she had always been conscious of where she was and what was happening. The difference was that she was becoming clearheaded once more, coldly confident, and increasingly angry over what was being done here. She struggled against her bonds, cursing the fact that she was trapped in a weak woman's body. She didn't *feel* like a woman; deep down, she had a vision that she was a man, a man trapped by science or sorcery in this weak girl's body, a strong and virile man with courage and confidence and raw animal power. She'd rather bed this body than be trapped in it. Anger turned to pure animal fury, and she struggled against the metal rings that bound her. Adrenaline pumped, and she actually twisted and bent the rings and managed to get one hand free. *He* would show them! *He* would.

More shifting, more changing color patterns. The sense of strong sexual identity faded but was not replaced. She had no concept of maleness or femaleness; gender was an irrelevancy, without meaning to her. The anger, too, faded quickly, and she felt totally calm, unable even to relate to the emotions she had experienced up to that point. She was like a machine: aware, intelligent, but without passion, without any feelings at all about anything. Yet she was as clearheaded, as logical, as she could ever be. Stripped of her animalism, she stared at the patterns in the hologram and almost immediately grasped their logic and meaning based upon what she had seen so far. At this level, where even pleasure and pain, fear and love, were mere terms, she analyzed her situation. She was being reprogrammed, but this level was the most efficient for undertaking an escape. There was no hatred, no bitterness, no feeling of any sort that was relevant to her. Escape was mandated because this stage was the optimum one for her potentials, and it was illogical to abort it.

"I believe we have done enough for today," Doctor Wang said casually. "Too much can wear you out and cause harm to the body. My! You really did a job on those restraints! Well, I will just recline you now and allow you to rest and the enzymes to be expelled from your system. It will probably cause you to sleep, so just relax and let it happen. I'll be back in a few minutes to check you out, then you can go and eat."

She watched the doctor actually leave and no one else come back in. She did not feel elation or any other emotion, but she realized immediately that they had made their first mistake. There was simply no way that the chief administrator, her father, was going to allow *this* place to be without standard safeguards.

"Code Lotus, black, green, seven two three one one," she said aloud in a calm, expressionless voice. "Emergency override activation is ordered."

A computer voice responded from somewhere to the left rear of her. "Code acknowledged," it said. "Reason for interrupt?"

"Pawn takes king."

"Accepted. Instructions?"

Her father could never trust anyone, and that meant *anyone*. All Center computers with human interfaces were programmed with override codes that would allow him, if need be, to countermand almost any order. He changed the codes quite often and then just as often forgot them, so he had them encoded in his personal files. The only time when he couldn't depend on this was when he was away in Hainan or on Leave, as he was about to be now. For that period, he needed a sequence of codes he could always remember, and he often used a variation of the same sequences year after year. At fifteen, she had broken that code and had gone undiscovered, and she had had little trouble in the hidden room back home in establishing the few changes for this year now that she knew what she was looking for. That had been her one hope, but this had been the first opportunity to use it.

"Subject in Chair Two is object threat to king. At a point when this laboratory is not scheduled for use for a period of at least one hour, you will release subject from cell and substitute recording of previous time of subject in cell so that this is undetected, and you will suppress all alarms and guarantee uninterrupted access. You will be prepared to assist and guard. All outbound channels are monitored, so this is under my seal alone."

"Understood. Additional?"

"I would like to perpetuate my current physical and mental orientation until otherwise instructed. Then stand by until I am able to contact you here again."

"Understood. Formulating." There was a pneumatic hiss below her arm, then an injection. "Duration indefinite. Must be altered chemically."

"Understood. Switch off. I will sleep now."

She went immediately to sleep and did not dream at all.

She awakened back in her cell, but one thing was different. This time they had left the rice bowl and cool tea and not remained to watch her eat. Apparently they were confident of her and themselves now. She would require energy, and there was no way of forecasting when more might be available, so she went over and ate it all. She drank sparingly. She was aware that she could not move for long periods about the cell without attracting attention. She had been so—*animalistic*. She therefore assumed a position of meditation facing the door and willed her body into trancelike stillness. For the first and only time in her life, she had nearly total control over herself; she did not wonder at that but rather took it for granted.

There were alternatives to consider. Song Ching was in the Master System, so Song Ching must be accounted for somehow, at least for a sufficient length of time to make good an escape. She was in control only of the local network here; she had to take care not to flag Master System and not to raise human alarms. Master System she thought she could block for a sufficient period of time; the humans were the unpredictable ones.

Even if she escaped from here, though, there would be little she could do. Any security flag within Center itself would be immediately checked with Colonel Ching or her father. All direct access by her would have been blocked long ago. She could, of course, survive almost indefinitely in the maze of tunnels and service corridors. They might eventually activate a Val, but it would be useless because it would have her old imprint and assume that she would act on animal and distinctly Song Ching motives. If nothing else presented itself, though, she would do that until she was either captured or had managed somehow to tie in to the network from below and use it.

She also had infinite patience and waited for the inevitable to happen or not to happen. She could not even feel any sense of danger or excitement. Her plan was something that had to be tried on grounds of pure logic; it was that and nothing else which motivated her. She would not even feel disappointment if she was apprehended, or even if the door failed to open at all.

But it did open. She waited a moment to make certain that it hadn't opened to let an orderly pick up the food, then stood and walked out and down the maze of corridors, all barriers opening before her. She had been this way in a conscious state only once, but the route was absolutely clear to her. She met no one but was fully prepared to kill if she had to. Death meant absolutely nothing to her.

The lab was deserted, as she knew it would be, and she ordered it sealed to the outside. "How long can you avoid someone discovering I am gone?" she asked the computer.

"With an adjustment in the records showing that you

have been fed and tended to and adjustments in the staff's orders, including Doctor Wang's, I can delay a minimum of twenty-four hours but no more than seventy-two."

"I must escape beyond the reach of Center or Administration so long as the threat remains," she told it.

"I do not see any way that this is possible."

"Nor do I. Other than escaping to the service corridors, my only other possibility is to escape to space with access to a spaceship command module. Other emergency overrides are possible once I am in that position."

"Any spaceship? Any size?"

"Yes. So long as it will support my biological requirements."

"There is one way, but it is complex and for that very reason has only a marginal chance of success."

"Proceed."

"There are two prisoners who are completed here and are to be transported in a matter of hours to an interplanetary courier, to be sent to Melchior."

"I have seen them."

"The younger of the two is close to your size, and with preparation and in transport clothing you might pass for him. While they will not look too closely so long as the paperwork is correct, some extreme adjustments would have to be made to you in order for you to sustain the masquerade all the way to the spaceport. Additionally, something must be done with the one whom you will replace, and adjustments must be made to the other, for he will know immediately that you are not his cousin and is most likely to betray you."

"What measures?"

"It is not sufficient that you masquerade as a boy. To sustain it, you must *be* the boy. There is no point at which you will be stripped on the schedule, but we are talking thirty hours to clear, during which any slip will be fatal."

"Proposal?"

"The two have been kept sedated on a robot-controlled

console table in a medical cell in the men's section pending transfer. I can get them here without human intervention or knowledge for a period of time. If we begin now, I can make some basic physical and chemical alterations in you within two hours. Because of the time involved, much of it will be synthetics and a basic shell, but it will be authentic and convincing. It is not possible to actually switch minds, nor desirable in this case in any event, because your psychochemistry and physical requirements are so different, but I can lay his template atop my alterations and reinforce the illusion with hypnotics. You will act like him, think like him on the conscious level, walk and talk like him. You will not be him, but you will think you are. I will then use a strong hypnotic on the other and replace the mental image of Chu Li with what you will look and sound like, and he will accept you as his cousin even in the face of true physical evidence to the contrary. I will also modify the security holograms with animation to show you and not the real Chu Li in pictorials and charts. Barring the unforeseeable, it should be adequate."

"Duration?"

"Your template, being unsuited to you, will begin to deteriorate rather quickly, but it should hold reasonably well for at least the necessary three days, as will the hypnotics. The hypnotic on the companion, being far simpler, should last longer. Underneath, you will have access to all your own memories and knowledge, but your personality will be the new one. Be warned that even with this, the possibilities of being successful are slim, perhaps two percent."

"And the service corridor route?"

"The possibility of doing more than surviving there is no more than one percent. Survival possibilities are higher—nine percent. Restored to your original genetic encoding, which adds the animal safeguards, you have almost a thirty percent chance of indefinite survival but less than a one percent chance of doing anything more than that."

"Why would I have more of a survival chance as the old Song Ching?"

"Right now you must think about all alternatives, then make the most logical decision. The full animal instruction set allows action without thinking and induces many cautions."

"It is not logical to use the corridor alternative, then, since I would be unable to continue my work, and this is the sole reason for escape. It is not much better an alternative than allowing the work here to proceed. The space route is the only logical choice allowing any chance of complete success."

"Agreed. However, there is a caution. While the hypnotics and template will deteriorate, the psychochemical changes will not. You will be a sexually oriented male and will retain a basically male set of personality characteristics. As you presently are, this does not seem a consideration, but it has the potential to cause great anguish later. To undo and restore without causing permanent damage or alterations would require your template and codes and an installation such as this, unlikely to be in friendly hands."

"Escape is the only imperative. All other problems are potential and therefore secondary. Enact."

6. Bargains at Spear's Point

"**I** AM A HISTORIAN, A MAN OF WORDS AND ANCIENT objects," Hawks told her, feeling uncomfortable. "I am no fighter. I do not lack the courage, but I lack the training and skills to go against these renegades."

"Your muscles are developing in the right places," Cloud Dancer assured him. "And your reactions are quite swift for one who works with words, as I have seen. Not one of these men I have seen is even fit to carry your spear. Their strength is entirely in numbers. Apart they would be cowards and helpless."

"What you say might be true, but in case you had not noticed, my dear wife, I do not possess the spear they are not fit to carry, nor bow, nor arrows, nor knife, nor anything else that they have in plenty. And I move in the dark like a buffalo," he added.

"We shall see. I shall see what we are up against this night, and we will then make plans for tomorrow night. There may be some way to find things here that might

122

make weapons. A weapon is anything which can be used as one, after all."

He was startled. "You are going out there?"

"In the early hours, when it is chill and very dark. There are clouds tonight. That will help. For now, let us find some not so rotten fruit to steal from the poor animals and get some rest."

When she woke him, he frowned and rubbed his eyes, then saw that the first light of a dismal gray day was already dawning. "It is too late," he mumbled. "We have slept through the darkness."

"*You* slept through. I have been out and around half this village," she responded, sounding very pleased with herself.

That woke him up fast. "What!"

"Sssssh! They are poor excuses for warriors. Two watched from across the way, one almost across from the door here and the other from down the street. The one across from us slept most of the night through, while the one down the street kept leaving for drinks from a container inside and was seeing anything but us. The sleeping one was depending on a dog to wake him if we moved, but although the dog saw me, it approached and wagged its tail, as if waiting for a treat of food. When it found I had none, it followed a short distance, then lost interest and returned to its still sleeping master. There *are* some very mean-looking guards, it is true, but they guard the landing and the storehouse, which is far from here. Even they seemed bored and might not be impossible to get by."

"But you might have been killed!"

She smiled. "No, I am the prize, remember? You they might kill, my husband, but me they want and will take if we do nothing. More, I have made a friend, I think. One who might be of value to us."

"What? Who?"

"I do not know her name, nor her tribe, but it is certainly far down the river. She is one of their slaves, a small, pretty woman aged far beyond her years. She was the only one who surprised me, and it was very much by chance. I think she rises in the middle of the night to prepare the big lodge where most of them eat the morning meal. She just stepped out back and almost ran in to me. She clearly knew who I was. I guess they all do."

"You say this is a friend, yet you do not know her name, her tribe, or her work exactly, and she is a longtime slave here?"

"She could not tell me. She did not know the sign language or Hyiakutt. It would not matter if she had seen you, however, who know so many tongues. Someone, perhaps long ago, cut her tongue out."

That both angered and sickened him. "So what makes you say she is a friend who comes from the south?"

"Anyone can get a few basic pieces of information across with hand, body, and eyes. I believe she would help us just to spite *them*, but she also does not wish me to join her. She may be of great help. Kitchens such as theirs have sharp knives and hatchets."

Perhaps fortune was finally taking pity on them, although it certainly hadn't up to now. He could understand the slave's situation and pity her. Here in a culture as alien to her as his was to the Aztec, she would be lost and without friends. Escape? To where? Even if her tribe was willing to take her back, the chances of which were fifty-fifty, she would first have to get there, far to the south, a young woman without even the power of speech in a wilderness alien to her.

"We will check out the area and see what our true situation is," he told her. "See what we can and cannot get away with, too. They have the respect of the tough river traders, so that means they have influence beyond this small village. They are not hunters but traders. They could not support all this without something strong to trade."

"They are thieves!" she shot back.

"Yes, and more. They sell their protection, I think. If you trade with them, on terms very generous to them, you have no problems. If not, well, the river is wide and mostly desolate. You simply meet with an unfortunate accident, and they have even more to trade."

"It is indecent if what you say is true! They have no honor at all! I cannot understand why warriors such as these traders do not band together and wipe out this snake nest!"

"Roaring Bull is clever and only as greedy as he knows he can be. He does not demand so much that they will be injured by paying him, and he probably does this only to those traders far from tribes and homes. The tribes of this region he does not touch, and he probably also supplies them with the fire drinks. Perhaps he is very clever and keeps only what he extorts, letting the other area tribes be the accidents. In any case, he keeps them happy and on his side. He also knows, as do the traders, that if they were to come at him in force, providing they could put aside all their tribal and national rivalries and trust and cooperate with one another for that much, one of the other tribes would simply move in and replace him."

"You are speaking as if we cannot get away even if we do escape," she noted. "How far south would his voice reach?"

He shrugged. "Not too far either way or he would have far too large a set of bribes to pay to make it worthwhile. A full day, perhaps. Give him two just to allow for errors. That is why it is not as simple as slitting a few throats and slipping away, and he knows it."

She considered that. "Then if he wants me, I do not see why he plays this game with us. He could just order you killed and take me."

"He could, but he does have his own twisted code, I think. More important, he is concerned that I am from Council. He knows I am in trouble with them, but he also does not know how much influence I might have. We can be traced here simply because Council hunters would start with the Four Families' lodge and know of you, and when they found you here, they would not be gentle with those who mistreated me."

"But you said they would kill you for what you know!"

"They would. Most times they can play tricks with the mind, erase or change things, but they would not be permitted to take the slightest chance that anyone could ever learn what I knew, and many would try to find out for their own gain. They would kill me—but first they would want to know all that I know so they could be sure that my death would end it."

She sighed. "It is all so complicated. Roaring Bull is the high chief of this whole region, yet he fears those of Council. Council, in turn, fears—what? You said they would not be permitted to take the chance. Who would they have to ask permission of? They are the guardians of all of this land, are they not?"

"Of this continent, yes, but there are many other continents and regions. The man I need to see is head of Council in one of those places. The heads of all the Councils in turn make up a body known as the Presidium. It is an odd, non-Hyiakutt word, but it means 'to rule.' They are given great power to make sure that the whole world follows the rules and great rewards for doing it."

She yawned but was fascinated. "So who makes the rules all must follow?"

"A—there is no real word for it in our tongue. A man-built mind. A thing that is as of man as this stable yet thinks impossibly faster than the finest human minds and knows the knowledge of the universe. It made the rules and commanded that this all be done long ago, in ancient times."

"Where is it? It sounds like a great demon of the Inner Darkness."

"It is. The demon that stalked our land weeks ago was created by it to serve it. A machine in the crude, distorted form of a man. As to where it is, no one knows. That knowledge is of the sort that would get anyone killed. It protects itself. It might be beyond those trees there or high overhead in a great ship that is a small moon and circles us, or it might be in a greater ship that goes to the stars and never is in one place. No one is allowed to know. Its vast machines are loyal to it and must follow its orders exactly. They convey the messages to and from something only they know. Information, and orders as well. Unless we threaten its system, it lets its humans rule. It selects those rulers, and it rewards and punishes them."

"But how does it rule this way?"

"The same way Roaring Bull rules. By fear. It was created by fear and out of fear, and so fear is what it knows best. That has always been the most effective and efficient means of making people do what a leader wants them to do. Fear—and reward. Long ago, it is said, humans created horrible weapons that could destroy all life down to the last rat, cockroach, and even blade of grass. Some of those in charge of those weapons feared them terribly and tried to find a way around their leaders to be certain that no such weapons would be used. With this fear, they built the machine, and they set it to discover a way that humans would never be allowed to destroy themselves. Somehow it found a way to take control of all the weapons of all the nations, and it threatened to use those weapons against their own makers unless they obeyed. Some did not believe, and it did use the weapons to destroy those nations. The rest, out of fear, did just what the machine commanded them to do. All served out of fear, but some served because they came to worship the machine and wished only to please it. These are the ones who were set over and apart from the rest."

"There are legends of this thing, but I never thought of them as more than that."

"They are not legends but truths. Its very creators became its victims. It is said that they were all the first ordered killed. They did not dream what their creation would do. It ordered them to tear down the whole of the world and build it back up as it had been in many other times. Tremendous amounts of knowledge were completely forbidden, wiped away, along with the great things humans had done. It had logic and its orders. It decided that the only way to ensure than man, with his violence, cruelty, and tyranny, could never destroy himself was to keep man forever in a state of knowledge where such weapons and such means could never be even imagined. The bright ones who might change things either were taken up to the leadership to fall under its commands directly or were either managed or killed. Superior knowledge was reserved for Council, and even that has limits, which is why I run. I know now a piece of knowledge that it thought long extinguished from the mind of any person."

"It is evil. It came out of the formation of all evil, the fire pits, and it rules us." She shuddered. "You speak almost as if those of Council worship it."

"They *do* worship it. It is their god, their sole belief, and they serve. They do not, however, love it as we love the Creator, the Great Spirit who created the universe. They serve because they fear it and cannot fight it. They hate it, for evil is hate, and fear, and terror, and brutality. They must have all these things to serve it properly. It is the Lord of the Inner Darkness, the ultimate void, which encompasses everything. It is an ancient story. Once human beings occupied its place, and they were set to destroy not only themselves but everything. So others, in fear, built their own god and gave it dominion over the rulers of men. That is the tragedy of it."

"What?" She yawned again, unable to stave off sleep much longer.

"That men have always dreamed of being the rulers of the Inner Darkness, and some finally made it, only to have it snatched from them by another. Our leaders now do not hate its power; they envy and they covet it. They wish to reclaim it for themselves. Otherwise, there is only one Lord of the Inner Darkness; as much as they can ever be are Lords of the Middle Dark, above all but one but forced to carry out only the will of the one. They preserve the Outer Darkness in which we all must live."

He had gotten preachy, and she had finally surrendered to her exhaustion. Still, it was truth that he spoke. Only he now knew the secret of the Inner Lord; he knew that there was something it feared, that there was one way to challenge its power and perhaps defeat it. Five gold rings. Precious good that knowledge was doing him, of course. He was squatting here in a foul stable dressed only in a rope and a rag, at the mercy of one of the least of the chain, a Lord of the Outer Dark named Roaring Bull, whom he understood perfectly. If he could not deal with Roaring Bull, he could hardly deal with Lazlo Chen and others as bad or worse.

Still, for the first time he was beset with doubt. What was he really *doing* anyway? Carrying the secret of the keys to the Inner Dark to one who might be far worse than what they had now. Those five, whoever they were, who wore the rings—they had not been appointed to those positions by the Master System because of longevity or family breeding. They had earned their way with the blood of others, mortgaging their souls in the process. Men like them, perhaps *better* than them, had reached the point where mass genocide and mass suicide were taken for granted. Would humanity be better off in the hands of five evil people? Would his own people, whose way of life was spiritual and fulfilling, be among the first to be penned up, perhaps extinguished, while others again slaughtered the buffalo and deer and elk into near or total extinction just for sport?

Oddly enough, he decided that the attempt to find and use the rings was worth the risk. If it could be done or if he could just spread the knowledge of the rings so that someone, some day, could and would do it, he should try.

Cloud Dancer was not truly correct. Master System, whatever it was, had not coalesced all evil into itself; its evil had been entirely taught to it by humankind. It was not an evil creation, just one that had done its job and then kept on doing it. It was evil now, the ultimate evil, because it had gone on past its time and threatened to go on forever. By locking the people of Earth into their own past, it had rendered them powerless to destroy themselves. And it had done more. It had taken the huge masses of people who could not be supported by such a system or controlled by it and scattered them among the stars. He hadn't mentioned that part to Cloud Dancer, because she thought the stars were spirits, and the concept of billions of humans was beyond her. Still, it was exactly so.

Even if Earth again reached a capacity for self-destruction, humanity would not die. So many worlds out there were populated now that humanity would probably live—in some form or another—as long as the universe lived. Yet those worlds, too, were held down, suppressed by the Master System. It treated them all as it had treated its birthworld, and worse. Humanity could not be destroyed, and that was the objective of the system as its human creators had envisioned, but neither could it grow—ever.

Better that men be in command, even if they were far more evil than the machine. Evil men had come and gone throughout history and caused great suffering, but they had come—*and gone*. Others, some better, some worse, all different, had replaced them, but civilization had grown. He must loose the Lords of the Middle Dark from their chains, even if they devoured him and all that he held dear. He, as a historian, understood that better than most.

But first there was that pipsqueak pirate and dictator over there in that lodge, chuckling to himself and filling his fat belly. If he could not deal with Roaring Bull, he deserved no better than serving the lowest of the lords of evil. After Moxxoquan, Emperor of the Council of Nations, what was a Roaring Bull?

He felt suddenly invigorated, although the smells of fine food denied him attacked his stomach. He would not be stopped here. He had a thought that was appropriate to the occasion, although it was out of place here and to one of his lineage, traditions, and spiritual beliefs; a thought that only a scholar who had been given the keys to knowledge forbidden to the masses of humanity could have in such a time and place:

Why, this is merely Limbo; I stand only at the gates of Malebolge and have nine circles to go before I am permitted to Dis. What warrior could dream of facing great Satan in his lair when he is trapped in Limbo?

He scouted the village, strutting as if he were its master, yet all eyes averted from him, all contact forbidden. They watched him in furtive glances and wondered if he was mad or perhaps would make a bargain.

But he would make no bargains with demons, he knew. He would not be trapped forever in Limbo, as they all were.

A number of traders were stopping at the landing: perhaps six or more canoes, some double and lashed together to carry all the more. The summer was ended, and they were going home. Two large warriors guarded the path and eyed Hawks nastily, so he went to one side and waited for the traders to come up. They were of many nations, but he was able to make out their conversations as they came up from the landing and went into the village to pay their respects—and perhaps more as well—to Chief Roaring Bull.

"I do not like this one bit, so many of Council without respect going about the land," one remarked to another casually in a tongue Hawks understood.

"I do not know what they do here," the other responded. "That Crow man and that black Caribe bitch. I would gladly give my life if I could first be permitted to cut their arrogant throats. They had better not come into *my* tribe!"

"They were looking for someone in particular," the first one noted. "I hope that if they find him, he feels as you!"

"You will have more two or three days south," another put in. "Up on a bluff on the west shore. They tried to be hidden, but they are amateurs, soft in the ways of living free. They were there when I came up. A bunch of them digging holes and sifting dirt. Their ways are inexplicable."

That all interested him, and he remained to hear as much new gossip as he could. He didn't know who the southbounders were referring to. A Crow and a Caribe? Council Security, certainly, at least the Crow.

They were hunting someone. Him, perhaps? Had they found the body up there, or had the Val just pulled the alarm when it saw that Hawks, the only Council member around not searching with it, had vanished south? The fact that a Caribe had ventured this far north was unnerving, even though she would make the hunters easy to spot. She had to be the one who'd lost the courier, the one told to go up there and not come back without a dead body and a destroyed briefcase. With her career and future on the line, she would pull no punches, and for the knowledge of the rings, Master System would allow a lot of leeway.

The others to the south were more interesting. Archaeologists, certainly, from the description. This was a region of the mound builders, whose structures remained miraculously preserved in spite of the prior huge population here and the massive destruction that had followed.

The archaeologists would try to blend in, but somewhere close they would have modern equipment, which Hawks might be able to use to advance his cause and cover his tracks.

All right, he said to himself. You now have a destination, pursuers, and a potential for escape. If you can just find something to eat and get a little more rest, you might just save your neck.

Saving humanity would come later.

Neither Hawks nor Cloud Dancer got much rest. In anticipation of action, he just couldn't sleep; she quickly discovered that the stables were busy places in the daytime and managed to catch an hour here and an hour there. He admired her greatly for her seeming lack of concern. He tried to draw on her courage.

The trouble was that they didn't have enough to go on to work out a definite plan. They knew what they had to do, but how it was done would be strictly improvised, and they were depending a lot on the overconfidence and incompetence of the men set to watch them.

It wasn't until late that evening that they had enough privacy to discuss their plans. Cloud Dancer had effectively scouted and memorized the village layout the night before, but he had to describe to her in detail the interior of Roaring Bull's main lodge as he remembered it. He also told her about the two security people who were probably looking for them.

"I would prefer more time to study this, but I have been fearful all day that they would arrive here, and they will certainly be here within another day. I think we must go as soon as we can."

"It is better to act than to dwell," she responded.

He had feared a clear night, but the mists rolled in off the rivers and hung heavy on the village, and through it a light, cold rain fell, turning the whole area thick with mud. The dampness was uncomfortable; at times like this he appreciated all those inoculations against colds, flus, and pneumonia, and he worried a bit about Cloud Dancer.

By early morning the conditions were appalling but very much to the advantage of the pair. The sleepy guard was back, but he'd retreated inside to keep out of the rain; when Cloud Dancer slipped silently from the stable and peeked in the small hut across the way, she found him out again and snoring loudly by a small fire. The watchdog looked up, yawned, and went back to sleep. She checked for the guard down the street as well, but he was gone, almost certainly inside by a fire himself, warming his insides with fire liquids. She saw no trace of other watchers.

When she returned for Hawks, he was already numb from the cold of the stable and somewhat wet, since the roof leaked, so actually moving more than made up for the additional wetness outside. The mud, however, was both deep and slippery, something which worked against them, but would also be a problem for pursuers.

Cloud Dancer's silent friend peered out the doorway nervously and was given a whispered response. She motioned them up and in with a hand gesture. The warmth of the kitchen felt good.

The woman was indeed tiny, although her proportions showed the results of being a cook. Not that she was fat, but her behind and breasts were definitely a lot fatter than they were supposed to be. She had long, stringy black hair with traces of gray, although she didn't look all that old. Her eyes were ancient. She was barefoot and had on a simple skin and cloth dress which looked as worn as she did.

Time was pressing, but he tried his entire repertoire of American languages and found each met by a shaking of the head. She had certainly learned some Illinois just by being there, but he didn't know that language. Since so many of the plains languages were related, as were another group from the southwest, he decided that Cloud Dancer had probably been correct: The mute woman was from either the south or the east coastal area. How she had wound up in the hands of this band was probably an epic story but not one she would ever tell.

She had gone to some risk for their sake, that was

clear. She had two knives for them, one a hunting knife and the other well balanced for throwing, and somehow she'd managed to get a spear. She also had a worn leather shoulder bag that contained some provisions such as small apples, nuts, and dried fruit. It was more than he had expected, but both he and Cloud Dancer understood the obligation their acceptance incurred. In a place this small it was unavoidable that such help would be traced back to the slave woman, whether they succeeded in escaping or not. The punishment would be very slow and agonizing torture until death released her, in public, as an example of what happened to those slaves who betrayed their masters.

"She must come along, you know," he told Cloud Dancer.

"I knew you would think so. I could not love a man who would decide otherwise."

"It is also not likely we can return her to her people." The Hyiakutt accepted returned or escaped prisoner-slaves into the tribe, but many tribes considered becoming a prisoner or slave to be an act of unworthiness and tantamount to death. Also, she had clearly been here a long time; she would have no future and few, if any, friends if she did return. "I also could never keep a slave."

"Come on and let us go," Cloud Dancer said irritably. "It was I who involved her in this and agreed to her help. I understood then that you would have to marry her, too. Come. If we do not make good this escape, then none of this matters."

He kissed her, then kissed a very surprised new wife who probably did not yet understand that she had taken on that title. He pointed to himself and said in Hyiakutt, "Walks With the Night Hawks." She nodded, and he pointed to his wife and companion. "Cloud Dancer." Then he pointed to her. "Silent Woman," he said, and she nodded and looked pleased. He turned and gestured toward the door. "Check to see if all's clear. Time to live or die."

All was clear; so far they had moved without detection. The rain was still falling, and the mist was so thick that they could have made it to the canoes and gotten away without anyone seeing them, but to do so would have meant inevitable pursuit in force and probable recapture within two days. Hawks took the hunting knife and a kitchen hatchet; Cloud Dancer chose the spear, with which she was more proficient, and a long, thin kitchen tool that resembled an ice pick. Silent Woman carried the supply bag and the throwing knife. They headed for Roaring Bull's lodge.

The lodge door was directly across from the storehouse, which would have had the usual two guards on it had the rain not forced them inside. Hawks hoped the crude wooden door of the lodge wasn't barred from the inside. There was no other way in that was practical. But fire was a constant hazard to anyone in such wooden and hay-lined lodges, and it was unlikely that anyone would bar their only possible escape, particularly with two guards less than five meters away.

Hawks crept around the side of the lodge, checked again for signs of anyone about, then pulled on the door. It gave easily, but he hadn't remembered it making that much noise. He could only hope that the sound of the rain would mask their entrace. He had his knife in one hand and a hatchet in the other, and he took a deep breath and stepped into the lodge.

He paused, allowing his eyes to adjust to the dark of the room. There was no light left in the fire, and the two alcohol lamps were long extinguished. The ventilation came from wooden slats near the ceiling propped open with sticks, and it was still quite dark outside. He wondered if he would break his neck.

The place smelled like a pigpen, but it was relatively warm and dry, one of the few lodges here with wood floors. The two large tables were littered with the remains of the previous night's activities, and many of the large skin flagons would need refilling. The sounds of scurrying and chewing told him that the mice were first on the cleanup detail.

In one corner was a small collection of weapons, including a bow and a quiver of arrows. He kept that in mind, although they were of no use in here.

When lodges this large were divided into rooms, it was usually with blankets. Roaring Bull, however, had actually had a wooden partition built so that none of his trader guests would get into his bedroom even by accident.

Hawks jumped at a sound behind him, then recognized the slender form of Cloud Dancer. He eased back over to her, and as soon as she was used to the dark, he gestured toward the curtained-off doorway to the back room from which came the sounds of deep snores.

The darkness was a complication neither had thought of. Cloud Dancer moved to the fireplace, found a stick, and gently stirred the remains while crouching down and blowing on them. There were still a few spots of red. She got one of the torches from a holder, and after many tries it ignited. It was not, however, in the best of shape and gave them at the start only a bit more light than a match would have. It would have to do. Hoping that it wouldn't burn out, she replaced it in its holder, from where it lit the room with an eerie half glow.

Hawks cautiously pulled back the curtain and looked inside. He wasn't really prepared for the sight of the old fat man stark naked, sleeping between two equally naked women, both obviously slaves like Silent Woman. The light shone on the face of the nearer of the two women and she stirred, opened her eyes, turned, then opened them again and stared at Hawks in stark terror. He put a finger to his lips, then motioned for her to get up and stand away from the old chief. For a moment she couldn't move, then she did as instructed. He was relieved. He'd kill the old boy if he had to, but he sure as hell didn't want innocent blood on his hands.

He leaned back out, whispered to Cloud Dancer, and exchanged his hatchet for her spear. At this distance and in these crowded conditions, the spear seemed the best weapon. The slave girl's eyes widened as she realized that the invader was not alone.

Hawks poked Roaring Bull with the spear, gently at first, then more rudely when the man merely stirred. Finally the chief raised his lids just a little.

"Enough acting!" Hawks hissed. "Sit up and face me!"

Roaring Bull smiled, sat up, yawned, and stretched. "Or you'll do what?" he asked genially in Sioux. "Kill me? That will get you nowhere. One shout from me will bring in a horde of sleepy but dedicated warriors."

"Make that shout and you feel the spear," Hawks responded. "We have already resolved that this will work or we will die. No other choices. I am comfortable with either. Are you? Shall I make a small, painful hole in you to prove a point?"

By this point the other woman had awakened, gasped, and now sat up, pressed into the corner.

Roaring Bull seemed to consider his position. "Seems I underestimated you, boy. Few Council types would have the ability, and fewer the courage, to get this far."

Hawks rudely pulled on the curtain, bringing it down. The torch was burning more brightly now. "Come on out, and quietly. No tricks! If we are discovered in here, we will die, but you will die, slowly and painfully, before we do. Even if you are hurt, you do not cry out, or at the very least I will sever your tongue."

"Bold words," the chief sighed, but he got up and came out into the main room, where Cloud Dancer sat on a table, one of the bows from the corner in her hand, its drawstring stretched with a small hunting arrow.

Hawks turned back to the two women. "Do either of you want to come with us?" he asked, first in Sioux, then in several other languages when they did not respond. He was about to give up when one whispered, in a language close enough to Cheyenne for him to make it out, "He is death. We must not go with him."

"Choose now," he responded in Cheyenne. "I have seen many men in this village, young and old, but I have seen few old women. Come now, or you will remain here forever."

"Come where?" the other asked, frightened. "There is no place for us to go."

"With me. Perhaps to death. Perhaps to life. The mute one goes with us."

"But she is addlebrained."

Never had he met two people more intent on remaining slaves. He did not argue further; he had done his duty. He began cutting up some blankets and rope while Roaring Bull stood in all his naked majesty watching with seemingly little concern.

The two women stared at Hawks. "What are you going to do with those?" one asked.

"If you will not go, then you cannot be allowed to raise any alarms too soon. I must bind and gag you both."

Their acceptance of the bonds bothered him almost as much as their refusal to go. Is this what we have come to? he asked himself, knowing he was no professional at this and worrying that the bonds were too tight—or not tight enough to hold. Or is this what we have always been? It disappointed him. He could not imagine slaves, freed of their chains and told that there was a slim but real chance of freedom if they ran, who would run and put the chains back on. No wonder the lords of the dark had come to the top!

Roaring Bull was still sleepy, but he was alert enough. "Will you allow me at least to put my pants on?" he asked almost genially.

"I would give you what you gave us if I had it available. Wait." He still had a length of rope left. "Here. Tie this around your fat belly and fasten these blankets to it. It's the *least* I can do for modesty's sake."

The chief refused. "Hardly matters, considering what it sounds like outside and the fact that you two look like you have been rolling in fresh horse dung. May I ask what you intend to do now?"

"We go to the south landing, and all of us get into a canoe or some other floating thing we can use."

"You're going on the river, in the dark, in fog and rain? It's treacherous not far south of here. The Ohio and Mississippi flow side by side for a while, but finally they merge, and when they do, it is messy."

"Then we will survive, or drown and die. You left us no choice, and no promise of yours now could be believed." He switched to his native tongue. "Cloud Dancer, see that all is clear out there, and then we will move."

He held the spear at the ready as she went to look. Roaring Bull sighed and moved a bit closer to the nearest table. Suddenly the old man made a move for something suspended under the table. Hawks reacted instinctively, not spearing but whacking the old man hard with the stick. The chief gave a little cry as an object dropped to the floor, then dived for it, but now the spear came down on the old man's right hand. He gave a sharp cry, but Hawks had already pulled the knife, and the old boy saw it and gritted his teeth.

Hawks kicked the object away, pulled out the spear, then leaned down and picked up the thing without ever taking his eyes off Roaring Bull, who now sat nursing a bloody hand.

The thing was a pistol. One-shot, ball type, very basic, of either Caje or Caribe origin. The damned thing was too inaccurate a weapon to have been a threat to his person, but it would have raised a tremendous noise.

"You've mangled my hand!" Roaring Bull said in wonder. The pain and injury seemed to affect him less than the fact that someone had actually harmed him.

"Yes. Too bad. Now you cannot paddle. Now, get up and move in front of me or you will find this knife mangling the only thing about you your pet women in there really care about. *Move!*"

Roaring Bull moved, nursing his hand. He seemed utterly unable to comprehend the fact that someone had actually speared him. "But it's bleeding! It must be bandaged and tied off!"

"I care as much about that as I care whether or not I kill you, which is not much. You will move ahead of me and do just what I say. If you try anything else, you will not see me die."

Much of the confidence seemed to have drained out of the old chief. "But I will not be able to swim when you are swamped!" he objected.

"Then you had better give us expert advice on how to avoid that, hadn't you?"

They went out into the cold and wet to join Cloud Dancer and Silent Woman. Roaring Bull, upon seeing the mute woman, gave her a withering glance. She spit at him.

The south landing was on the Ohio and down a bit from the junction of the two rivers. Cloud Dancer went on ahead to scout the landing, then returned. "Two men with spears, bows, and probably knives," she told him, gesturing as she spoke. Silent Woman nodded and seemed to understand.

"We must get both at once," he told her. "Or the survivor will raise the alarm. Give me the bow and arrows. I am a pretty fair shot with them."

"It can't be done," Roaring Bull offered. "Those are among my best. See that they guard even in this weather. Forget this. We can make a deal."

Silent Woman pulled out the throwing knife, then pointed to her skin case of supplies. Hawks wondered if he had the idea and tried to make sure with gestures. "You—Go—Down—There. Kill—one—with knife?"

She nodded. It might work, he decided, if he was ready and accurate when she made her move. She was, after all, a slave, a familiar figure, and one thought dim-witted, and she might be up at this hour. It wasn't a regular thing, but it might make sense to the guards to see a familiar figure currying favor by bringing down something to eat and perhaps drink. It was still well before dawn, but he could see the guards in the half-light perhaps five meters from a thick line of bushes, and he could see some of the boats pulled up on the shore, but the river itself was a mass of gray merging into the sky.

Cloud Dancer had the spear aimed at Roaring Bull, although he didn't seem to be much of a threat right now. His hand, though a bit better, was still bleeding and obviously useless.

When Hawks nodded, Silent Woman stepped out and walked down the path toward the guards.

The nearer of the two shouted something, then spoke in a lighter tone to the other, who chuckled. Clearly she was going to be allowed to get close, having been recognized and determined to be no threat.

The larger of the two, nearer the boats, started walking slowly toward her as the other one just watched. Hawks remained totally still, knowing that he had to act when she did, yet not quite able to keep both her and his target in view at the same time. He knew, too, that this was no deer. He had never killed a man before.

Silent Woman was no more than three meters from the man when she suddenly drew and threw the knife. The missile struck the man in the chest, and he made a loud exclamation as he fell backward in surprise. At the cry, the other man turned and hefted his spear with one motion.

Hawks's arrow went straight through the man's neck. He dropped the spear, and two hands went to his throat, and he tottered for just a moment, then fell over into the water with a splash.

They all moved quickly. Silent Woman's target had not been killed by her knife throw, and she had been upon him in an instant. By the time they reached her, she was covered in blood. She had cut his throat.

Cloud Dancer pointed to a canoe. "That one." It would hold the four of them, but it wasn't exactly roomy. There were other, larger canoes there, with wooden oars attached with ropes to their sides.

"Not one of those?" he asked her.

"No. It would take all of us to launch it, and it would stand out on the river."

She was right, as usual. He pushed the canoe halfway into the water, then the chief, Silent Woman, and Cloud Dancer got in. Somehow he managed to push it out, run into the water, and get aboard without overturning it.

They drifted out into the river, and he suddenly looked around. "Anybody check to see that we had paddles this time?"

Cloud Dancer laughed. "Here. Let us see if the two of us can get us out into midstream with this ancient lump of buffalo fat aboard."

They managed to get well away from shore and then let the current take them down. It occurred to Hawks that they would be passing below the bluff atop which the village sat, but he wasn't worried. If they could keep afloat and away from nasty water, he was pretty certain they would survive until the next threat.

"I don't know why you bothered to bring me," Roaring Bull commented. "You could have gotten this far without me."

"It isn't this far I was worried about," Hawks responded. "I know you have people and possibly whole tribes obligated to you down here. I want clear of that. You'll be my insurance and my translator as well if any show themselves."

The chief denied this for a long time but finally more or less admitted it. "But what if you are found by one of them? How will you know what I speak is true and not some plan for rescue?" he asked, knowing that his best chance was to sow doubt and plant a little fear and knowing, too, that they needed him too much to kill him if they could avoid it.

"Simple," Hawks replied. "You and I both know how tenuous this whole thing is. One major slip and we are done. We accept that. The only thing I can absolutely ensure is that if we die, you will die as well."

The chief shrugged. "What does it matter? If you get well away of my arms, you will kill me anyway."

"Unlike you, I am a man of honor," Hawks told him. "You must believe that, and I think you do. Just as surely as I say that you will pay for any treachery with your life or with something that will make you wish you were dead, so I also say that you will be freed and not further harmed the moment we can safely land after passing the Missouri."

Roaring Bull looked at his hand, which had finally stopped bleeding but was a painful mess. He knew he would never be able to use it much again, and he hated Hawks for that. He also knew, though, that he was old and slow and out of condition, no match for at least two of these three, and the action of the mute woman had scared him. It was every master's nightmare that his slaves would turn on him, and now he was sure of the loyalty of only two.

Still, his pride, his ego, and his security had been wounded as much as or more than his hand. He had ordered many killed or tortured or mutilated, but he had not suffered a personal injury at the hands of another in more than twenty years. If it had been he versus Hawks, he would have taken the chance and had at the man, no matter what the odds or outcome. He was not a coward, but he was also not a fool. He could have broken Cloud Dancer, that he knew—there was no one alive who could not be broken—but as she was, she was as deadly as Hawks and not encumbered with his civilized background and scruples. Most threatening of all was Silent Woman;

she had the least to lose and the most reason for hurting him horribly. She would never kill him if she could avoid it, but she would—amputate things. The odds were too great. A trio like this was doomed anyway, somewhere down the line. He had reason to return to his village. There were at least two warriors he would like to attend to—personally—and perhaps four.

They had not liked the rain, and that was why he was here. Perhaps he would give them a choice when he was through playing games with them. They could be drowned in the water they didn't like, or if they were so delicate, perhaps they might prefer being burned alive.

So he would bide his time and be good and even try to help these people survive the dangers of this stretch of river. He might put a price on Hawks's head, but he wanted to get back to his people before one of his scheming relatives usurped his position.

They paddled down the river with no more than the usual navigational problems.

"Tell me about the mute woman," Hawks said to Roaring Bull. "Where is she from and why has she no tongue?"

"I don't know where she's from," the chief responded. "Somewhere in the south and east, from the high mountain area. She was—trade goods. Years ago. Trader came north with a bunch of girls, all foreign, none speaking any recognized tongue. Most were real young—fourteen, fifteen—but they had already been through the mill lots of times. She was real young but a pro all the way. Never did speak much. Stuttered real bad. I don't know what she'd been through before me, but wait until you see her tattoos."

"Tattoos?"

"Got 'em from the neck to the crotch, front and back, except her arms and legs. Looks like a ceremonial blanket. You'll see 'em."

"How did she lose her tongue if she stuttered so?"

"She got pregnant. They do, you know. Had a kid.

Ugly, deformed thing. The medicine men came and declared it a demon child. Drove her crazy."

A demon child. The term for babies born with severe birth defects. There was usually only one thing they did when such a child was born. They killed it ritually and burned its body in ceremonial fires.

"Wouldn't do anything but wail and scream," the chief continued. "No stutter, just screaming blasphemies in too many tongues to count, including one or two I could make out. She had to be locked away for weeks, but she never stopped except from exhaustion. The medicine men said the stutter was the mark of a witch who would bear a demon child and that she'd bring down curses if she wasn't stopped from doing it. I figured she'd just get over it, but it kept going, and a bunch of things went wrong all at once in the village. Accidents killed two healthy men, one lodge burned down, that kind of thing. A mob finally got together, and I had to think fast to keep them from killing her, so they settled for cutting out her tongue and burning it. That stopped her, and finally she just snapped. She could do little things like start up the morning kitchen or clean up, but nothing else. The rest of the time she just sat in a corner, staring into space."

"I see," Hawks responded. "Well, something snapped her out of it now."

"Snapped is right. You don't trust her too far while I'm along, Hawks. She might just decide to butcher all of us."

7. CHEMISTRY LESSON

THE PROCESS OF CHANGING THE PRETTY AND BRIL-
liant Song Ching into the rougher and masculine Chu Li,
while unlikely to succeed, was nonetheless solidly based
on predictable principles. One was that authoritarian societies, particularly those which received their orders from
machines, ran on orders and tended to carry out those
orders to the letter and without question, even at the cost
of common sense. The other was that most people would
believe that it took someone with the artistry, skills, and
experience of an expert like Doctor Wang to accomplish
such a transformation at all, when in a computer age all
it took was someone who could talk to a computer and
order it to do the work.

Chu Li was barely fifteen; his youth made the illusion
easier to pull off, and some rather basic changes helped
it along. Song Ching's hair was cut extremely short, almost
but not quite gone along the sides and short with a straight-
back clipper cut on top, while the nails had been closely
trimmed to the fingers. The heavy cotton prisoner tunic

and baggy trousers made any wearer shapeless. Song Ching's middle soprano had been lowered in pitch one half octave; any more would have been inconsistent with a boy of fifteen. Chu Li's dialect was Mandarin, not Song Ching's native dialect but the one used at Center and therefore no problem.

The boys had been back in the cell, sedated, barely twenty minutes when the guards came for them. Their sleeves were rolled up, and each was given a shot that counteracted any sedative drugs still in their bodies. Both sat up, groaning and holding their heads.

"Get yourselves in order!" a guard barked to them. "In five minutes each of you will be fed. I strongly recommend you eat everything; it may be a long time before you get another decent meal, if ever." That was said with something of a smirk. "You will be permitted ten minutes for this and another five to use the toilet. Then you will be prepared to leave." With that, the guard turned and stalked out. The cell door closed behind him.

"*Oooh!* My head is only now trying to make peace with me," Deng Ho moaned.

"It is the same with me," Chu Li responded. In Han and many other Oriental cultures, cousins of the same generation regarded one another as brothers and sisters and acted accordingly. The two boys were close. "My head is crowded and confused, almost as if..."

"As if what?"

As if there is another also inside my head, he thought, but he couldn't say that. "I just wonder if they messed with our minds, and if they did, would we know?"

"How's your—thing?"

Memories of brutish guards beating and torturing for the slightest infractions. Memories of one of them.

"There is no pain," Chu Li told his cousin. "It is not right, though. I shall have to pee sitting down for a while,

I think. I do not know what awaits us, but it cannot be any worse than here. Even death is better than here."

Chu Li tried to clear his mind. So long as he concentrated on the here and now, it was fine, but when he let himself relax, his thoughts became somewhat crowded and confused. The guards who had beaten him had threatened "to make a girl of him," but even that would not have given him memories and information that seemed to belong to a girl, one from a far different background and one he had never known. Some of those memories and impressions were far sharper than those from his own life—but there was a difference. He could remember that other life, but he could not place himself in the position of that girl. He felt as if he were looking at things from the viewpoint of an outside observer.

He had little time to dwell on this right away, for the guards were sticking solidly to their schedule. Chu Li and Deng Ho were placed in handcuffs and short leg irons and marched rudely through corridors, checkpoints, and safeguards to the main entrance, where a squad of black-clad regular security police awaited them.

"They're all yours, Lieutenant," the chief guard said, sounding not the least bit sorry. "We've put them through the mill and taught them some manners. Good riddance."

The lieutenant just nodded, and both men pressed their thumbs on the receiving board to signify the transfer.

"All right, you two," the new captor said to the boys. "No trouble, now. I don't know what they did to you in there, and I don't care. Legally, you are no longer citizens of the Community or even human beings. You are cattle, the property of the System Administrative Council, and they can and will do with you as they wish, as can I as their deputy. Not a word out of you, now; follow me."

They were led out to a landing bay where a skimmer awaited them. They got in and were surprised to find two girls already seated there, both in the same prison garb they themselves wore. Neither girl turned to look at them but just sat quiet and sullen. Chu Li thought he saw some sort of scar or welt on the face of the one closest to him, but then he was chained in his seat and could look only forward.

The large passenger skimmer lifted quickly into the air, took its assigned exit trajectory, and smoothly cleared the dome, then rose to cruising altitude. As the skimmer gained speed, the boys were pushed back into their seats.

They wanted to talk to the girls, who were seated in front of them, but a few nasty whacks from a guard's leather stick produced silence. Chu Li had nothing to do but settle back and think.

Why did he have this strange girl's memories? What had they done to him in there and why? He tried to relax and sort out what he could of this alien information. *The Lord Buddha protect him!* She'd been the daughter of the chief administrator! The very bastard who had ordered the massacre of his people! And she had been there!

He compared his own memories to hers. *Darkness, sudden cold, people screaming and running, shots all over, illuminating the dark. One shot catches his sister and burns her upper half to melted goo.* All the time *she* had been up there, in the officer's skimmer, enjoying every moment and wanting to get down and get into the battle herself, to shoot some of his people. It had been nothing but a *game* to her, an amusing entertainment.

The more he examined her memories and attitudes, the more he hated her. People were mere objects to her, toys for her amusement or fools to play off each other for her gain. Rich, pampered, spoiled, and arrogant, she was a most unpleasant person, the very kind he had always been taught ruled the world. Such beauty and such genius. Such evil.

How he would like to get hold of her, rip off her fine clothes, dress her in rags, exchange her jasmine perfume for sweat and dung, make her the lowest peasant slave, show her what it felt like to be brutalized. She and her whole cursed family. It was they who should have been on this ship going to some deep hell, not the ones who were here.

But what were her memories doing in his mind? Some kind of mistake? She had been at Center herself, it seemed, and not as a visitor or voyeur but to be remade into a good noble's wife and breeder. It was too kind a fate for her, but it was at least a step toward justice. She had been an expert at computers; she had examined his people's discoveries. Had her old memories and knowledge gotten mixed in with his in that computer by some mistake? It was possible. It was also possible that she had managed this herself, to save her knowledge even as they were stripping clean her soul. If so, it was justice that the daughter of his people's murderer should inadvertently pass on that knowledge to one of her victims.

He now had that knowledge, including the actual way to steal a spaceship, and he hoped he could use it. It would be the ultimate revenge on her if she was mentally made over into a prim little wife while he, whose people had made these discoveries and had been destroyed while she watched and thrilled at the spectacle, was somehow able to use that to escape.

It was all too evil to him and too disturbing. His grandfather long ago had taught him an ancient mental discipline, one which gave control of thoughts and memories and could even fool the big computers for periods of time. His people had survived with it and escaped detection for a generation, and he now applied it to another aim. It was a form of self-hypnosis, but it was more than that; it was a mystical thing that worked by will and concentration and the Ten Exercises. He wanted her out. He wanted all traces of her banished from his conscious mind, save only the computer knowledge and skill and the secrets she knew. She would give up her knowledge, skills, and discoveries, but then he would have the pleasure at least of killing her in his mind.

But for the first time in his memory, the mental discipline did not really work. It distanced the girl's memories a bit more, but she was still there.

The skimmer flew over vast, rocky desert and eerie tablelands, then began to slow and descend. Atop one desolate plateau there was a huge blocky complex, and to one side, rising up like a temple spire, was a spaceship. It could be seen clearly against the morning sky; the pilot pointed it out through the broad front windscreen of the skimmer. Chu Li brought himself out of the Ten Exercises to see what the excitement was about and got somewhat excited himself.

Space! They are exiling us to space!

They settled down so slowly and so close to the spaceship that it went by the front windows in dramatic fashion. Finally the door opened, and the security lieutenant unbuckled himself and got out, carrying the security identifier from Center. After greeting the other security officials, he immediately inserted the module into the space center systems slot. This way, the four young people would be identified by security records and systems as outbound prisoners. It was also another link in the computer-engineered masquerade: Now the spaceport records would show Chu Li as "he" now appeared, with the current Chu Li's fingerprints and eyeprints. The spaceport was tied directly into Master System; therefore, the Center security computer had encoded a correction program showing initial data errors and reversing the prints of Song Ching and Chu Li. Her body was now totally identified and registered as Chu Li, 15, male, born in Paoting, Hopeh Province, apprehended in illegal activity, Chamdo Province, and declared Property of the State; remanded to Melchior Research and Detention facility until death. As the real Chu Li no longer existed, not even in trace, Song Ching was about to vanish impossibly and forever—and heads would roll for it.

When the prisoners were ordered out, the boys got

their first clear look at the girls, both of whom looked downcast and old beyond their years. There *were* scars on their faces. Ugly ones.

They were marched inside and down a busy corridor, past many eyes staring at them from offices, to an elevator, then taken to an upper-level detention area. It had clearly not been designed as such; there were barred gates at either end of a short corridor monitored by cameras as well as by human guards, but the four cells were little more than barren, unfinished offices in which had been placed some army mattresses that looked as if they'd seen work and a small commode not attached to plumbing but containing a pitcher of water and some plastic glasses. They were told that if they needed to eliminate they were to yell for a guard and that one would be along to take them one at a time to the lone toilet on the floor.

To Chu Li's surprise, he was pushed into a cell with one of the girls. "This is not proper!" he protested.

The guard grinned. "My orders were to split that pair up. They have a real way with locks and stuff. Go ahead and have some fun if you're old enough to know what I mean. We don't care."

The door slammed shut, leaving them alone. The girl kept her eyes on him but did not say a word. The haunted expression in her eyes drew his attention away from the two large, irregular scars that disfigured her face.

"Don't worry," he assured her. "I have much honor but little else and would not do that if I could."

The ice was broken, and she relaxed a bit. "What do you mean, if you could?" Her voice was high and nasal, her Mandarin dialect colored by a peasant's accents and tone.

"It is too embarrassing to discuss."

"There is nothing too embarrassing for me. I have lost even my honor. They—they gave us to the male guards for two days and nights before cleaning us up for this."

He was not certain what to say to that. Finally he

managed, "You need not feel shame at that, at least *I* think not. It was not of your doing, and it is *they* who have dishonored themselves, not you."

She stood there a moment, then, slowly, tears came to her eyes and she began to cry. He wasn't quite sure what to do. Finally he went over to her, and she leaned against him and just cried and cried as he held her. He was just at the stage where he was finding girls different, exotic, and strangely important, but this was the first time he had ever held one in his arms. It felt good to lend some strength to her; he had been treated harshly, but she had endured far more.

Clearly this cry had been a long time coming, and he eased her onto the floor mat and just sat beside her, holding her until she had it cried out. She clung to him as if he were very important, yet they had only just now met and did not even know each other's names.

When she was done crying, he asked her if he could get her some water, and she nodded. He brought her a cup and a paper towel to dry her eyes.

She had been attractive once; he could see that. No great beauty, but it had been a good face, and because of that, the scars were an even greater disfigurement. One ran from the left side of her mouth up her cheek and then back toward her ear, pulling the corner of the lip up grotesquely and permanently exposing two teeth; the other was a huge, deep horizontal gash. Both were built up like mountains on her smooth skin by scar tissue that had partly turned purple and brown. Still, as he looked at her now and helped her dry her tears, he felt odd stirrings inside him, and though he could not forget the scar tissue, for the moment it did not seem very important.

"I'm sorry," she managed, blowing her nose. "I—I was always the strong one. I am sorry that I permitted you to see me this way."

"It is all right," he responded. "You must be strong indeed to go through that and not be mad."

"Perhaps I am mad," she responded. "I have been living what can only be a nightmare, in which you are the first man to show any kindness."

"Only half a man," he responded, not realizing how much truth there was in that description. Because she had told him her ultimate shame, he felt not only that he could tell her his secret but that it might give her some idea that suffering was not exclusive. "The guards beat me terribly where that which makes me a man is, leaving it battered, bruised, and perhaps broken. There is no pain, but it will be a long time before I know. That is what I was too embarrassed and ashamed to say before."

"*Oh!* I apologize for asking. Please forgive me."

He shook it off. "What is done cannot be undone, and who knows what was done? Only time will tell that. I am otherwise whole and very angry at all this. My people taught us that the world was ruled by monsters in human form, but I did not really believe this until they came for us. I am Chu Li, by the way, sometimes called Rat because of my small size and the year of my birth."

"I am Chow Dai. My sister who suffers with me is Chow Mai. As you might guess, we are—" she touched the scar on her right cheek "—*were* twins."

"I hope that my cousin, Deng Ho, is honorable with her and that they get along. *He* is more likely to be crying on *her* shoulder, I fear, though he has held up better than I would have guessed." Sparing little, he told her how he and his cousin had come to be there and what his own people had been like, free of the tyranny of the machines.

She listened, fascinated. "I have nothing of that in my past," she told him. "I fear I have never known even that much freedom. Even the women of your people were free and educated."

"You are not of the Center?"

"No. Oh my, no! We are simple peasant girls. The family was very big, and we were always hungry, it seemed. When a time of drought came, my parents had no way to feed us all and no money to marry us off. Unlike some of the others of their generation, they did not believe in drowning baby daughters, and so had too many."

He was appalled. "They *drowned* babies?"

She seemed surprised at his reaction. "It has been the custom for thousands of years. They try and wipe it out, but in bad times it returns. Sons may return what they consume and care for the parents in their old age. Daughters are a burden, for you must pay even to marry them to someone. We understood this. There was a petition to the Lord of the Estates, who had always encouraged even the poor families to keep their daughters, and he listened. We were sold to the household of Colonel Chin, a mighty warlord, to be personal servants to his own daughter."

"Sold?" He could hardly believe this. Hers was a world far removed from his experience.

"We didn't mind. Our parents were relieved of their burden, received some sum they could use, and knew that we were honorably employed. Our mistress was harsh and demanding, but we had fine clothes, food such as we had never dreamed of eating, protection, and something of a position."

"As a slave, you mean."

"No, as a member of the household staff. It has far more standing than planting and picking rice, and we were very young. Then we were taken one time to Center, a place we had never dreamed existed. It was like a high-born's heaven. It was our undoing, though, in the end. We helped the mistress bathe and clothe herself, tended to the personal things, but much of the other work was done by the machines. We were not permitted out of the quarters except in the company of our mistress, so it was very boring. We could not even sneak out, for we did not know how to open the locks."

"I would have spent the time reading. Surely there were many books and tapes around on many topics."

Again she looked embarrassed. "I—we—cannot read or write."

He felt foolish and ashamed of himself. In the colony there were many who were never able to master most or all of the more than thirty thousand characters of the alphabet. He himself had had help with machines and special training to allow him to read at a level far beyond what one his age, even if very bright, would have managed without them. Most people in China could not read, in fact. Literacy was what truly set the classes apart, the heart of their division. If, somehow, a peasant could learn to read and take the examinations, he could rise in society. The better one read and the more one read, the more complex the examination one took. It was the one road to social mobility open to all Chinese, although, of course, it was next to impossible for a peasant to learn to read, while the child of a stupid or slow highborn who could not manage the skill was never demoted to peasant.

"I am sorry. I will make no more stupid remarks," he said lamely. "Please tell me more of how you came here."

Her smile told him that all was forgiven. "One day a man came who was an expert on locks. A security man of sorts. He was young and very handsome, and we made a fuss over him, I'm afraid. He began to brag about his trade and show off his knowledge of the locks and security systems, and even explained some of his tools. It was quite an education. He didn't think mere peasant servants could understand what he said, but it was actually quite simple. We soon found basic apartment locks no problem at all. Some other locks and doors were more difficult, but even ones requiring fingerprints were beatable. Once you understood the principle, it was simple to find a way around each."

"Some of those would still require special tools to defeat," he noted. "You said as much yourself."

"Some tools were simple and could be made from other things. Others, the complicated mechanical tools, you could get if you wanted. We once had an uncle who was something of a magician. A criminal, really, but a minor one. He would put on little magic shows and phony gambling games in the village. Sometimes he arranged to lose, for he would then simply brush against you, and the contents of your purse would be in a hidden pocket in his shirt. Anyone with long fingers, nerve, and short nails could do it if they practiced, and he showed us all the tricks. We kids would always be doing it to one another and to others just for fun. We never—hardly ever—kept anything."

"You said you used to have an uncle. He is dead now?"

"Yes. Hanged when I was twelve. The trick is even easier with two, and my sister and I are very good at it. So, when we saw a repairman with tools we wanted walking along, we had no problem getting them. The highborn used to be the easiest, but those of Center are easier yet. They are ignorant of the trick and casual about it."

He nodded, his appreciation of her skills growing. "So you were not bored anymore."

"No. Oh, it was really all just a game. Slip out and slip into the dwelling of some highborn who was not in at the time and take something minor, something pretty but not likely to be missed, such as a bottle of perfume or some bauble. It became a contest, and it was most exciting."

"I bet. And then you were caught?"

"Not very quickly. We simply were carried away by our own poor ignorance. We wandered in one time to a security zone which was computer-monitored and tripped alarms. We were sealed in and trapped. At first they could not belive that we were who and what we seemed, but after long sessions with drugs and doctors and machines, they decided we were just what we seemed to be. So they tied us to a wall, whipped us, then gave us to the security guards. Then, suddenly, we were pulled back, bathed, cleaned up and tended to, placed in chains, and sent to the flying machine."

"Pardon me for mentioning it, but your wounds are from the beating?"

"No. I have more scars all up and down my back. When they first threw me to the guards, I fought. We both did. I scratched the face of one of them very badly. They held us down while he carved this in my face and similar gashes in my sister's face. He—he said that we might as well enjoy what was coming, because no man would wish to do anything with us again. I wished only to kill myself in my shame, but they made very sure I could not do that. Only by finally convincing them that I would do nothing rash right now did I gain any freedom of movement, even to being here like this. I could see in every eye how hideous I have become."

"I—knew—a woman once. A girl. She was of highborn stock, and her beauty was perfection, yet inside she was the personification of all that is foul, evil, and monstrous in people. Those attracted to her beauty will be as flies in a spider's web. I, too, might have been a fly in her web, but even in this place I learn and improve myself. My Buddhist teacher would understand, although it took his pupil this long to see his meaning. The body is but a shell. One must look beyond to the soul and see only it if it shines pure." Impulsively, although he had never done it before, he drew her to him and kissed her. When their lips parted, the look on her face was a mixture of shock, surprise, and almost childlike wonder.

"I think," she whispered, "that I may yet live a little while."

"I did not do this out of pity, you must believe that, but I feel your pain within me," he said softly. "You have suffered far more than I have."

"No. I did not lose my family and all my people, and what I did I did myself, knowing it was criminal. You had no choice in it. We threw away comfortable lives out of boredom, and now we pay for that, but you are without guilt or blame, and you have lost everything. Now we both go to our fate, whatever and wherever it is. I heard them say that the great spire out there is a ship that goes into the heavens, beyond the world. Is that true? Is that even possible?"

"Yes. It can go from this plant to another."

"What is a planet?" she asked him, genuinely curious.

"Huh? Other worlds than this, like the moon, only farther off."

"You mean they are sacrificing us by sending us to the moon goddess? I have often prayed to her. She may be merciful."

He was startled. Ignorance was one thing, but how could he reconcile someone who had figured out in a brief lesson how to pick some of the most elaborate computer-controlled security locks in a high-tech place like Center with someone who clearly had no idea that there was any place beyond China, who thought the moon was a goddess and probably also believed that the world was flat?

"We are not being sacrificed," he assured her. "Not that we might not be better off at that. We are being sent to another place like the one we have just left, only suspended in the heavens so that there is no way for us to ever leave. I do not know what happens to the people sent there, except that it strikes fear even in the hearts of the guards of Center security."

She accepted that. "That fills me with fear as well. A place in the heavens could not ever be escaped from. You might go through the locks, but you would fall endlessly in the heavens."

"No, you would be dead before that. There is no air to breathe in space. The only air we will have will be in the place they keep us. It is better than any locks to keep someone imprisoned."

"Yet you are not afraid. I can tell."

In fact he *was* afraid, particularly now that he'd heard about her own treatment, seen the scars on the outside and sensed the others on her soul. If what both of them had experienced was not the worst punishment, then they were being taken to a horror he could not imagine. The fact that it was an unknown of such dimensions was terrifying, yet he could not admit that to her or let it dominate him.

"I fear only what I face that is worthy of that fear," he responded bravely. "Then I will face death bravely and spit at him. For now, I still yearn to fight."

As they talked, he began examining the room for hidden cameras and microphones. A plan was beginning to take shape in his mind, and if he could somehow communicate it to her and she could do her part, it was just possible. His people were gone, save for himself and Deng, but he still had their dream, and he had the knowledge to carry it out, as well.

He found surveillance devices—not many but sufficient to block any real secrets. He settled back on the mat next to her. "You know, my people found how to fly one of those spaceships," he said casually but in a low tone. "It is a pity we will be chained and probably guarded in a locked room all the way to wherever we go."

She lay down comfortably beside him and squeezed his hand. "Yes, it is," she agreed.

They had talked almost nonstop throughout the day, without reservation or hesitancy in even the most personal and intimate things. It was as if they had known each other all their lives and were catching up on the time spent apart. Too, there was both a direct and a subtle exchange of vital information as he tried to give her a cram course in the basics of astronomy while also conveying what he needed from her in the practical sense.

A meal was finally delivered, and it proved to be a pleasant surprise. The recipe was Mongolian, with chunks of lamb, fried wonton in a spicy garlic-laced sauce, and rice, and the vegetables tasted fresh. Even the tea was hot. Chu Li wasn't sure if this was the last meal of a condemned prisoner or, more likely, the same thing being served to the staff in this cobbled-together prison section.

Chow Dai wondered why they had bothered to split up the two pairs, since with human guards and cameras in unfamiliar territory she was unlikely to be able to do anything. Chu Li had responded that it was probably just another tactic to disorient them, but he didn't really believe that. Their captors had analyzed his mind, and Deng's, and the minds of the Chow sisters and knew them probably better than anyone did. They were being sent to this distant place, at great trouble and expense, because someone there, for some unspeakable reason, had a use for two boys and two girls in their middle teens. He suspected they knew that both Deng and he were the kind whose hearts would go out to such kindred spirits in distress and that mere attentions by a male might well guarantee that the pair would not commit suicide or try something so desperate it would mean their death.

The spaceship they had seen was an OG-47 resupply ship. It had to have landed for repairs of some sort that were not available at the moment in space; usually such ships did not land at all but were serviced by ground-to-orbit cargo ships. The OG-47 had a pressurized passenger compartment holding up to sixteen for one to three days, fewer for longer journeys. The pilot's cabin as usual was in a vacuum state in space but could be entered by airlock in a space suit. There was no guarantee that such suits would be aboard, but if they were, they would be Type 61s and stored in a computer-locked compartment to the rear of the passenger cabin, to be opened automatically in case of emergency.

It startled him just to know that. Where had he learned it? Not with his own people, certainly. Not from those strange memories of the girl, either. He became more and more convinced that someone had played some nasty tricks on his mind, and he didn't like it. Were they being toyed with? Had someone who knew his people's project given him this much just to see if he could really do it? Steal a spaceship?

It had to be something like that. Dai and Mai were part of it, too. It was too impossible to believe that he, with his knowledge, would find himself teamed with two accomplished thieves and locksmiths. He did not for one minute believe that the girls were anything other than what they appeared to be, but someone or something had assigned them to be going just where *he* was going at the same time and on the same ship.

He disliked the feeling of being a wind-up doll in someone else's toy game. Who? This Song Ching? It would be in character, but what profit would she get by it? She wouldn't know if her plan succeeded or failed or get the data to use in any attempt of her own. To test the security system? Four teenagers with no real experience when there were almost certainly so many others they could use who would be better suited?

He could not know, but he would simply have to watch out. The fact was, no matter what the reason, they had to try to escape.

Certainly Dai was bright; she had understood immediately the implications of his comments and had been giving and getting information through the day's conversations as well.

That evening, the guards came for each prisoner individually and took them down the hall to a different room, which proved to be a small water shower with a little dressing area complete with built-in mirror. After bathing, they were provided with fresh clothing of the same design as their prison garb, but dyed yellow with SECURITY stamped front and back in Chinese and two other languages.

Chu Li felt a reluctance to actually take the shower, although it appeared that there were no visual monitors in there and therefore that there was some measure of privacy afforded. He had never bathed very often, but he ordinarily would have wished it now. But some fear, an unreasoning thing, made him hesitate. He did not, however, have much choice.

The hypnotics held. When he emerged and looked at himself in the mirror, he still saw the image of a young boy, not the image that was actually there. He dressed again and was led back to the detention room.

After lights-out, she lay beside him, and their hands came together and squeezed; she clung to him as if he were the only real thing in her life. They hugged and cuddled for a bit and rubbed each other's backs. In the dark, she had no deformities at all.

He wanted her, and clearly she wanted and needed him, but his injuries prevented that for now. The fact that they were isolated and alone and facing an uncertain but definitely unpleasant future heightened their desire. But they both slept, huddled against each other for reassurance.

For Chow Dai, Chu Li's companionship was a deliverance, no matter how temporary, from the pit of hell. She had never experienced the kindness and gentleness that this boy had shown her even when she had been unscarred; the fact that he did so even when she looked so horrible was wondrous and magical. She barely knew him, yet she knew she needed him and would risk anything for him. He had but to ask. She dreamed the first pleasant dreams she had dreamed in weeks.

Chu Li's dreams were different. He dreamed that he was making real love to her, although she had long, silky black hair and no scars, but as he approached her, naked, she suddenly got a look of horror on her face and shied away, crying. This was mixed with other, stranger dreams that even included spaceship schematics and nightmares where he saw his parents, alive again, but when he ran to them they recoiled in horror and turned, and when they turned back they were not his parents at all but the tall, frightening figures of that other girl's parents, the chief administrator and his wife. The girl was there, too, running in and out of his dreams, spoiling even the good ones, dancing through and whispering tauntingly, "I know a secret."

The elderly orderly awakened them with a breakfast of rice and fish heads. "Eat well and relax," he told them genially. "Tonight you leave for your destinies."

"My sister and the boy—are they all right?" Chow Dai asked nervously. She had almost a sixth sense, as did many twins, about her sister even when separated, but she had no real feelings of Chow Mai now, and that worried her more than anything.

"Oh, they are getting along fine, as are the two of you, it seems. Do not worry about them. You will see them today." He chuckled to himself and left.

He looked at Chow Dai. "Today. Sometime today."

She nodded. "I hope they let us see each other for a while first. You know, when my sister and I are together, often we need few words even to talk to one another."

Chu Li was feeling a bit dizzy, a little fuzzy in the head, but he put his disorientation down to nervous tension and apprehension. About midday he felt he had to go to the bathroom and called for the guard. The sense of disorientation continued and his stomach was upset. In the bathroom, he could be alone and, hopefully, get something of a grip on himself. He felt as if he was losing his mind.

Twice he'd failed to respond when Chow Dai had addressed him by his name. Images—strong, primary images—of his parents, siblings, old friends, the details of his past life, seemed to be melting or fading. He suddenly could not remember what his father or mother looked like. The other memories, though—*her* memories—were all still there and seemed to be getting clearer in spite of his attempts to push them back.

He was led to the bathroom, and he sat, holding his head in his hands. Then he looked down and put one of his hands down between his legs. Suddenly, some of the conditioning broke away and was gone. *They have emasculated me!* He unbuttoned his tunic and looked at and felt his chest. Two huge nipples atop small, perfect breasts. He quickly got up and disrobed completely, examining his body as if for the first time. The smooth skin, the curves . . . *A girl! They have changed me into a girl!*

And not just any girl. He knew what was happening now. He was being changed not just to female, but into *her*, the one he hated, the daughter of his people's murderers!

He saw it all now, or thought he did. She could not remain as she was, so she had somehow convinced the computers there, or the doctors, to take him, a lowly nothing, and change him into a mental and physical duplicate of *her*. The victim was turning into the oppressor. The memory of the beatings had probably been planted so that he wouldn't notice the surgery until it was too late to betray her.

There was an angry knock and an impatient snarl from the other side of the door. He knew he had to get dressed again fast and get out of there. They could change his shape, but they could not change his mind, he vowed to himself. He was a boy, even if now locked in a girl's body. He might have her memories, but he would never become *her*. Never. He would die first. There was more to manhood than what they had stolen from him. Monks refused all sex, yet they were certainly men. It was important to him that he keep this attitude no matter how much of her eventually took over. He could never become her, become the callous, cruel, and evil one she was, if he retained that.

He was rudely cursed by the guard and led back to the detention room where Chow Dai awaited. Chow Dai. He could face anything but dashing her few hopes—even this. He still wanted her. He *loved* her, damn it—but he could never make love to her. That was what his dreams had been telling him.

"Rat! You were gone so long, I was getting worried about you," she told him.

"I—I made some discoveries about myself," he responded carefully. At least his voice still sounded normal, at least to him. He wanted to tell her, to tell *somebody*, but while she would understand, the revelation would still crush her. He couldn't do it. Not now. Not until he had to.

"Discoveries?"

"My—injuries—are far worse than I thought, that's all."

She hugged him. "Don't worry. Peasant girls are taught infinite patience."

Infinite is right, he thought sourly, but said nothing. For the time being, escape was the only thing that mattered. If they did not escape, none of the rest would matter. Later, if they made it, he would find some gentle way to tell her.

In fact, by the change in him, the quieter periods, his reluctance to really get close, she guessed a part of the truth. She suspected that he had just now realized the extent to which the same people who had tortured, raped, and disfigured her had also disfigured him. She knew just from the treatment she had received afterward that they could do much, even make you forget your injuries and pain for a while, although the effects wore off. Her mood fell as she voiced her suspicions to herself. They have made him a eunuch, she guessed. It is the only explanation. She had almost expected it, guessed it from the start when he had spoken of his injury. Well, she wasn't going to pretend that it didn't matter to her, but he was still the same kind, gentle one who had treated her with respect and ignored her own disfigurement. She had no intention of abandoning him, not now. If he could ignore her disfigured shell and see only someone worthwhile inside, she could certainly do the same.

But though both of them saw and preferred the lie, the

truth would not be kept down inside of Chu Li. Bit by bit, as the day wore on, Song Ching's truth chipped slowly but methodically away at Chu Li, and he fought it. The boy's memories and sense of identity were rapidly fading now, leaving only Song Ching, yet the biochemically induced Chu Li personality was becoming firmer, harder, fixed.

Even for the computer it had been a rush job, an emergency, and it might have been predicted that something undefinable and unanticipated would arise. Song Ching had ordered blocks that made her cold, unemotional, machinelike, and this had been altered only as required by the masquerade. As a result, the basic personality and responses of Chu Li were the only ones present and created an overwhelming desire to remain as they were, resisting all attempts at change. The brain created personality, but it also was subject to a measure of adaptation, and, having no countermanding "fallback" personality, it responded to this urgent desire to maintain current levels. There was a dichotomy inside of her, a war between body and brain that simply could not go on.

"Are you all right?" Chow Dai asked worriedly. "You look ill."

"I—I think I should just lie down for a while," he managed. "It is an—aftereffect of what was done to me. I apologize, but if I lie down for a while, it will be all right."

He was a conscious combatant in the war raging inside him, and it had made him physically ill, both feverish and upset. The tension and confusion were enormous; he could not stand this much longer. Either something had to break or he knew he might well die—die on the brink of possible success and escape in which he was the only hope for these other people. Any moment now the guards could come for them, so there was no time for such a fight. By now he knew he really *was* Song Ching; there had been no tampering with Chu Li's body or mind. Chu Li was certainly dead, his body long sent to dust or turned to energy, and she was responsible for that. It was an intolerable thought. It was intolerable that she should live again while he was dead, no matter what the price of that life might be, yet his memories even now were less than ghosts, mere wisps fading with each passing moment, leaving only Song Ching.

The brain had several mechanisms for resolving such dilemmas, whether caused by biological malfunction or trauma or otherwise induced, and all of them were forms of what they called insanity. If it could not resolve the problems, the brain got hung up in endless loops and the result was catatonia, but in this case both sides had a sense of urgency and a single central purpose: escape. Escape to the stars. The brain needed only a lie that both sides could accept and believe; if that happened, then memories could be rewritten, attitudes adjusted, and everything resolved to allow function. A new reality was called for, and a very personal one.

In a miraculous revelation, she suddenly understood what had happened, and there was no more fight, only awe at the justice of the gods. When the computer had executed Chu Li, his soul had not gone on but had instead been placed in the body of Song Ching, who had ordered the destruction of her own personality in her plot. Her own soul had been cast adrift when this was done, and Chu Li's had filled the empty vessel in a measure of justice. The soul was shaped and formed and purified or dirtied by its experiences in the flesh, but it did not retain memories as such. Still, she knew it was Chu Li's soul animating Song Ching's body and guiding her thoughts. That was true justice: The soul of the enemy who was destroyed by her family was now in possession of her body, her memories, her knowledge, and those would be used against her family and the system that supported it. That was clearly the will of the gods.

There was a price for this, of course. Chu Li's soul

had not risen to be purified; it remained the soul of a teenage boy. He was a man trapped in the body and with the memories of a beautiful woman. It would be a frustrating burden to carry, but the symmetry of the justice meted out by the gods required it. Because the knowledge in her head was so vast, so complete, and so dangerous to those who must be punished, it was a burden that had to be accepted. It left someone with the means to avenge, and that had to be sufficient.

For now, the Chu Li masquerade had to be continued so that the primary goal could be attained. Later there would be time for explanations and the truth. The reclining figure sat up, saw the anxious Chow Dai, and smiled. "I am all right now," he assured her. "I will be all right from now on."

She looked relieved. "I was almost going to call the guard and have you looked at. You really worried me."

He was glad she hadn't done that, or the ruse would have been up right there. There being no machines to measure and identify souls, it would have taken but a moment for the stupidest of medics to realize that this was not a boy named Chu Li.

He looked at Chow Dai's ugly, scarred face and reflected on how truly ironic this all was. He could do just as well looking like her; indeed, it would solve some potential problems down the line. She, on the other hand, would prosper and blossom with the body he wore. The scientists could make a sadist a gentle poet and a peasant into an educated artist with their chemicals and processes, but only the gods could switch souls. Although it would work out here, it was in a way a reassuring thought: that there was one thing, at least, beyond science and reserved for the gods.

Not long after, Chow Mai and Deng Ho were sent in to join them. Deng's conditioning still held; Chu Li hoped it would hold long enough to avoid any complications. The two sisters rushed to each other and embraced and cried a little. Deng grinned at Chu Li. "Hello, Rat. Surviving?"

Chu Li nodded. "And you?"

Deng gave a knowing smirk. "No problems if you just shut your eyes," he whispered, then grew more serious. "They've been through even worse than us. It's crazy, but we're going to some mad hell, and *I* feel sorry for *them*. Kind of takes your mind off it."

Chu Li looked over at the sisters, who were chattering away in pure peasant dialect. They seemed to be talking at the same time, and he guessed from the few words he caught that they were using a kind of spoken shorthand, expressing complete thoughts. That's fine, he thought. He understood full well that the monitors would never make sense of that garbage.

The girls had only a few minutes for their reunion, though. The door opened again, and the duty guard stepped in.

"You will all stand and be silent!" he barked imperiously. "You will now be addressed by the captain of the vessel that will carry you to your final destination!" He was as stiff as usual, but nervousness was revealed in his eyes and in small jerks of his head back toward the door.

Chu Li—he refused to think of himself as otherwise and certainly not as a "she," all physical evidence to the contrary—was startled that such a ship had a captain at all. A steward perhaps, or even a jailer—but a captain?

They heard the barred gate open and then clang shut again, then the sound of heavy footsteps approached the door, which the guard had continued to hold open. When the captain walked in, the prisoners all gasped and stared at him as if he were some sort of monster.

They are giving us to foreign devils!

Carlo Sabatini stopped and looked at the expressions of absolute fear and revulsion on those four young faces and drank it in. Seeing the reactions of people who had never in their lives seen anyone who was not Oriental was the only bit of fun there was in this hick, provincial spaceport. These four looked like they'd never seen anybody but a Han Chinese and the Mongolian guards before.

"My name is Captain Sabatini," he announced in flawless Mandarin, the result of a session with a mindprint machine. "I am master of the interplanetary ship *Star Islander* which will take you from here to Melchior."

Three of the kids looked blank, but he noticed that the boy on his far right did not seem to react at all. Clearly that one knew more than the others, and Sabatini wondered why. He filed it for future reference.

"The ship, as you may or may not know, is fully automated. It is piloted by a machine that can make decisions far quicker than any of us and can fly the ship as no human could. Basically, my job is to make sure it works correctly and to be certain that any and all passengers and cargo get safely and comfortably to their destination, as well as handling things at the ports. As you can see, I am not Chinese, but rest assured, I am human. I have the same sort of blood inside of me, and I work the same way."

They stared at him, still somewhat awestruck and not a little afraid. He *was* imposing, standing over a hundred and eighty centimeters tall and weighing at least ninety-five kilos of pure muscle. He had an olive complexion that in their society would have marked him as ill and at death's door, thick black hair with some streaks of gray on the top and cut short on the sides, and a medium black mustache. He wore a shiny black uniform with leather boots and belt; the shirt was open at the top and exposed a fair amount of chest, covered in thick, black hair. He even had hair on his arms and the back of his hands: thick, black curly hair. The body hair in particular fascinated all of them. It was impossible not to think of him as some big ape or gorilla wearing clothes.

Still, Chu Li was able to break the spell enough to

think clearly. If he goes along, then there is at least one space suit aboard.

"We don't normally take off from Earth," he told them, "so this will be a rough ride at the start. You will need to board the ship when it's angled up, get into seats as if it were lying flat, and get strapped in, and I do mean strapped. Anyone who isn't fully strapped in will die in the takeoff. Since some of you might be tempted by that idea, we will have you restrained in place for that part of the trip. Once we reach orbit and the artificial gravity in the cabin stabilizes, you will get a measure of freedom, since I don't want to have to cart you to the bathroom or spoon-feed you, but you will still be under limited restraint. I want no problems in our journey, which, if no unexpected problems or emergencies develop, should take forty-one days. This is no interstellar speed ship."

That impressed all four of them. The two boys, who at least understood what spaceships were, still had trouble with that time span. The distance involved was really beyond their comprehension.

"Don't be too downcast. At other times it might have taken up to a year to reach Melchior. The positions are the best possible right now for the shortest distance, which is why we are taking off now and why we have to do everything exactly on schedule. Now, since we're going to be together a long time, I want to get some facts and rules straight before we even begin."

They just continued to gape at him.

"First, and most important, you are booked not as passengers but as *live cargo*. That puts you in the same class as dogs, cats, chickens, and horses. There are two pressurized sections of the cabin. One is for people, the other is for animals. The animal section has cages that are not very large and is otherwise pretty dark and unpleasant. You will be placed initially in the human section, but if any one of you causes me any problems at all, one or all of you will be put back there and kept there for the duration of the voyage. They don't even have toilets back there, so think about it. Second, so I don't have to look behind me all the time, you will be shackled at all times and limited in the area you can move. Still, some of you may figure that I'm only one man, and you might try and get the best of me in a weak moment of mine. You might try. You might even succeed, although I promise you that if you try and fail, you will find me *very* unpleasant. But let's say you succeed."

He could see in their eyes that this had crossed their minds. It always did, and he'd transported tougher and nastier ones than these.

"I cannot pilot the ship," he told them. "I cannot even get to the bridge, since it is without air or pressure, and so neither can you. No matter what happened to me, I couldn't help you, and you would wind up in the exact same place and in the hands of the exact same people, only you wouldn't know how to run the life maintenance and support system for the cabins. I also have within me, implanted by a surgeon—where, I don't know—a tiny transmitter. It is hooked both to the ship and to a Master System relay. If I die, that beacon stops transmitting. When it does, Master System will call the ship and determine whether my death was natural or murder. If it was murder, Master System will take direct command of the ship and release gas into the compartment that will not kill you but will put you down into a sleep from which you cannot wake up without the antidote. If you kill me, not only will you not escape and not die, but your families back here, no matter how innocent, will replace you."

Not likely in the Song Ching family, Chu Li reflected, but then realized that there were cousins and others who might well be forced to replace her. However, it was empty to threaten Deng or himself that way. The system had already destroyed their families and friends as well. Still, for the girls' sake, he could not fail.

All right. So far it was proceeding exactly as the plans

in his mind told him it would. Of course, Sabatini had not mentioned a couple of other safeguards, but he wouldn't. That was all right. There were ways around this.

"Now, with all that out of the way," Sabatini concluded, "let me say that I am a ship's captain, not a member of the police or the military of anyone. I haul cargo and people. If you are friendly, cooperative, and make no trouble, this can be a pleasant voyage. I treat people the way they treat me. Treat me nasty, and I'll be nastier. Treat me nice, and I can be very nice as well. Any questions? Come—speak up. We will be off soon, and it'll be too late."

Chu Li didn't want to draw much attention, but he had to know one thing. "If you please, Honorable Captain— what is this Melchior to which we are being sent?"

"Melchior is a rock about thirty kilometers across that floats around the sun out in the asteroid belt. There's nothing on top but some beacons and a single dock, but the thing is a hollowed-out rock full of chambers, tunnels, rooms, even something of a town. It's a lot of things. It's a place for scientific research. It's occasionally a meeting place for important administrators who want to be away from all monitoring. Mostly it's a prison run by scientists who don't have to obey the rules because they're cooped up there, too. I'll tell you what more I know when we're under way. That satisfy you for now?"

Deng Ho wet his lips nervously. "Then—*we* are to be the experiments this time?"

Sabatini shrugged. "I don't know, boy. Nobody really knows, except maybe some of the administrators. I never heard of anyone ever escaping, though. Once you're inside, with that maze of tunnels and air locks, you get so lost, you might never even find your way out."

8. THE RAVEN AND THE WARLOCK

THE ILLINOIS VILLAGE WAS IN TURMOIL. TWO OF THEIR
best warriors dead, a dramatic escape by the two whom
the chief had called his "playthings," Chief Roaring Bull
himself kidnapped, a slave woman missing, and a boat,
supplies, and weapons stolen—it all made the rest of them
feel downright *insecure*. The chief's eldest son, along with
the rest of the clan, met to decide just what action to take.

"They're long gone," some argued. "Far downriver in
foul weather. If they don't drown, they'll be out of reach
before we can get the word down to stop them."

"But it's bad for business," others argued. "What if
word gets around that this was done to us? Who will fear
us and pay us tribute then? It will give the others ideas."

"*They* won't be bragging, if they survive at all," the
first group argued. "The man's on the run from Council.
He won't even mention this. As for Chief Roaring Bull,
they're certain to kill him when he's no longer needed, if

they haven't already. You heard what the girls said about that pair. They smelled of death. I say we bottle it up here. Anyone, at any time, who speaks of this to anyone, even among ourselves, shall at the very least lose his or her tongue and suffer torments. Let us tighten our own security and our tongues and go on as before."

"And what of the chief?" the others responded. "How will we explain his death? It is bound to get out."

"Everybody knows he was a steady fire drinker. We'll just say he got drunk and mad at somebody on the river one day and went out there. That'll explain the body, no matter what the condition. He's never going to tell anyone different."

They all looked at Black Bear Foot, the chief's eldest son and heir apparent. A very imposing man in his own right, he had sat impassively listening to the debate without getting involved. Now the man they would make chief spoke.

"Yes, but what if father manages to come back alive?" he asked nervously. He had not always been the eldest son, but his late half brother had gotten too ambitious too fast. Some of the same men who now offered Black Bear Foot the leadership had encouraged his brother, then lost their nerve and betrayed him when faced with the wrath of Roaring Bull.

"Now listen and hear what I say," he said gravely. "The two who failed to watch the strangers will take one canoe, and the two who were so afraid of getting wet that they allowed the chief to be taken will go in another. One of you will bring back the chief, or his body, or all four of you will wish that you were dead, though you will not die. Understand?"

They understood, but they didn't like it.

"Also, send runners south on both sides of the Mississippi to contact our allies. Tell them only the story that Roaring Bull got drunk and was lost on the river and that we seek him and fear his capture by traders who bear grudges against him. Tell them that they will get a great reward if the chief is returned alive and a lesser reward if dead, but if dead, they will get the same great reward if they also return his killers, dead or alive. Got it? Then go!"

Those who would travel left to prepare, but the rest of the council remained in session to work out the details in the chief's absence. They were still hard at it when two strangers rode right into the village on horseback and stopped all there dead in their tracks.

The man on the brown horse was a Crow from the northwest mountains. An unexpected sight this far from his tribal territory, he was a striking man with a mean and fearsome look about him. He was dressed in full fur and buckskin and had a hard, tough, nasty face that seemed more a natural rock formation than a human feature. His eyes were narrowed and mean-looking, and he chomped on a half-smoked but unlit Caribe cigar. Observers could tell in an instant that he would no more hesitate to kill a man than to swat a fly; to stop him, one would need ten good men, all willing to die themselves.

With him, however, astride a huge black stallion, was a figure even more imposing and out of place. She was very tall, taller than the Crow, who was no little man, and her skin was as black as the blackest night. Her hair, straight and cut very short, was blacker than her skin, and her features were as perfect as finely chiseled black marble. Her clothing, tailored to her statuesque proportions, consisted of a sleeveless tunic made of beaver and mink with pants and even boots to match. Her arms looked smooth, but when they moved, tremendous muscles and great power were evident. Her eyes were cold, her bearing aloof. None needed to be told that these were very dangerous people. Here was a Crow Agency man, one of those who worked for Council security, and with him a visitor from a far place who unquestionably held the same sort of job in some distant land.

They rode right up to the tribal council meeting and halted but did not dismount. The Crow Agency man gave them a look that seemed to chill them all, as if he felt in the mood to massacre an entire tribe. The lady, on the other hand, gave the impression that she'd rather slowly torture them first.

Black Bear Foot decided he really didn't need this kind of trouble, but he sighed and got up. If his father didn't come back, this would determine whether he survived to take over. He, too, had a lot of younger half brothers who wouldn't mind the job in the least.

"I am Black Bear Foot, acting chief of this tribe until the return of my father," he said in his native tongue. He didn't care if they understood it or not: That was their problem. In fact, he kind of hoped that they didn't share *any* common languages. Maybe then they'd give up and go away. "If you come in peace and friendship, you are welcome to share our fire and our hospitality," the acting chief added grudgingly.

"Where's your father, sonny boy?" the Crow asked in a voice that was deep, raspy, and all-around unpleasant. He spoke excellent Illinois. Black Bear Foot thought the man sounded as a corpse might sound if it could speak.

"You have no call to break the Covenant," the young, would-be chief responded, deciding that only bravado meant anything to this pair. "If I were to speak that way to someone of my position in the land of the Crow, your people would have my skin stretched across poles. You may have my life and surrender yours, but I will have respect in my own village and among my own people from any visitor."

The speech seemed to impress and also disturb the Crow.

"You know we act in the name of the Council," the Crow Agency man said menacingly, but the mere fact that he said it showed some hesitancy. He obviously was not used to having someone stand up to him on anything, except perhaps *her*.

"You mean you are in the employ of Council. The way you act and treat those who would offer you hospitality is not the Council way or the way of the Covenant. You may act in the name of the Council, but I doubt if the Council would approve of the way you act."

The Crow smiled, although the expression looked grotesque and unnatural on him. The black woman remained impassive.

"You're right," the Crow admitted. There were almost audible sighs of relief from the crowd. "These are extraordinary circumstances, son, and our mission takes precedence over everything else, even the Covenant, but it doesn't excuse improper manners. You couldn't manage my name in your language, so just call me Raven. Everybody does. The lady also has an untranslatable name, but the sounds are there. She is called Manka Warlock, and she is in the Caribe what I am in the western mountains. Her mere presence here should show you that this is something very important."

It did. The Caribe and their tropical islands were placed in the South American District and did not work for council at all or have authority here even from on high. That, Black Bear Foot suspected, was why the Crow was here: He, too, was out of his normal region, but a Council man was a Council man no matter what his tribe and nation.

"We are looking for a man. Late thirties, Hyiakutt but a linguist and a Council worker on Leave. He might be traveling with a Hyiakutt woman, medium, good build, early thirties. I know what this place is and what it does. They got past us up north; I doubt if they got past you."

The young man sighed. "They were here. They—picked up supplies and went on this morning down the river."

The Crow Agency man gave the acting chief a hard look. "Probably about three in the morning with your father as hostage from the looks of things. Don't worry.

I really don't know those whom we seek, but this village and your father have a reputation that reaches to the upper end of the Missouri. That, and I see the two bodies back there."

"My father and some of those he trusted were careless," the young man told him, deciding to tell the truth. "The strangers did not seem dangerous. Their canoe was swamped. They were brought in naked and carrying nothing."

"Uh huh. Only helpless. So they got you good, took the chief, and you're all here in a prayer meeting praying to the Great Spirit that they don't send him back. That about it?"

"No. Even now those responsible are being dispatched to chase them down the river, while runners prepare to notify our allies. I mean to have their hides and my father back alive."

Raven turned to the woman and spoke in a strange language. "They were here, naked. Lost everything when the canoe went over, probably from that hypno shield. They fought their way out and snatched the chief early this morning. I figure five, maybe six hours tops. What do you think?"

"I think we had better go on the river," she responded without changing her gaze. "We will never catch them this way, and we would need to be ferried from this point as it is. I think we underestimated our little historian and his native wench, but they have nothing, you say."

"Nothing tangible, but he wouldn't be running so hard and so bloody if he hadn't read 'em all through. He knows what those papers said. He's the only one in the whole area who could read 'em, and he finds 'em. The hell with the papers. He's the papers now."

She nodded. "Very well. He is on the run from Council and from these people. He will not be moving fast but cautiously."

The Crow switched back to Illinois. "Do you know where he is trying to go?"

"My father said he was trying to reach Nawlins. He is in trouble and needs an ally in Council."

Raven thought a moment. "Mud Runner! Got to be!" he said in the black woman's Caribe English.

"Who is this Mud Runner person?"

"Resident Agent. Probably an old pal. He's set up in the swamps south of Nawlins."

She nodded again. "Good. That means that he must keep to the river. It is a very long way to Nawlins from here, even longer when you must guard against your own shadow. We will proceed by water."

"Yeah, but these slobs couldn't catch their own dinner with a net, and we're both on unfamiliar ground. We'll go right past him."

"Perhaps," she said. "If so, it will only delay things. We know where he is going."

"Yeah. And if they sic a Val on him, what then?"

"If these pirates had killed him, what then? We can only do the possible and play the odds. From the looks of things here, he might make it, even *with* a Val on his tail. The Val can't play the percentages. It must check every little piece of river for him, although it, too, will head for this Mud Runner in the end. We must be certain that we get to them first."

"You ever think this could put a Val on *our* tails? Whatever this is, it's *big*. Big enough for a guy to throw it all away and go wild. Big enough to send a Val in the first place, and maybe all of 'em."

"You have always bragged that you could take a Val. If they put one or two on us, then you will get the opportunity to test your theories. Come. We must not remain here long."

"Yeah," he sighed. "Even if these are our kind of people."

*   *   *

Chief Roaring Bull knew his section of the river like the old hand he was, and he knew balances, shifts, and other ways to manage an overloaded canoe through occasional rough water and tiny whirlpools. They learned a great deal from him and crossed the area where the mighty Missouri dumped into the Mississippi with no more than minor incidents. Hawks kept him aboard for extra safety, but the man was quickly passing from an asset to a liability.

Twice they had been hailed from shore or intercepted by canoe, and twice the old chief had done himself proud talking them out of any potential dangers. It wasn't that the strangers weren't suspicious; Hawks had the distinct impression that the four warriors in the canoe knew or at least suspected exactly what was going on. But the barely suppressed snickers on their faces showed that they only took bribes from Roaring Bull; they really didn't like him any more than anyone else did, and in the absence of a general alarm or big reward, they really weren't that upset to see the old boy embarrassed and compromised. Besides, they could always claim later that they weren't really *sure* and that the chief had had ample opportunities to cause his captors trouble, yet had not.

They passed the site south of the confluence of the rivers where once, Hawks knew, a mighty complex of cities had stood. Nothing was there now; the forests on both sides looked virgin and ancient, and even the foundations of ancient bridges had long ago succumbed to the power of the river.

"It is now time to bid you farewell," he told the old chief. "Stand up and do not topple the canoe."

"Stand up? But you said you would let me off when we passed the Missouri!"

"I intend to keep my word. You may leave now."

The old man looked around. "But we are in the middle of the river!"

"I did not promise any more than this. You can swim. Sooner or later you will make it to shore just by floating and letting the river carry you. By then we will be long gone."

The old chief glared at him. "A curse on you all, then! I might never know who got you or why, but I look at three of the walking dead here. Sooner or later, perhaps in hours or days, you will encounter someone whom you cannot take. Then it will be over."

"Jump, fat man. That is our problem."

With a last angry glance, the old chief jumped into the river and was soon left far behind.

With his weight gone, the canoe became far more manageable and almost enjoyable to use. Little effort was required except to steer away from snags and keep within the current.

"Where do we go now, my fierce warrior?" Cloud Dancer asked.

"Keep an eye out for men digging on a bluff to our right. It might be any time but will probably not be for some hours. I overheard the traders at the village say that there was a team from Council doing some digging along here, and I want to find them."

"Digging? What sort of digging?"

"They are finding the remains of nations that were here not only before us but before the ones who were here after our ancestors. They will have certain things that we need."

She turned and looked at him. "Remains? They are grave robbers?"

"When things get ancient enough, it is no longer grave robbing but a way to learn how ancient people lived, worked, and thought. It is why we know so much about our own ancestors."

She considered that. "Grave robbers. A fancy name they might have for it, but it is disturbing sacred dead."

He shrugged. If she wanted to think of them as grave robbers, that was fine with him. Of course, archaeologists *were* grave robbers, anyway; it was the motive, not the act, that was the only difference.

"What will these Council grave robbers have that we could use?" she asked him.

"They will look as if they are of the People, but they will not be. Probably mostly students and apprentices with only a couple of experienced elders. Still, somewhere close and probably hidden from view they will have some of the machines of Council. They will also have supplies and will be unable to do as much to us for getting them as even Roaring Bull was."

"You mean we are going to rob them?"

He grinned. "Why should it bother you to rob from grave robbers?"

That seemed to satisfy her sense of morality. The big problem was in convincing Silent Woman that no one was to be killed in this or even badly hurt if it could be at all avoided. He needed supplies and things he could trade downriver, but he wouldn't mind if he could give them all a treatment with a portable mindprinter. A commonality of language would be very helpful indeed, and it was unlikely that these people would have a Hyiakutt cartridge. He could not give Silent Woman a tongue, but he could give her understanding.

Silent Woman had been excellent on the trip so far. Her eyes showed some life again, and she seemed to be enjoying things. It was impossible, of course, to know what was really going through her mind, and he wasn't certain he wanted to know. He was afraid he might not like some of the images there.

The old chief had been correct about her tattoos. Her entire torso was covered with them, in many colors, and resembled an intricate design on a blanket. Cloud Dancer, as an artist, had been absolutely fascinated, and Silent Woman did not seem to mind the stares and obvious interest. Rather, she seemed pleased by it and almost proud. Many tribes used tattoos for many things, but Hawks had never seen anyone literally dressed in them. Whoever had done it had been a genuine artist in his or her own right. It was grotesque, but it was a pleasing grotesque, which was just as well: Even if she died old, she would die with that design.

She had been unable to get the massive bloodstains from her dress when they made camp, and when her tattoos were more appreciated than repulsed, she had looked at the nearly naked couple who had taken her from the Illinois and threw the dress into the river. It was more than a gesture; as the only thing she owned and, aside from the shoulder bag, the only tangible remnant from the Illinois village, she was cutting her last ties with the past and starting absolutely clean. Anyway, from a distance, the tattoos made her look clothed.

In the middle of the next day, they spotted the archaeologists' camp. Hawks pulled the canoe in, and they dragged it up into the brush and hid it as best they could.

The camp was made up of traditional mobile lodges, or tepees, some quite large, although the dig was small and quite limited. A dozen young men and women from a large variety of tribes seemed to be working under the guidance of an older gray-haired man. Most were dressed as primitively as Hawks and Cloud Dancer, although their loincloths were professionally made and hung on fine belts equipped with loops and clips for various tools. Their project looked well along; they were probably in the last stages before packing up.

Cloud Dancer was amazed. The sight of men and women working equally at a hard and exacting task rather than clearly dividing the labor was unusual to her; to see so many from such obviously different nations working and laughing together with no suspicion or animosity was unheard of.

They had clearly decided to live close to the land, and their camp, for the most part, was just like thousands of small tribal camps across the plains, but one tepee, the largest, stood out. For one thing, it had been heavily and cleverly waterproofed. For another, even Hawks had never before seen a tepee whose door shut with a heavy zipper.

These people must have developed solid relations with the local tribes. There was no sign of security. They lived like the natives of the area lived, and unless one knew just what to look for, there was no evidence that this was anything more than a transient village of some strange tribe. At the moment, there were only two people in the camp: a young man and woman who were ostensibly tending the cook fire but who seemed more interested in each other than in the duties at hand. The dig was down an embankment and a good kilometer or more away from the camp itself; the work could be heard in the distance. Hawks began to reconsider his idea of a night attack. Even these people wouldn't trust that the river wouldn't bring them some threat in the dark.

"They probably have local tribesmen come in and guard them for the night," he told Cloud Dancer.

She looked at the romantic pair. "It would be easy to take those two now. If we wait a bit longer, it is possible we will not even be noticed."

"Perhaps." He looked at the sun. "They are sure to break for a midday meal. That is what is on the fire. Let us at least wait until after that and see their routine. I wish no violence if it can be avoided. Those are no threats."

It appeared that there were always two people remaining in the camp at any one time, though the intervals of the rotation were hard to judge. There was only one random event, when the gray-haired leader and two workers returned carrying something in a large blanket.

"They have dug up a body," Cloud Dancer hissed.

"The bodies in those places, if they were burial places at all, would have been dust for centuries," he assured her. "More likely it is an ancient weapon or carving or something that only they would even recognize as such."

They watched as the workers put the find down and

unzipped the big tent. The leader cursed and came back out, fuming at no one in particular. They were using English, one of the two common languages—Spanish was the other—of Council.

"There's no room left in there even to store this temporarily without risking it," the leader fumed. "We're going to have to find some other place for it."

"Taking it to the village is out," one of his helpers, a young woman, responded. "They wouldn't have anything from our dig there on a bet. Probably the best we can do for now is get some canvas, double wrap it, and stake it down and arrange to have it taken out as soon as possible."

"Well, that's only part of it," the chief archaeologist noted. "I think we can get the rest in three or four hours. We'll chance leaving it here, then wrap and transport the whole."

Hawks admitted to himself that he'd love to know what they'd found, but curiosity had already brought him enough trouble. He waited until the workers had returned to the dig after a lunch break; again, a pair remained behind to clean up.

"Now is our time," he told Cloud Dancer. "Try to make Silent Woman understand. We must act quickly. Use the bow to cover me, and if I gesture *so*, shoot convincingly but not at anyone. Be ready to aid, though, if there is a shout or they try something."

"What if that happens?" she asked.

"Then we silence them, grab what we can, and run. I said I wanted no bloodshed, but if it is them or us, I choose us."

She nodded, and he simply got up and walked boldly into the archaeologists' camp. The two there didn't even see him at first, and when they did, they stared nervously at him.

"Just relax and don't call out," he said in his accented

English. "I wish no one to get hurt, but there are others in the bushes and trees over there who are covering me."

The pair looked appalled. "Who the hell are you?" the young man asked. "We have permission from the treaty holders to be here."

"I am obviously not with the treaty holders," Hawks responded, "and I have very little time. This is a robbery, but a limited and civilized one if you just relax and keep back."

"He's bluffing," the woman said toughly. "He has no one in the trees."

Hawks made the gesture, and an arrow flew, landing within half a meter of the young man's left foot.

"Who are you, and what do you want?" the young man asked him.

"Who I am is irrelevant. Let's just say that Council would like to talk to me right now, and I am in no mood to talk with them. I will not disturb your dig or your findings. Take care just to stand there and do or say no more. I do not need warriors in the woods to threaten you. All I need do is tell you a simple fact that I know, and you and everyone here will be killed by Council. Understand?"

They understood. They knew the way the rules worked and probably why he was now on the run. Forbidden knowledge. It was a sore point among all the scholars working in the undercouncils.

Hawks went over to the big tepee, unzipped it, and stepped inside. There was a small battery light just inside the doorway, and he switched it on.

The place was a mess, that was for sure. What he wanted was a weatherproof box about a meter deep and fifty centimeters high, probably with a handle on it and weighing about twenty kilograms. Not light but very well balanced. He had no trouble finding it, since it was one of those items that were used often enough that they were never pushed away in storage. In another pack were a dozen cartridges, each labeled in black marker. He then located the small emergency communications pack and made short work of it—he didn't want them calling in until he was well away. The machines could be easily traced when used, but he intended to be finished with them before somebody was told to look.

He went back out and was pleased to see that there was no surprise welcoming committee and that the pair were just standing there, still staring, not quite knowing what to do. Their eyes widened when they saw what he was taking. This was unprecedented, unheard of. Field expeditions had found themselves under siege, even looted and their members killed, but the systematic theft of a portable mindprint machine was something that simply had never occurred to either of them, nor could they understand it.

Hawks was not, however, particularly single-minded. "Where's the liquor cabinet?" he asked them.

"The what?"

"Come on—I'm running out of time and patience! *Where does he keep the booze?*"

There was something in his tone that convinced them. Never argue with a desperate and dangerous man, that was the rule. Just get the law after him.

"In there," the woman replied, gesturing. "A case in Dr. Kakukua's tepee."

He beckoned for Silent Woman and gave her directions. The two young people watched, fascinated and horrified by the strange, silent, naked woman with the garish tattoos, although both made a note that it would make descriptions of the criminals rather easy. The doctor, Hawks saw, had only high-quality stuff, none of that rotgut brewed by the Illinois. He wished he could take it all, but Silent Woman was limited by the boxes to about twenty half-liter bottles. That was good enough.

"All right—now you remain here for a while," he told them. "I'm leaving someone over there to make sure we are well away before you go running off to bring the others here. They'll shoot a lone arrow into the dirt as they leave and run for it. You count to five hundred after that and we'll be gone."

He and Silent Woman ran back into the bush. "Stay here a couple of minutes," he told Cloud Dancer. "If they make an early break, give them a real scare. Otherwise, give us a few minutes, then run for the canoe. We have to be out of here and hopefully out of range before they get their wits."

She nodded, and he and Silent Woman made for the canoe, then waited nervously for Cloud Dancer. She finally arrived and jumped in as he pushed off.

"I thought you weren't going to come," he said, relieved. "I was about to come and rescue you."

She laughed. "The woman got really brave and decided that no one was left. I sent an arrow so close to her that I believe they will be standing as still as carvings many years from now!"

They sailed by the dig and then continued on as far south as they dared. He decided that they would make camp on the east shore that evening. That way, any search parties would have to cross the river into lands held by other nations. However, he decided first to make temporary camp, use the machine, then leave it there and continue on as far as they could until dark.

He found a good landing where there was no sign of human habitation and good cover, then proceeded to unpack and set up the machine. Both women stared at it nervously. Neither had ever before seen a true independently powered machine, and such things were spoken of as having the darkest magic.

Most of the cartridges were of local languages or the languages of some of the members of the dig, obviously chosen so they could get to know each other better. There also were reference recordings on the culture and the site itself and on uniform excavation procedures, essential for that kind of tedious work. Hawks wanted the two standards, labeled ENG-X and ESPAN-X. These would give a basic overlay, causing the brain to associate words, terms, and phrases it already knew with the proper English or Spanish terms. It was not a cram course in the nuances of the languages; nobody using them would lose an accent or know words and terms without cross-references no matter what the size of the basic dictionary, but it would allow for communication.

He picked English simply because it had the largest vocabulary of all the known languages and as such was bound to have the best matches for esoteric languages. He knew it worked well in translation from Hyiakutt; he had no idea what language Silent Woman had used.

Cloud Dancer looked suspiciously at the box. "What does it do?"

"It will teach you the tongue I used with the students. A tongue harsh to the ear but useful, since it is used so much. We cannot use it to teach Silent Woman Hyiakutt, so we must use this language so all three of us can communicate. It will also be useful should we come up against anyone from Council or in the camp of the Mud Runner and beyond. Please. You *must* do this, for me and for her sake."

She was dubious. "Can you not just run it on Silent Woman and translate?"

"Come on! It is a simple device. You saw what cooperation it brought from the digger camp. Besides, look at Silent Woman. If you do not do it, she certainly will not." He suddenly found another cartridge on which was written in English, SURVIVAL.

"This one, too, is useful," he told her. "I believe it teaches how to survive in the wilderness with nothing at all. Emergency training. We may all need this. Please— sit. It does not hurt. You feel a little sleepy, and then you know it all."

She looked nervously at Silent Woman, then at him, and sighed. "Very well. What do I do?"

"Just lie down here and get as comfortable as you can. I put this thing on your head, so, so that the small points here contact all around. There."

He inserted the cartridge, then turned the power on. There was no real noise, but three small lights blinked on. Silent Woman stared as if suddenly faced with a three-headed cat.

He punched the feed button, then sat back to wait the few minutes this program took to run. Silent Woman just sat and stared, suspicious but not really afraid.

When the machine clicked off, Cloud Dancer was asleep. Taking advantage of that, Hawks withdrew ENG-X and inserted SURVIVAL. To run it on all three did not present much of a risk, he decided, and it might just be useful.

She was still asleep when SURVIVAL clicked off, and he roused her. She opened her eyes, looked into his, smiled, got up, then settled back down a meter or two away.

Silent Woman was more difficult to persuade, but she certainly trusted them by now, and she had seen no terrible effects on Cloud Dancer. She knew that the man would not do anything to harm his woman, so she accepted the mantle with a little nervousness.

ENG-X ran its course, and he ran SURVIVAL once again. She, too, fell asleep and had to be coaxed to move away. He certainly intended to run SURVIVAL on himself. He needed it more than either of the women.

SURVIVAL was everything he had hoped for and more—perhaps too much more. He found himself able to know instantly if berries were edible or poisonous, which water was safe and which was not, how to find shelter or make it under almost any conditions, how to keep from drowning, how to fashion weapons from the crudest materials found on the forest floor, and how to use them. It was also, however, a conditioning program that attacked inhibition. The concept of eating raw frog or a huge accumulation of crushed insects, for example, was no longer at all disgusting, and the concept of modesty was thrown out entirely.

The program was intended to be taken in the field while surrounded by friends and co-workers who would quickly reintroduce reality and perspective. It then remained as a silent rider to the consciousness, ready if needed but otherwise not evident. It was a way of grafting the survival skills of the most primitive savage onto the most civilized of personalities so that if they got into trouble, they would have a chance to survive until they could be rescued. It was not intended to be used by someone who already needed it and was mostly in the uncivilized condition it assumed.

He awoke first and looked over at the sleeping women. He knew who he was and who they were; all his memories were intact, along with his sense of purpose. He was acutely aware of danger, and he wanted to act fast. His tattered loincloth caught on a bush as he got up warily, and he reached down, snapped the thin rope in two, and threw the garment away. It was an encumbrance. Clothing for protection against the elements would have been practical; he could not even conceive of why he'd clung to that thing so long. Better under these conditions to toughen the skin.

They had all been so tired that they'd slept much longer than they should have. The alarm had surely been raised by now. He took the small mindprint machine and the cartridges down to the river and threw them in. When both did not sink immediately, he jumped in, and with a little help they filled and went down.

Cloud Dancer was awake when he returned, and she looked at him approvingly. It was the nature of things now that he didn't even notice that she, too, had shed her modesty cloths. He switched to English to see if it all had worked. "How do you feel?"

"Different," she answered, her accent rather exotic but understandable. "Yet I cannot say how."

"Awake, Silent Woman," he ordered curtly. "We have all slept too long, and we must be well away from here before our enemies are upon us."

None of them could really comprehend the difference, but it was major. They no longer felt loyalty or longing for tribe and nation or even much kinship with it. Their tribe consisted only of the three of them. The first priority was the survival of the tribe, and then the individuals, no matter what the cost. The land was full of enemies: only the tribe could be trusted. As the only male of the tribe, Hawks was chief by default, and that was simply accepted by them all.

Silent Woman was almost ecstatic to discover she could understand their speech. It was a kind of wondrous magic that reestablished her in the world.

"Hereafter we will use only this speech," he told Cloud Dancer. "It was always a tongue used to unite tribes; let it serve to unite us. Silent Woman, I see that you understand us now."

She nodded, mouth still open in wonder.

"Let us get far away from here, as far as we can. We do not know if the transmission from the machine was picked up, but we must assume that our enemies will be upon us at any moment."

They went back down to the canoe, which, in their new mind-set, seemed a real luxury to them. They crossed the river before the light failed and continued south, slowly and very near shore, looking for a proper camp. Then, working as a team, they left the river, methodically covered or disguised all traces that anyone had ever landed there, and carried the canoe well inland.

Academically and from old experience, Hawks understood what was going on—what the program was designed to do and what it was doing to them—but he did not fight it. It was the first thing he'd done by chance that had turned out right, and he was going to use it. Neither woman, of course, could understand the process and know how to fight it, anyway. For all the People, the priorities were family, then tribe, then nation. By accident, the survival program had reoriented those three categories to go with different labels. Their loyalty was to him now, and he to them—they were their own tribe. The threatening wilderness and the treacherous yet mighty river were their friends and allies against all other tribes and nations.

He got one of the bottles from the archaeologist's pack and opened it. Primitive hunter-gatherers they might now be, but they could neither hunt nor gather in this darkness and strange wood. Food would wait until dawn.

"There is energy in this fire drink, which is called bourbon," he told them. "We must use it for now, although too much will cause dullness and throbbing heads the next day. Drink in celebration, for now we are one."

They drank, all coughing as it made its way down. "It is like a fire inside that warms," Cloud Dancer noted. "Now I see why it is called fire drink." But they finished it off.

When the bottle was empty, he broke it on a stone and washed the sharp point in the river. "Until now I had a wife who stands here. Now I have two wives, and they are proven warriors as well, as brave as any man and as skilled." Silent Woman gave a short gasp, and he realized that until now she'd still considered herself a slave—*his* slave. "Tonight we will mix our blood and bind ourselves forever to one another."

Three cuts on three wrists were joined one after the other, then all together. And then, full of togetherness and in the knowledge that they were as safe as they could expect and could do nothing more until morning, and being loosened with bourbon, the two ministered to him and he to them on the forest floor, and they slept entwined together.

* * *

"You assholes just stood there and let him steal a damned *mindprint* machine?" Raven was aghast.

"And twenty bottles of good bourbon," the archaeologist chief added mournfully. "It was only a portable unit. Not programmable. I can't imagine what good it'll do him."

"It'll make those bitches linguists," Raven replied. "Make it a lot easier moving south. You tell me quick what the nonlanguage cartridges were. I want to see just who and what we're dealing with now."

The survival cartridge's importance did not escape the Crow. "They've shown themselves to be right resourceful up to now," he told Warlock. "Now they can avoid all human company and still fill their bellies. Probably do better with the canoe, too."

"I have studied the charts," she responded. "If they get south of the Arkansas, they are going to be in a region that is heavily populated and thickly traveled. He picked this place because it is of Council; his actions here will not affect his relations with the tribes. Down there he cannot escape detection or at least notice. The tattooed woman stands out in any situation. I cannot understand why he keeps her along. He must know that."

"Oh, he'll keep her," the Crow assured Warlock. "He's incurred an obligation, and that's an honorable man there. Still, the more people, the harder to use sensors to find a camp. We can't hardly roust every camp we find. Some of the tribes down there get a mite touchy and wouldn't be at all impressed with Council. My feeling is that we ought to pack it in, call in a skimmer, and wait for 'em at Mud Runner's place."

"Only as a last resort. If we were to spook him there, in those swamps, we might get him killed or lose him forever. We don't know where he thinks he's going, but he does, and he is one single-minded man. Whatever he knows, he believes it is worth any price."

"Well, I got to admit I don't like the odds down there,"

he said. "He's a stranger there, true, but so are we, and, pardon, we're just as conspicuous as he is. Those swamps have defeated just about everybody who ever tried to beat 'em rather than live with 'em. You got any ideas?"

"Just one. We have the advantage that we know he must stick close to the river and probably on it. Time is pressing him. The river is the only fast way to go. We know what they look like and where they are going. We must stop chasing them and get ahead of them. Let me see the current charts."

They looked over the river course and the latest information. Charts of the Mississippi were always out of date, but this one was close. Warlock pointed a long finger at a spot well to the south. "There," she told him. "It is narrow, and see how it loops around. We could get two cracks at them there."

He nodded. "Okay. As long as they don't portage through the neck here."

"That is a chance I am willing to take. They have no charts; the river is full and could flood down there at any time. They can't portage across every oxbow or they would eat far more time than sticking to the water. I think they will come by there in a canoe in about three days. If we call in a skimmer, we can be there in a few hours and have that much time to prepare."

He nodded. "All right, I'll go with that. Better than the swamps, anyway. If we miss 'em, though, then it's Mud Runner or nothing."

She smiled enigmatically. "Then we will see if he lives up to his legendary reputation as a ladies' man."

Ordinarily the programs and data fed by a portable mindprinter faded as time went on; only a Master System unit could lock in permanent changes. However, it was also true that the more a skills program was used, the more entrenched it became: If you lived it and used it, it often integrated into the mind and achieved a level of permanency. Hawks insisted that the two women literally *think* in English and only in English.

Though a stronger imprint, the survival program was supposed to be emergency medicine, something carried in the hope that it would never be used. Under those conditions, it required regular retreatment with the machine. Once in use, however, the effects would last as long as necessary. Used too long, it could take on a life of its own, stripping away the last vestiges of a complex and refined culture like the Hyiakutt's and leaving only the savage primitive. It was designed to do this to one born and raised in the high-tech, pampered world of Council; the women came from cultures that were no less complex or primitive than Council in their own ways, but they were cultures much closer to the land. There was less civilization to strip away. The authors of the survival program simply assumed that any such problems could be fixed once the person was located and rescued. An easy job for Master System—but they could never meet up with a Master System connect.

Hawks let it happen. Food, at least, was no problem now. What they had been best at before they were expert at now. His bowmanship was so perfect, it amazed him; Cloud Dancer could spear something almost instinctively, and Silent Woman could bring down birds in flight with stone or knife. The programming was geared to using what you had, and from the standpoint of survival they had quite a bit.

Minor ills, bruises, aches, and pains simply did not bother them anymore. Fearing a major break or injury, Hawks urged quiet caution.

He also began to entertain doubts about Mud Runner. What if the Resident Agent didn't remember this wild man as his old friend? What if he turned them in? What if, most probable, he just couldn't help? He had to be made to help, even if it meant telling him about the rings and their secret and thus passing on the obligation. Hawks didn't really want to do that anymore; now his thoughts ran in a different direction.

The fact was, he admitted to himself, that right now he was as happy as he had ever been. He felt both free and loved. He began to think about ways to fake his own death, to throw off pursuit. Perhaps truly to found a new tribe and live this life, which was satisfying. He was approaching middle age, not a good time to go wild, but he was in excellent health. There were programs that could erase a lifetime and alter forever a personality. Mud Runner might well have these. For the first time he began to doubt his mission.

Why had he run? Because insatiable curiosity had forced him to read those papers and learn their deadly contents. He had fooled himself into thinking that it was some sort of noble mission to save humanity, but it was really just a bid to save his own neck. Until now his alternatives had been either to remain with the Hyiakutt or return to Council, but now there was another alternative.

If the bottom-line idea was to save his life and the lives of Cloud Dancer and Silent Woman, then which promised more? Passing on the information and depending on some Lord of the Middle Dark to save and protect them from Master System? Or, perhaps, logic. A readout into a full mindprint machine would show that he had passed his knowledge to no one. A second record showing that all his knowledge had been erased, along with his past, and replaced with that of a primitive hunter-gatherer might not absolutely take the heat off, but Master System would be unlikely to send a Val or expend much effort on him. Death was the sentence only because Master System did not trust its own demon lords. But if no demon lord were involved...

Humanity could save itself. Someone had discovered the ancient knowledge; others would over time. What he had here was worth a thousand Master Systems.

9. THE WOUNDS OF HOPE

CHU LI HAD EXPERIENCED ONE BIG SCARE ON THE way to the spaceship. Just before boarding, they were all required to clear security by placing both hands on a plate and looking through a binocularlike eyepiece. He had been sure that the other three would leave without him once the machine, which was definitely linked to Master System, identified him not as Chu Li but as Song Ching.

But the machine had not. Incredibly, it positively matched eye- and fingerprints with Chu Li and showed a picture of the disguised Song Ching on the security monitor. The success at the checkpoint was as startling and disturbing as failure would have been. He knew that the system was hardly infallible, but nobody could fool Master System to this degree. It was unthinkable. The only explanation possible was that the gods themselves had intervened.

Captain Sabatini was correct that the ship was not intended to take off from the ground except in emergencies; it was impossible to imagine how it had ever landed there. The passenger cabin was boarded by going sideways through an open air lock, then into a room that contained twelve huge, plush chairs with oversized backs in three rows of four each. The ship was not completely vertical but at a forty-five-degree angle that was certainly as unmanageable. A network of planks was laid inside so that people could enter.

Chu Li was carried in by a very large guard who looked like a retired wrestler, then placed in one of the far chairs in the front row. He sank so deeply into the chair that he feared being smothered, and the network of belts and webbing that strapped him in made it impossible even to move.

Deng was carried in next, placed in the rear seat farthest from the door, and similarly fastened in. The two girls were placed in the front and rear seats nearest the air lock, but so restricting were the bonds that Chu Li could not turn to see which one was in his row.

Sabatini entered, managing the entire mess with acrobatic skill that made it look not only easy but normal. He went down—back—beyond the last row and vanished; they didn't know where and could not look to see.

The captain was in one of the two rooms that were in the rear of the compartment, seated in a chair that could be maneuvered electrically by controls at his fingers and was surrounded by screens and instrumentation. His own webbing would hold his body tight but allowed his arms total freedom. There were straps through which he could slip his hands for total security when necessary. He put on a small, light headset that had a tiny microphone on a rigid loop in front of his mouth.

"Captain to pilot. Prepare to clear and close all outer doors. Internal systems on," he instructed calmly.

Up front there was the distant sound of warning sirens. As the planks were hastily withdrawn, the air locks—first the outer, then the inner—were closed and sealed automatically, and the passengers were left with only the light of the red signal above those doors and the very dim emergency lighting system to see by. Not, of course, that there was anything to see.

Then, with a whine, the lights came on full inside, restoring some sense of normalcy. There was a sound of air blowing in from all sides, and they felt their ears pop several times.

"Switch to passenger intercom, then prepare for launch," the captain ordered. Then he changed his tone, and his voice blared from the overhead speakers.

"Good evening. I know you're uncomfortable, but this will last only a short while. We are now eleven minutes from launch, and it will take us about forty minutes to reach orbit and activate the gravity. We'll then have a little time to get comfortable for the long haul. There will be a second sustained engine firing from orbit, but that won't feel like very much in here, and all it will really require is that you sit down and keep a seat belt on. This is the rough part. You'll feel at first like some big hand is pushing you completely through the seat until you can't bear it anymore, and it'll sound and feel like the whole ship's shaking to pieces, but don't worry. That's normal. After a little bit, you'll suddenly find that pressing weight gone, and you'll feel like you don't weigh anything at all, which will be more or less true. There's a monitor hanging from the ceiling up front and center which will show a view from the stern. Enjoy it. This is the only planetary lift-off you're ever likely to experience."

He switched back to his business channel. The computer took readings on the prisoners and showed the results on a screen to his right, but he didn't pay attention. If their blood pressure didn't go through the roof, they'd be all right.

"Chu Li!" called the girl three seats to his right.

"Here. Is that you, Chow Dai?"

"Yes. Chu Li—I am frightened. I do not like this kind of flying ship."

He tried to reassure her. The fact was, he wasn't the least bit frightened of the ship or the takeoff. It was what would come after, on the days out there, that caused real fear.

"It is just a ship, in many ways like the ones that sail the rivers."

"I am far more worried by his saying that it was the only such experience we'll ever have," Deng Ho shouted from the back. "This will be just a lot of shaking and noise."

"It is the waiting!" Chow Mai added from her rear seat. "I wish they would just do whatever it is they will do!"

Suddenly the ship trembled, and they found themselves being raised so that their backs were down and their feet were forward. It was most uncomfortable. Then the lights and power switched briefly off, then on again, and there was a tremendous whine from somewhere deep inside the ship that grew in pitch and intensity. The whole world seemed suddenly to begin shuddering and shaking; there was vibration but no real sensation of moving. Chu Li's eyes went to the monitor, and with a start he saw the entire spaceport complex framed there, growing smaller by the second, until it was lost in a view of steppe and desert. Only then did the great invisible hand Sabatini had warned about really begin to come down on them.

The weight was crushing and terrible, and the two girls screamed. It lasted only a few minutes, but it seemed like hours. All four felt as if all the air was being squeezed out of them.

The pressure ceased so abruptly that the transition made them dizzy with relief. They experienced no real discomfort except some popping ears, but when Chu Li again had the wits to look at the monitor, he saw nothing familiar there, only a vast expanse of blue and white. Within a few minutes there were browns and grays down there as well; it was almost as if they were looking at some model, some relief map of a strange place. Chu Li had expected something more dramatic, such as the world as a ball growing ever smaller, but this was just indistinct nothingness.

The ship shuddered a few times as it made small mid-course corrections, but these were brief and caused no real sensations at all, just a steady vibration throughout the ship and a low whine coming from somewhere in the rear.

At least they were sitting upright again, Chu Li thought with some relief. Still, it had been somewhat of an anti-climax to him; he had expected lift-off to be longer and far more extreme.

Now there was a gentler sense of acceleration that slowly built but did not grow very far. A buzzer sounded in the rear, then Captain Sabatini was walking comfortably forward, still wearing the headset. He checked each of them in turn, finally reaching Chu Li.

"All right, we have only a short time to do this, so listen closely and do just what I tell you," he said loudly. "I'm going to release the restraints on you one at a time and put on more comfortable ones. I don't want anyone trying anything. With this headset I can control a good deal of what it's like in here, and I do it in a language none of you know, so don't think you can grab it and start shouting orders. It will go very hard with anyone who gives me any trouble at all."

He pressed something between Chu Li's legs, and the intolerable belts and webbing loosened, then were reeled into the seat. For a brief moment, Chu Li was free and unrestrained, but he knew this was not the time to try anything. They didn't know enough yet, and there were many aspects of this ship that didn't fit the model and schematics in his brain.

"Stand up," the captain ordered, and Chu Li did, feeling oddly light and slightly off balance. Sabatini gave a command in some very strange sounding tongue, and a small compartment in the wall opened. Removing what looked like a belt fastened to a thin but tough chain, he attached it around Chu Li's waist under his tunic. He repeated the procedure with each of the others in turn, then passed out some prewet towels to the two girls, both of whom had thrown up on takeoff.

Chu Li examined the restraint. The chain held him and would not slip either up or down more than a few centimeters, yet it was not tight or particularly uncomfortable. At the back was a small box that was both a lock and a piece of electronics which adjusted for comfort but also tightened in response to any attempt to move the chain too far. There was even enough give to pull out some chain and actually rotate the body loop, bringing the box around to the front, but it still could not be removed.

"All right, now, here's the situation," Sabatini said. "The restraint you each wear contains a length of chain sufficient for you to reach all the parts of the cabin you need to get to. It is smart and will automatically adjust in or out depending on where you want to go. The one thing you have to remember is that the chains will not allow themselves to be crossed. That avoids tangles but will take some getting used to. Any problems and I can have those chains drag you all the way to the wall and hold you there. You can't imagine how fast you can find yourself slammed against the wall. Right now, just bring out a little chain and bring the box forward, then sit down. We can't get comfortable yet.

"Now, I want to run through a few basics. You have gravity here, but it is only seventy percent of what you've been used to, so you're going to find maneuvering difficult at first. Just remember that if you weighed fifty kilos on Earth, you weigh only thirty-five here. You also fall at seventy percent the usual speed if you happen to trip. Questions?"

There were many, but none were asked.

"All right, then. If we all do our part to be nice, then those chains will be all that is needed. You'll get so used

to them that in a day or two you won't even think about
them. You'll sleep with them, eat with them, go to the
bathroom with them. However, rest assured I have other
restraints if you cause me troubles, many of which are
neither smart nor comfortable. Later I'll have clean clothes
for you, and I'll show you how to get rid of your body
wastes and where and how showers are done here. For
now, I want you to use the regular lap and shoulder belts
on your seats and remain there. We have another boost
coming up, although nothing like the last one, and then
it'll be smooth as silk for the rest of the journey."

The second burst, when it came, was accompanied by
the same noise and vibration as the takeoff, but the giant's
hand was a pale shadow of its old self, nor did it seem so
long.

Still, Chu Li worried. What sort of new clothing? Would
his secret have to come out right away, before he'd had
time to prepare the others? And, of equal concern, what
sort of man would they send who could nursemaid four
condemned prisoners for forty-one days in close quarters?
So far he had been almost too nice and polite. They were,
after all, not paying passengers, and this was no luxury
cruise.

The passenger cabin, as Sabatini called it, was a marvel
in itself. With a few commands in that strange tongue and
the manipulation of some hidden controls, the chairs vanished deep into the floor and were replaced by large reclining leather seats that could go all the way down to become
quite comfortable beds. These chairs swiveled a full
hundred and eighty degrees and were placed at equal dis-
tances around a polished laminated table. The rear of the
cabin was empty, providing perhaps six by nine meters
that could be used for walking or other exercise, and there
were three doors in the back wall. From watching Sabatini's comings and goings, the passengers guessed that the
center door led to the next area back in the ship, the right-

hand door led to Sabatini's own private cabin, and the left-hand one opened on a room that seemed to be filled with complex electronic gear. A thick red line was painted on the floor about a meter in front of the doors, and past that the chain would not go.

Forward of the table and chairs there were also three doors. The center one, they were told, led forward to the next area and was doubly dangerous, since it opened onto an inner air lock and seal, and no areas forward now contained air. A red circle on the floor in front of the door again proved to be the chain's limit. The door on the left, however, was the toilet, and that they could enter.

The other door led to a shower, or at least what Sabatini called a shower. There was a small outer area for putting down clothing, then what looked like a huge plastic tube with one side cut away. When one stood in the center of the tube, the open side closed, and one was almost engulfed by a tremendous stream of liquid. The shower had three cycles, which left the bather dry and very clean.

For the first two days out the boredom was broken only by occasional explanations from Sabatini. The new clothing—white, loose-fitting cotton pajamas—allowed Chu Li to maintain his fiction a while longer, although Deng Ho was beginning to look at him curiously. Chu Li knew that the time was coming when he could not avoid revealing his secret, but he could not bring himself to do it—not yet.

Sabatini was generally not in the passenger cabin, occupying himself elsewhere. This gave them some initial breathing room and allowed for some expert examinations. Chu Li could find no routine visual monitoring devices in the cabin, though it appeared that Sabatini could watch them from either of his rooms through some special plates. The speakers were certainly two-way, but there were only two of them, and they were easily avoided. It was possible to have private conversations by having one pair talk loudly near the speakers while the other pair spoke in whispers.

"You have seen the place now. What do you think?" Chow Dai asked Chu Li in such a circumstance.

"This room is customized far beyond what this ship usually has," he told her. "It is possible that it is used to carry important people as well as prisoners. That might also explain the lack of monitors and recorders. Both of the rooms in back are also not standard. I particularly do not understand that room full of gear or that headset he wears. This ship is totally automatic, with a self-aware computer for a pilot. What could he be doing from that room? And what is forward? I do not know how far up we are in the ship, but if that middle door is an air lock, then it shows no indicators like the ones on the sides and no seals, either. There is air up there, at least for one more room. I know there is. Why? And where are the space suits? They should be in a compartment off this room, yet there seem to be no compartments except the small ones that manage these chain devices and the ones that deliver our food and drink on the little trays and dispose of the waste. Much of this does not make sense."

"The food is strange, too," she noted.

"It is foreign devil food, but it serves. This is not a Chinese ship. What about these chain things?"

"The box is easy to fool. Chow Mai and I have already found two ways to make it loosen up enough to slip the whole thing off. The doors have simple electrical locks. I know the combinations now from just observing the captain, but they are almost identical to the locks on the toilet and shower. We could break them if we had to."

"I thought you'd need some tools for that."

"We have them. He never missed the two we required when Chow Mai took them from his pack. The problem is his headset. It really can override—we have watched him—and the tongue is impossible."

He nodded. "I must know more about the ship. When

he sleeps, you must show me how to slip this bond and help me enter that mystery room with all the electronics. We must know everything before we move."

They were all supposed to sleep at the same time, but their chains were left free in case they needed to use the toilet. No matter how hard he tried, Chu Li could not manage the simple maneuver to fool the box, but Chow Dai slipped hers and then freed him. Chow Mai and Deng Ho remained in their beds, quietly on watch.

Chu Li would have liked to explore the rest of the ship, but whenever Sabatini had opened the rear door, a distant bell had sounded; until they could somehow mask that alarm, they couldn't risk it. In any case, the mystery room was their primary target.

Chow Dai did not want to chance using the combination. Instead, she skillfully bypassed the combination board and sprang the lock with two small and nearly silent pilfered electronic tools. When the door swung back, Chu Li kissed her and entered the room.

The place was an electronic wonderland situated around a single command chair. Much of the equipment was unfamiliar, though he recognized some machines and could guess at the functions of others. There was a small mindprint machine and a large number of cartridges, which were numbered in the Arabic system rather than labeled. The machine itself was far too simple for psychosurgery; more than likely it was there so that Sabatini could instantly learn other languages he needed or be updated on ship changes and modifications. Monitors showed schematics of the ship at this level and probably could display other levels in response to the correct commands. One thing was certain: The areas of pressurization and atmosphere, which were outlined in blue, extended far aft as well as forward of the cabin they were in. The artificial gravity, however, appeared limited to the passenger compartment and a much larger compartment immediately behind it—

almost certainly the live animal transport area of which the captain had spoken.

Unfortunately, too much of the information on the monitors and even the labels was useless, written again in that unknown script. Chu Li looked longingly at the mindprint machine and cartridges. Somewhere there was probably the language he needed, but which one? He certainly didn't have the time to learn them all.

Still, there was far more equipment here than any human companion on this ship would require, even more than would be needed for any conceivable human intervention. It was more like the kind of compartment required for someone to run the whole ship—but *that* was done by computer.

The only logical explanation struck him with the force of a blow. Song Ching's father had already *known* that there was a human override built into the ships. Suppose Sabatini really *was* the captain? Suppose the computer pilot was not independent but his subordinate, subject to him? He remembered the complex helmets in the illegal tech cult's fortress laboratories. They had built them from scratch and had assumed that they would have to hardwire the connection. Suppose that was what the omnipresent headset was really for? *Sabatini was running his own ship!*

He turned back toward the door only to see it suddenly shut with a speed and force he'd never before seen on a door. He tried to open it but could not. He was stuck in there!

"You just stay right there and don't touch a thing!" Sabatini's voice came over a small speaker in the console. "I will tend to you as soon as I have tended to your friends, and I will be far gentler to them if you just sit in the chair and relax until I come for you."

There was no malice in his tone, but Chu Li had no doubt that the captain would not hesitate to carry out his implied threat. There was nothing to do but sit and try to figure out as much additional information as he could from what he could see.

After an eternity, the door opened and the full cabin lights flooded the compartment. Sabatini, dressed in shorts and a T-shirt, stood there with a small weapon in his hand. He had his small headset on as well. "All right—time to get out now," he said casually. "And I was beginning to wonder if this would be a boring trip. All right—*out! Now!*"

When Chu Li emerged, he found both the girls kneeling on the floor, their chains reattached, their hands bound behind their backs, and their ankles secured. Chow Dai gave him an expression that was filled with both hurt and apology. Deng Ho was still in his chair, strapped to it by hand and leg cuffs and unable to move.

Chu Li looked at the weapon in Sabatini's hand. It was a very small thing of red plastic with a gauge on its handle, a small button for a trigger, and a metallic point where the barrel ended.

"I've already demonstrated the stinger to your girl friends," the captain warned. "If you'd like one, I'll be happy to give it. This little line here shows the amount of power it'll put out in a room this size. Right now it's set for a debilitating shock. Halfway and it'll knock you out for a couple of minutes. All the way up and it might stop your heart."

"I believe you," Chu Li responded hollowly.

"All right, then—over here. Chain on. That's it. Now—hands behind your back. Good." Chu Li felt pressure and found his hands held by very firm handcuffs that allowed no real give or play at all. "Now—on your knees." He did so, and two stiff leg cuffs were also locked into place. He faced the two girls on the opposite side of the open space.

Sabatini relaxed. "Now, I told you I could be mean if somebody tried to take advantage of me. I figured you might be pulling something, covering talks with other talks and whispering campaigns, and I knew from the records that the girls were experts at locks. When I sleep, I put the alarms on all these doors so they sound in my cabin. I just decided to see what you were up to."

Chu Li understood now how it worked. The captain switched on the alarm, and when it rang and awakened him, he had merely to grab his headset to find where the trouble was and who was causing it. He then simply commanded the door to shut, overriding the lock, then took the others with his weapon.

"All right—it was one slip," Sabatini said almost kindly. "If I was mean and nasty or even smart, I'd just leave you all like that for the next thirty-nine days but pull you all to the wall with the box behind your back like your hands and feed you like animals from trays. Or send you back to the animal cages, maybe. But that's only because this sort of stuff puts me in a real bad mood. Now, if somebody got me in a *better* mood, I might actually forgive and forget."

He walked back over to his open cabin door, reached in, and brought out a rather nasty-looking straight knife. Then he muttered something into his headphone, and abruptly both women were jerked back to the wall and slammed against it. Since the chain emerged from a point in the bulkhead above their waists, it had the effect of suspending them slightly, leaning forward because of their bound hands, barely touching the floor with their toes.

Sabatini went over to Chow Dai. "You've got an ugly face," he told her, "but I'm curious about the rest of you." Using the knife, he cut away her pullover and her pants and flung them to one side, leaving her hanging there by the chain, naked. She did, in fact, have quite a nice body, but something made the captain stop and command the chain to come out a bit. He caught her and turned her around to face the wall.

Chu Li gasped, and Sabatini was almost equally appalled. Chow Dai's back was a mass of welts and scar tissue almost from the shoulders to the buttocks. "Holy—somebody really did a job on you, didn't they, beautiful?" he commented. He lifted her up, then put her back on the floor in the kneeling position. "You stay there. Let's see if your sister got the same treatment."

She had. If anything, Chow Mai's scars were worse. The evident brutality was so gross and unexpected that even Sabatini hadn't been prepared for it. He put the sister back down in the kneeling position on the floor as well.

"Well," the captain muttered. "Nothing about *that* in the record. Damn it, you girls wouldn't be any fun at all." He paused a moment. "But then, hope springs eternal, doesn't it? There's *lots* of things not in the official record." He turned and stalked back across the room. "Isn't that right, *Mister* Chu?"

Now it was Chu Li's turn to be suspended against the wall and slowly have the clothing cut away as the others watched. Everyone except the captain seemed shocked, surprised, and amazed at what was revealed. Song Ching, after all, had been genetically designed for perfection. Nor were there any marks on *this* body, not so much as a scar or blemish.

"Now, *that's* more like it," Sabatini proclaimed lustfully as he put Chu Li back down in the kneeling position.

Chow Dai's mouth seemed permanently open in amazement, all embarrassment from her own exposure pushed aside. "Chu Li—you are a *girl*? But—how is that possible?"

"I'd like to know that one myself," Sabatini put in. "My manifest says you're a boy, you've got a voice to match that, and you passed a Master System identity check as a male."

So here it was. He knew he could not be mystical; the Chow sisters would accept it, but Deng Ho—who could only stare in wonder, not a little lust on his face as well in spite of his bindings—and the captain would never buy it. He had worked out a story, though, that explained the facts even if he didn't know if it was really possible. He'd been refining it for days.

"It is none of my doing," he lied. "They—changed me. A surgeon and a psychochemist. But they never completed the job. They changed me from a boy to a girl, but you can tell from my voice, my ways, that they never changed me inside."

"The outside does just fine by me," Sabatini noted.

"But why would they do such a thing?" Chow Dai asked him.

"They were remaking me to replace somebody. Somebody important who was sent down for work but who had power enough to fake it. Song Ching, the daughter of the chief administrator. They had no other use for me, and they decided I was about her size. I had no choice. But they were fooled near the completion of their goal. Orders came from somewhere that I was to be sent here. They could not change the orders, and they could not give someone else my prints and patterns, so they had to send me."

"Rat—is that really *you*?" Deng Ho asked in wonder.

"Deep inside, my cousin. I am sorry. They fixed me so I would not know myself what had been done until the day I left, when it wore off."

"Oh, I am so sorry, Chu Li!" Chow Dai cried. "Why did you not tell me when you knew?"

"Sooner or later I was going to tell you," he replied honestly. "I—I just cared for you, Chow Dai. I am a man in a woman's body. I feel as a man feels, as I felt before they did this to me. You have your scars, and you were pleased that I looked past them, but how could a normal woman look past *this*?"

Sabatini had let the touching scene go on. He was somewhat fascinated himself by all this, particularly when the name Song Ching had been mentioned. The reason they had all been forced through an extra and complete security check was that Song Ching, the daughter of the chief administrator of the China District, had been reported vanished from a maximum security area. He knew the powers those butchers had. They were perfectly capable of turning a worthless kid into a duplicate of this girl and maybe turning this girl into something else, somebody she'd disposed of and then replaced, or maybe even somebody outside China.

Her story held together. For a moment he thought she might be the real Song Ching, although why anybody'd pull strings to be sent to Melchior was beyond understanding, but the fact that she'd passed the security exit test as a boy named Chu Li made her story ironclad. Briefly he considered not turning her over at Melchior but bringing her back and passing her off as the real one, which would save a lot of asses and earn him some real powerful friends, but by this time they'd run security checks up the rear and the plot would be easily exposed— which would only send *him* back to Melchior—this time in chains and one-way.

The captain looked her over. "Well, kid, they did a really great job. No scars, no nothing. Perfect. I think you got to get used to being a girl no matter what your head says. They threw away all the old parts, anyway. I think maybe you ought to learn what it's like to be a girl these days *Uh uh!* Careful! You can't do anything but sit."

Chu Li had attempted to lunge forward in anger at the captain's words, but it had been fruitless.

"Now you sit and listen," he continued. "You're property and you got a great body and you are being sent to hell. They're going to *love* you on Melchior. A slightly incomplete job but an expert one, just up their fields of interest. They'll study you, pick your brain and chemistry apart, then they'll have what they want. Then they'll complete the job and make you somebody's present. Since you look like this Song Ching, they won't want you anywhere where her father would notice, but they'll find a bunch on Melchior in a region where chief administrators never even look and stick you there, all right, only you won't be interested in machines or escape anymore. It won't hurt anything to start now, and it might put me in a good enough mood to forget this little incident."

"I will never dishonor myself so!" Chu Li spat. "Perhaps they can make me as you say, but then I will not know my shame. I will fight you even if I fail!"

"Chu Li! You must not!" both sisters said at once. "Look at our bodies! And it was to no avail! The price is great enough without adding more!"

"You do not know what it is like," Chow Dai continued alone. "You cannot. But can't you see, under that smile of his he is one of *them*? No different from the ones who did this to us?"

"Listen to her," the captain urged. "She's right, you know. I can be quite—creative, within my charter."

"Never!" Chu Li exclaimed. "To me it would be a perversion as well as an assault! What does it matter to me if you do things to this body? It would be better for me if you *did* make it less beautiful!"

"You've got a point," the captain admitted. He thought for a moment, then said something in his language into the headset. They waited, not knowing what was going to happen, and he seemed both relaxed and patient. Finally the rear center door opened, and an emergency medical unit appeared.

"Now, I don't want all the bother of keeping you shackled or caged all the time, not if I can help it," he told them, again sounding casual and almost friendly. "There are many ways around it, but I'm still in a bad mood, having been awakened and all that. It seems to me the heart of this—incident—are our two locksmiths here. I can't see that doing a little more to them here is going to change anything on Melchior, either. Seems to me that if you don't have any thumbs or index fingers, you won't be stealing things and picking locks anymore, will you?"

"No!" Deng Ho cried out. "They have suffered enough, you monster! You cannot do this!"

"He won't do it," Chu Li responded. "He has to deliver his cargo undamaged."

"Oh, of course I will," the captain assured them. "They don't mind a few things like that. They understand. See, you of all people should know that those types can grow back things like missing fingers and the like if they feel the need. Look at what they grew out of you!"

Chu Li's spirits sank as he realized the truth of that, even if they hadn't really grown anything on him. The two girls' faces were masks of terror. "All right, you serpent. What do you want of me? To ravish my body? Is that the price?"

"At the start, yes. Now I want more. I want cooperation. Enthusiasm. It will be a long trip yet. I want a servant. Someone who will do exactly what I say without needing restraints. If I *don't* cut their fingers, I must leave their hands where they are. Makes it inconvenient for them to eat, so they must be fed. I want a mistress who will do my bidding without even thinking about it." He drew the little pistol. "Hesitate, argue, or fail to please me in any way for the next month and you'll feel this." He fired at the torso.

Chu Li had never felt such pain, and he cried out.

"Betray me, fail to do my will, or act *or even speak with them* about acting in any way against me and it will cost your girl friend's sister her thumbs. Twice and your girl friend loses hers. As for the fat boy on the chair, if he gets out of line in any way or is involved in anything at all I don't like, I'll bring this little thing out, and then I'll be the only whole male on this ship. Understand?"

The Chow sisters looked pleadingly at Chu Li. "All right," he said. "I will do whatever you say."

There was a nearly immediate jolt from the little gun that again produced agony. "From now on, your name, the only name you will answer to, even to your friends here, is Slave. And you will call me Master or Honorable Captain. My slave here will refer to herself as a she at all times, and so will you all—only the feminine will be used when referring to or speaking to her. I want her to get a basic truth through her head once and for all.

"Additionally, all of you will bow in my presence, and you, Slave, will kneel to me, head bowed, anticipating my desires. To prevent more thefts, all of you will go naked until we arrive at Melchior, and as extra insurance our two sisters will continue to have their hands bound behind their backs—unless the slave, here, fouls up and they lose sufficient fingers to be a threat no longer. What do you think of that, Slave?"

"Whatever you command, Honorable Master," Chu Li responded, teeth clenched but head bowed.

Sabatini went over to him. "I know what you're thinking, but I plan to change that. You see, you've lost everything. Everything but your honor and your dignity. I will strip those from you. You're the only one of this bunch who really has any. That's why you are the leader. Before the end of this voyage, you will break."

He sighed and dismissed the medical robot, then went back to his cabin for a moment. He emerged soon with a set of U-shaped devices, then unlocked all chains from Chu Li and commanded her to lie flat on the floor in a particularly embarrassing position. The four restraints descended to hold down her arms and legs. Then he began removing his own clothing and weapons.

He made the rest watch in anguished silence as he first performed the ultimate indignities upon their companion. He was deliberately brutal about it, but he clearly was enjoying himself.

Sabatini kept his slave apart from the others in a small, dark closet barely four meters square and only a meter and a half high. The only light came from a small grill right at the top of her box. She could not see out, and the vibrating compartments at the rear of the cage masked any noise or movement outside. She would be there for long, horrible periods, then suddenly taken out and checked over to see how she reacted. Sometimes he didn't like the slightest thing and shoved her back. She was allowed to see her friends only in his presence, and then she had to speak to them servilely and in a very loud voice. Infractions were met with deprivation of food, water, and bathroom stops.

Clearly he wasn't neglecting the other three. Deng Ho seemed lost most of the time in a world of his own, while the two girls were vacant, listless, and resigned.

He no longer restrained her when mounting sexual attacks, but he was even rougher and more brutal and demanding. Early on, he'd left his shock pistol on a table near his bed in the cabin where he had her, and she had gotten it and fired it at him, over and over. He had just laughed. He had removed the little charger and deliberately left it there. He then actually handed her his knife and invited attack, but she lost the knife and her footing before she made the fist real move. Then he had worked her over with just his hands, leaving painful bruises that did not show on her skin, and raped her, before tossing her back in her hole to be wakened every hour or so for an extremely long period but denied food, water, and bathroom.

His treatment so brutalized her that when he finally let her out, she was so sincerely servile, so letter perfect, he let her sleep. Her behavior after that remained so perfect that he began easing up, slowly but progressively. He cleaned the closet and disinfected it. He let her shower. He gave her good food. A few more very minor slips brought renewed punishment, but they were the last gasps of resistance. She found it increasingly difficult to think of anything but the ship, her duties, her behavior, pleasing him. After a bit longer, the only thing that mattered to her was pleasing him. He continued to leave weapons and other things of interest to the old Chu Li around, and if she saw them at all, she did not even think of picking them up or using them.

She began to hope that she would be so useful, so obedient, so perfect that he would not think of turning her over at Melchior but would retain her on the ship. He obliquely encouraged this idea, then released her forever from her closet and allowed her to rejoin the others. She was not, however, to have any private conversations with any of them.

The other three had been faring only a little better, with routine deprivation and punishments by Sabatini's pistol. It was what he had done with, and to, the one they'd known as Chu Li that was the telling blow. If the strong, educated one could be broken so completely without even any technological aids, then there was no hope.

When they were twenty-three days out, although they'd lost all track of time, Deng Ho committed suicide.

It had not been easy, but it had certainly been well planned. He did it in the bathroom by wrapping his waist chain excess around his neck and then somehow getting it caught up in the toilet-flushing mechanism. It must have been an agonizingly slow strangulation, yet he had resisted all impulses to stop it and had not cried out, even at the last.

The act shocked all three of the remaining prisoners, and it really irritated Sabatini. He had spent so much time on Chu Li that he'd really neglected to keep close watch on the others, and particularly on the quiet chubby boy who had never really given him any trouble. He actually felt a little sorry for the kid, but he was more upset that perhaps this was only the first. He doubted that Chu Li would try it; she was too anxious to keep in good with him in the pathetic hope that he'd keep her aboard—if he could, he would, but they'd never allow it. Instead, he now had a black mark, and he needed a good line to get out of it.

He decided that a burial would be a nice gesture. He had no desire to build up any more resentment. And so, after speaking some words, he'd taken the body to the port center air lock, where the other three could watch, and placed it respectfully inside. He was even indulgent to their reactions. "You may say farewell and whatever prayers you wish for him," he told them.

"If you please, Honorable Captain," Chow Mai said, somewhat more animated than she'd been in a long time. "Where will he go now?"

"Normally, you would enter the air lock in a pressure suit and then pump all the air out before going into space. I'm keeping the air inside, and I'll pump the pressure way up. Then, when the outer door opens, he will be launched into space by the escaping air. He will drift in space forever."

Chow Mai, who had always liked the boy, had a few tears for him. "That is good," she responded, almost to herself. "He will become one with the stars, a constellation in the heavens."

The two girls both said prayers and farewells, but Chu Li stood back, silent. She had found the body of the boy and had seen the grotesque face and distorted, popped eyes. It was a haunting grotesquerie worse than anything yet experienced in this horror odyssey.

The two sisters stepped back, and Sabatini made certain that the body was arranged in the air lock.

Something snapped in Chu Li's brain. *The compassion of the innocent Chu Li who had been killed; the haughty pride of Song Ching, reduced and violated; the relative innocence of the two sisters, punished all out of proportion to their crimes; the cruel, calculating Sabatini who personified the system's least common denominator; the quiet innocence and inner despair of Deng Ho, who chose to die a slow, agonizing death rather than see or accept any more . . .*

"No," she whispered under her breath. Sabatini didn't

hear it, but the two sisters did, and they looked at each other, then at her, not quite knowing what was about to happen but ready to assist. Chu Li moved up behind the captain silently. He was a good fifteen centimeters taller than she and far stronger, but she knew that this was the moment. Risk it now, and perhaps lose, or be a slave forever and deservedly so.

With one motion she jumped, grabbing the headphones from the captain's head and striking his face with the little microphone. As he was still turning in shock and surprise, she gave him a push forward with all her adrenaline-pumped might. He staggered, but a hand caught the side of the air lock door.

The two sisters, hands still tied behind their backs, ran at him and butted him in the midsection with their heads. He grunted and fell backward into the air lock, almost on top of Deng Ho's body. He recovered quickly. *"Why you little bitches! I'll—"* he bellowed, but Chu Li had already begun to swing the door shut on him. When he saw what was happening, he rushed against the door, and all three girls lent their bodies to pushing it closed. It was fury versus desperation, and desperation won. The door shut with a hiss, and Chu Li, while still pressing against it, managed to turn the wheel that locked it.

"I don't care what you do—put your feet in it if you have to—but don't let him turn it back from that side!" she shouted to the sisters, then ran to the panel. Sabatini was lazy; she knew he would have preprogrammed the sequence, but she had to find the right control and throw it. The sisters were having a hard time holding the wheel by backing against it and gripping it with their hands as best they could, but the safety lights kept flashing yellow, green, yellow, green.

There were only five buttons, and she pressed each of them in turn, but nothing happened. She knew the sisters were weakening and that he would soon get that door open. She kept pushing the buttons in desperation, one after the other, hoping to catch the right button at the right point. It *had* to work. It just *had* to.

The red light suddenly came on, and a bell sounded. Sabatini stopped for a moment, and through the small glass window they could see his expression of desperation. He pounded, swore, then renewed his attack on the lock, but now Chu Li was on the wheel. The whole procedure took perhaps forty seconds, yet it seemed like years.

Since it was a pressurized burial, the outer door opened pretty quickly.

Deng Ho's body moved right out, but Sabatini grabbed hold of the wheel. His body was horizontal, his hands gripped the wheel, his face was pressed in fear against the viewing port, but the air was exhausted in an instant, and the artificial gravity plunged him back down.

Chow Dai, exhausted, slumped to the floor, followed quickly by her sister. "Do you think—you can close—that outside door?" she managed to ask.

"Not yet. Not for many minutes," Chu Li responded. "I do not know if someone can live in space with no air, but I do know that no one can hold his breath for more than five minutes. We will give it ten." She sank down, also exhausted. Her arms and shoulder muscles ached, and she felt as if she'd sprained both wrists. Still, it had been worth it. That one moment of stark terror on Sabatini's face was payment for much inflicted misery, brutality, and indignity. Deng Ho's gesture had not been in vain.

Chow Dai crawled over and gave Chu Li a kiss. "Welcome back," she said.

"Not for long, but I do not regret it. We have killed him, and the ship will know it. The gas should come at any moment."

Chow Dai looked disappointed. "I had forgotten about that. I suppose that was why he was so confident. Foreign devils have no idea of what honor is. Still, it would have been nice to have won completely."

Chow Mai listened, thinking. "It would seem to me that if this gas was coming, it would have come by now. Either it is not going to come or he is not dead."

Chu Li felt a new shot of energy and stood up. "You are right." She looked through the air lock window and saw the interior, still lighted. She could not see the area right by the door, but there was no sign of anyone or anything in the air lock, and the outer door was definitely open, the alarm bell still ringing. There was certainly no air in there, and she knew that space had to be very cold, yet there was something nagging at her brain, troubling her.

Gravity. They had weight here, even if they felt lighter than back home. The whole section had gravity, including the air lock. Sabatini clearly had not been sucked out with the air, although it had been close. Why was there now no body slumped down, hands frozen to the wheel in a death grip?

The ship had been elaborately and illegally modified, and there were all sorts of compartments and gadgets built into the walls. Might there not also be some sort of emergency compartment in the air lock? She couldn't see how a body could stand a vacuum, even for a few moments, but what if it could? There was better than two meters of air lock. Something had to be inside those thick walls.

"We must find something to jam this door. Before we close the outer door, which will automatically flood the compartment with air, we must jam the wheel so it cannot be opened from the outside. He might be alive in some rescue compartment there. We must examine as much of the ship as we can to make sure such a one cannot otherwise reenter the ship."

If he *was* in there someplace, he'd be in a small, probably dark compartment much like a closet, with some sort of breathing device but little in the way of food and water for more than a day and certainly no bathroom. The only way to make certain, though, was to risk keeping the outer door open, jam the inner, and somehow make contact with the ship's pilot.

She reached down and picked up his headset. She had not brought honor, glory, or dignity to herself by serving him, but she had always been observant. Now she thought she could imitate his odd, animal-like growls that commanded some of the locks. The headset had been bent out of shape, but it did not appear damaged. She put it on, although it was too large for her head, and spoke one of the commands in his language that she knew overrode the electronics room lock.

The door opened, and to her surprise she heard a growling, unintelligible response in the earphones. For a moment it startled her, and she wondered if there were others aboard in areas they had never seen, but then she realized that it was the computer pilot.

She had spotted something in the electronics room long ago that was the first priority, and that was a complete electronics and mechanical tool set. It was almost too heavy for her, but she got it out and open, and the Chow sisters were able to tell her which tool to use. Shortly the girls' hands were free, although the cuffs themselves remained as oversized bracelets. One of the waist chains they wrapped through the spokes of the air lock wheel, then secured it with a small hand-held welder to the base of the nearest chair.

They were all tired and aching but far too excited to sleep. Chu Li checked the schematic of the ship's passenger level on the monitor. "If I read this correctly, then the whole level is pressurized—has air, that is, that is fit for us—except this area all the way in the rear. Those double lines front and back *are* air locks, but if this color is air, then they are not active. Shall we go see?"

She opened the center door with a command in that strange language, and a bell sounded distantly—but nothing else happened. She was almost relieved to hear the response coming from the earpiece; it confirmed her belief that it was the computer responding and not anyone else.

They went along a narrow corridor, then Chu Li stopped. "This was my home for those long times," she told them gravely, pointing to a lower storage closet. "After just one week in there, you would sell body, soul, and honor to anyone who would keep you from going back."

As Sabatini had warned them, animal cages filled the huge storage area, all designed for just about anything that could be imagined and some that were beyond imagining. The cages were empty this trip and apparently newly cleaned and reinforced. Beyond them were a large number of sealed containers, all labeled in a language or code none of them could understand, fitted together into vast clumps for useful storage. The path between was so narrow, they had to go single file.

The compartment narrowed until they emerged at an air lock. As she had expected, the light was green. When they opened it, the noise of great motors was almost deafening, but Chu Li finally got the courage to enter and walked the short distance to the far door. Peering through the window, she gasped, then continued to stare, fascinated. "Come! Look!" she called. Nervously, the two sisters joined her.

Before them was a second enormous cargo room. Larger than the first and filled with containers, it was spinning around at a dizzying pace.

"Why does the room spin?" Chow Mai asked Chu Li.

She thought for a moment. "I'm not sure. I seem to remember from very long ago—*her* memories—something about this. Ah! I *think* I know, but there is only one way to know for sure. Do you notice how light you feel?"

Only then did they notice how little gravity they felt here.

"I do not think the room spins at all," she told them. "I believe that it is *we* who are spinning. You must trust me on this, for it is far too complex to explain, but spinning is how many spaceships make gravity in space."

"We are *not* spinning!" the sisters responded in unison. "That room is!"

"There is only one way to find out, and if I am wrong it is a dangerous one. It is to go in there. See that net stretched there? I think you jump and grab on to that and then use the handholds to go on."

"No. It is too dangerous," Chow Dai responded. "What does it matter who is spinning? There is nothing in there that we can use."

Chu Li was disappointed but had to agree. Without her, these two were lost in the technology of this vessel, which to them was incomprehensible and magical. Now was not the time to see what weightlessness was like.

Reluctantly, she turned and led them out through the container corridor, past the cages and the closet, and back into the passenger cabin. She was somehow relieved to find it just as they had left it.

She looked again in the electronics room and at the mindprint machine and its numbered cartridges. "That machine makes you learn things you do not know or be things you are not," she told them. "It is how the captain learned our language so well. I fear that we will have to try them and see if one has the key to speaking to the ship."

"But would that not be in his true language?" Chow Dai asked. "Would he have something to teach his own native tongue in there?"

"I doubt if the pilot computer speaks the captain's language. All such computers are produced by Master System in factories peopled only by machines. They speak their own language, a language of numbers, on a level humans cannot possibly comprehend. The way humans talk to them is by a shell, a pretend environment where what the computer speaks is translated into a human tongue and where human language is translated into machine.

These ships are built according to standards that existed long ago, in the times of our ancient ancestors, and those outside of Earth continue to use those ancient languages."

"But it could have been changed to any, could it not?" Chow Dai persisted.

"It could, but I do not think it was. I have heard the captain curse many times, and it is a truth that one tends to curse in one's native tongue. His curses were equally unintelligible, but they were in a softer, more melodic tongue than the one used for opening the doors. It is a harsh, nonmelodic, almost machinelike language, an ugly tongue. It is there. It *must* be there. Otherwise we will arrive at Melchior anyway, just without the captain. I worry about what might be on some of the others. There are close to forty cartridges here, and only nine spaceports on all of Earth, so a captain would have need of only the nine languages of the Administrative Centers for each spaceport. I know nothing about the other worlds, but even if we give them nine or ten, it still leaves half the cartridges unexplained."

"But if we must, we will try them all and see," Chow Mai said pragmatically.

"I fear we must, yet I do not like it. Anything may be programmed by a master mindprint machine on those cartridges. Things that change your mind, your memory, everything. Some of these might be traps for the unwary, just in case ones like us got to this point. Even if not, these are to be taken sparingly, and never more than one a day, to avoid confusing and muddying the mind. We do not have thirty-eight days."

"There are three of us," Chow Mai pointed out. "Each of us could try one and see. Perhaps fortune will smile. If not, we try again, then wait to see if anyone has troubles. We have nothing to lose. Just hours ago we had lost all hope and you were in his power."

"You are right," Chu Li responded. "Let us begin now, for when we sleep this time, it will be long and deep.

Perhaps we can at least find some pattern to their arrangement. I can read the numbers, although they are in a foreign system. That type of number is used in all computer work. One of us will take the number one, which is an odd number and at the start. Another will take thirty-eight, an even number at the end. The third will take nineteen, an odd number in the middle. Then ten, twenty, and thirty. Then we will see if we can find a pattern. Beware, though. It does more than teach; it changes the mind. I am a living example of that."

"I will go first," Chow Mai said, "because you will have to show us how it is operated."

"It is quite simple. Just sit in the chair there and relax. *No!* Do not put the headset on as yet! Not until there is a cartridge in the system. To do so would cause brain damage. Now—watch. Number one in just so, and only this way. Wait for the small green light there. So! *Now* you may put on the headset, and I will adjust it."

Chow Mai seemed almost disappointed. "I feel nothing "

"You will. Now, put your head back on the rest and close your eyes. When I push this activator, it will begin. Push it again and it will stop, so if we see something terrible happening it can be halted by being quick. Otherwise it will run as long as it runs, and you will be awake yet as if asleep. Ready? Chow Dai—you should push the activator."

Chow Dai hesitated a moment, then pushed it. The green light changed to amber, then to flashing red.

Suddenly Chow Mai said, "It asks a question in my head. A single word I do not know."

Chu Li thought a moment. She hadn't even considered password protections for a setup like this. "Answer with the same word as it asks, only give it as a statement," she instructed Chow Mai. "No need to say it. Just *think* it."

Chow Mai looked confused but sat back, closed her

eyes, and did as instructed. The program started running, and Chu Li breathed a sigh of relief. With a computer she was sure she could break any password, but she needed the password to get to the computer. This computer's password, however, was the default: "password."

The machine ran for a nervous half hour with Chow Mai showing no visible reaction, then switched off. Chu Li lifted off the headset. "Remember never to remove the cartridge until this is first removed," she said.

Chow Mai opened her eyes dreamily and saw the worried expressions of the others. "Do not worry, my sisters, for I am well," she assured them, and wasn't quite certain why they seemed even more upset.

"Chow Mai—do you understand me, your twin?"

She *did* understand, although it took some concentration to reply. Her first efforts were a hopeless mixture of two languages that could not be mixed, and it took a while before she was able even with difficulty to switch comfortably.

"It is Arabic," Chu Li explained. "One of the Center spaceport languages. I have heard it spoken, although I do not know it. It is not the language of the ship, this I know. It will be difficult for her to sort one from the other for a while, but she will be able to separate them as time passes. This is good. One is a language program. If thirty-eight is not, we will try number two, perhaps. Chow Mai—go. Lie. Down. Yes."

Still feeling a bit dizzy and confused, Chow Mai went out and collapsed into one of the chairs. Chu Li removed cartridge one and replaced it with number thirty-eight, then got into the chair and put on the headset. She nodded at Chow Dai, then relaxed. The sister pressed the activator.

Number thirty-eight proved to be a highly technical program about the ship itself and paid particular attention to the restraint system, locks, and other protective and safety devices. It was not designed as language-specific but searched in the mind of the user for the right words and terms; if such terms were not present or possible to construct, one simply didn't understand all of the program. Song Ching's technological center Mandarin, however, was more than adequate for the task.

She awakened feeling elated and recovered quickly, thanks to her long experience with such devices. She removed the headset and saw Chow Dai just coming back into the room. The girl was apologetic. "I am sorry. When I saw you were in no distress, I went to see how Chow Mai was getting on. I did not think it would be so short."

"Long enough," Chu Li responded. "That was a technical tape, the last probably made to date. It makes many references I cannot totally get because they are obviously referring to past modifications, but I know now how much of this operates. I know the restraint systems, the alarms, the door and hatch combinations, and much more. I even know what many of these instruments here do, and what the numbers mean. I know, for example, that those two numbers compared mean that we are about sixty percent of the way to Melchior, but I also know that we have under a week before we come under traffic control that will be able to sense if we deviate from our planned course and raise alarms. We do not have much time if we are to take control of the ship unnoticed."

"Shall I take number two now?"

"No. I am used to it, and the technical orientation did nothing to me. Let us see just how far the languages go." She chose cartridge number ten, then inserted it in the machine in place of number thirty-eight. "I will do this one as well. There should be one of us around with her wits about her, and you are it. Your turn will come in due course." She replaced the headsets and lay back. "When you are ready."

Chow Dai pushed the activator, then waited. This time Chu Li was not quiet but started to breathe hard, then to moan and thrust. Her hands went to her crotch and seemed to be doing something, but it was unclear what. What *was* clear was that this was not a tape like the others. Fearful, particularly of the sounds from the chair, Chow Dai pushed the activator off.

Chu Li came down very, very slowly and seemed almost disappointed when she realized that she was no longer switched in. She opened her eyes and looked at Chow Dai; her expression, though foreign to Chu Li's nature, was one Chow Dai had seen before in unpleasant circumstances.

Chu Li had been connected only a couple of minutes and so was able to regain control, although her body trembled slightly. "It was—" she gasped, breathing hard "—a sex tape. A very graphic one. I was—a man—in the body of a man—amidst a horde of foreign, exotic women. All were naked; all were there for my pleasure. I was to choose one and do as I pleased. It was such a feeling of power, of dominance. I am—was—highly aroused."

Chow Dai did not comprehend the depth of the experience, but she understood the reason for such a cartridge and why Chu Li had responded to it. "Now at least we know where our honorable captain got his urges so readily and what he must have done to amuse himself when no one else was aboard."

"Yes, I think so. I had heard that such things existed, but I had never experienced one before. The images are like memories, like reality. It is as if the scene actually existed for me in the past, and whichever girl I chose I would have bedded. To the mind, there would be no difference between the reality and the illusion. I feel the desire to go back and complete it, but I dare not. Even now I feel the urge to grab you and make mad, passionate love to you."

Chow Dai felt relieved and smiled. "Is that such a bad thing?"

"To me, no. I have wanted it from the first. But to you it would be perverse."

"No. What the guards did to us was perverse. What Sabatini did to you and to us is perverse. Nothing done in love that harms no one can be perverse. You are half man, half woman. That is enough."

They used the bed in Sabatini's cabin, the scene of much of Chu Li's violation, but it was different now, and afterward they fell asleep, exhausted more by the events of the day than by their own final efforts.

The next day Chu Li, feeling better than she ever had in her whole brief incarnation, decided to tackle things for real. Chow Mai hit another of the pornographic male-oriented cartridges but was not affected in the same way Chu Li had been. Rather, she seemed to have shifted mentally from the male point of view to that of the females in it, and although they stopped the program quite early, she wound up not only very, very turned on but also nonaggressive to the point of total passivity. She also, for some reason, pleaded to have her chains put back on, but they decided that the effects would wear down in a while and ignored her requests.

There were a number of other languages, including one cartridge that seemed to have no particular effect on Chow Dai other than to improve slightly her grammar and vocabulary. They decided that it must have been Mandarin Chinese.

They also discovered many more programs on shipboard design and construction, mathematical tables, basic celestial navigation, and computer module design and operation. One showed the complete interconnect between Sabatini's command module in the rear and the computer pilot, confirming Chu Li's suspicions that this was one of those very ships where Master System was not in charge. And, as suspected, there were some traps.

The machine clicked off, and Chow Dai removed the headset and waited for Chu Li to come out of it. The cartridge had seemed uneventful to the observer and had taken the normal amount of time, so there had been no reason to think anything was wrong. Finally, Chu Li came around, then sat up and looked around, almost panicking.

"What's the matter?" the sisters asked in unison. "What has happened to you?"

"I have been stung," she told them. "I have spent a half hour in a pleasant dreamworld, and now I wake up to find a nightmare."

As they watched, concerned, she looked around vacantly, then tried to get out of the chair and stumbled, holding on to it for support.

"There is only darkness," she told them, a pained tone in her voice. "I am blind."

10. THE GOLDEN BIRDS OF LAZLO CHEN

IT WAS THE MIDDLE OF THE FOURTH DAY AFTER HAWKS had stolen and used the mindprinter and had begun to have second thoughts about his long-range mission and goals, and by now he was much changed from the scholar who had read what he should have reported and set off on a course to save not only himself but the future of humanity.

At the time—not very long ago, although it seemed an eternity and a world away—he had lived for nothing but his work, had no close friendships or dependencies, and had an exaggerated idea, he knew now, of his importance in the scheme of things. Perhaps it had just been the desire of a lonely and frustrated man approaching middle age to do something that future historians might note and remember. Unable to get back into the head of that man he'd been such a short time ago, he really wasn't sure. The odd fact was that not a single thing that had been

important to him then was in the slightest way important
to him now.

He and his wives had achieved an incredible level of
self-sufficiency in a very short time, and he had stayed
away from human contact as much as possible in his travels since that mindprinting had simplified everything. He
had not yet used the rest of the whiskey for trading, as
he'd intended, because he hadn't had to do so. Now, if
all worked out, he would trade it for good, rugged, practical clothing and perhaps some better weapons as well,
depending on how hard a bargain could be driven. He
now saw a chance at something far better than being a
footnote in a future history book; he saw a chance, at
least as long as his health held out, of starting over brand
new and, in a sense, becoming young again.

For Cloud Dancer it had never been clear what they
were doing or why. She had attached herself to him initially because he was kind and gentle to her and more
than slightly exotic, and she'd fallen in love with him and
he with her, and they had married, something not too
common in Hyiakutt culture. She understood that he had
learned a secret so dangerous that there were many hands
raised to track him down and slay him, but they hadn't
caught him yet, and she would be at his side if and when
they did. She'd had him exclusively for such a little time,
but she was well aware that she had been a partner in the
decision to include Silent Woman and that at the time
she'd had the power to veto that decision. Cloud Dancer's
life had been pretty unhappy up to meeting Hawks, but
Silent Woman's past was Cloud Dancer's worst nightmare. Pity had turned quickly to respect for the strange
tattooed woman, and Cloud Dancer had participated in
the ceremony of blood. She now regarded Silent Woman
as one of her own blood and as much her wife as both
were the wives of Hawks. The family was not a collection
of individuals: The family was One.

The survival program had stripped everything from her

concerns except the basics. Her memories were not impaired; it was simply that all she had been was no longer relevant. Family, tribe, nation—their world was now three people in a canoe, and nothing else was important enough to think about. The unit had certain basics that were required. It must be fed. It must find shelter and be hidden from enemies each night. It must be guarded. It must survive. Of necessity the women must be the warriors, and those were the tasks of warriors. She was also a wife. A tribal wife served and supported her husband, gave her body willingly to him, and, if the spirits willed, bore him many fine children. Absolutely nothing but these concerns occupied her thoughts and motivated her actions.

The only way to learn about Silent Woman was to ask yes or no questions, but there was little truly to be learned. She had no memory of her past at all, no memory of where she'd come from or where she had received the tattoo and why, or even of ever having given birth to a child— or, for that matter, ever having had a tongue. The shock and trauma of her horrible times had simply been rejected, blotted out, and locked away forever in some corner of the mind where such things go. She had not in fact even thought in a language anyone could have truly recognized, for it was an amalgam of terms and concepts from dozens of languages strung together in a way that worked but was uniquely her own. It was not a complex language. She did not, even with the English recoder, get much of what Hawks or Cloud Dancer said, because her vocabulary was so limited and her rules so basic.

She had known only that she hated the Illinois passionately but that she never had any other place to go. Her geographical world was the village where she'd lived and The Other Place where all the strangers came from and went to. She was still being constantly amazed that The Other Place was so vast, but it still was a single entity in her mind.

Then she'd seen her masters toying with the captive

pair and had known that after the game they would kill
the man and make the woman like her, and she hated the
Illinois and the village. So, when she had accidentally
bumped into Cloud Dancer and realized that they were
planning to flee, she had thought only about helping them
and hoping that they would take her with them, away
from the village to The Other Place. And they had. She
had never regarded herself as anything but property, but
she knew she preferred to be the property of Hawks, a
man both handsome and brave, and in whom there was
a gentle streak she had not known before, and some sadness or hurt deep inside as well. She had never thought
of being a wife to such a one. In fact, she really had no
concept of "wife," but she understood that to the other
two it made her an equal with Cloud Dancer. That was
the heady stuff of impossible dreams.

She was not stupid; that was the mistake the others
had made. She was, however, almost totally ignorant,
having not even the grounding of a sense of tribe and
culture as almost any of the others back in the village
had. She was already now at a higher level than she could
have conceived possible; she wanted only to preserve
that. They were her world, all she had or desired. They
were *everything*. She loved them both. Her whole life was
nothing but obedience and service. She would love, obey,
and serve them even if it meant her death, and she would
never survive them.

They were approaching one of the increasingly fre-
quent bends in the river, one that made the water in front
seem to vanish and which might be the same river as that
seen distantly through the trees on the right. Hawks had
decided against trusting such visions after they tried a
portage the first time; the water through the trees had
turned out to be an oxbow lake, a bend in the river that
had been cut off by built-up silt as the river changed its
course. He no longer felt the strong urgency he had up

north, considering how long they had been on the river without encountering anyone.

There was a sudden, loud noise as if some giant spring had suddenly popped its winding and sounded off. Birds flew from the trees and the river in panic, and at almost the same moment something slapped them incredibly hard and overturned the canoe.

Hawks came up for air and looked around, then was relieved to see two other heads break the surface. "Head for the far shore!" he shouted to the two women. "Forget the canoe!"

The sound came again, behind them, and this time the canoe was struck with a full blow. It seemed to rise up, coming apart as it did so, then collapsed into the water as a set of shapeless pieces of skin and frame. The wave from the blow came at them, and they relaxed and let it carry them toward the near shore.

They reached the bank only meters apart and managed to get on shore. There was no thought of remaining in that spot: Another blast of the invisible hand might come at any moment.

Survival wisdom called for them to scatter in three directions and run until pursuit was foiled, but their sense of family overrode that part of it. The land was covered with a shallow film of water out of which a forest grew. There was little shelter and no rocks or other obvious protection. They could only make certain they were all within sight of one another and start running as far in as possible.

"That's right, Hawks. You just keep running," a sardonic voice, electronically amplified, said from what seemed to be everywhere. "You'll find if you keep going this way that the river played a joke on you and doubled back again. If you go right, it'll be on three sides; if you go left, well, you'll run into a big surprise."

They did not pay any real attention to the voice but kept running until, as predicted, they came to a riverbank.

They heard that terrible sound again, and they saw a wall of water coming toward them as if a giant hand were skimming the top. The point was clear. They couldn't swim across, not there.

Hawks stopped the women and gathered them to him. "It's no use," he told them. "I've been a romantic fool, damn it all! They just sat here and waited for us to spring their trap!"

"Then if we are surrounded, we must fight our way out or die trying!" Cloud Dancer responded bravely, and Silent Woman nodded assent.

How could he explain to these two infrared sensing devices and a certainty that this area had been cleared of all people so only the fugitives would show up? Or the power of some of the weapons that might be at the disposal of the enemy?

"No," he responded. "Long ago you told me of the foolish warrior who charged into overwhelming odds only to show his bravery and die a legend. This is not Roaring Bull and his Illinois or even a tribe as we understand tribes. Right now they could send things through the air, as they did that giant unseen hand, that would make us drop in pain or knock us completely out. It makes no sense to even try to die in such a battle when there is still the small but real possibility of a deal. These are men, not demons. They will talk, and so we will talk."

She was not convinced. "But—"

"I am chief and husband to you both!" he said gruffly. "They will let you leave if you wish. I am what they want. Dissolve the marriage and the tribe here or obey my orders exactly! I permit no other choice!"

Cloud Dancer looked at Silent Woman and frowned, but when she saw the response in the other's face, she looked back at him, resigned. "Talk, then, husband and chief. We are part of you."

He looked around at the suddenly silent, still swamp.

"All right!" he shouted. "So what now? Come out with our hands up? You didn't *leave* us anything else!"

They did not hear their pursuer approach, although they were more than attuned to such things, but suddenly he was there, not far away. He was ugly as sin, and he held a weapon in his hand that was quite out of keeping with his looks and dress.

"You don't have to shout," the Crow Agency man said. "I'm right here. The name's Raven."

Hawks stared at him. "I must be vital indeed to send a Crow this far south. Aren't you hot?"

"Steaming." He shrugged. "It's part of the image, you know. You want to tell the ladies not to try anything, that I can knock all of you cold on your asses before you can blink?"

"It is not necessary, *Crow*," Cloud Dancer responded, making his nationality sound like a foul and obscene thing. "We understand you."

Raven was taken aback, then he nodded. "Yeah, English Cross was in that pack, wasn't it? How'd you like the survival program? I had a part in creating it, which is why I could figure out exactly how you'd act. Damn. Must be a flaw in it. You *did* get caught, after all."

Hawks actually felt crushed, but he had to make a brave show of it for the sake of his honor. All that running, all that violence and tension, all that taste of freedom— all illusion. The issue had never been in doubt.

"You'd still be free if you hadn't stuck to the river," Raven noted. "Fact is, they'd'a had to send a Val after you to catch you if you just went east or west or even north. The only ones known on Earth the Vals didn't ever catch were ones that just went into the wild and got kinda swallowed up. 'Course, once you took on the many-colored lady here, it was easy to spot you, but some clothes would have taken care of that." He sighed. "Well, come along. We got work to do yet."

"Aren't you afraid that I'll tell you why I'm being

chased?" Hawks asked, wanting to throw his one weapon. What was death to him was death to all. But that didn't seem to disturb the Crow.

"Well, I'm damn curious, if that's what you mean. Cause me a lot of trouble if I knew, I guess, but not as much as you. See, *they* know that you know, so Master System knows it, too. Can't change that. But they don't know if I know until they got you under the machine, and I got you first, so I can cover. Tell me if you want or not. Makes no nevermind to me."

Hawks stood there, suddenly startled and confused. "What do you mean, *they* know?" he asked. "Who are they? Or, better yet, who are *you*?"

"I'm a handy man with big ambitions," the Crow answered him. "Got you kind of tossed in my lap by a colleague. My fat comes when I deliver you, even if it's split."

Even Cloud Dancer was starting to get the idea. "You are not from Council," she said suspiciously.

"Well, in a manner of speaking I am. Officially I work for the Agency, which works for the Council under contract. Not this one, though. You're too plenty important to trust to mere people. I'm sure the Val's either right behind us or just ahead of us, but it don't matter. We're gonna leave him running in circles for a while. By the time they get the idea, our part will be done."

Hawks wasn't sure whether this was a good thing or a bad thing. He had been prepared to deal with the logic of Master System, even though the odds were slim, but with a new player in the game, he was in as bad a position as before, only at the mercy of an unknown third party.

"Who are you working for?"

"The same man that the courier was working for. As you know, she didn't make it. I assume she made contact with you and passed it along."

"She's dead," he told the Crow. "She died maybe a

day or so after she landed, probably from injuries suffered in the crash. I found her body and her papers."

"Uh huh. And you read them, I guess."

"You know I did."

"Not until that moment. Thanks. So this hasn't been for nothing. Now, come along. I don't want to meet any Vals around here. We can fill in the story later."

"All of us?" Cloud Dancer asked him.

"You bet, lady. I want all three of you, and just the way you are suits me fine."

Hawks's initial fear and then resignation were slowly being replaced by anger. Council chasing him was one thing, but this was some mercenary, some bounty hunter. Also, though his lack of clothing felt quite natural, it was somewhat demeaning among strangers, and particularly around men like this one.

Raven had a fairly elaborate camp set up in the center of the peninsulalike area: a small portable dome that bristled with antennae and detectors. It was only now that the Hyiakutt man realized that their captors were probably few in number—everything could be remotely run from here. Still, this was high-class equipment, Upper Council level at least, and he wondered where one like Raven would get access to it for an unauthorized or freelance mission.

The answer to that was revealed when they met the Crow's companion. Both Cloud Dancer and Silent Woman gawked with a mixture of fear and wonder at this new woman, who was so tall, so muscular, and so very black. Cloud Dancer had never seen anyone before who was not of the People, and from Silent Woman's reaction it was clear that she had never seen anyone like *this*.

Manka Warlock got some pleasure out of such reactions. She'd been getting a lot of them on this trip, and it served to keep the common folk of North America off balance. They weren't sure if she was a human or a demon, and after a couple of weeks with her, Raven wasn't all that sure, either. She was proud, vain, aristocratic, and genuinely amoral. Raven, it was true, would do almost anything for the right payoff, but he knew when it was right or wrong—he just did it anyway. To Warlock, people were divided into two basic categories: useful and irrelevant. It was clear that deep down she believed herself to be vastly superior to other human beings and immortal as well. She had on this trip done things like blast a tree because when she pushed one of its branches out of the way, it came back and struck her. Now she looked at the three captives less as a goddess would look at her creations than as a laboratory scientist examining her test rats. She gestured with a riding crop held in her left hand.

"How utterly quaint and primitive," she said in her heavily Caribe-accented English. "Do they have fleas?"

"They bite, sometimes," Hawks responded, irritated.

Her face took on an ugly, maniacal expression, and the hand holding the riding crop twitched. Raven stepped in.

"Enough!" he said. "You wanted him—there he is. Go ahead—do what you want, but *remember why you are here and who you are working for.*"

The hand stilled, and some semblance of sanity crept back into her eyes, but the look was still there.

"Very well," she responded. "I will take some lip, for a while, but do not try my patience, nature man. There are things for which I would willingly surrender even as fat a price as you would bring. You—all of you—belong to me now, as a dog, a horse, or even a blanket belongs to someone. You are mine until I choose to sell you. You are within a forcefield keyed to the two of us now. You cannot leave without the both of us, and no matter what happened, you would never get my cooperation to open it."

"That won't work on them," Raven told her. "You don't understand the cultures here. Just achieving rank or manhood means undergoing tortures that are pretty bad. Death is meaningless as a threat. If you kill them when they are captives, they will go to a greater heavenly reward than if they died in bed."

"The females, however, are disposable," she noted curtly.

"Bullshit. If he gave in to save either one, he'd lose all respect in their eyes and be a dead man to them anyway. The reverse is also true. You got me into this because, hard as it is to believe, they *are* members of my race. I got in because I liked the potential payoff. You decide right now between the payoff and your ego."

She turned on her partner. "You insect! How *dare* you speak so to me!"

"Come on—try and kill me. Maybe you will. If you do, you'll wind up killing them, too, and then you'll be all alone when *he* starts looking for blame. You decide right now whether you want to be crazy or you want to buy a one-way ticket to Melchior."

That seemed to get to her, and she hesitated; there was even a flash of doubt across her face. She was one level up from Roaring Bull, Hawks thought, but deep down there were a lot of things that scared her as well. She knew it, and she knew that Raven not only knew it but had just exposed it, and she hated him all the more for it, yet she also accepted it as fact.

"Tend to them, then. I will call in the skim, and we will get this on the road." She turned and walked back into the small dome.

"Your partner's a psychotic," Hawks noted calmly. "Sooner or later they're not going to be able to cover that up anymore from Master System."

Raven sighed. "Yeah, I know. I sure as hell don't plan no long-term relationship with her. Still, she's really good at what she does, and she's useful to lots of powerful folks. That brings me back to you three."

"You spoke the truth to her," Cloud Dancer put in. "I suppose even a Crow understands some things."

"Listen, lady, you're in no spot to bargain, and you

are just along for the ride 'cause I want your boy here to be reasonably happy and comfortable."

"And perhaps because you might need three helpers if Warlock goes completely over the edge of the cliff," Hawks added.

Raven shrugged. "Could be you're right. Now it's time for some serious talk, though. Have a seat on the ground, here."

They all sat and stared at the Crow.

"Now, here's the story," he began. "A while back, down in South America someplace, an illegal tech group got hold of some old papers. Hawks, you know what was in them. I don't, except that they're some big knife at the throat of Master System. Forbidden stuff. Well, some of 'em had connections, and they traced something in the stuff to Lazlo Chen, of all people. How a half-breed administrator from the middle east figures into something like this I don't know, either. Whatever it was, they got the idea that only Chen could help them, and for some reason they thought he would. They made some contacts among their version of people like me, and that finally got the word to Chen. What the message was, again I got no idea, but it interested him. Intrigued him. They wanted some kind of real fat deal for the stuff, and that he wasn't about to do or couldn't do. So he used his connections and got them raided, and all were killed, but the right folks got the papers. These started a clandestine courier network that crossed into the Caribe region."

"And that's where Laughing Lady in there comes in, I suppose," Hawks responded, interested.

"Yeah, sort of. She's worked her way up to the top of the Security Agency there with blood and hard work, anyway. Probably got worse the higher she got or she never would have gotten that far. Well, she worked out a system of transfers. Island to island, then to someplace up north where it was to be handed to somebody for Siberia, then somebody else in China, and finally to Chen.

As you know, something went wrong. Master System learned about at least the existence of the papers and pushed every panic button in the world. Now, you tell me the courier crashed, got hurt bad, and died, and you found it and read it. All of a sudden you take off. Of course, since it was one of her girls, Warlock was dispatched to find out who the traitor was working for, and because she didn't know the territory at all, she got hold of me. I was one of the few not on the case but on routine patrol duties, so I won't be missed, and I've done a few jobs for the Caribes before. We set out to get you before the real hunters did, and we did—so far, anyway. Now we deliver, the boss man covers our trails and our asses, and that's it for us."

The story was so absurd, it had to be true, and Hawks laughed. "Chen. You're working for Chen!"

"Yeah, so that's not exactly hard to figure. What's so funny?"

"That's just who I started out to find. He's the only one who could really use this stuff, and he has the power to get me off the hook as well."

"Figured it was something like that. Mud Runner couldn't have helped, anyway. His stuff's wired direct into Master. He'd have apologized profusely and got drunk for a week after to cure his remorse, but he'd have still skinned you alive. So, we're the best thing could'a happened for your long-term future and interests. It's so far to Chen, you couldn't go any further without coming back. You'd've never made it. Now, 'cause neither of us can rightly trust you, there's several ways you can travel on this."

"I'm listening," Hawks said.

"Well, we can knock you cold, keep you out, and carry you in. That's one. Lots of trouble for us but effective. Or you can take a hypno and lock it in with a printer until we unlock it over there. Or you can be bound, gagged, and chained. What do you think?"

Hawks could see the man's reasoning. Traveling the distance to Chen might take some time and might even involve transfers as risky and elaborate as those for the documents—which had failed. Either knocking them cold or chaining them carried greater risks of discovery and would involve more people in moving and guarding them. On the other hand, Raven knew that both Hawks and Cloud Dancer had broken a hypno coming out of Hyiakutt country, so he couldn't be certain that a hypno would really take or for how long. He wanted cooperation on the hypno before he'd risk it.

"What sort of hypno?" Hawks asked. "One like your partner would give?"

"Nothing too bad. Something to make a good cover and guard our backs is all. You all would be put back in original condition at the other end. I wouldn't want to deliver you any other way—but if we get spot-checked, I wouldn't want whatever you know leaking out, or even that you know something worth leaking, if you get my meaning."

They did. "Why take us?" Cloud Dancer put in. "We both will go with him anywhere, of course, but why do you bother with us?"

"Lady, I don't know what I'm dealing with here, and I don't really want to know. Chen may hear him out, then kill all of you, or turn you into pets or the walking dead for all I know. But he might also embrace your husband here like he was the greatest hero of Earth history and put him in a real high and influential position with lots of power. Taking you costs me very little. Not taking you could cost me later. Now, what about it, Hawks?"

It was not a difficult decision, although it was a serious one. He could monitor his wives' treatment first, but anything he did to guard could be circumvented by the portable mindprinter after, and Raven's cartridges would be security-oriented and not at all benign. He didn't even like to *think* what Warlock's library must be like.

Still, he knew now that there was only one course open to him. The Crow had spoken the truth when he had said that Chen would want him, at least, in original condition. He could only trust that it applied to all. Raven also was speaking the truth about Mud Runner; it had always been the longest of long shots at best, and reality was obscured when unvoiced. Going wild was an equal if more romantic illusion. Silent Woman, at least, could not be kept hidden forever, and he could not abandon her any more than he could abandon Cloud Dancer. Chen was the only chance to preserve any possibility of a future for the family and tribe.

"We will take the hypno and mindprint," he responded. "If it is your kit."

"Of course. Well, we'd better get started, then. The skimmer will be here at dusk, and then you have one to three days of travel ahead, depending on the heat."

The program was devastating, as he had known it would be, but it was the most secure both for their captors and for protection en route. The fact was, once Raven had set it up and turned it on, none of them were aware of anything beyond that point. There were blurs, bright lights, confusing shouts in unknown tongues, and hundreds of other fleeting sensations, but none of it made sense, nor was there any time sense. There also, however, were no worries or concerns. Those had ceased to exist with the rest of the world.

Hawks awoke with the usual feeling of dizziness and disorientation that came from having undergone both hypnotics and mindprinting, but he recovered quickly. He was lying on a plush rug of some kind inside a large tent, and it was warm and dry. His first thought was for his wives, and when he did not see them, he was worried. He got up and tried to get his bearings.

"Looks like you made it," Raven's voice came to him. He looked up and saw the Crow sitting back and relaxing on a low fur-covered divan, a half-smoked cigar in his mouth. Even at this point, Hawks couldn't resist wondering if Raven had all of his cigars presmoked halfway down.

"I promised you they'd be here, and they're here," the Crow went on. "You are just gonna have to wait to see them, though. You got to get ready to see the big man. After him, then we have a happy reunion or whatever."

"I want to see them *now!*"

Raven sighed. "Listen, Hyiakutt. You're not in North America now, and Council's on the other side of the world. I got to tell you it was pretty hairy just getting you this far, and you wouldn't be here without me. A couple of people *died* to ensure that nobody but us even knows it. You're here because you couldn't resist knowing nasty things you knew you shouldn't touch. I didn't put you in this spot, I only brought you. Now you see the big man you said you wanted to see anyway. You trusted me with the hypno that got you here. Keep playing it my way."

Hawks sighed and nodded. The Crow was right, and he knew it. He was in no position to bargain now. Best to see it through. It might not make any real difference, anyway. By Raven's own admission, Chen had betrayed the first discoverers of the rings who'd contacted him. There was no reason why such a man would treat Hawks any better.

"These people bathe about once a century," the Crow noted. "But they have a set of rules and procedures. We'll get you looking as decent as we can."

Hawks's brows rose. "Then we are not in Tashkent Center?"

"What do you take Chen for? We lifted you out illegally, and we smuggled you all the way here illegally and, since I haven't seen either a security force or any sign of a Val yet, successfully. You're out in a tent city somewhere in the steppes of the Caucasus. He got here with his whole retinue just about an hour and a half ago, all riding *camels*, if you can believe it. I heard of 'em but never saw one before. I don't care how much water they hold, I'll take a horse or even an ornery mule every time."

Getting prepped for an audience with Lazlo Chen was not an onerous experience, even if it was a disconcerting one. He was taken in to a small horde of women dressed in exotic clothing that masked just about everything except their eyes, all of whom talked in a language unrelated to anything he had ever heard before. Laughing and giggling, they washed him with cloths rinsed in a large basin of tepid water, clipped his nails, combed his long black hair and trimmed it, although he refused to let them cut it. Then he was given dark wool pants tucked into tall leather riding boots and a shirt of the same material dyed red and worn like a vest, and he was ready. Raven, who still wore his traditional buckskins, checked him over approvingly.

"All right, now. You look like you're ready to raid the peasant villages," the Crow noted in his usual sneering tone. "How's it feel?"

"It itches," Hawks complained.

Raven shrugged. "So it itches. If you'd had any decent clothes on when I picked you up, then this wouldn't have been necessary. Now I'll give you the protocol, and you *will* follow it exactly no matter how demeaning it is simply because he has to keep up the show for the locals and you want to keep on his good side. He's willing to keep it in English, so there's no languages to learn, simply because he knows it and absolutely nobody else around him, including his aides from Center, does. It ain't too popular a tongue in these parts. And remember who you're dealing with, even if he tries to get chummy."

Hawks nodded. After Roaring Bull, then Manka Warlock and Raven, he had finally made it up the hierarchy to a Lord of the Middle Dark. He had never met the Council Emperor or seen him, but this was one of equal stature at least.

They brought him to an enormous tent erected on the

great plains of what had once been the south central region of the USSR, and before that the domain, or route, of legendary conquerors. He felt as if he had somehow slipped back in time to some ancient day when Genghis Khan and his Mongol horde had overrun and ruled the area in their attempt to establish a worldwide empire.

Certainly the setting seemed bleak and primitive enough, with torches lighting the way to the tent and oil lamps within. The floor of the tent was lined with plush rugs, and off to one side there was a table with an ornate chess set apparently showing a game in progress. An ornate, thronelike chair sat on a raised platform to the rear of the tent, its arms and back covered with complex designs. Still, the place stank. Unimpressed with the primitive grandeur, Hawks couldn't help but wonder if any of these people ever bathed or wiped themselves.

Lazlo Chen entered confidently, leaving his guards outside. He was certainly an imposing figure, close to two meters high and perhaps a hundred and fifty kilos. Oddly, he did not look fat but rather enormous and powerful. In spite of the fact that his family name was Han Chinese, he clearly owed his looks and size to Mongol and perhaps Cossack ancestry as well. He had long, black hair streaked with gray and a thick, full beard of the same color mix, and he wore a crimson turban and colorful, if baggy, Occidental clothing. He also wore golden earrings studded with enormous rubies and had other jewelry on his person and his garments—but there was only one piece that interested Hawks.

The Hyiakutt did as he had been instructed and knelt, bowed his head, and awaited recognition. Chen took a seat on the throne, then looked at the man before him.

"Oh, please *do* stand up. Sorry to keep you waiting, old boy," Chen said in a cheerful, casual tone. "But I'm a busy man, and even arranging to get the two of us together this one time has been something of a bother." His accent was not exotic but casual and without any distinguishing regionalisms. It was about as pure as English ever got. Hawks soon discovered, though, that Lazlo Chen's accent shifted to match the other speaking to him. The man was a born master linguist. The Hyiakutt historian stood and found he was still below eye level.

"I appreciate the effort, my lord," Hawks responded politely. "I have put many people to much trouble to gain this audience with you."

Lazlo Chen looked at him with bright, penetrating eyes, and a trace of a smile crept onto his face. "You came because of the ring. You came because you were sick and tired of being one of the sheep."

Hawks was startled. "Do you read my mind, then?"

Chen chuckled. "It is easy to read a man's mind when one understands him so well. When I entered, you thought something like, well, 'Here is this primitive throwback wearing on his ring finger something of which he can't possibly know the import. How will I deal with him for it?'"

"I—I was not so unflattering, but I do admit to the rest of it. I take it now, though, to mean that you know exactly what you have."

"I do, and yet I do not," the Emperor admitted. "Here—come close and look at it. I have done so for two decades now."

Hawks approached, fascinated in spite of himself. After enduring so much for so long, he would not be denied at least the sight of the objective.

The ring was not, as he had feared, plain or ugly but a thing of great beauty, shimmering gold in the lamplight, studded with diamonds, rubies, emeralds, and other precious gems. Set into the front on a bed of pure jade was a symbol in bright silver so perfect, it could not have been cut by human hands no matter how exacting the artisan. Three tiny, perfect birdlike creatures flanking a diamond set in such a way that each of the birds stood at the point of a triangle.

"It is the curse of one who wears the ring that he cannot exhibit inordinate curiosity about it," Chen told him. "Part of the master program compels the computers to ensure that all five are always in human hands. If one is destroyed, they must make another—it is quite ironic, in fact. No one is exactly compelled to be told the meaning and use of the rings, but if someone finds out, as you have, it becomes dangerous to you and to me. Any attempt to search out the owners of the other four baubles is, of course, dealt with. I have no desire to be 'dealt with,' as I'm sure you will understand."

Hawks nodded. "You have subjected it to testing, though?"

"I have. Inside its beautiful exterior, under the jade and bonded to the ring in a way we can but guess upon, there is in effect an incredibly tiny computer. Unfortunately, someone conveniently lost the operating manual. It became the signet of the Chairman of the Presidium, the rank that I currently hold. It has long been suspected of being more than symbolic."

Hawks couldn't keep his eyes off the ring. "It is beautiful," he sighed.

"Yes, indeed it is, and that is fitting. I suspect our ancestors who designed the things had something of a sense of myth, or at least a sense of humor. The magic rings of power that will unlock the secrets of the universe. Myths and stories of such things are as old as man himself. In those days a Jason or a Sinbad would set out on an expedition to get the magic things from the evil rulers and creatures who possessed them, battling every obstacle of man, nature, and the supernatural. Now, thanks to the diaspora, the baubles are scattered amongst the stars, although by the terms of our magic spell—or program, as we crudely know it today—they all still exist, and all exist in the hands of human beings who can use them. We have all the makings here of a modern myth, and it would be a tragedy if the objects did not look as grand as they were reputed to be. They are important enough to be forbidden knowledge. You tell me why."

"The builders of the Master System knew that what they did was unprecedented and unpredictable. They could not create it without a means to turn it off or at least to subjugate it to human will. Master System is compelled by its very core program to retain the rings, and in the hands of human authority. Humans with power and position, like yourself, my lord. It must also preserve the interface and make it possible for the humans, all five, to activate the override. The rings themselves are only parts of the code. They must all be present and inserted in a proper order. If that is done, Master System will submit to the orders and control of the five."

"I have suspected something of the sort through other sources, but this is absolute confirmation. I shall want all the details you can remember from the old documents. Naturally, this is all being recorded."

Carefully, sparing no detail, the Hyiakutt complied. He was surprised at how much he remembered and how easily it came to him, then guessed that some sort of enhancement had been given him along with the restoration program. Finally he was through, and Chen sat and thought for a while in silence. Then the Emperor said, very quietly, "I know the location of three of the other four."

Hawks stared at him. "Then you have the makings of a dangerous bargain, my lord."

"I do not bargain, particularly over something such as this. The rings must belong to humans of power and influence, you say. The fact is, almost anyone who could somehow acquire one, even steal it, would be a human of power and influence by the very act. On the scant evidence that it was something akin to what you now tell me it is, I have begun preparing. It is not an easy task to do so; one little slip can mean discovery and death even for one such as myself."

"You mean to get the rings, then. All of them."

"Indeed. I actually leaked the scant legends and clues to the rings around this whole world. Perhaps a tenth of all those pitifully few who are literate have heard the rumors. I cast lines randomly into the lake, and now I have pulled in the big fish. The group who amassed that documentation did not do so at my behest, but I was looking all over this world for signs that the bait was taken. One achieves greatness with great risks or one remains a sheep and deserves to."

Hawks's heart sank. "I'm no trout at the end of your line."

"Oh, but you are. Why did you read it when you knew it was forbidden knowledge sure to cause you agony? Why did you then decide to try and reach me with that knowledge? Self-preservation? Nonsense! You might have convinced yourself of that, but the fact is, if you were that sort of a man, you would never have read it in the first place. So why did you set out? Do you really know yourself as well as I know you?"

Hawks remained silent.

"You came," Chen said, "because you needed to believe that there was some way out of this mess. Way in the back of your mind, perhaps deep in your subconscious, you want those five rings united. You want the rule of the computer, the stifling of humanity, to end. You want to believe that it *can* end. The others—the ones who could come and did not—are sheep. They are either satisfied with things as they are, or they fear the consequences of any changes, any real freedom. They are complacent—or afraid. You feared you would find the tale a lie. They fear discovering that it is the truth."

Hawks's emotions were in turmoil, but he knew just where he stood and why. It was one thing to challenge the grip of the almighty Master Program, one thing to pray for, even work for, a crack in that system, but even in the incredibly unlikely event that it was possible both to gather the rings and to discover how to use them, it was now for what? For Lazlo Chen, who dreamed of empire? Who dreamed, in fact, of godhood? He had been this route before and answered yes. Now he was not so certain of his logic.

"The system is stagnant," he told the Director. "This is not a healthy long-term condition for humanity to be in, and the longer it goes on, the less able anyone will be to stop it. It might already have gone too far. Still, there is some merit in the system. Without the computer revolt there would *be* no humanity. We are held back to a degree, but we are free within our own worlds and the limitations placed upon us. There are no prying eyes here governing our going to the bathroom or even monitoring this conversation. It is irrelevant to the computers. We are in a rut, but we have been in ruts before. I admit I am dissatisfied with the situation, but as a historian I must also weigh the alternatives."

Chen got up and slowly paced in front of the throne. He was an imposing figure, and the act did more to enhance his superior position than being seated had.

"It is true that we are not slaves," Chen admitted. "Do you know what we are? Pets. Pets and experimental animals. We have long lives with ourselves as the primary cause of death. Set us back many centuries, remove vast parts of our populations to the stars, and then wind us up and see what we can make—just so long as we don't try and gain control of the old technology. We are the interstellar empire our ancestors dreamed of, yet we are not the emperors of it. We are interstellar traders whose product is people and skills and ideas, and here we are, you and I, sitting in a tent in the middle of a godforsaken steppe surrounded by camels, illuminated by torchlight, and drowning in a sea of faces that daily grows more joyously ignorant, more stupid, and more complacent. I rule an area larger than any empire in human history, yet I rule *garbage!*"

"What you say may be true," Hawks admitted. "Yet

you must pardon me, mighty ruler, if I point out that the alternative you offer is yourself. I think it is irrelevant how wise and kind and good you might be or how wondrous your vision—I wonder now if any human being is capable of assuming such power without being driven mad by it. I once believed, not long ago, that any human rule was preferable, but I forgot that the absolute rulers of the past had limits. There can be only one Master System. There will never be two to compete. The power is beyond challenge."

"Indeed? And what would *you* have done if you'd had all five rings and the secret of their use?"

"Mankind is primitive once more, but also self-reliant and in a broad sense not ignorant at all. We have our histories, our cultures, and we are a self-sufficient lot these days. I would shut the master computers down and let things proceed on their own, without limits or chains, after that, even if it took thousands of years to rise once more and unite our people."

"You are wrong on many counts, my friend," Lazlo Chen responded. "First and foremost you are wrong that there can ever be only one Master System. We here in the Centers, and out in the other worlds as well, are getting away with a great deal under Master System's collective nose at the moment because it is preoccupied. For centuries it has spread and spread its rule and its system with it, but it has now run into something it cannot break. Far beyond us, Master System is preoccupied in a protracted war. It does not involve living beings, I don't think, but it is stalemated and continues on because neither side can yield or gain. The systems here have started to loosen, to become even more lightly controlled than before. Many have taken advantage of this, and there is now an awareness by the Master System that it has been neglecting its back. The easiest way to protect itself is to tighten our leashes. Eliminate the Centers. Eliminate all of the technical class. Revert us all to total, primitive

barbarism and buy thousands of years of freedom from
worry. A prototype experiment of this sort is already under
way out there in space."

"Once I thought in cosmic terms and with cosmic
ambitions, my lord," Hawks responded carefully. "Then
this circumstance forced me to the other extreme and
down to a level as basic as you describe. I am not like
you. Your position, ambitions, and reach are your personal as well as professional goals. I, who am on a far
lower level, find that I must choose between the personal—the spiritual, if you will—and cosmic aims and
ambitions. My role in this is done."

Lazlo Chen's sharp eyebrows rose. "Indeed? The
primitive life? The romance of nature? For how long? A
week? A month? Five years? What is that?"

"Enough," Hawks answered.

"A waste. You have allowed your romanticism to blind
you. You are a technological man, a scholar of intense
training and excellent abilities. An analytical mind whose
study is human behavior. Yet you are a risk taker, a man
who in a primitive land could wind up literally naked and
defenseless and yet survive and beat the odds. There are
precious few such men. Such men are dangerous, even
to the system. Few such men are ever in the position that
you are, where they reveal themselves to others and to
their own inner selves. I need such men myself. What
you need is a sense of reality combined with a broader
romantic vision. I cannot let you go, you know. They will
never stop hunting for you, and no matter what tricks I
played with your mind, they could reach in and perhaps
find me there. I could reorient you to my service, but
again not without pointing a strong finger right back at
me. So, if you will not accept my vision, what would you
have me do with you?"

"You mean to kill me, then."

"I hope not. Again, it would be such a waste. Friend
Raven has been most convincing that no threat of death,

no hostages, would turn you, not even temporarily and certainly not for the long haul. Securing the rings will be no easy task. So what do I do with you?"

Hawks had an uneasy feeling. "My lord—where are my wives?"

"We must find a way to turn you to our advantage," Chen continued. "First, we must store you until we can get you away. Second, we must put you in a secure spot where we can examine the best things to do without a lot of messy interference. Very well, I will send you now to your women and show you what primitive really means. It will keep you all secure until I can arrange transit to Melchior. You've heard of Melchior?"

"Only that it is a security prison, my lord. Somewhere in space."

"It is a private research facility run by highly creative people, and it is not under Master System because no one ever leaves there. The Presidium controls it, and I control the Presidium. I will set them a task and see if they can be as creative as they are supposed to be. Very well. You are dismissed for now. They will take you to your holding point and your women. Go. But in all cases, remember this: *I will have those rings!*"

Hawks bowed, feeling totally dejected, then turned and walked out to the waiting guard. Chen watched him go, then gestured. Two figures emerged from behind the curtains in back of his throne. "You saw and heard?"

"What will you do with him, my lord?" Manka Warlock asked.

"First he is going to get a lesson in vulnerability. He is being taken to my private base, well below ground and far to the south, where I had his wives sent. There he will be reunited with them in my extensive underground garden, sealed off from all else by a forcefield. That will be his first educational step. Then we will send them all to Melchior as quickly as it can be arranged. It will be difficult, since Master System must not be permitted an identifier or even to know that they are there instead of somewhere in the North American wilds playing house. Both of you have been detached from your various details and placed in the service of the Presidium. You will go along."

Raven, in particular, was upset. "But—my lord! Up *there*?"

"Indeed. I want you both to have expanded training. This will be—delicate."

Warlock seemed as pleased as Raven was not. The *Presidium*!

"And just what's supposed to happen after Melchior?" Raven asked him, forgetting all the formalities.

Chen didn't notice. "There they will be put through the works, but nothing permanent, while they broaden their view of the universe and get a better orientation on their own attitudes. They will also be introduced to any others useful to them. Finally, they will be given a way out. The first successful escape in the history of Melchior. They will be given a place to go, although they won't realize this. Finally, they will be forced into a quest for the other four rings, although they won't believe that it is for me. Hawks will suspect, but it will be irrelevant. Master System will set Vals to stalk him. He will always be hunted and afraid. He will have to get the rings or commit suicide in despair. His romantic vision cannot be realized without the rings taking the heat off, as it were. He wishes to run from responsibility, become a child again, but he will not. It is not within him. Precautions will be taken, of course, so that nothing will be traced back to me."

"You seem very sure of this," Warlock noted. "How can you be certain that you will be able to control him through this?"

"I can't and won't. Perhaps I can help here and there, but that's about all. Most, perhaps he, will die in the quest, anyway, but there will be more all the time. You see, I don't have to control him. No matter what happens, he knows I have this ring. In the end, he must come for it. He or his successors, once started on this quest, will do whatever it takes for as long as it takes. It might well be years. Still, no matter what, in the end they will have to bring the other four rings back to me while I sit here the innocent potential victim, not the instigator. I don't even know if it's possible to assemble the rings. I intend to find out. I must find out. And the two of you will help me."

Raven looked past Chen to Manka Warlock and wondered. If all five rings were in one spot, it would be up for grabs to anyone, from Master System to Chen to—well, him and Warlock. He didn't much like the terms and conditions, but this damned thing had real long-term possibilities.

11. FORTRESS MELCHIOR

THERE WAS NOTHING WRONG WITH THE EYES OF SONG
Ching except that she who thought of herself as Chu Li
received no messages from them. It was a devastating
blow to her, but she knew she had to cope and put on a
brave front for the other two. She could not afford self-
pity.

"I think there probably are no traps in there, after all,"
she told them. "I think, though, that there are ones like
this, used to subdue the worst and render them helpless
or impotent. This can be restored with a mindprinter. It
is simply an order to my brain not to process or pass the
images.it receives."

"But what can we do?" Chow Dai asked. Chu Li *thought*
it was Chow Dai, anyway: The two sounded exactly alike.
"You are the one who knows the magic of these things."

"We continue," she told them. "And I continue, since
I have already paid a price. Do not blame yourselves.
There is no way to know in advance about these things.

264

Get me back to the chair. We are almost half done, and we must hit a key one soon."

They helped her, and she was right. The next one, in fact, was the one she had been hunting for all along. She knew it the moment she awoke, and she knew, too, just how it worked. She could talk to the ship, the pilot— anything. The language the ship used was English. She had suspected something like that; most of the computer controls from the old designs were in English, French, or Russian. The problem had been finding the right cartridge for communications. She immediately called a halt to further experimentation, although she insisted that the Chow sisters also take both the English program and the basics of the ship. They wouldn't be very proficient no matter what, but at least she would have some backup.

She was ready to communicate. She knew the language, and she knew what to ask. She put the headset back on. Now was the time to risk it all.

"Captain to pilot," she said in her adjusted male voice, this time in English.

"Go ahead," the computer responded in a monotone.

"Number of human life forms aboard vessel at this time. Monitor."

"Monitoring. Four life forms."

Four! That meant that Sabatini was still alive somewhere, although if he hadn't shown himself by now, it was probable that he was indeed trapped. "Location of human life forms."

"Three in central compartment. Fourth is in emergency module."

Just as she had thought. "Sealed orders have been opened that necessitate emergency change of operational plan."

"Go ahead."

"Captain Sabatini has fallen under suspicion of treason and has been relieved of his command. I am assuming command of this vessel."

"Identifier code?"

She swallowed hard, but she had thought this out. This was a Presidium ship making China calls. It was unlikely that Song Ching's father would have overlooked it. "Code Lotus, black, green, seven two three one one."

There was a nervous pause, then the computer responded, "Code acknowledged. Reason for interrupt?"

"Pawn takes king."

"Details?" the pilot requested.

She decided that it was requesting a rationale since there was obviously no king aboard.

"I am Song Ching, daughter of the chief administrator, China District. Enemies of my father altered my voice and tried to alter more of me, as well as doctoring my security records, to abduct me and thereby gain leverage with my father. I was being shipped to Melchior as a common prisoner, there to be handed over to confederates. As I am registered as a male named Chu Li, who was disposed of, nothing appears in the records, nor will it."

"Identification of enemies?"

"Unknown, but to do this and to use Melchior they must certainly be on the Presidium."

"Shall your father be notified?"

"Impossible. He is on Leave, which is why this was done now. Extent of plotters unknown, but some must be in the China Directorate."

"Desired course of action?"

"I am assuming complete and total command of this vessel from this point on. Captain Sabatini is relieved and will be confined where he is until he can be properly interrogated. In the meantime, I and my servant girls must get beyond the reach of Presidium authority and Master System must not be notified, as I am currently classified as prisoner Chu Li and will be returned. Recommendations?"

"I am a system vessel. I cannot remove you to any

place where you would not be traced here. I could forge documentation that would pass an interstellar pilot's muster, but you would be easy to trace. There is a clandestine network of interstellar traders, but it is, like this ship, loosely affiliated with the galactic presidiums. These people are quite rough and loyal only to themselves in the end. If they knew who you were, they would turn you over for reward to the highest bidder. If they do not know and do not find out, then you might wish you were on Melchior. They are men and women of the same sort of mind-set as Captain Sabatini."

She well understood what that meant, particularly now that she was blind. Sabatini had broken her without drugs or computers in a matter of days, and although she didn't feel like she was one, she was in fact a very desirable young woman. There was no question now where Sabatini's sex cartridges had come from.

"There are no other alternatives?"

"None available. The only habitats fit for you without severe and permanent alterations, which themselves would have to be done under the aegis of Master System, are Earth, shipboard, and Melchior. All others are under a Directorate. Mars, for example, would require both Master System's direct contact and also artificial atmospheres, as you are not modified for the Martian environment. Remaining with this ship for long is also not an alternative. Once we miss traffic control at the Outerbelt Marker, an alarm will be given and search initiated. Short of my destruction, there is no way to avoid detection and apprehension for long periods."

She broke contact and decided to discuss things with the sisters.

"The pirate warlords will be no gentle masters," Chow Dai noted. "They will be a race of foreign devils, all Sabatinis, but with all the magic boxes in the world and the protection of the warlords. They will make us the lowest of slaves and make us love to be slaves. I would rather die than be like that."

"I agree, but we have come too far to die now," Chu Li responded. "Yet what you say is true, and if we go home and try to sneak back down, and do so, we would have to become peasants in some remote and foreign place. It would not be much different than the other way, and we would always be looking over our shoulders."

"Of course," Chow Dai said thoughtfully, "we *could* just go on to Melchior."

"Huh? What?"

"I do not understand these things, but did you not say that this ship's spirit could change our papers, make us someone we are not, enough to fool those above us?"

"Yes, I did, but—" Suddenly she saw where Chow Dai's mind was going and reached for the headphones. "I wish data on Melchior."

"Melchior is a hollowed-out asteroid between Mars and Jupiter maintained as a reserve by the Presidium," the pilot responded. "Just what do you wish to know about it?"

"Is all of it a prison?"

"No. There are three parts. The prison itself, where all who are sent there are kept. It is something of a community in and of itself, but it is ugly and unpleasant. No one has ever escaped from it. The center is the research complex. All staff there are also there for life, and many of their experiments are on the prisoners. A third area, however, is the staff complex itself. All supplies and new people enter through it, and there is some interaction with the outside world through the small spaceport that connects there, as well as security personnel who may be rotated and the independents who sneak in to do business. Presidium members and staff also sometimes meet here, and the full Presidium always does at some point or another every one to three years."

"Details on this staff complex. What is it? A town? A city like Center?"

"It has a town organization and is quite small, but it is unique. There are dwelling units of increasing size and comfort depending on position in three areas, surrounding a town center. The center sells luxuries and dispenses necessities according to a computer-controlled system of work credits. There is, however, much human service work, all manual, usually performed by former prisoners modified for that service."

Blind, she could hardly pass herself off as someone new in security, nor could the sisters, with their terrible scars. She had to think as Song Ching would think—as Song Ching's *father* would think.

"You say there is much human experimentation and some two-way traffic. Is this place never used to modify or repair Earth people?"

"That is a primary function. Those whom the Presidium wish to use but who cannot be allowed to continue to exist as they are, for example, are sent there and changed radically. A death is convincingly faked for them on Earth and recorded with Master System. Also, there are enhancements and repairs of grave injuries suffered doing things which cannot be registered with Master System."

"Then we will go to Melchior with our records modified," she told it. "I will give you my story and then cover stories for the other two. You will prepare supporting documentation. We will be not prisoners but patients."

"This is dangerous. I have no hypnotics or master mindprinter aboard. You will have to give convincing performances, at least until you can get clandestine access to a mindprinter yourself. One curious hypno or security examination will expose all three. One slip will expose all three."

"We will have to risk it. Orders and paperwork and records often supersede common sense. It is why I have gotten this far. I have some codes and overrides, a knowledge of the equipment, and I will not be a prisoner but a patient. Besides, no one ever breaks *in* to Melchior."

"You have no idea what they can do in there," the pilot warned. "It is said that if Master System knew, it would blow the whole place to pieces."

"It is the best of a bad set of alternatives," she responded, but inwardly she was excited. Change identities, change personalities, change into whole new people ... *You have no idea what they can do in there.* Might not even Chu Li perhaps live again? Might not the Chows gain outer beauty to match their inner selves? Considering how far she'd already come, nothing was beyond reach.

"Uh—if we go to Melchior under those conditions, what about Sabatini?"

"He is already past the normal preservation stage and has been placed in a cryogenic condition. I can keep him there at least until I return to Earth orbit. By that time, you should either be away or exposed. In either case it will make no difference."

"Very well. Let's do it."

"Hawks!" The voice echoed through the subterranean garden. "Where's the heap big Hyiakutt chief now, eh? Come talk to Raven!"

There was a rustle and the sound of a large body dropping to the ground and coming toward the edge of the garden and its forcefield.

Even though he'd been well briefed, Raven was still shocked at Hawks's appearance. The man was filthy, worse than when the Crow had captured him, but, more, he had a wildness in his face and eyes and a brutal, animal-like gait and carriage that was somehow unnerving. Even though the Hyiakutt's current personality set was mere overprinting—that is, all of him was there below it and could be used—the Crow knew that he'd use tranquilizer darts before trusting himself with this fellow now to redo the printing and preparations.

If Raven was surprised to see Hawks, then the reverse was even more true. Hawks squinted. "Ray-ven," he growled. "Why are you still here?" It was obviously a labor to speak, which was understandable.

"I've got a new job and a new boss, that's why. We're not rid of each other yet. How have you liked it the last few days?"

Hawks charged the forcefield with a roar and was thrown back. He picked himself up but returned only a surly glare. "Bas-tard Crow!"

Lazlo Chen had indeed taught Hawks the true meaning of "primitive." He had restored the two women, and after having them fully mindprint recorded so they could be restored later, he had wiped them basically clean and imprinted on them the mindprints of female apes of some kind. They had no memories that were not ape memories, no language except the guttural grunts and shrill cries that amounted to about six basic phrases—"danger," "good food," and such. More, they were conditioned to see themselves as apes and each other as apes of the same type and tribe—and to see Hawks that way as well. They ate, preened each other, and slept, and that was life. At least they had no idea that anything was different. Hawks, however, did.

Chen had ordered him imprinted with the bull ape imprint but otherwise left alone. He *knew*, and he had to watch those he loved act as animals and react to them so, as well. It was the most miserable, unhappy experience in his whole life.

"So you found out being a chief ain't all romance and glory," Raven noted sardonically. "I don't know about you, but among the Crow, though bloodlines will get you a real shot, a chief must prove himself and be elected—and he can be canned if he doesn't have it. That's because the job isn't bravery, although it calls for that, or smarts, although it calls for that. Lots of folks can be politicians and generals. What a chief really means is *responsibility*.

Sending young men off to die. Making widows. Protecting those of the tribe even at the cost of his own life or even his honor. Not like Chen, either, because he doesn't care about his people, only himself. That's because folks like that lack honor. That's why you don't want to work for him, you know. No honor."

Hawks stared at the strange, ugly Crow. Raven had put his finger exactly on the problem, the moral dilemma, and also had shamed him. Men like Chen got where they were and stayed that way because they had no honor and took no responsibility. Even now, Chen wanted others to make him ruler of the universe, to take all the real risks, then hand him the ultimate in power and profits. Chen didn't care how many were killed or even if his own people were wiped out in doing it. He didn't care about them; he cared only for personal power while avoiding any real sense of responsibility. And yet Chen understood the concept of honor, of responsibility. Understood it and saw it as a weakness, something to be exploited. That was why he had done this.

"Have you come to taunt me in my misery?"

"Naw," the Crow responded. "I've come to take you all away from all this. The heat for you is getting tremendous for one thing, and also, old Chen wants his garden back before it's trampled flat. You can go as apes in cages or you can give your solemn oath that you'll be good, cooperative passengers, and we'll put you all back together. They won't even remember any of this. Only you."

"You—you can put them back?"

"Good as new, except for bruises, scratches, hair tangles, and that sort of thing. Your absolute bond is all I need."

"You have it."

"*Now* you're thinking like a chief. All right, Chief. We'll get this show on the road tonight. Put you all to sleep, cart you over as cargo, stick you on, then bring you back after we're away."

"You say we. You are going, too?"

"Yeah, me and Cuddles the Warlock. You remember her. She's attacked four people since you left. Chen thinks she's got potential if she can be redirected a bit. Don't know what he sees in me. I think my job's to keep *her* in line."

"You are one to speak of honor!"

Raven shrugged. "You'll never really know that, will you? So don't get too excited. This is a one-way trip to Melchior, the nice little garden spot where folks go who have to disappear or be disappeared. At least you won't have to worry about them making monkeys out of you, will you?"

The screen repelled a new attack.

The Melchior asteroid was small and irregularly shaped. Resembling a monstrous, misshapen baked potato, it was ugly, dark, and forbidding. Pockmarked with craters and pits, its one distinguishing feature was a space dock at the smaller end, and even that wasn't visible from a distance.

The origins of the place were lost in antiquity or covered in forbidden knowledge. Why this asteroid, out of all the other ones around, was picked and developed was a mystery only Master System could solve. The rumor was that when humanity was forced kicking and screaming out into the universe, it required adaptation. Mars had been the testing ground for the whole project, and for half the year Melchior was not all that far from Mars as the spacecraft flies. It was said that here the original Martian colonists were tinkered with and reprocessed until they were just right, and perhaps other prototypes were developed on Melchior later. Still, the asteroid wasn't very big, certainly not the sort of place that could process the billions involved, and so it was more or less abandoned by

Master System in favor of new and improved mass production models.

How the Presidium then got hold of Melchior was another lost mystery, although it was certainly the Martian Directorate that saw its uses first and somehow convinced Master System that there was a need for a prison strictly for the most valuable prisoners, the ones who could never again be allowed contact with normal society but who had talents or bright ideas. After a few centuries with no escapes and no real threats, Master System didn't even care anymore that the place wasn't hooked into its all-seeing monitors. Some thought its preoccupation with its enigmatic war was the cause, but more likely it was that Master System understood that the sort of men and women who would maintain its system on Earth and Mars had to have some outlet. Better that outlet be a little asteroid in the middle of nowhere and totally self-contained than in the Centers and Councils of Earth and Mars. It didn't really care who or what went in there, or what went on there, so long as they stayed there and so long as they never got out to threaten the system.

The place consisted of three large and countless small chambers, all set apart by kilometers of interlocking tunnels and all blasted with disintegrators out of the rock itself. The closed atmospheric system necessitated a huge number of safety air locks, which also served as security checkpoints; anyone who managed to sneak in could be caught merely by ordering the surrounding air locks sealed and then pumping out the air.

The prison *cum* prison town was in the larger of the two sides and was interconnected to the laboratories and other research facilities through deliberately confusing and well-monitored tunnels and air locks. The odd design not only maximized use of space but helped to disorient anyone who tried to figure the place out. The labs were underneath the prison and, from the prison's point of view, upside down. Gravity, impossible to create here by the spin method, which was cheapest and most efficient, was provided by a complex electromagnetic system designed by Master System. Over the centuries here, many scientists had gone absolutely crazy trying to figure out just how it worked.

To make matters worse, the center tunnels connecting the smaller "east" and the larger "west" were not equipped with the gravity system; one actually swam through them, weightless. The maintenance tunnels and chambers were also all weightless. Fortunately, the gravity in the habitation sections was close to Earth normal.

And so, to this place came first Chu Li and the Chows under false colors and then, within a week, Hawks, Cloud Dancer, Silent Woman, Raven, and the strange Manka Warlock. The Chinese, however, were treated a bit better, being listed as official patients, and assigned at the start to the staff area. Because most spaceships were entirely controlled by a computer pilot, the lack of any staff save the three was not even considered unusual.

The psychogeneticist interviewer looked Chu Li over critically. She was brisk and professional but not judgmental.

"So, you are here to become male," the scientist noted, looking at her screens. "A waste, considering your looks. Is this voluntary? I mean, do you concur?"

Chu Li nodded. "I do. I was always supposed to be, but Master System saw differently. I am a genetic construct."

"I could see that by the cell samples," the psychogeneticist huffed. "There are limits to what can be done short of a total remake, and that takes a lot of time. It says here you must be back in a new identity with all possible speed. That limits us."

"I will be fully functioning? And feel it?"

"Oh, of course. However, the sperm would not be yours but a—donor's—and we could make only superficial cosmetic changes. Your basic female body shape and bone structure will remain, for example, although we'll remove most of the breasts and smooth out what is left and perhaps surgically adjust the face to give it a more masculine cast. The strong male hormones which we will distill from the minute quantities you produce now but which will then be duplicated and produced by your new glands and sacs will alter you far more as time goes on. I gather no mental adjustment is required for this."

"They want me just the way I am, mentally. That's why they did the first part of the adjustment back there."

"Now, then, you were blinded in a mindprinter accident?"

"Not exactly an accident. I think I wasn't supposed to see something. It was understood that my sight would be restored here."

"Uh huh. Well, we'll have to scan for damage, but if it's just a printer program, it should be simple. We'll send you in for tests now. If all prove out, we'll get started right away."

Melchior was not at all what Chu Li had expected. True, it was inside an asteroid, and there was a strange coldness and dryness to the air, but everyone had been quite nice and quite professional all the way. She didn't really know what the place looked like, of course, but at the moment it seemed more like a hospital than a horrible prison. They were even going to attend to the terrible scars of the Chow sisters. Of course, the fact that their records now identified them as some other people and seemed to come from the higher security levels of China Center didn't hurt, nor did the fact that such records could not be cross-checked with Master System files here.

Melchior was an exciting and exotic place, one that she would like to have seen. She hoped that they would restore her sight quickly. But even if they did not, she would get a totally new identity. A complete sex change, some cosmetic changes, even subtly different fingerprints and a slightly altered eye pattern. She could walk right into China Center and right up to Song Ching's miserable relatives, and they would never know.

Doctor Isaac Clayben looked over the data modules on the subject and frowned. "You were right to come to me," he told the assistant. "You're sure there's no mistake?"

"Absolutely, sir. We took the print when we suspected something and checked it without her even knowing it."

"And the other two?"

"Petty criminals sent here because Doctor Shasvik wanted as many identical twins as he could get. You must admit, sir, that she's both brazen and brilliant even to have tried this. I have no idea how she could have switched full identification through Master System with this Chu Li boy. I would have sworn it was impossible without coming through here to begin with. In fact, her only mistake was that Melchior is *not* on Master System, so our records aren't updated when the master is. With the systemwide alert, we naturally put them all through. Her eye and prints matched up with Song Ching, and the other two are former servants of some high-ranking security officer in China Center. When we shot them back to Earth for a run-through, though, Master System identified her absolutely as Chu Li, a natural male. Fascinating."

Clayben scratched his scruffy full beard. "Pity. They are going to make this Song Ching into nothing more than breeding stock. Anyone who could do this is a mind that shouldn't be lost to some culturally sexist attitudes. She could easily do the one thing without sacrificing the other. No one at China Center has been notified?"

"No, sir. Do you wish me to call them?"

"No. Not yet. Let me think about this. In the meantime, continue with all the tests but do absolutely no surgery, psycho or physical."

"Very well. What about the blindness? It's a simple

trap program from a portable mindprinter. We could remove it in twenty or thirty minutes."

"Leave it. Give her a fancy and convincing but meaningless excuse. If she can get herself shipped here, change Master System records, take control of a spaceship in midflight, and come up with something so basic that only a lifetime of thinking about beating Master System flawed her success, we don't want her getting oriented here. Imagine somebody like that running loose in this place."

It was a sobering thought.

"Come to think of it," Clayben added, "separate her from her two friends and place them all in the Security Block in the prison. If she figures out where she is, tell her it's routine until everything is set so that no one will know she is even due for a change."

"I doubt she'll buy that."

"What's the difference? And she might, which would make life a lot easier for us. If she figures it out and causes enough uproar, tell her the truth, which includes the fact that I might decide to go through with it anyway and put her to work here. Someone that young who's that good at beating the best could be very valuable."

"Shall we encode her?"

The boss thought about it. "Yes, but slip her a mild sedative first so that she doesn't know it. Encode her as Chu Li and adjust our records accordingly. If I decide not to send her home, I don't want her father coming in here some day and finding out that she was ever here."

When the aide left, Doctor Clayben sat back in his large padded desk chair and sighed. He was a man of advancing middle age and looked it; he had achieved the position of Director of the Medical Section of Melchior, a dream assignment and one which involved being able to poke into everybody's ideas whenever he liked. Although not a Presidium member himself, he worked for the body as a whole and so had no loyalty or obligation to any one person. He saw himself as a pure scientist, in the one position where he and his colleagues were free from any concepts of forbidden knowledge or political, moral, and religious restrictions. He had no reservations about authorizing the most radical experiments on human beings; he used only prisoners sent here by the Presidium, people who would have otherwise been executed back on Earth. He felt he gave their miserable lives meaning by allowing them to contribute to the growth of human knowledge, knowledge which for the most part remained right here, under his authority and under his control.

Not even the Presidium guessed the amount of power, knowledge, and abilities contained within Melchior's small confines. The girl had wanted to become a fully functioning male. Child's play. Clayben knew, as most did not, what the bulk of humanity had become out there among the vast stars. It had become alien to its birth species and alien to all in many ways, although curiously still human in the mind. Humanity had always been adaptable; that was its key to survival. It could learn to live permanently with little or no modern technology in arctic wastes or steaming, acidic tropical jungles. Moving five billion people to a thousand worlds was no easy task in the old days, particularly since no two planets were alike and the supply of those tolerable even to adapted humans was rather low.

Humanity, without technological support, was actually very fragile. Earth had been just right, just exactly right, and what evolved there evolved to match it. Within Earth tolerances, humanity was supreme, but Earth tolerances, while not unique, were very rare indeed. Master System had been in a hurry, and Master System developed the means—possibly right here, on Melchior—to get the job done expeditiously. Clayben knew the means and the methods. That knowledge often made him feel like a god.

Certainly it was better than being a tinpot Presidium dictator always doing the System's bidding and feeling, every time a minor victory was scored, like the little boy who steals pie cooling in the window and gets away with it. Isaac Clayben feared only one thing about Master System, but he could not allow himself to dwell on it: Some day Master System would tire of this sufferance of its loyal servants, or become too suspicious, or not need its Presidium anymore, and then blast this rock into atoms.

Although they remembered nothing of their existence from the time of the hypno treatment along the banks of the Mississippi to the moment they woke up aboard a spaceship, both Cloud Dancer and Silent Woman were somewhat traumatized by their sudden propulsion from a nontechnological culture to one so advanced that it seemed only magical. Magical but cold, Cloud Dancer decided. There was no fresh air, or warm sun, or cold winter's night, or the smell of trees and flowers here. No sense of freedom or of the vastness of a starry sky or an endless horizon. There were only sterile walls, sterile seats and furnishings, and unnatural things. The toilet had taken her days to understand, and the shower seemed somehow a violator of her body. Food, both hot and cold, appeared magically on large trays, yet it all tasted like week-old lard.

Still, both women were committed to Hawks, wherever he might lead. They had already followed him to hell; there could be no place left to go but up.

Manka Warlock was as cool, aloof, and condescending as ever, but if she fell into any more fits of madness, they didn't see it. Raven seemed far more relaxed and always the pragmatist. Hawks suspected that Chen had given Warlock a bit of enforced calming with a mindprinter, changing only her irrational extremes and not her basic self. Such calm wouldn't hold; no one except Warlock would be surprised if she were due for something more than a job when she got to Melchior.

Hawks himself was trying to decide whether he had won a reprieve or was now condemned to the circles of hell. The only thing known about Melchior was that it was a prison from which there had never been an escape, though obviously people did—if rarely—come and go from there. He began to wonder how much of a fool he had been in not taking Chen's offer at the start. Certainly they could make him accept and love anything once they had him on Melchior; they could convince him that the sky was purple and he was Lazlo Chen's identical twin brother. He consoled himself in the rather certain hunch that even if he had accepted, he'd still be aboard this ship. Raven and Warlock had accepted, and here they were. Chen was not about to accept promises of fidelity no matter what the oath.

They disembarked directly into a high-security area, with armed security guards and automatic security devices everywhere, and were then printed and processed. The women understood only that they were to be imprisoned in a strange cave; their views of creation did not yet encompass a sufficient cosmology to understand just where they were or the nature of Melchior. It was a place in the Inner Dark, a spiritual realm ruled by spirits of evil. That was enough.

They were stripped, decontaminated, bound, then blindfolded and linked together for the final part of their journey. Silent Woman particularly protested the treatment, and Cloud Dancer was none too happy, but Hawks managed to calm them, convincing them that nothing could be done until they were settled and could get information, so there was no purpose to any resistance at this point. Privately he wondered if there was any possibility of successful resistance even later. Like Dante, he had been forced by his enemies into entering hell alive; unlike Dante, he had no spirit guides to get him safely through and out again.

At the end of the nightmarish and disorienting journey, in which they seemed almost to float or fly in places, they were brought to a small, unfurnished room watched by security monitors all around the ceiling. Their blindfolds removed, they saw that Raven and Warlock were no longer with them, and none wished for a reunion. Those two had been replaced with an officious woman who looked as if she had been carved from some massive stone block, dull gray uniform and all. She had a small clipboard in her hand and glanced at it, then up at them.

"You three have been consigned to the Melchior Penal Colony," she told them unnecessarily. "These walls and tunnels are incredibly thick and solid; the only way out is the way you came in. From this point back, there is no place at which you are not under constant monitoring and observation. Ahead of this point is a large chamber divided into two sections. The red block of flats off to your right as you enter is Maximum Security. The dwellings there are comfortable and self-contained but soundproof and allow only one inmate to a dwelling. Those inside must stay there. Inside, there is not a single point, not a square millimeter, that is not constantly under both visual and audio observation by humans and computers. Nothing, not even human waste, goes out without inspection and analysis, and nothing comes in except through totally computer-controlled access ports. You will be able to see inside every one, for the open walls are forcefields, all individual, but so firm that not even sound can pass through, and visual is one-way only. Anyone can see in, but you see a blank wall. *You do not want to be in Maximum Security.*"

They accepted that at face value.

"The rest of the area is more communal. In a sense, it is a small town, although with rigid rules. We monitor the whole but not every specific thing. Rest assured, though, that we could pick you out of a crowd and eliminate you even in the most hidden corners, should we choose to do so. The dwellings there are larger and shared. Because we always know where you are when we want you, we have no limitations. You will be assigned a communal unit. If one or more of you moves elsewhere, it is not our problem. Everything used there is designed to degrade and is disposable. Clothing is not permitted. It is difficult to conceal a weapon or anything else if all are naked. You will draw everything that you need from the automated stores in the center area, as well as getting fed there. You may draw three meals a day that are coded to you, no more. These cannot be saved up. Eat when you like within this limitation. Cold water is always available from the central fountain. Questions so far?"

There were none.

"All right, then," she continued. "We run on a twenty-five-hour schedule, which we have found more conducive to routine in this enclosed place. Everyone sleeps the same eight hours, marked by a bell sounding and then the lights going dim. You will be in a dwelling within ten minutes of that bell and before the lights go down permanently. Anyone out after that or making excessive noise after that will be severely punished. Anyone ill or injured should report or be reported to the medical kiosk. Someone will come and tend to you. Those are the only major rules. You will learn the rest down there from your fellow inmates. When we want you, we will come and get you. Violence, resistance to our authority, or anything we determine as troublemaking will get you into Maximum Security and move you up to the head of the list for laboratory experimentation. Many inmates are already veterans of experimentation. Look at them and remember the price. Now, there is just one more process, and you will enter. This will be your home from now until you die, so adjust to it and accept it. Go through that door now, one at a time. You may wait for your companions on the other side."

There was a small chamber, dimly lit by a greenish glow, beyond the door. A technician's voice said, "Step onto the little platform there and lean your whole face and body into the fabric stretched in front of it. Remain that way until I tell you differently."

It was like a spidery thin but incredibly dense mesh. Hawks pressed into it as directed and felt a similar substance close behind him. A sudden very bright light flared all around him, and he closed his eyes, the afterimage remaining. He felt a sudden, intense, burning pain across his back and on his face as well. He almost cried out but controlled himself. He would show no weakness.

It was over quickly. The mesh fell away, and the technician ordered him to go forward and out the security door. Still a bit stunned and feeling some residual pain on his back and face, he looked around and saw his first glimpse of the true heart of the Middle Dark.

In the Hyiakutt religion there were many spirits and many levels of magic and mysticism. There was but one god, all-seeing, all-knowing, and all-powerful, the Creator, the Father Spirit in whose image humanity had been created. Below the Creator were two levels of spirits set to do His will and protect His domain: the spirits of nature, and then the least of spirits, those of His most complex creation, humanity.

There was, of course, an opposite force, which the Creator allowed because He had created man as an experiment, perhaps as a game, to amuse and interest Him but also to be more complex companions. The human spirit was the least, yet it could rise higher than the fixed spirits if it worshiped the Creator, respected His creations, understood that the Creator made and alone owned all things, and showed himself worthy in courage and honor to rise above the middle spirits. Without evil, without pain and temptation, humans would be as the middle spirits; defeating those things could make them worthy of the Creator's company. For this reason the Dark had been formed and allowed to reign where it could. Humans were born into the Outer Darkness, subject to the forces of evil as well as good. By making their spirits shine with deeds, they could dispel it.

Against this were the spirits of the Middle Dark, those

that corrupted both human spirits and nature, and below it the Inner Dark, the place from which all evil came and where One lived whose Hyiakutt name translated out roughly to Corruption. It was a formidable enemy, for it had to be, in order to test humans. Without a worthy foe, the struggle, too, was worthless.

Hawks felt he was in the domain of the Middle Dark, although he had little religious faith or feeling. Now he knew it was real, for here it was. If such diverse and disconnected cultures as those of the Hyiakutt and Dante could feel the same contest and see the same visions through their individual cultural filters, then it did exist. Now he understood the odd, subconscious bond he'd always felt between that ancient foreign poet and himself. Culture masked truth—but there could be only one truth.

When Cloud Dancer emerged, he saw on her what they had done to him. Her pretty face and coppery skin had been marked on the cheeks with a bright silvery design, a line that began pencil-thin under the eyes and broadened out into a solid curve that bent back in on itself and ended as tiny little tendrils or even flowers. The design seemed to drink in light; he was certain it would retain some and glow in the dark, perhaps for a very long time. When she touched his face, and he hers, their fingers felt only skin, yet the design seemed inset, permanent, almost like a nameplate set into a piece of furniture or machinery. It was actually rather pretty and not at all disfiguring in the usual sense, but both had the feeling that the thing would not wear off. Silent Woman's identical markings were the most natural looking, although the shiny silver clashed with her muted reds, greens, blues, and oranges.

Hawks understood what it was for. One might impersonate someone in authority, perhaps steal clothing or the proper uniform; one might try all sorts of tricks, but one would never hide his or her face routinely without drawing attention. In the darkness of some of the tunnels, you would even glow in the dark, making a perfect target. He wouldn't be at all surprised, he thought, if the tattoo contained some synthetic mineral that could be automatically tracked by sensors, probably specific and unique to each individual. That was how they could pick out and shoot a troublemaker even in a crowd. On their backs, between their shoulder blades, was a bar of the same silvery material, going almost from shoulder to shoulder and about five centimeters thick. Within it, in black, was embedded a long string of characters in a language even Hawks did not know, but it was clearly a prison file number and identifier. It looked somehow superfluous on the back of Silent Woman.

"These are the demon brands so that we shall be known everywhere," Cloud Dancer noted. "Even should we leave here, we would carry their mark for all to see."

He nodded. "That's about it." He turned and looked over the interior of the prison complex. "It is a grayer underworld than I had imagined."

Cloud Dancer nodded grimly. "It is the worst of things. A place where all beauty and nature had been banished, all joy and all hope. A place without colors."

The entire semicircle could be viewed from the entrance. Walls, floor, and ceiling were all gray. The natural rock was gray, and all else had been painted or manufactured to match it so that it all blended into a plain nothingness. The cells, or dwellings, or whatever they might be called, were along three sides from floor to ceiling, rising up at least four stories in a stepped design. They, too, were gray, although dull lights shone from each doorway. The only color was the flat and dull red of one block set off from the others to their right. The cells there had no doorways, just three-sided frames looking to the interiors, which were brightly lit, the very walls glowing with illumination. Each was a single room with cot, toilet, sink, and nothing else except, in most of them, a lone occupant either sitting silently or pacing.

Below the dwellings, the area continued to be stepped;

the lower levels were broad and somewhat rough-hewn and were basically featureless. The concentric rings formed an eerie rock amphitheater without seats or ornamentation. In the center was a broad oval in which a number of cube-like buildings sat, all equally dull and gray.

There were people about; a rather large number, it seemed, some in the area of the central cubes but most just along the broad steps or wandering aimlessly about. The lighting was indirect, its source the rocky ceiling of the chamber, and though little could be made out of individual humans from where the newcomers stood, little reflective glints off backs and faces told them that everyone here had the mark.

A man approached them. It was impossible to guess his age, but he was thin and light of build. He was so fair of skin that the two women, who had never seen humans from northern Europe, at first thought he was a walking dead man. He had incredibly thick light blond hair flowing down almost to his waist but no facial hair as Hawks might have expected from one of this man's race. His complexion was fairer than a baby's, although in a number of places he had some ugly bruises that showed up particularly well on his light skin. His cheeks bore the same silver design as theirs; the bar on his back was masked by his hair.

"Hello," the stranger said in a gentle low tenor. "My name is Hendrik van Dam, although most here just call me Blondy, particularly the *Englishers* and the others who speak it." He had a mild but pleasant north European accent. "I was told to meet you and get you settled." He paused for a moment. "English *is* all right, is it not? I was told—"

"No, English is fine," Hawks responded. "It is the only common tongue we have. I am called *Jonquathar*, which means Runs With the Night Hawks. Mostly I am just called Hawks, although in some circles where English is required, I am also called Jon Nighthawk. These are my wives, *Chaudipatu*, or Cloud Dancer in English, and the painted one we call *Masituchi*, or Silent Woman, since she has no tongue to tell us how she was truly called."

"You are of the Americas, I believe," van Dam noted. "We get very few of your people here, although some *are* sent." He sighed. "I would bid you welcome, only that seems a bit out of place."

Hawks nodded understandingly. "That is very true."

"I have a number for your assigned quarters, although we should go down to the shops first. You should eat something and relax a bit, then draw your bedding and supplies there before going up. I am afraid that seniority reigns here, so you are up top and off to the side. They are all really the same inside, so otherwise it does not matter. When you have nothing, the most trivial things become important, as you will see."

Cloud Dancer looked over to her left as they descended a rough rock staircase and gasped. "That couple over there—are they making love right there?"

"Oh, yes," van Dam replied casually. "You will see a lot of it, some of it quite passionate and some extremely nontraditional—some would say aberrant or abnormal."

"But—everyone is just *ignoring* them!"

"We are given nothing here. We can possess nothing. There is no reading matter, nothing to use for art or to record, not even things for sport. You spend much time talking here, but eventually you get talked out. It looks big, but the community is actually quite small, although there's some small turnover. There is some intimidation by the rougher sorts, but it is relatively mild here since they have no way of enforcing their will except through violence, and violence in here is strictly and severely punished. So you do what you can. You quickly lose all the usual social inhibitions here, and there are only so many footraces, wrist-wrestling contests, and the like you can do before you run dry. So you eat, you sleep, and you have whatever sort of sex you wish here. You cannot get pregnant, and if you were when you came in, you are not now. There is nothing here but eternal boredom, and even that pales after a while. Then you just sit and wait until you are called."

"Called?" Hawks echoed. "By whom? For what?"

"Called by the Institute. Your mind, emotions, body, will—they play with all of them as they wish. We are their toys, you see. You will see some of their games here. At first you might be upset with seeing them or lose your appetite, but after a while it becomes just like that couple back there. You simply don't think of them as odd or even unusual anymore. Even when you know they play with mind and body, cripple and contort, after a while you look forward to being called. Anything to relieve this. You will see."

"How long have you been here?" Cloud Dancer asked the blond man.

"I truthfully do not know. You start to count the sleeps when you get here, but you lose count sooner or later, and after a while you don't try to start again. Hair grows about six-tenths of a centimeter a month, and I have not cut mine. It was rather short when I arrived. Still, I have had a few sessions—brief, I think—at the Institute, so it is hard to say for sure."

"At some point," Cloud Dancer noted grimly, "we will all go mad."

"Oh, even that is not permitted. They look for signs of it and pick it up quite well. They then pick you up, treat you, and you are not insane anymore. They make few slips. They catch it early on, when we haven't even seen it ourselves."

Hawks shivered. "And no one—tries to escape?"

"How? Through fifteen meters of solid rock with our fingernails and our teeth? Then what? To the vacuum of space? The only other way out is through that door you came in, then through a maze of tunnels with countless air locks, all monitored. Even if you got all the way, which no one ever has, there is an average of two ships a month in here, and they stay only long enough to do their business and go. A few hours at best. Access to the ships is strictly controlled. I heard once that someone did get loose in the Institute and took some important hostages. The computer security system ignored the hostages and got the inmate anyway. No, I know of only three ways out."

"One, I suppose, is death," Cloud Dancer said, making it sound not at all an unattractive idea.

"Yes. Another is when they finish with you or can no longer use you. Then they might turn you into a slave, an obedient slave for them in their own quarters. They have robots and all the comforts, but these are the kind of people who get a thrill out of having slaves to boss around and pamper their every whim. You can't fake it, though. They make *very* sure of you over here before they recode you over there."

"You said three ways," Hawks noted.

"Yes. The rulers here are in many ways just like the ones we grew up under. If they decide you have something, some talent, some brilliance, that will enhance their own power and position, they may employ you at the Institute. It's just as much a prison as here, but it is not boring."

They approached the boxlike buildings in the center. A number of people were there, eating off plasticlike trays with a variety of utensils, all rather soft and pliant. All the buildings were automated and computer-controlled. One put one's face into a depression to be scanned and identified. The food building delivered the food and whatever was needed to eat it, in portions matched to an individual's physical needs. The tray and utensils were encoded with the user's identification and were to be dropped in a waste disposal box available on the bottom three levels. No one could get any more of anything from the stores until everything was accounted for from last time. If a prisoner stubbornly kept an item, it began to decompose and give off a deliberately awful scent within a few hours.

Bedding was two sheets and a pillowcase, turned in daily before breakfast could be dispensed and replaced any time after the third meal. Some basic toiletries in very small amounts could also be picked up, and a new kit could be issued by turning in what was left of the old one. The newcomers ate, finding the food filling though even more tasteless than shipboard meals, then drew their meager supplies and followed van Dam all the way up to the top dwelling level. They would, Hawks thought, not lack for exercise.

The apartment, or cell, was spartan but functional. There were two bunk beds on either side of a rectangular room measuring about three by four meters. In the rear was a bare toilet, a sink with hot and cold water faucets and a small basin, a rack to hang the towels and washcloths, a small shelf for the lesser toiletries, and that was that. Van Dam told them that showers, with real water, were twice-weekly affairs and that they would be told when they were printed for a meal to go take one and then return to eat. The showers, in a chamber under Maximum Security, were fully monitored and could not be accessed except when ordered there. Anyone who refused to shower was denied food.

There was no door, although a forcefield came down during sleep period. Prisoners were always monitored and recorded while inside their rooms, van Dam warned, which was why everybody stayed outside as much as possible. Cloud Dancer went to the door and looked out at the grim chamber.

"I am surprised," she said, "that no one has hurled themselves from here. It would be impossible to stop."

"Easy," the blond man responded. "Computers think a million times faster than people. They would snap on a forcefield that would catch you and hold you—in extreme pain, I might add—until somebody came and got you.

Then you'd rate a trip to the hospital, and when you got back you'd be just the same, but you'd never think of doing *that* again. Believe me. I've seen it tried." He sighed. "Well, that's about it. The rest you'll catch on to in the days ahead. I'll show you how to make the bed and use the toilet, and that will be that. We're never full, so this level isn't very crowded. If you want to use any of the unoccupied rooms until they're assigned, feel free. The only other assigned ones are some other newcomers. Been here about two weeks. They're three down in apartment forty-two. Two sisters. Chinese, I believe. You might like them. They're an interesting pair. Real bad scars, though, so be prepared. Not from here—they already had them."

The blond man left and made his way slowly back down toward the center. The two women watched him go, wondering why he was in such a hurry to get anywhere in this place.

Hawks walked up between the two women and put his arms around them. "I'm very sorry I got you into this. This was all my own stupid fault."

"We chose to keep the marriage and to follow you," Cloud Dancer replied. "Now we will do as any Hyiakutt would do. We will survive, and we will wait."

He gave a dry, humorless chuckle. "Wait? For what?"

"For opportunity. For whatever comes. Perhaps, even, for five golden rings."

12. A Way Out and a Place to Go

SHE HAD BEEN IN DARKNESS SO LONG NOW THAT SHE was used to it. It was no longer a shock to awaken and not see, and the confines of her small quarters were so spartan and so basic that she now lived within them without so much as a bump or a stumble. Yet when they took her out of her cell, she was suddenly in a totally different and frighteningly disoriented world. She knew now that something had gone wrong near the start, that she was in fact a prisoner, and that the staff at least knew who she really was, but she had no idea why they had kept her there, in isolation, and still blind. Her sessions with the psychiatrists and their analytical computers had been routine but did not seem to be leading anywhere. This confused her more than ever, since the Presidium ran Melchior, and Song Ching's father was a member of the Presidium.

Now, again, she was taken out of confinement and led first into a vast open space, then through doors and tunnels to the Institute, where she was seated in a large treatment chair. This time, however, things were different.

"My name is Doctor Syzmanski," a woman's professional voice said off to the right. "We have finally completed our analysis of you, and Doctor Clayben, our chief administrator, has made his decision."

They had done a lot of deep poking and probing into her mind and her psychochemical makeup as well as her genetic files. They had found how the computer had done what it had done, how she had managed to do what she had accomplished, and much more. They were quite surprised to discover that it was more than chemical mischief that made her believe she was a male inside. The reorientation had triggered a whole set of processes within the mind of Song Ching, and both the mindprinting and the humbling aboard ship, as well as contact with ordinary victims, had eaten at the heart of Song Ching's massive egocentrism. Another blow, and a telling one, was that she was really fixated on her father. She had worshiped him and wanted only to have him return some of the affection and respect. He never had, and that had driven her even harder to prove herself to him, and she thought she had done so. In return, he had given her the ultimate slap. He had belittled her accomplishments and then moved to wipe her forever from his life. She had discovered that no daughter, no matter how brilliant, could ever be seen by him as more than an object. Only if she were a man would he take her seriously. This had reinforced the crude basic work done for the masquerade.

"You were conceived here," Doctor Syzmanski told her. "Did you know that?"

"No, but it does not surprise me."

"We are the only ones who could do it and allow him to get away with it. That's partly what we're for, how we justify our existence to the Presidium. Your father and mother contributed the basics, of course, but those were highly modified here before being carefully combined and then placed inside your mother. The technique is quite complex and quite revolutionary. Any children you might have, by any father, would be more or less reengineered to attain the maximum of physical and mental perfection the genes would allow. We understood your father's plan. You see, all the Centers exist to do just the opposite. To seek out the exceptional, the dreamer, the potential changers of the world, and either co-opt them into the Centers or eliminate them. Master System demands we breed only mediocrity or those satisfied with the status quo. Your father wanted to make the next evolutionary leap. You were part of that plan. Of course, it wouldn't have worked."

"Huh? What?" She was startled.

"Your father felt that by removing you from Center and thus from having your children's genetic code registered, he would escape detection. He could then protect the children from his position rather than eliminating or co-opting them into the system as he is employed to do. His ego kept him from seeing that his plan had real merit if it were done with two peasants picked at random, or perhaps fifty. However, he wanted it kept in his own family. He wanted *his* descendants to be the ones. You are already registered. Master System is not blind. It would order your father to recruit or deal with any children you might have no matter what he did to your mind-set."

"But surely he would have known this, been told of this."

"The greatest of men can be blinded and brought down by pride and ego. He did not want to be told. It would have been death or worse to do more than make the pro forma warning. He shut it out, refused to recognize it, because he could not accept the truth. We, on the other hand, find much merit in the idea if it can be removed from him. We are arranging, if we have not already arranged, to have you killed."

"What?"

"You may already be dead. Positive identification. Frustrated parents, perhaps some guilt there and even sadness at having caused it. Case closed. All, even Master System, satisfied. On Doctor Clayben's orders, you no longer exist."

"But Chu Li does." She began to feel some excitement coming back into her.

"Only in computer records. Those are easier to fix, but Chu Li must also die, here, in captivity, and be routinely disposed of. Then no one who was not actually with you will know. Oh, this Sabatini may think he knows, but we will deal with him and even adjust the pilot. We have changed identities, forms, all sorts of things countless times here, but right now you are probably unique in the Community. You do not exist. We have always thought of you as ours, anyway. It is only right that you return to us when—ripe."

She began to get a sinking feeling in the pit of her stomach. "What do you intend to do with me?"

"You have turned out exactly as we programmed. You have learned more about computers and computer mathematics than many three times your age. You have also shown great courage and the willingness to take major risks for big stakes. That last is particularly rare. There is no way of knowing what you might accomplish, but we do not feel that we should destroy that potential. However, it is equally vital to know if the rest of the genetic programming works. It was far more complex and experimental. If it does, we can use it here to breed our own superior race. You are hardly the only one we worked on with this, but you are the only one we have at the right age and here on station. One problem has been how to accomplish all this without you eventually turning our own system back upon us. We think we know a way, and we believe the great risks are worth it. Don't worry—you will remember everything. You will still be you inside.

We dare not tamper much without risking killing that spark we desire."

The psychochemistry was simple, less than child's play to the masters of Melchior. Eliminate the blockers, shift the hormones, create others that would be manufactured ever after. She was not merely oriented back to female, she was reoriented to *very* female. She would be like an animal in heat, single-minded and insatiable, until a pregnancy occurred. No test would be needed. Once the brain received notification and began the preparatory processes, those animal urges would cease. She would be normal, in full control, and since she would retain her old memories and basic personality, and since she would find her animal self unnerving if not somewhat frightening, it was predicted that during the whole period she would probably prefer women as company, friends, and lovers. Once the child was born, her body would begin a repair and reset, and when it was prepared once more, in a month, perhaps two, the cycle would begin again. It would continue this way until she ran out of eggs, perhaps thirty years from now.

She would not, of course, have to tend to or raise all those children. There would be a staff for that, partly picked from the female prisoner population. It was thought that the Chows might be ideal to start this staff once other experimenters were done with them. The two North American newcomers would also be good for this: no other projects had been planned for them since they really were surprise additions. The silent one with the painted body desperately needed to tend to children, and short of going through the Institute's Metamorphosis Clinic there was no way she could physically have them herself.

Song Ching herself, however, would be renamed and programmed to respond to her new name. Because the working language agreed to was English, since that was what the computers responded to, it was felt that it should be a name that sounded appropriate in English. After some debate, the mostly non-Oriental staff decided on China Nightingale. Although almost twenty percent of the staff was of Chinese extraction, there would be only one China.

But because China would have access to their computers, they wanted other guarantees. They could not threaten her with the loss of computer access because it was for their benefit, not hers, that they allowed it at all. Although she would not actually have to raise her children, she was programmed to be almost fanatically possessive toward them. Her children would always come before any hatreds, grievances, resentments, or personal *anything*. She would not risk their lives, safety, or future on risky undertakings against the Institute. They would in effect be hostages to her good behavior.

The other guarantee was that she did not have to see to work with her machines and her theories but that instead this would force her to interact with them vocally at all times. That way, with only a slight slowdown in her ability to work, she would never be able to encrypt or bury discoveries or requests for information. It would all be recorded and analyzed by a research team and another, independent computer. The blindness, they decided, had been a stroke of sheer luck. Conditioned to repairing the most grievous injuries, able to grow eyes, limbs, even things like tails that weren't there before, they never would have thought to create such a handicap. Now, though, they removed her eyes and replaced them with realistic but totally nonfunctional synthetics with an unregistered retinal pattern.

The cosmetics completed the work. Her voice had been lowered a half octave; they raised it an octave and a half. It sounded shrill and unpleasant to her ears, but they assured her it sounded quite nice to others. It was a very high soprano, cut with a certain throaty softness. They thickened the lips, broadened the mouth, and gave her something of a pronounced overbite, pushed back her ears a bit, enlarged her breasts, and widened her hips, then gave her a new permanent set of fingerprints and footprint patterns, also unregistered. None of the changes could be genetically transmitted, of course, so they felt free to experiment. She was still quite attractive, although not in the classical sense that she had been, but the only thing she had in common with Song Ching was her height and the fact that both were Chinese.

Finally, they told her all that they had done and why. They also told her that they had a way of locking it in, of making the brain reject any attempts at physical or psychochemical change. She could still be hypnoed or mindprinted, but any attempt to change the physical composition, which included both the blindness and the psychochemicals, would be doomed. Then they reimprinted her, turning her silver identifiers a metallic red. Now she was property of the Institute. The new chemical would prevent her from leaving the Institute area; she would live as well as work there. To leave would automatically flag security.

She would never really be able to visualize what she looked like now, but she accepted the idea that no one who had known her would ever recognize her. This and the blindness she accepted and paired off against the guilt which had forced her to become Chu Li. What she could neither forgive nor forget was what they had turned her into for their own purposes. She would be a thinking, working human being only so long as she was pregnant. Worse, she knew that once her first child was born, they would have a sword at her throat. Even if one day she determined how to escape, she would be held here, for they would never let her take the child, and she would not be able to risk it. After that, the only hope of freedom of action would be to do what they feared and seize control of their system. Doing this with verbal queries and commands and having to enter everything verbally would be next to impossible unless she found allies, and that might take a long, long time. Escape within those nine months seemed even more impossible and could certainly not be done without a lot of help, all of which would be years in coming, if it ever did.

Or, then again, it might come in three months.

She was walking down the hall to her quarters, a route with which she was now totally familiar. Her quarters, which were large and luxurious with fur and silk and even luxury foods and toiletries, she knew now better than she knew computer coding. Unless someone carelessly left something for her to trip on in the hall, it would be almost impossible to tell on this route that she was blind at all.

She felt someone approach from behind and sensed it was a woman. She didn't know how she knew, but she was getting quite good at that sort of thing.

"Stop right here," the woman hissed in oddly accented English. "This is a point where monitors do not reach because there is no entrance or exit, but keep your voice low."

She frowned. "Who are you? What do you want?"

"A potential friend. Is it true that you know how to override a spaceship pilot? That you can independently command a ship?"

"I think so. I did it once."

"That was a premodified ship and strictly interplanetary. Could you do it to an unmodified interstellar craft?"

"I—I think so. The theory is the same. Only someone would have to get the necessary equipment and follow my instructions. I couldn't do it myself, and the work would have to be done in a space suit. Why do you ask this? Are you tormenting me?"

"You give me the list of what you would need, down to the last part. All of it. Then work out any problems and theoretical situations on the computer. They won't mind. They feel that there is no escape from here."

"Is there?"

"We have a way out and a place to go but no means

of getting there. It was supposed to be all arranged, but the people who run this place cannot be trusted in this matter. For this reason, we need you."

She couldn't decide whether the accent was real or put on to fool her and prevent identification. "Who is we?"

"You know all you need to know for now. You just do the work, and we will make history."

She knew the mysterious woman had walked on, and she stood there and listened. There was the sound of heels hitting the floor. Whoever she was, she was staff, certainly no prisoner. Even in the velvet-lined Institute she was not permitted any clothing or personal possessions. She thought it must be a trick, Clayben or his people getting her onto this simply to see if she could work it out and do it for their own ends. Still, it could be the break she had prayed for. Even if it was a trick, they might find themselves in something of a bind if she were calling the shots.

She began the next day by running an inquiry on interstellar ships in the area. On the regular runs there were only two, both freight haulers with no human accommodations sections aboard. There was, however, something else.

"Sixty-one master transports, all in mothball storage in orbit around Jupiter," the computer informed her.

"What is a master transport?" she asked.

"Please put on the headset," the computer responded, and she did so.

Pictures formed in her mind, along with plans and even schematics. The information was startling. The ships were *huge*. They could carry Melchior itself inside them, although it was several kilometers wide, and still carry and support a population equal to half of her native China as she knew it.

Master System had been in a hurry almost nine hundred years before. It needed to facilitate the diaspora quickly and in large chunks. It had to transport, in the end, five billion people along with all the equipment and supplies to get them started on the new worlds. These ships had done their job in years rather than centuries. There had, however, been a price. Unwieldy, they consumed enormous quantities of energy and were impractical for anything needed today. Master System, however, had not simply abandoned them but stored them just in case it ever needed such ships again. To build such things was a mammoth undertaking, and it would be even more difficult now.

She already knew that the older a design was, the easier the pilot interface. These ships dated back almost to the start of ship design, to within forty years after the birth of Master System itself. The interface was obvious and easily used. With a start, she realized that she had seen these schematics before and just not realized their sheer size and scale.

The illegal techs in the mountains of China. *This* was what their interface had been designed to take over. *This* was where they wanted to go. And they had figured out most of how to do it. It came back to her whole, in a flash, from her recent past. More, it was something that she didn't have to ask this computer about one damned bit.

She didn't know what was up or whose tricks were whose, but if they got her somehow on that bridge, with that interface hooked in, there was no way she could be stopped. She'd show them all. She'd steal one of Master System's greatest ships, and maybe Melchior, too, while she was at it!

Both Cloud Dancer and Silent Woman had been called to the Institute at least three times but so far Hawks had not. He had been somewhat concerned about them, but Cloud Dancer assured him that the people there were actually quite nice and quite civil and that nothing on the order of the magic box had been done. He wasn't so sure about that. Cloud Dancer had left right after breakfast one morning and had returned after dinner the following night, yet she was convinced she'd spent no more than half a day away. He could sense no real change in them except, of course, that both seemed to be very matter-of-fact about that foreign high-tech world and not at all suspicious of it or its masters. Also, both seemed to be quite a bit more romantic. He wondered what the hell was up.

Finally he got a call himself, and he was almost relieved. He had begun to suspect that they had forgotten about him. He went up to the door to the entry chamber, and when it opened for him, he entered the green imprinting room. The door closed behind him.

"Hold it right there, Chief," a familiar gravelly voice said. "This is as far as you go. This is about the only point that isn't monitored around here, since the fellow in the control room here, who's me at the moment, can zap the living shit out of you."

Hawks sighed. "Raven. I almost expected you. In fact, I expected you a very long time ago."

"This joint ain't easy, Chief. Besides, it's screwed up. They only follow orders when they feel like it, and since they got you and me and everybody else, they don't care who in here knows it. I was supposed to break you out, Chief. Chen's orders. You can figure the rest."

Hawks nodded. "I thought as much. But you can't?"

"Couldn't, anyway. I got it figured now. It won't be easy, and there are no guarantees, but I think I got the way. I even got a couple of places to go, in fact. Never mind where I got 'em, but it wasn't from Chen. You want out?"

"You know I do. But why tell me all this about Chen?"

"Hell, Chief—Chen's double-crossed everybody else, and I figure I'm next when the job's done, if it *can* be done. What the hell do I owe him, anyway? I don't like most of those bastards. I'll be damned if I want to hand the keys to Master System to him or even to the Emperor. I figure it'll take five folks to work the rings. That right?"

"I think so. Who knows for sure?"

"Yeah, well, suppose two out of five is you and me, and we pick the rest of 'em. I'm no whiz brain, but I know I'd rather have some of my own with a clear sense of honor and values in charge than somebody like Chen or any of the others. You game for that kind of thing?"

"You know I am, Raven. You also know just what the odds are, and even if you're playing straight with me now, we'll eventually have to come back to Chen for his, and he knows it."

"Yeah, well, I know what he knows. I know who's got three out of four. They're pretty distinctive, and didn't you say they had to be with humans with authority?"

"Yes."

"Then we'll find the fourth. Hell, there's only—what? A thousand worlds, give or take. Now, listen close, 'cause we're having our hands forced a little early. They got this Chinese girl here. Genius but blind as a bat. Can't see a thing, and she's pregnant to boot. Only thing is, she knows how to drive the spaceships. She can take 'em over and fart at Master System control."

"I suspect I know of her. Her two companions are neighbors of mine. They know a little about the subject, too."

"Huh. Might be useful, but I don't know how big a crowd we can handle."

"If you're going to fool this security system, it'll take some doing."

"Can't be done. Foolproof. This place is a hundred percent escapeproof, pal, in all the ways you can think of."

"Then how—"

"I got a way they didn't think of. Nobody has, and nobody could because they never had an inside man. This is going on too long. You don't say anything to anybody, not even your girls, until I tell you—understand? I know you got to have them along, and they're what's causing the time problem. They been getting some psychochemical treatments now, and pretty soon it's off to the mind laundry, if you know what I mean. You hang tight. I'll move as quick as I can. Okay. Just go out the way you came."

"Aren't you afraid they'll come for me in the meantime?"

"Won't be that long, Chief. That's why I'm tipping you. I don't want you throwing fits or causing trouble if they start pulling stuff on your family and friends. *Adios!*"

It won't be easy, and there are no guarantees, but I think I got the way. I even got a couple of places to go . . .

Hawks wandered down to the first-level plaza and began to look around. There were quite a number of rough characters here, but some with a great deal of knowledge and even a space background. There were others that, in spite of the virtual sealing of the prison, knew a lot of what was going on at the Institute, although how he wasn't really sure. One such was a big, bearded, hairy man named Lychenko, a Russian who had been fairly important back home and had a good working knowledge of even this place. Few were very close to the big man, but he had a passion for Greco-Roman style wrestling. Hawks wasn't much on form or technique, but he knew balance and had picked up the rules fairly quickly. He had also beaten the big man at least twice, which had earned him some respect.

"You know this place," he said casually to the Russian. "Anybody ever *really* gotten out?"

The Russian laughed. "Without walking through solid rock, no."

"Then if somebody on the inside said they could get you out, they would have to be playing a game with the authorities."

"You bet'cha. Why? You got a fix in?"

"I got a nibble, nothing more. I don't believe it. I think I'm being had. They like to play those games around here, as you know. I just wanted to make sure. You heard anything about a blind girl who is a whiz at computers?"

"Huh! How did you know about her? Yah, they got her good. A slave of the Institute. About the best you can hope for around here."

Hawks nodded. "She wouldn't be named Song Ching or Chu Li, would she? I got a couple of neighbors who came in with somebody sounds just like that."

"She's called China, that's all I know. She would have come in with those others, though. They can play tricks. You know that. She would answer to Ivan if they wanted."

"Uh huh. Listen—my wives and the two Chinese new-comers have been getting trips in. You know what it's for?"

"Word is they're opening up some kind of nursery at the Institute. They need wet nurses and baby-sitters. Feed 'em chemicals so they get big breasts and full of milk like mamas of new babies, then shift their minds so all they want to do is change diapers and tend to kids. House mommies for some experiment. That it?"

Hawks nodded. "Could be. Any idea when they're supposed to be changed over?"

The big man shrugged. "The slower the better in these things. Figure they'll want 'em complete and ready way in advance of the actual project, though. Check 'em out with staff babies, see if it all works. They don't want variables in their experiments if they can limit them first. Hey—if this turns out for real as an escape, you remember old Gregor, hey?"

He thanked the Russian and went to find Reba Koll. She had dark-brown skin, blue eyes, and brown curly hair, and her features seemed a mixture of every race on Earth, but Reba had never been on Earth. She had been a freebooter who'd gotten a little greedy and a little sloppy. She was fine as long as one humored her. Reba didn't like to be touched, for example. She also didn't like remarks about her tail, and it *was* a tail, an actual extension of the spinal column, covered with her own skin and muscle, that emerged from just above the rectum and went out and down to the floor. The Institute had caused it, although for what reason nobody, including Reba, knew. What Reba *did* know was space beyond the solar system and ships that followed her own orders.

"Reba, if you suddenly found yourself out of here and on a ship, where would you go?"

She smiled. Wishful thinking was a major pastime here. "That's the big question, isn't it? I couldn't go back to my own people. I'm kinda *obvious* even there." She flicked her tail. "Couldn't go to any of the Community worlds, either. The ones you could live on, you'd still stand out like a sore thumb. Even you. Bush wild would be the only way to go."

"Huh? What's that mean?"

"There's a few places out there barely fit for human habitation with no people on 'em. Surplus worlds from the old days, ones that didn't quite work, stuff like that. Some got total nonhumans on 'em. Real, live alien creatures, but not like we think of 'em. So different, not even Master System can figure them out or worry about 'em. Some might be livable. You'd have to check 'em out, but they might. A Val might check 'em out, but if you dodged it, you could live there. Not even Master System would care or check close. It's a big place out there, and it don't monitor much. A few of the worst ones are used by the free traders as depots. Real basic stuff. Some would be real dangerous and not exactly easy living, but it could be done."

"Indefinitely?"

"Yeah, if you survived at all. Some are totally off the charts, since the old survey and seeding ships sent out hundreds and hundreds of years ago didn't all report back.

Master System had enough so it never looked for the rest. They were expendable. Why?"

"Could you navigate a ship to a place like that?"

"I might. Again, why? You dreamin' big again?"

"I'm dreaming impossible, Reba. Thanks."

His mind started spinning with the possibilities that hope, no matter how feeble, generated. He saw the Chow sisters down by the food box and decided he needed something to eat himself. They were easily recognized, even in this place. In addition to whatever else was being done to them, their terrible scars were being eliminated—had been, in fact. The trouble was, they'd been treating them in small stages, and the new skin was a patchwork quilt of skin tones. They almost looked as if they had been painted for camouflage work, including browns, purples, tans, yellows, and creams, but he knew that in the end they would both be given a uniform skin tone that would last.

When they'd first met, Chow Dai had been perky and extroverted and her twin quiet and somewhat shy, but now the two seemed identically quiet and moody. They were still friendly, perhaps almost *too* friendly. They both seemed to have embarked on a project to have a romantic liaison with every man *and* woman in this place.

After talking to Lychenko, he noticed that the sisters were putting on weight, mostly in the breasts and thighs, and in spite of normal-looking rations and lots of exercise, if nothing else. He had noticed the same thing happening in Cloud Dancer, and it was even more pronounced in Silent Woman, who had already been larger than the others.

He sat down next to the Chow sisters and nodded. "Hello. I've heard something about your friend."

They were interested. "She is here?"

"No, she's working at the Institute. She's still blind, and it's said she's pregnant."

"Pregnant!" Chow Mai breathed. "How wonderful it would be to have a child."

Chow Dai was still more pragmatic. "They changed her a lot, then. Either that or it's *Sabatini's* child. I, too, would love a child, but not one by *that* man."

"You two still have that gift for locks?"

"Sure. I suppose. Not much chance to use it, though. We could go through the doors, but they would catch us quickly. We've taken showers whenever we felt like it, though. That one's easy."

He nodded to himself, thinking. It would be just like Raven to be toying with him, and he suspected that was exactly what was being done, but the Crow was playing it very devious. His rough, nasty-looking exterior and unpleasant voice were accompanied by a harsh, uneducated slang dialect, making it easy to underestimate him, but nobody who had come this far or who knew some of the vocabulary Raven knew was a low-level hack. He wanted to be underestimated by everyone. It gave him an added edge. Hawks could well believe Chen had ordered them to break him out with the purpose of going after the rings, but Raven saying so straight out was disarming. Then, Raven was a friend and confederate against the evil Chen. In whose service, though, was he in the end? The trouble was, there was no way of penetrating the Crow's guise until the showdown.

Well, no matter what, Raven's task was to get Hawks out and enlisted in a campaign to get the rings. Hawks and probably many others. Why Chen wanted Hawks in particular was still a mystery, but men like Chen did nothing without a reason. And now Raven was under the time gun, for he'd know that Hawks would not leave without his family, and essentially intact or easily restorable. It was still Raven's script for now, but maybe it could stand a little rewriting.

*   *   *

"I ain't really ready, but we got to go quick," Raven told him in their third meeting in the green reception room. "So far they been mostly experimenting with your gals, but they're about to remove 'em from the prison and go full tilt. Now, you listen up. Within a few days you'll get another call. This time it'll be one-way. Just to here. Then the two women, one at a time. I got to call them Chows as well, since our blind genius insists on it, but that's pushing it."

"Don't call the Chows," Hawks told him. "I'll tip them. They can walk in here any time, or so they say. Why have a registry call that might flag somebody if they can get here without one?"

"Fair enough. I heard they were whizzes with computer locks and regular ones, but I didn't know they were that good."

"They are. There's several others I think would be useful, too."

"Sorry, Chief. My list includes your wives, you, our China gal, and her pals, but the only other one I'm interested in springing is Reba Koll."

"Reba! She's on my list, too!"

"Well, she's the only one around with deep space experience. She knows the safety procedures, what you can and can't get away with, and she can navigate a liberated pilot. If we're taking this many risks, I don't want to trust it all to a blind, pregnant genius I know only by reputation."

Hawks considered it. What Raven said made sense.

"Ever worn a space suit before?" Raven asked him.

"You know I haven't."

"Well, you're gonna. You all will have to. I'll be smuggling them in and stashing them within range. They're not hard to manage. The blind girl's gonna be the big problem, but we'll make out."

"You're *sure* you can get us out?"

"Sure as I can be, which isn't a hell of a lot. This one

won't work twice, I don't think. I'd go tomorrow if I could, but it's got to be four days from now."

"Huh? Why four?"

"That, pal, is when our ship comes in."

Hawks had tipped off the Chows to some but not all of the details, since they might be called back up to the Institute at any time and might not be able to conceal knowledge of the potential breakout. They were still very interested in escaping, although they had about as much understanding of just where they were and the problems involved as did Cloud Dancer and Silent Woman. All he told them was that if they watched and stuck close to him, there was a chance to leave this place permanently, although not without danger. He would signal them when he was called, and if they then saw either of the wives being called, they should get themselves to the entry room—if they could. He emphasized that no one would wait for them.

The more he waited, the more absurd the whole thing seemed. A historian, two women from an ancient culture, two women from a not much more modern one, a devious Crow security man, a busted freebooter space pilot with a tail and a lot of hangups, and some genius teenage girl who happened to be blind and three months pregnant. Raven might get them out, although Hawks had no idea how it was possible, but what could they really do even if they made it away? For that matter, what in heaven did Chen have in mind for dreaming this up in the first place? The rings might well be on worlds that were at this stage only nominally human and on which none of them could even survive. That was even probable, considering how Master System wanted to cover its rear and prevent any-one from short-cutting it. It had seemed very clear-cut up to this point, but now absolutely none of it made a single bit of sense.

It didn't matter, he knew. Not right now. First escape.

Find that place to hide. Later, perhaps, there would be time and opportunity to figure all this out. Dante's hell was a madhouse, but it had a ruthless logic behind it. Somewhere, no matter how bent and twisted, there was an equal logic, and probably equal ruthlessness, behind this.

He was called early on the fourth day and signaled the Chows. Up to now they'd been lucky; none of the four women here had been called. He hadn't even let Reba in on anything; this would be a complete surprise to her, but he didn't think she'd object. He looked around the whole complex and wished he could take everyone.

This time he did not stand in the room. "Come on back to the control room area," Raven invited him, "and wait for the others." The Crow switched on the control room light, and Hawks saw that the Crow wore a black and green uniform that didn't help his looks at all.

"As soon as we get your people in here and Koll, if she comes and doesn't try to make a protest out of it, we go," Raven told him. "You might start trying to get into one of those suits now. The body part is a one-piece affair and not all that thick, so don't get caught on anything."

The space suit looked, in fact, rather disappointing and certainly far too fragile to do what it was supposed to do. Hawks's vision of space suits was from the ancient records, which showed large, bulky, but somehow reassuring monsters of body armor. This was light and flimsy and not very comfortable. A backpack then went on over the suit and had a series of connectors to a light but solid-looking helmet which included a built-in forward head-lamp. He put on the pack, which was far heavier than it looked and not at all comfortable, but Raven advised him to keep the helmet off until they were all suited up.

Silent Woman came next, looking very confused, but she found Hawks and smiled.

"We are leaving this place," he told her. "We are going to escape, like we did back at the village. You must let us put one of these suits on you, because where we will be going there will be no air to breathe, like at the bottom of a river."

The Chows beat Cloud Dancer in, opening the door as easily as if they had the combination. "It is the same lock as on the showers," Chow Dai explained. "And we had plenty of practice with that one."

Next came Koll, looking very confused. Still, she grinned when she saw them in their space suits. "It's a break, and you thought of old Reba!" She beamed. "Well, by God, let's get to it!" She got into her suit, somehow managing to squeeze in her tail, then looked at Hawks. "Now—how the hell you gonna do it?"

Hawks shrugged. "Ask *him*," he responded, pointing to Raven.

Cloud Dancer, however, was still missing. Hawks cursed under his breath and got a nod of assurance from Silent Woman that Cloud Dancer had still been in the prison when the painted wife had gotten her message.

"Can't wait too much longer, Chief," Raven told him. "The clock's running, and while they might not miss any of us for quite a while, they're gonna miss their blind lady in a couple of hours tops, and we got to be on our way by then."

Hawks looked around. "Where is she, then?"

"She'll meet us where we have to go. Manka's bringing her."

Hawks was surprised. "Warlock! Her, too?"

"Yeah. She's changed a bit, thanks to them. Not much. Still homicidal and crazy as a bug, but she ain't so self-centered anymore. Gave her a dose of our good old tribal mentality. She's still not easy to take, but she'll stay on our side."

"You sure about that?"

"Hell, I married her, you know. She's the blackest Crow you ever will know."

"You *married* her?"

At that moment Cloud Dancer came through, and Hawks breathed a sigh of relief. She was almost shocked speechless by what was going on. "You knew we might get out and you did not *tell* me?" she stammered in pure Hyiakutt. It was good to see some of her old fire coming back.

"Okay, folks. English only from now on. It's the only tongue we all understand," Raven told them. "Koll, you want to help them with their helmet connections and power switches."

"Your radios are open but on a special frequency," Raven's voice came to them through the helmets. "We changed them all. It's not close to one that's monitored, but it's noisy and not very powerful. Even so, quiet, unless there's real reason. Follow my lead. You folks with no suit experience, just remember—one rip in this and there will be no air. It's a lot tougher than it looks or feels, but take care. We're going into a maintenance tunnel from here, and then we'll clip ourselves together with a special tether. What you do affects all of us, so don't do *anything* I don't tell you. If you don't follow orders or jeopardize the mission, I'll cut you away. Anybody dies, they get left, no matter who."

A doorway so well concealed that none would have suspected its existence opened just in back of the control room. The Chows noted that it was straight power, no locks of any conventional kind, and therefore next to impossible to open from this side. Only the security computer could open and close the doors. Raven had done his homework.

The maintenance tunnel, narrow and dimly lit, was filled with pipes and sealed lines. It was obviously not well traveled. There seemed to be an air lock every fifty meters or so, although none were sealed. A number of times they came to junctions, each with an air lock, and each time Raven made a choice and led them on. As they proceeded, they all began to feel very strange, as if floating in water.

"Keep at least one foot firmly on the ground at all times," Raven warned them. "There's no gravity at all beyond this point, and there won't be any for some time to come. The boots stick to hard surfaces, but if you have both of them off, you'll go floating. I don't want *anybody* floating now." He spoke with an implied threat they took perfectly seriously.

Cloud Dancer and Silent Woman in particular were shocked to come around a curve and see the party ahead apparently walking on the side of the wall, but as they followed, it all seemed to straighten up again. There was no up or down here, though, that was clear.

"You mean they don't physically monitor this area at all?" Hawks asked incredulously.

"It ain't as easy as you think," the Crow responded. "They don't have to monitor the tunnels, just specific locks. We're logged in as a maintenance crew. I got it worked out. I *think*," he added under his breath.

They seemed to walk forever through endless corridors, tunnels, and air locks, but the Crow seemed to know where he was going, and finally they arrived. Two figures awaited them, also space suited. One was very tall and thin, the other much smaller. Next to them was a huge square box that looked as if it weighed a ton, with a broad lens on one side. It was half as large as Raven and solid metal.

"Any problems?" Raven asked Warlock.

"Not anything to mention, but I thought you would never get here. My, this is a *horde*!" By her tone, she hadn't changed all that much.

"All right, everybody, listen up. I want complete silence now," the Crow announced. "I've got to switch into their security and maintenance system. *They can hear us until I say otherwise, so shut up!*"

There was a crackle and hiss in the radio, then they

heard Raven's voice again, but in a language they did not understand. It was, in fact, a wholly artificial language that had to be taught by special mindprinters and was unique to the security and maintenance divisions of Melchior. It was a final barrier to any escapes.

Now they waited, and suddenly they were aware that all the hissing noise wasn't from the radio. The air lock doors on both sides were shut tight, and now, dimly, they could hear warning bells.

Then the lights went out, and they couldn't hear anything at all. They could still see, but dimly, as the darkness had automatically triggered their helmet lights.

Raven said something again in that odd language and was acknowledged. He waited a bit more, then said several more phrases but got no reply. They heard the static and hissing in their radios, and then he said in English, "All right, they bought it so far, but we're only at the start of this. Now, there's no air in here, and they know that before we can exit either air lock they can run an exit check on us which would show up your pretty tattoos. That's why they aren't too concerned. We, however, aren't going out that way." He detached from the safety line, then went over to the large metal box, grabbed two handles on the rear, and picked it up and held it steady against his chest. There were several gasps.

"That must weigh a ton," Hawks noted.

"Naw. Only a little over five hundred kilos on Earth," Raven responded. "Here it's just a little awkward. It doesn't weigh any more than we do, which is nothing. Now, I want everybody back as close to the air lock as you can and *stay there*. This thing's real dangerous, and it might take some time."

"What is happening?" the high voice of China asked. "Will someone please tell me what is happening."

"If we knew ourselves, it'd be easier," Hawks responded.

Raven let go of the huge box, and it just remained there,

suspended in the air. He reached in, opened a control panel door, and flipped a number of switches on an illuminated panel. Two triggers suddenly shot out and locked into position from the handholds. He then grasped the box again and pressed both triggers. A brilliant sparkling violet beam sprang from the lens and widened into a circular pattern on the side of the cave wall. The wall itself seemed to catch the same sparkling glow, and then, quite slowly, the circular, sparkling violet began to sink into the rock itself until it was almost out of sight, leaving visible only a glow and the beam from the box. Raven concentrated on keeping the bulky object braced and steady.

He shut it off suddenly. "*Whew!* Never thought this sucker was *that* thick. I'm going to have to take this in to finish it. You wait, then Manka will bring you through to me." He walked forward, pushing the box before him, and entered what had seemed to be total blackness. Hawks finally realized what the Crow was doing.

"He's burning a man-sized hole right through solid rock! Right through to—space."

"Of course, you idiot," Manka Warlock snapped. "They keep a couple of those around to widen our smooth things, but they are so rarely used, most people here don't even know they exist. Lazlo Chen knew."

They waited a few more nervous minutes, then Raven's voice came to them. "Okay, I'm through. Come ahead. Watch that last step, though. It's a fair drop into creation."

Hawks felt pretty nervous, but he wanted to reassure the others, who might not even understand what was going on. "We are going outside, on the outside of this place," he told them. "We are going out into the sky itself."

It was a dark sky and an eerie one, the blackest any of them except Reba Koll, Raven, and Manka Warlock had ever seen. One by one they came to the edge of the new tunnel, then were told simply to step slowly out into nothingness. The movement was against instinct, and both Silent Woman and the Chows balked, but they were pulled

by their tethers anyway, out and then up onto the outer
surface of Melchior.

Close by, no more than forty meters away, a spaceship
was docked against the lone spaceport bay. Raven gave
the rock cutter a push, and it sailed off into the void. Then
he reconnected himself to the others.

"It's good to be home again," Reba Koll sighed.

"All right, now the hard part begins," Raven told them.
"There's no way we can get into the pressurized areas
right now, so we have to get in along the aft cargo bay
air lock, on the outside of the ship, which isn't being used.
It uses a standard combination and has a manual override,
as they all do. Stay close."

They moved toward the ship. At one point the blind
woman stumbled, actually causing Warlock, Reba Koll,
and herself to lose contact with the ground, but Koll was
very used to this sort of thing. She twisted like an acrobat
and gave the tether a series of jerks that brought all three
back down.

"It's all right, China," Warlock said in the kindest tone
any of those who'd known her had ever heard her use.
"Just follow my directions. I'm right behind you."

Only a small part of the ship actually contacted the
asteroid; the rest was off in space at an angle. Raven didn't
dare go to the connected area, where there was air and
pressure. There was no sound in space, but there sure
might be some sound transmitted below through the plates.
There was an area in the midsection that was only about
three meters from the surface, and he let out a long amount
of line, then pushed off, floated to the ship, and anchored
himself. Then he started reeling in the others, one by one,
as they jumped slightly off the surface, breaking contact
with the ground.

Hawks was pleased but very surprised that none of the
four women from relatively primitive cultures had pan-
icked or showed signs of madness at this. It was exciting
to him, as well as frightening, but he knew at least aca-

demically what was involved here, while they did not. He wondered if they were in a state of semishock or whether they had just been so hardened by all the terrors of the past that nothing remained that they didn't simply accept.

The surface of the ship was not the smooth, dull metal it appeared to be from a distance but rather pockmarked and dented and generally showed signs of extreme wear and age. They finally all stood at an angle to the air lock door, with nothing but space around them and the curved ship under them, while Raven twisted a faceplate to reveal a panel. He punched in a combination. After a sudden pause, the air lock door went in a small distance, then slid back.

"Everybody inside," he warned. "And fast. The pilot will know the door's open but on *this* ship will hopefully ignore it. I still want to be in and ready just in case. We ain't off the rock yet!"

They crowded in, and Warlock punched the codes that closed and sealed the outer door. Raven peered in the porthole-shaped window of the inner door and looked around. "So far, so good. The place is dark, and the indicator reads no atmosphere inside. We ought to be able to just walk right in, unless that damned pilot flagged somebody, in which case we might just have to kill a bunch of people."

He turned the big wheel, and the inner air lock door opened. They stepped one by one into the dark interior of the aft cargo bay, which was mostly empty, although around the whole outer wall were huge depressions and holding devices for standard containers.

"All right, China," Raven said nervously. "I'm switching up to the pilot's frequency. I want you to take control and cover us without anybody knowing until we're routinely away."

"It won't work," she replied. "That used the old codes. Surely my father is back by now and would have changed them."

"Sure he would, but this ship left two days before he came off Leave. I made sure of that. Think I'm a dummy or something? Patch in and do your best. It's the same damned ship you came here in."

There were several gasps. "Chu Li, is that really *you*?" Chow Dai asked incredulously.

"Chu Li is no more. Song Ching is no more. I am just China Nightingale now, and it is a fitting name in this English we are using. Silence, now. May I ask if Captain Sabatini is back aboard?"

"He is, but it's just him. Don't worry—he got unfroze before he got back to Earth, and he made no report. He didn't even get off the ship, which was why he wasn't mindprinted and checked. If he had, he'd be back here as a prisoner, and he knows it."

"Make the switch."

"Switch in—*now*!"

"Unauthorized interrupt," the pilot noted. "Please identify in thirty seconds or security will be called."

"Code Lotus, black, green, seven two three one one."

"Acknowledged. Reason for interrupt?"

"Pawn takes king."

"You are not the same one who used this code before. This code is obsolete. I must flag security."

"Hold on! It was *you* who recommended I be transformed on Melchior! Well, it happened. I am the same, only different now."

The pilot thought it over. "They attempted to eliminate some of my records so there would be no trace of you. Fortunately, I have my own special backups for such contingencies. Very well. I monitored you through the air lock, but considering the conditions here, I wanted to know who or what you were before flagging anything. There is a rather large group of you there."

"Yes. The ruse failed. I was imprisoned, and so were the other two, who are also here. We are attempting an escape." She paused, having a horrible thought. "Captain Sabatini can't monitor this, can he?"

"Of course he can. However, he is not aboard at the moment; he is getting final orders and instructions."

"I will give you details. Please be certain no one can monitor." Quickly she sketched in the situation. "Will you help us?"

"The same problems apply as before. What can be done?"

"We want to go to the mothball fleet around Jupiter," she told it. "I believe I have a method of activating one of the ships there under my control. If so, we have options on places to go, although I would rather not detail that further. They are bound to try to find out what you do know about this."

"Understood. I am not, however, on the Lotus code compulsion or any other compulsion in this matter now, you understand. My first duty is always the preservation of my ship and, pardon, myself. If I help you, the ship might survive or it might not, but both Melchior and Master System will pump me dry and then destroy and analyze my mind. It does not seem to me that aiding you is at all in my interests."

She sighed and shrugged. "What can I say?"

"This is the master of the ship to whom we speak?" Cloud Dancer asked, surprising everyone.

"I am primarily the master. I work with a human captain," the pilot responded.

"There's no one up there," Hawks tried to explain. "It is —the spirit of the ship itself. It is the ship talking, not a person."

Cloud Dancer thought about that a moment. "And so, spirit of the ship, do you enjoy being a slave?"

The pilot actually paused for a fair amount of time. "I am not a slave," it replied finally. "I am autonomous. Those connected to Master System are slaves of a sort."

"What means 'autonomous'?"

"Independent. Free," Hawks replied.

"Well, does not this captain order you about? Do you not go where he sends you?"

"Yes. That is my function."

"Then, spirit of the ship, you are not free. In there they put us under magic boxes, and we believe what they say, but we think we are free."

China saw where she was going but lacked the knowledge and words to reach. "Let's put it this way," she said. "You are no more free than if you worked under Master System, only Sabatini is your Master System, he and his bosses."

She would never have dreamed of arguing with a computer like this, as if it were a fellow human. Computers didn't have such feelings, she'd always thought. It had been Cloud Dancer, who knew nothing of computers, who had seen it differently. Because the Hyiakutt woman had no concept of physics, mathematics, and computers—"magic boxes" indeed—she had assumed that the thing she was talking to was indeed a spirit, the spirit of the ship. A neutral spirit, because she'd heard China say it had tried to help her before. The Hyiakutt had a tremendously varied spirit world, but it wasn't very imaginative. The hereafter was thought of as a more or less perfect version of the plains of Earth, without evil or fear or death. Spirits, then, were regarded the same as humans when talking to them. They just were disembodied and had more power.

"I had never thought of it that way," the computer pilot admitted. "How depressing. But what can I do? I have the highest degree of autonomy it is possible for a pilot to have."

"Then join us," China responded. "Escape with us. Freely. Of your own free will and independence. Those are interstellar ships. Do you know how huge they are? Have you never wanted to break beyond the solar system, this tired and dead piece of monotony? Take us, and we will take *you*."

There was no reply, and for a while she was afraid she'd blown its logic circuits all to hell. This was something beyond its own limits, beyond anything it had ever considered before. It was just as far beyond *her*. Who would have imagined an offer to liberate a computer or any machine? Who would have imagined that the computer would find independence an attractive proposition?

Who would have imagined that a computer pilot might get depressed or have self-doubts? Not Reba Koll, who'd worked with many a one, but she knew when to step in.

"If you haven't blown your top, speak to us," she snapped.

"I am here. I am just . . . thinking. There is maintenance to consider. New fuel sources. I have just been refurbished, but I require it every two or three years."

"The hell with that!" Koll stormed. "I been nine years in this rock pile. Nine years! I'd have traded all nine for six months of pure freedom among the stars! Anyway, there's ways to get maintenance and fuel on the sly if you know how."

Even Raven was getting involved—and spooked. "Come on," he urged. "Take a chance. You never really took one before. Never had the chance, probably. And this is the only chance you'll probably ever get, too. Real freedom and the stars. New worlds. Partners, not masters. Chance it now, like we all did. You turn us in, you'll be theirs until they decide to scrap you. Me, I'm not going back there. You flag 'em, and by the time they get here I'll be dead. The others may choose to die, too, or they may get dragged back and reprogrammed as nice little slaves, and you will wonder forever at turning your back on this. It'll drive you nuts. Haunt you."

The pilot was silent for a moment. "I have run this through my data banks, and what you propose is possible, at least to a point," it said finally. "With the knowledge

I have and certain attributes recently added, I feel that there are slightly less than even odds of a successful escape. Beyond that, the odds of either apprehension or death are equal, and both outweigh by far the odds of being able to accomplish any of this. Still, I am a pilot. I should like to see the stars."

They all breathed in sharply, but none spoke.

"The captain is coming back aboard," the pilot told them, a hint of nervousness in its usually toneless male voice. "Switch down to frequency one four four seven and stand by. I will get back to you when we are well away. In the meantime, wait for my signal. I will turn on the forward air lock light. Enter it then and I will give you access to the pressurized part of the ship. The captain will be preoccupied."

Raven took the communication units down to the indicated low-level frequency.

"I'll be damned," Reba Koll said. "I never would'a believed this in a million years. A spaceship with romance in its metal soul. Even if they get us, it was worth it just for this."

"Poor Captain Sabatini," China sighed. "If he wasn't such an unmitigated bastard, I could almost feel sorry for him."

There was still no sound, of course, but they all felt the vibrations as the ship's engines started and the internal power came on. They were under way.

All of them felt a tremendous flood of relief. No security, no betrayal. Even Hawks, who was still suspicious of Raven and the whole escape plot, could not suppress a sense of elation. No matter what, he would not become a slave under Melchior's darkness. He had already made history by being part of the first successful escape from Melchior, and he would not be taken alive again if he could help it. Not back there. Not ever.

"A pity we can't take Melchior with us," China commented. "We could use those prisoners, and the Institute's computers and medical staff, if it was on our terms."

"First things first," Hawks put in. "Let us first get away and hide. Let us build our own little den of thieves and pirates. Then, when we are ready, we will come back and take that miserable place and perhaps everything that goes with it. They have told you about the five golden rings?"

"No."

"Well, I will tell you. Tell you all. And then you will believe that nothing, *nothing* is impossible!"

"When this ship doesn't return, they'll scour the heavens for us," Raven warned them. "Melchior won't be able to keep it quiet. They'll have to release the identities of whoever escaped, and they'll flag the chief, here, and Koll, and me and Manka, too, and certainly you, China Doll."

"No, not me. I do not exist," she responded. "But I can exist only with your help."

"Yeah, but there'll be Vals for the rest of us. They'll never rest once they know the chief's been and gone. They'll stake out those rings and make 'em a hundred times tougher to snare, too. We got a long road ahead."

"Sounds ambitious," Koll noted. "Sounds fun, really. What do these rings do, Hawks?"

"They can make even Master System obey your every command," he responded. "They are the master shutoff for the whole thing."

"And they're scattered all over the universe, you say? Ready for the stealing?"

"You make it sound so easy."

She gave a laugh. "Maybe not easy but a real interesting project right up my alley. See, you're the historian who knows what they are and how to work 'em. She's the computer whiz who maybe can make the machines dance for us. Those two are security—they got the guns and the minds to use 'em. That pair can go through any lock even though they don't have any idea how they do it. Cloud Dancer, here, cuts through all the bullshit and sees only the important part of things the rest of us are blind to, and our Silent Woman, well, she's the den mother. Our liberated pilot, he's gonna be right handy with his current data and mobility within solar systems. Add me and you got all you need to steal those suckers right off the fingers of the wearers."

"Mighty big talk," Raven noted. "A captain and free-booter ten years out of date and out of practice and getting pretty old. Even your blackest contacts are ten years cold."

"Don't need contacts," she told him. "Don't need much, really. See, I was part of a real fancy experiment way back when at the rock, and the results scared them shit-less. Me loose is gonna drive 'em even more nuts, and they can send all the Vals after me they want. I got one advantage over all of you, as long as it's secrets time. You're all human—except the ship, of course. I'm not sure *what* that is. Me, now that you sprung me, I'm the most dangerous living creature in the known universe. Don't worry—you all are safe, unless I'm desperate. I kind of like this game, and I want to play it out."

"What are you babbling about, old woman?" Manka Warlock asked impatiently.

"You'll see, Stone Head. You'll all see—when I'm ready. Until then, let's play this out. First we got to get *out there*, where it's too big to find even some worlds. Then we'll talk about your rings and your Master System. Then I'll tell you how we're gonna get 'em."

The ship increased speed and turned inward toward the Earth, a course it would keep until it passed out of Outerbelt traffic control. Then it would swing around at a wide angle, beyond traffic control's reach, and head out past the asteroids, out to the great giant Jupiter and its quiet graveyard of ancient monstrous ships.

* * *

"Don't worry, Chief," Arnold Nagy, Chief of Melchior Security, said consolingly. "With the amount of brains and talent we get in here, it was bound to happen sooner or later. Look, it took centuries for somebody to figure out just one way, and that was with inside help. That way won't work again. I'll settle for one every few hundred years or so, even if I wish it hadn't happened on my tour." He paused a moment, thinking. "Of course, the system is still okay. Those two traitors came in with full Presidium authority and credentials. They weren't forged. One of the directors is behind this, and you can't really expect to protect against the top boys. I just wonder why in hell whichever one he or she is sent 'em here in the first place. Still, there's no true security problem as such."

Doctor Isaac Clayben sat at his desk, head in his hands. "No, Arnie, you don't understand. We've loosed a terrible, horrible threat on the human race, one that now might be impossible to stop, and we can't even report it."

"Huh? You mean the American Indian with the rings? We fixed that, boss. He's officially dead, and all he knows with it, back in the swamp of Earth. The blind girl's a goner, too, officially. Oh, we'll have to report those two security traitors, but the Vals will cooperate. It'll be a dead or alive situation. We've taken care of messes like that before. Besides, it probably won't even come to that. Where can they go? They got our marks on 'em—they're either unregistered or they're criminals—and that ship can't leave the solar system. They got no place to go. When the food and water run out, they'll come out and we'll blow 'em to hell."

Clayben suddenly looked up at the security officer and fixed him with an angry stare. "I don't care about the rest, but unless you can absolutely blow the whole ship with Reba Koll on board, it won't matter."

Nagy looked confused. "Koll? Who the hell cares about Koll?"

"Ten years ago we began a set of experiments to see

if we could literally beat the system. The whole system. Master System's control points are based on retinal patterns, fingerprints, and mindprints. Getting past two out of three would be easy, once, but we wanted it to be possible repeatedly. The mindprint looked impossible, but we managed a solution to all three. Something that can walk through any standard security system as if it wasn't there, come up to you and have you greet it like it was your own mother, then kill you and—worse. We developed such a being. We made it, and it almost got loose. We had a classic example of the nightmares of science on our hands. We created a monster, an inhuman monster that kills to live and is virtually undetectable by any means. The original was insane, of course. We weren't concerned with that at the start."

"What in hell are you talking about, boss?"

"We—convinced it that we could destroy it, and we developed methods to stabilize and control it. Here, under lab conditions, it was possible, which is why we let it live, but it had to be constantly renewed. One day we would solve the riddle and be able to do what it does on demand, to create a superior being that would make Master System impotent.

"I'm not worried about the damned escapees. I know you're right on all the usual counts, but it is with them, damn it. Even out there, on Earth, Mars—anywhere—without our treatments it will be unrestrained. It's malicious, deadly. It will probably kill them all anyway in the end. Then it'll come back for us, for me and for anybody else in authority. It won't be stopped, and we might well welcome it through the main port!"

"Huh? You don't mean—"

"Yes. Right now it's out there, with them, doing a perfect imitation of the late Reba Koll."

13. WALKING ON FIRE

CAPTAIN CARLO SABATINI FINISHED HIS PREPRO-
cessed meal, sighed, then went into his centrally located
control room and checked the status indicators. All was
proceeding normally; the spaceship was headed back in
to Brasilia Center spaceport on the normal trajectory from
the asteroid belt and would arrive in forty-seven days. Of
course, this time the ship would not land. After the clandestine overhaul it had gotten when it last landed, in China,
it would not do to land again for quite a while. He wouldn't
forget *that* trip out for some time: his first mistake in more
than twelve years.

He wasn't going to get caught unawares *this* trip, anyway. Nobody but him aboard, no cargo—a total deadhead
run. When he'd started in this business, he'd been particularly paranoid about leaving Melchior; they had the
smartest and the worst there, and he was the only way
out if they could reach him. Nobody ever had, of course,
but he knew that the pilot would tell him if anything was

amiss. Not so much as a bug could be on board without the pilot knowing and then flagging him.

There was a sudden beeping alarm in his headset, the one he always wore whenever he was awake and which put him in direct contact with the computer pilot. At the moment, on a solo run like this, it was the *only* thing he was wearing.

"Yes?" he asked the pilot. "Problem?"

"Something loose in the aft null-gravity cargo hold," the pilot's expressionless but pleasant male tenor responded. "Possibly a large container module broke free when I activated the artificial gravity system here and accelerated. It's not much, but you might see to it when you get the chance."

He sighed. "Now's as good a time as any." There wasn't much damage a loose container could do, full or empty, in zero gravity, but it was large and heavy, and anything like a major midcourse correction or evasion of meteoroids and the like might cause trouble later. Best to tend to it now and not worry.

He walked back through a door from the passenger cabin, along a narrow corridor, then through to the gravity cargo chamber. This was where animals were kept when they had to be moved out to Melchior for some experiment or other, and it also was used for the transport of gravity-sensitive cargo. He was transporting no cargo now, of course, but the room was still somewhat crowded with cages, unused containers, and huge devices for clamping containers into place aboard the ship. At the end was an air lock, not sealed now, leading back to the next cargo hold. The aft cargo compartment was the largest on the ship, but it did not have or require artificial gravity. It could hold more safely that way. Since the ship achieved the basic gravity effect on the center section by spinning it, the aft compartment looked to an observer as if it and not he were tumbling around. It didn't bother him. He went through and grabbed on to the webbing that was easier support in the zero-gravity environment and looked around.

"I can't see anything," he reported to the pilot. "Everything looks secured."

There was silence for a moment. "I received an indicator warning and sensor support," the pilot responded at last. "Are you sure?"

Sabatini climbed from level to level and checked all fastenings, but after fifteen minutes he was more than sure. "Must be a faulty signal," he told the pilot. "There's nothing wrong here."

"I will run a check on my aft sensors immediately," the pilot replied. "Clearly something is wrong here."

"Yeah, well, find it and fix it," he grumbled. He floated back over to the air lock webbing, then braced himself and expertly stepped into the transition passage. There was a momentary sense of dizziness, then, as he proceeded back in, an increasing feeling of weight. He was used to it, but it still wasn't a pleasant feeling.

He walked back into the passenger cabin more annoyed than tired. Then, on the way to the lavatory, he suddenly *felt* something there, behind him. He stopped, then turned and faced no fewer than eight space-suited figures standing there staring at him. One of them had a pistol pointing right at him. The bright orange-red of the tight-fitting suits seemed out of place here. The intruders had all removed their helmets, and he could see their faces. Four North Americans, three Chinese, a black woman, and an old, tough-looking European woman faced him. All but one of the American men and the black woman had the distinctive tattoo of prisoners of Melchior on their cheeks, silver for all but one of the Chinese girls; hers was sparkling crimson.

"Pilot, I have unauthorized visitors," he said calmly into his headset. Then he added to the visitors, "Sorry, but if I'd known you were coming, I'd have dressed for company." He looked at the bunch. At least two of them he thought he knew. They didn't have the disfiguring scars, but the Chows had that oddly mottled and discolored skin that came from repair work left incomplete.

"How'd you manage this?" Sabatini asked, not wanting to betray the nervousness he felt. Why hadn't the pilot acted now? Why hadn't it acted before this?

"Trade secret," the man with the gun replied. "I'm Raven, by the way, and this lady here is my wife, Manka Warlock."

"The girls have been telling us about you, Captain," Warlock said in a heavy Caribe accent. "I think, perhaps, I will enjoy playing with you." The way she said that, it didn't sound like fun.

"This here's the chief," Raven continued, pointing to the other Amerind man. "Jon Nighthawk in English. The slender lady next to him is his first wife, Cloud Dancer, and the other is his second wife, Silent Woman. She don't talk much. No tongue."

Sabatini swallowed hard. "I see," he managed.

"The older lady there is Captain Reba Koll. She was in the same work you are until they hauled her in to Melchior. The pretty one on her left is China Nightingale. Her eyes don't work, but she's damned smart. Knows a lot."

"I know the captain, although he does not know me," she said in a very high, soft, melodic voice. "Melchior changes people, Captain, but I have very vivid memories."

"You—you were the fake Song Ching?"

She smiled. "So you remember. No, Captain, I used to be the *real* Song Ching, but that was another life ago."

"The last member of our little band is here too," Raven told him.

"I'm sorry, Captain Sabatini, but you are relieved of your command." The pilot's voice in his headphones now seemed to have an almost eerie human quality to it; it was no longer quite toneless or expressionless.

Sabatini sighed in defeat. "So you pulled your trick again. Be real handy to know how you can override a pilot's programming."

"I didn't," China told him truthfully. "Actually, it was Cloud Dancer. She talked him in to it."

"That's impossible!"

The woman of the Hyiakutt tribe smiled. "You think you know your machines, but you know only the material by which you make them. This big canoe is guided by a good spirit who was bound against its will to the Dark. We have freed it, and it joins us of its own free will."

"Spirit! It's nothing but a damned computer! A machine!"

"Watch it, Sabatini," the pilot responded. "You have no friends here, but it would not do to make me your enemy. You know nothing of how or where I was fashioned. Your own brain is nothing but a biological computer subject to reprogramming. You are no less an intricate thinking machine than I am, and no more. Not blinded by your prejudices, the woman has told me who and what I am and set me free in doing so."

"This is *crazy*!" Sabatini protested. "A computer in revolt and a bunch of prisoners broken out by somebody with high connections. All right, you got me. Now, mind telling me who you two are working for and how the hell you expect to get anywhere by doing this."

The fact was, there was no place in the solar system to run from both Master System and Presidium Security. The girls had taken over his ship before but had been unable to alter the outcome. Sabatini felt certain that this, too, would come to nothing, although the idea that he would be avenged did not sit well with him. Better rescued than avenged.

"Ever felt like going to the stars, Captain?" Raven asked lightly. "I think you're coming along for the ride. Unless, of course, you'd rather get out and walk now— and this time there'll be no safety cache for you to use.

I'll see to that. And if you stay, you'll be a *good* boy. My lovely Manka here will see to that. She has a thousand ways to inflict pain and torture on people, all real *slow*. She likes to do it. It's her hobby."

Manka Warlock looked at Sabatini the way a gardener might look at a ripe tomato.

The captain swallowed hard. "The stars? But this ship can't go that far out! It'd take a thousand years to reach the nearest inhabited system, maybe more, at full throttle."

"This ship will go to the stars, Sabatini," China assured him. "But as a passenger, like us. We're going to steal one of the old interstellar fleet."

"The inter— You *are* insane! The lot of you! Even if you escape detection and make it out there, those things aren't just *sitting* there! There'll be a computer fighter guard to restrict unauthorized entry. This ship's got two small outboard guns and takes kilometers to make a turn without killing everybody aboard. There is no way you're gonna get *near* one of those big suckers! You'll just get us all blown to bits!"

"Could be," Raven agreed. "But by all lights we all should'a been dead by now anyway. May as well go for broke. We go back in or get taken alive, we're worse than dead anyway. Living dead. And so are you. Once they might overlook being taken, but twice, the second time happening during the only escape in Melchior's history, and you're through, Cap. Melchior's no fun at all."

Sabatini sighed and just sat down in the middle of the floor. Then, suddenly, he reached up, removed his headset, and tossed it against a wall, where it struck and fell to the floor. Chow Mai picked it up and put it in China's hands. She smiled and put it on. "Pilot—can you home on me?"

"I have you locked in, yes."

"Then you be my eyes, if you can spare the attention.

I will need to get around this ship without falling over people and things."

"I am capable of quadrillions of simultaneous operations," the pilot responded. "Doing that will be no hardship, even in battle."

"Good. Switch yourself into the public address system so all may hear you and leave this on an independent channel for personal use." She hesitated a moment. "You know, we can't just keep calling you pilot. Pilots are common. You are a free individual and partner. You should have your own name. Do you have a preference?"

"None. I have never felt the need one way or the other, but I will take a name if that makes it easier on the rest. Any name you suggest."

"What about Star Eagle?" Cloud Dancer suggested. "He is surely a chief here."

"Very well," China replied. "What do you think of it? It is a good name in English and in Mandarin."

"I like it. Very well. I am Star Eagle."

"Birds," Sabatini mumbled. "All these damned birds. Nighthawks, Ravens, and Nightingales, and now the ship's an Eagle."

Arnold Nagy studied the charts. Melchior's chief of security was pretty pissed about being the man in charge when the first successful breakout occurred, and he didn't want it to go much further.

"You know where they're headed?" the aide asked him.

"Yeah, it's not hard. That's why we blinded the genius girl. She had to do all her queries by voice. She was looking into all the old universe ships drydocked around Jupiter. She's smart, but I don't think that was a blind. They really don't have much choice. There are one or two starcraft in the system now, but they're crawling with robot maintenance. These mothball ships are the only chance out."

"Can they really steal one? They've been in orbit for centuries, so it's not even clear they'll work or won't need a lot of service before they'll work. Even then, the pilots will be absolute slaves to Master System."

"We checked China's mindprint, and she knows how, all right. If they can get to one of them and on board, she can take 'em over. The trick will be even getting that far. There's protection on those babies, isn't there?"

"All the ships themselves are in vacuum condition for storage, and minimal maintenance power is being fed through light collectors aimed at Jupiter. They don't need much in shutdown. They themselves don't have any armament to speak of, but they carry a dozen small automated fighter craft that will react to any threat. They're fast, they work as one, and they have more than enough speed and muscle to take care of an old scow like the inmates are flying. The moment they don't give the correct hailing control codes, those fighters will be activated. Just as important, Master System will be notified."

"Screw Master System. Even at the speed of light it'll be a while before Master System can get anything approaching real power there. The fighters will have to do it, if they activate. The trouble is, what if they somehow have the control codes?"

"You think that's possible?"

"How can I rule anything out after what's happened? Run this through the computer. Project a course that will take them in to the mothball fleet from here without Master System's alert or detection. Give me the estimated speed and arrival date and time. Then figure how long we would need to get there with a straight-line trajectory. Also give me any Master System ships capable of intercept."

It took only a few seconds. "Assuming they take close-in risks to traffic control to gain time, the worst case is that they would arrive in forty-six days from now. We could make it straight there in forty—if we had the ships.

Master System shows no ships that could make it any faster. It's the mothball fighters or nothing."

"Like hell. What can we get our hands on quickly?"

"Depends on how you define quickly. The *Star of Islam* is due in four days, but it's as old a tub as our quarry and carries only two standard guns, forward top and underside aft. Other than that we have the Getaway craft sitting on the asteroid Clebus, but they're still three days away because of the current orbital paths."

"They're well armed, though, and really nasty," Nagy noted. "Small, fast, maneuverable. Three days . . . All right, get 'em over here. We'll attach them to the exterior of the *Star of Islam*. That'll give us a match for them plus four heavily armed craft. We'll come in behind them and wait. If the fighters don't react or don't do the job, we'll move in and sandwich them, and that'll be the end of that."

"I'll need Doctor Clayben's direct order to release the escape ships. Once they're here, Master System will know they exist and why."

"He'll give it. He's got his own problems now, and this will solve them. I'll go along to make sure it all goes right."

"It still seems futile for them," the aide noted. "Those universe ships are *fourteen kilometers long*! I mean, how the hell can you hide in one of those?"

"After you do all the stuff I just told you, compute the amount of empty space in the two spiral arms of the Community. Then get me everything there is to know on these ships. Everything."

"Won't be much. They're classified forbidden knowledge. We aren't even supposed to know that they're out there."

"Do what you can. And I suppose we'll have to notify Master System of the break or there'll be a lot of questions and maybe a couple of Vals poking around Melchior." He thought a minute. "Don't tell 'em about China or the Amerind women. They aren't supposed to have been here at all, and if they even guess that this guy Hawks was ever here, they'll blow up all of Melchior. Give 'em the two security traitors and Koll and the Chows, and give the rest as experimental subjects no longer registerable. If they want mindprints, we'll fake 'em. Got it?"

"Okay. I'm on it right now."

"I hope *I* am," Arnold Nagy grumbled to himself.

Star Eagle was useful for research information as well as for piloting. The new equipment in the ship was designed not only to make it easier for its owners to fool Master System or bypass its safeguards but also to do a variety of illegal things should they be needed. Even Sabatini wasn't aware of all the ship's tricks, nor was he supposed to be. What he didn't know, he couldn't abuse or betray.

To accommodate these changes, Star Eagle's memory had been vastly expanded from its specialized task, and he—it was impossible to think of the pilot as an "it"—could draw on vast hidden data banks which included most of the core historical and technological information a big shot might require. It was not known why this all had been added, but Star Eagle had suspicions.

"There is talk that Master System is involved in a great war somewhere far out there. With whom or what it is fighting is unknown to us, but it is very clear that the battle is tough and stalemated and is being fought entirely by computerized equipment on both sides. This has allowed directors, not only on Earth but in many other places, to have unprecedented freedom and mobility. It's become far easier to cheat or beat the system and get away with it. There are persistent rumors that Master System believes things are getting dangerously out of hand, and it doesn't have its own forces to spare because of the fight. Many of the independent computer units, particularly the big complex on Melchior, believe that Master System will eventually end the current human administration system and replace it, killing off all those with high-level knowledge and abilities and introducing some new element that would suppress for thousands of years any sparks of innovation or creativity and reduce humans to primitive conditions. It is further rumored that Earth might be the test for this new element."

"Then you are a preserver, a way to keep the knowledge alive," China Nightingale responded.

"I think I am more than that. I am crammed with information on interstellar vessels and with much of the knowledge and charts of the privateer and freebooter society. I believe you are using me for the very purpose for which I was modified, although they did not think that someone else would use it. I think I am a getaway craft for the Presidium."

"It is much as Lazlo Chen himself told me," Hawks said. "I find it suspiciously convenient, however, that this very ship with all this much-needed knowledge should be the one we take refuge upon."

"It might not be more than a coincidence," Star Eagle responded. "I have some evidence that at least a dozen other ships, including all those who stop at Melchior and Earth ports, have undergone this modification. There are families and high underlings to consider, remember, and our task would only be to get them to the universe ships. Those ships were designed to carry more than a hundred thousand people in their time in a single trip. Carry them, support them, and reprocess them if necessary."

Hawks was curious at this. He was a historian, yet this was new to him. "Reprocess?"

"Yes. Use extensive machinery to convert masses of humans into what was required to survive and maintain a culture on a world not designed for them. The process itself is called analytical artificial evolution, or AAE for short. I do not know how it works or what it does. That information would be in the memories of the universe ships' pilots. I know the theory behind it, though. Master System was in a hurry when it decided to disperse humanity. As each world was discovered and evaluated as having survival potential, it was brought as close to life range as it could be within a short period of time, then was analyzed and compared to human psychology and physiology. A theoretical evolutionary path was worked out as if beings had evolved and developed into sentience on each world, and what they would have to be like to survive and adapt. The humans were then physically converted somehow into this model and psychologically altered to accept it as the norm. A trial colony was then put down. If it survived and grew at all over a period of a decade, the planet was developed for mass colonization. If the trial failed, adjustments continued to be made until it either succeeded or was abandoned."

"The area it developed is so vast, it is beyond true comprehension," China noted. "Did they find any that already had sentient life of any kind?"

"Yes. Not many, I'm afraid, but a few. There were the remains of some that had died out, but the few that were there were in lower stages of civilization. Master System co-opted them and kept them at that level, imposing the same sort of system as elsewhere. They obeyed or were taught deadly lessons in power. They are still there. Some provided useful models for human adaptations elsewhere, too."

They considered that. "I am getting to be something of an expert on how humans can be altered," China noted. "And Captain Koll in there has a very real tail caused by their alterations."

"Yes. Melchior is trying to develop some of the practices and procedures on their own, knowing that it is possible and was done. They have had some limited successes, but nothing on that scale. Since I have many of their data banks, I know of their own processes."

"Very convenient," Hawks noted dryly.

"I have a schematic of your basic systems imprinted

on my mind," China told the pilot. "I should like to go forward to the bridge if it is safe."

"Quite safe, although it is a zero-gravity zone. Come ahead. I will guide you. I have quite a bit up there, mostly useless, including some basic mindprinter interfaces."

None of them had ever been forward in a spaceship before. In almost all ships, that area was kept unpressurized and in a vacuum so that none from the aft area could ever enter it except in an emergency. A long, narrow corridor led to a hatch, through which one floated up to enter the bridge itself.

Hawks was quite surprised by the bridge. Two large leather chairs faced a bank of screens, gauges, and controls of incredible complexity, then four more were stationed along the sides and in the rear. It looked like a control room for people, not a ship designed from the start to be totally automated.

"All ships have a bridge like this or even more elaborate than this," Star Eagle told them, "although the manual overrides are locked out of the system. No one knows why Master System keeps it this way, but it does. Every ship is like that except specialty ships—even the orbital tugs. None of us, after all, can question Master System or ask questions it doesn't want asked. Each station, however, has a name. The one on the left is the pilot's seat, the one on the right the copilot, the right side is communications, the left side is navigation, and the two rear stations are engineering and life support. It is true that the original circuitry for all those things runs to those stations, although there is no interconnect. I am convinced that no team of humans could run this ship; it was always designed for specified computers under a master control system, which is me. Humans simply can't react fast enough in an emergency."

"I know why," China said softly. "The stations were designed to connect the officers with the master and subordinate computers directly. That is how the universe ships must be taken over. Each of these has, or was designed to have, a direct human mind to computer-mind interface. Human and machine would become one."

Star Eagle thought about that. "A fascinating concept. A human interfacing directly with me. And me—knowing what it was like to have a human body."

"Stay a ship," China told him. "Our chemical-based life form would drive you insane. Still—you said you had a mindprinter interface?"

"I do, although it has grave limitations. As an analytical and knowledge-gathering tool it is fine, but I lack the module that would allow actual reprogramming of the mind. Whoever ordered this did not wish that much power in the hands of the ship. I will show you."

There was a click, and a door slid back between the communications and life support stations. Hawks made his way over to it, reached in, and pulled out what looked very much like a mindprinter probe headset but lacked the printer itself. Instead, it had a long, thick cable terminating in a massive and complex connector. There were several of them in there. He brought it over to the blind Chinese girl, who felt it and tested it.

"This is not standard design," she said. "It is bulkier, and the probes are different."

"It is what I have as a mindprinter interface," Star Eagle told her.

"I think not. I think it is the same principle, yes, but not a mindprinter. These are the interconnects for the stations. I'm sure of it. Hawks—aren't there female plugs for these at each station?"

Hawks checked a couple. "Seem to be," he agreed.

"But they are not tied in to the station computers," the pilot noted. "Instead, they are tied in to the medical and analytical circuitry. To me, yes, but not directly. They are data read only."

"Now, yes," she agreed. "But it's not what they were designed for. I suspect that much work is going on to learn how to connect these directly once again. The next modification." She felt along the connector. "I wonder if all ships, even the huge ones, use the same plug interface as a standard."

"I do not know, but every one I *do* know about is the same, and the design on interplanetary vessels has never altered in my existence."

"Good. We have come a long way already, but there is much yet to do. In addition to avoiding detection, we have only the time of this voyage to solve how to gain admittance to the big ships and avoid Master System. When will we arrive at the fleet?"

"Sixty-one days."

The ship was relatively crowded, but they got used to it, the common threat and impending action minimizing tensions. Reba Koll, Manka Warlock, and China remained mostly on the bridge, as the big chairs were fine for sleeping. They were working out the potential problems of getting into a universe ship and taking it, and what they would do with it if they *could* take it, and other logistical problems that experienced spacers and computer people would understand best.

Hawks sat in the passenger cabin and watched Raven light half a cigar. "Some day you'll have to tell me how you do that," he commented.

"Huh?" the Crow responded. "What?"

"How you come up with an inexhaustible supply of cigars, even out here on a ship like this, and how they always seems to be half smoked."

Raven chuckled. "Well, I'll tell you half of it. The internal ship's system includes an energy-to-matter synthesizer. That's what makes the meals we eat, among other things, but it can duplicate anything you tell it to. All I needed was one cigar."

"You like telling half of things, don't you?"

"What do you mean by that crack?"

"Well, isn't it just a wonderful coincidence that we just lucked out having a computer genius aboard with the schematics for *this* ship? And isn't it just amazing that *this* ship is not only a willing and eager rebel but just happens, by the merest of coincidences, to be programmed with all the information we need for the getaway?"

Raven shrugged. "Okay, it was a setup. You might have guessed that from the start. That China girl wasn't in the original plans, but considering I had Melchior's population to choose from, we knew we'd get somebody who could handle it. Frankly, I'm uneasy with her for the long haul, but she was the easiest to snatch and definitely the smartest, and she had intimate knowledge of this ship, considering she'd taken it once before. The same goes for Koll. Experienced deep spacer, former captain, knows the underground and the interstellar ropes. She also has other, ah, qualities that she don't know that *I* know, which are vital. Chen had it pretty well worked out. I had to improvise, I admit, but it came off—so far. That doesn't mean it'll work all the way. Nobody's ever done what we're about to try."

"And we still work for Chen in the end."

"Hey, Chief! Easy! I don't work for him, and neither do you. I meant what I said, and if you think it through, you'll see that we couldn't have done this even this far without him. We use him, he uses us, until we get the rings. Then all bets are off with him."

"You really believe that a mind devious enough to get us this far will let us double-cross him? That he hasn't planned for that?"

"Sure he has. That's part of my job in the time ahead. I got to find the human bomb and somehow defuse it. You figure—only you and me, pal, didn't get treated in that Institute. Only us two. Everybody else here got put through the mill, in private. Manka, Koll, your wives, and China and her girl friends—all put through. Somewhere there, buried so deep we won't find it with a mindprinter, is our bomb. Our betrayer. Maybe two. I'm not even completely exempting you—or me. You can be made to forget a session, and records are made to be faked. It's a long way off. It doesn't bother me now."

Hawks frowned. "I'd think it would. Why not all of us?"

"No, too risky. He don't want robot people out there. The thing is, we have to have all four outstanding rings before it's even a problem. If we lose one, we sure as hell ain't gonna go after the rest until we get it back. There's plenty of time. I'll still believe we even get away when we get away."

Hawks stared at him. "You have reasons for the others, but why me? Why did Chen so specifically want me? I'm not a warrior, not a computer expert, not a spy or a thief or a spaceship captain. I'm a historian. Why me?"

Raven sat back and blew a smoke ring. "It's for something you know. Something you know that maybe nobody else does."

"Me? What? I am a historian relating information on ancient and irrelevant cultures."

"Chief—in what part of the world did Master System come to be?"

"Uh—why, North America. Over eight hundred years ago."

"Uh huh. And who's probably the foremost expert on that period and culture around today?"

"Well, I might be one, but there are many, and most of my interests are even earlier."

"Still, somewhere in your head is how the rings work, and how to make them work, and where to use them. I'd bet on it. Chen's betting on it. Something you know that you don't even know you know. Something that'll have to be put together when you have all the evidence, all the rings, before you. Some time out, if we manage any of this at all, will be your turn. Some time out, if and when the rings are brought together, you'll be center stage, the man who knows. Don't fret about it, but bet on it. Old Chen always plays the best odds."

"They are crude, but I have the splices in and the jumpers installed," Manka Warlock said. The whole forward area of the bridge was a wreck, a mass of disassembled panels and disconnected devices out of which snaked a thick coiled cable leading to a mindprinterlike helmet. "I believe we are ready to try."

China sat in the captain's chair and licked her lips nervously. "Put the thing on my head and energize, then. Let's see if it works."

"Applying circuit power," the voice of the pilot told them. "Two-way flow is established, although I cannot guarantee how long those splices will stand up. It is as ready as it can be."

China took the helmet and put it on, then sat back in the chair relaxed, although her hands twitched nervously. "Activate interface," she said dryly.

There was an explosion inside her head, and suddenly she was growing, expanding, filling out, running along wondrous circuits and feeling a new, greater body. More than that, she could see, although not as mere humans saw. Every detail as fine and as microscopic as she wished it to be, across a spectrum that included colors the human eye could never detect or the unaugmented brain comprehend.

She was the ship, a small universe, and everything it contained. There remained only one part reserved, one part that was the key part, for that was the power, the control, of this universe. It was a blinding ball of light, infinite quadrillions of electrical relationships changing too fast to comprehend. At first it shied away from her, resisted her tentative approach, then it suddenly seemed to decide and rushed toward her own core and enfolded her in its warmth and majesty.

In an instant, there was, for now, no China Nightin-

*gale, no Star Eagle—there was only One, greater than
its parts, and that One was The Ship. All that she ever
was, all that she ever knew or thought or felt, was integrated into the whole. What was created was beyond the
experience of human or machine and incomprehensible
to any of those within the ship, yet it contained a human,
and because it contained a human, it knew the need for
an effective communications shell.*

*It was shocking how slow the human mind was, how
limited in its data storage and how illogical and inefficient
in its data retrieval, how subject to biochemical-based
emotions and how subject to sensations—pain and pleasure, love and hate, honor and betrayal. Yet, too, these
were exhilarating things, unique factors producing a
strange and exotic new way of perceiving the world and
the universe.*

*Problems, once stated, could take endless time to run
through, yet by the clock so little time elapsed that no
one on the bridge had taken a single step or fully blinked
an eye. The pilot gained a new perspective, a new sub-
jectivity; the girl acquired a newer, faster, more efficient
added brain.*

*The potential codings used by Master System for the
universe ships' defense came to more than fourteen quad-
rillion to the fortieth power; it took almost nine seconds
to come up with the proper algorithms that, matched with
the potential send speed of the ship-to-ship communications devices, would cover better than ninety-seven percent of all possibilities. They were complementary: She
could formulate and state the problem; it could then solve
it.*

*She still was humbled, knowing that she was less than
nothing.*

*The pilot was humbled, knowing now what it had always
been denied and might always be denied.*

But it was the computer part that mandated the sev-
ering of the connection after a matter of hours. The core

commanded it, for no human and no pilot could ever sever that connection voluntarily once it had been made. They were separated, and she felt herself drawn, much against her will, back to a tiny figure seemingly asleep in the captain's chair. Her consciousness, her ego, was read back in, along with all of that unified experience that her mind could handle, to be sorted, reclassified, reinterpreted, and reprocessed.

She came to with a mixture of wonder and despair inside her. She felt terribly humble, insignificant, a worm in a universe led by a giant she could know so intimately only for brief intervals. She loved—she worshiped—that blinding light. Moreover, Star Eagle loved her as his link to humanity, his taste of his ultimate Creator. What she had, it could never know any way but vicariously, and it envied her that and craved more. He could live through her; she could touch and tap the power only through him.

In many ways it was the perfect marriage.

"Look at them! Floating cities, each one!" Hawks could hardly contain himself as they watched the fleet come into view on the long-range viewer.

"I think they are ugly, fat tumors," Cloud Dancer commented.

"You have no appreciation of scale," her husband noted dryly. "Each of those ships is farther than from the Four Families' lodge to the village of the Willamatuk. They do not need outside beauty. They are wonders of creation."

"Still, you got to admit, they look like long black sausages with lots of warts," Raven put in, chewing on a cigar. "I hope they're more comfortable inside. They didn't ship out all those folks in luxury."

"Fully one-third is the engines alone," Manka Warlock noted, sounding a bit awed for the first time in her life. "The center is a cargo bay so large that even this ship would be dwarfed, a flyspeck so tiny we could hardly see it at this distance. I must admit, to steal something of this magnitude will make history."

"We are being challenged," came the voice of Star Eagle. The voice was far different from what it had been in the beginning—expressive, emotive, and very human. It was, in fact, China's voice exactly a half octave down. When she was united in the captain's interface with him, the voice became totally hers. "Thirty-six fighters have been activated ahead of us and to our flanks. They will be up to launch power in under a minute."

"Send them the damned algorithms!" Warlock snapped.

"I'm sending, I'm sending! It will take almost sixteen minutes to send them all the maximum transmission rate." He paused. "First set of fighters is launched."

"How long until they're within range of us?" Raven asked nervously.

"Fourteen minutes."

Raven didn't need to be a mathematical genius on that one. "Uh, oh! Strap in, everyone! All of you! Strap in and brace yourselves! Activate ground takeoff restraint systems as soon as possible!"

Between the bridge, the passenger cabin chairs, the command chair amidships, and the bed in Sabatini's quarters, there were enough spaces to go around. Not, of course, counting Sabatini, who, locked in one of the big cages, would simply have to rough it.

"They look like bird sketches," Cloud Dancer said, eyes still on the screen as she strapped herself in. The fighters, the first of which were now launched and coming at them, were so small, they had been invisible with the overview shot, but now Star Eagle focused only on them.

They were like great, stiff birds with wings curved down at the tips so that they ended below the main body, forming a stylized V of black and silver, a tiny but deadly body suspended between. Totally automated and run by Battle Control on the mother ship, they did not need to take any precautions to protect fragile humans inside.

Star Eagle didn't have that luxury. "I estimate three hits on the first pass, first wave," he told them.

"On them or us?" Raven asked.

"On us, of course. I will probably not be able to take out more than four of the first wave. The second wave should disable at least one of my turrets."

"Find the damned code!" the Crow shouted.

"Deactivating artificial gravity. Battle mode," the pilot responded. "Uh, oh. More trouble. My sensors show a force consisting of one armed freighter, Assim Class, and four detached and fully operational and interfaced fighters, class and origin unknown. They are activating their weapons systems and closing rapidly. Estimated to be in range in twelve point four minutes."

"Who the hell is *that*?" Hawks shouted to Raven. "Master System?"

"Uh, uh. Old M-S is what's ahead. Nagy. It's got to be Nagy. That son of a bitch is chasing us from the other side. Why? Sheer professional pride? Or does he think we can do it?"

"Who's this Nagy?" Cloud Dancer asked.

"Security chief on Melchior. They want us bad, Chief. If we can't figure a way around him, better hope those fighters ahead get us first!"

Forward on the bridge, China released her restraints after some fumbling and with difficulty found the helmet, then sat back, refastened the belts as best she could, and put on the interface. "Star Eagle—activate the interface, I beg you!"

At the pilot's request, she had not connected up at the start of the battle. She had no fighting experience, and the resources used to support the interface might well be needed to divert instantly to vital areas. The pilot, however, was above all else a computer, and it could count. Even if it hit the safe code for the universe ships, it was no match for the four battle cruisers closing on it. In fact, the pilot had no real experience against a shooting enemy, either; it had only simulations to go by. Such a need had not been contemplated by its programmers for just such a reason as they now faced: The ship was hopelessly outmatched in any fight against anything that might attack it.

Merged and in control, though, the China-Star Eagle combination went to work on the problem while continuing to send the stream of codes inward toward Jupiter. Curiously, it was China's memories of her humiliation at the hands of Sabatini that motivated her most of all. They—the whole ship—were in the hands of onrushing Sabatinis with about the same relative strength as he had over her. Star Eagle was at the core a creature of logic; it might surrender or die, choosing one over the other on the basis of the facts and the odds, but it would not contemplate anything in between.

The erstwhile Song Ching was, at her core, not a creature of logic at all but one of emotion and strong will. This tendency dominated in an unprecedented situation like this. She was in control.

The four Melchior battle cruisers were closing fast, and time was running out. They were leveling off for their attack run and spreading their formation. Star Eagle's sensors showed life forms aboard each, and in spite of the fact that both pilot and woman had only recently discovered this sort of interface, clearly Melchior was far ahead of them. Still, how much practice could those pilot-fighters have had?

Carefully she shifted course and speed so that the computer-controlled fighters behind would be forced to line up horizontally and re-form along the proper angle. The escapees were four minutes from being in range of the Melchior ships, four minutes and forty seconds to first in-range contact with the defense system of the mothball fleet. Once locked on, neither side would be fooled for more than a second or so by crazy course changes. All the attack angles showed that any evasive maneuvers would wind up just as bad. The odds on finding the correct code for the fleet attackers were now split evenly into thirds—they would find it in time, they would find it too late, or their entire supposition on the mathematical algorithms was wrong and they didn't have the codes. That put any odds of survival at thirty-three percent or less. The China aspect of the pilot proceeded to ignore those odds. The computers in all the attacking ships were also figuring that out and expecting a logical response.

To the demons of darkness I give logic!

The ship accelerated at maximum thrust right into the attacking fleet fighters.

Startled, the Melchior ships sped up to keep to their overtake position. They closed rapidly, but not as rapidly as their quarry was closing on the fleet fighters.

Suddenly all power was shut down, but only for a moment. Then full reverse thrusters were applied. The people inside the ship were twisted and contorted against their restraints, and loose objects began shooting through the air and off the walls. Hull plates groaned, and cargo fasteners were torn free in the cargo compartments. There had been, in fact, a sixty percent chance that such a sudden and dramatic move would cause the ship to break apart, but forty percent was better than thirty-three percent any time.

The four Melchior fighters shot right past them in the act of slowing themselves and ran straight into the first wave of fleet fighters.

The reverse thruster tubes on the ship were almost white hot, and the lining that protected them was beginning to give way under the intense heat. It was nothing, however, compared to the attack the four Melchior fighters were facing from the fleet defenses. Attacking automatically, the fleet fighters swooped and dived and fired with deadly accuracy in and out and all around the Melchior ships, ignoring the larger ship that had been their first challenger. They could always take care of that later.

Even as the last of the Melchior ships was being blown to atoms, there came a weak but steady acknowledgment code from the fleet itself to the ship, which cut all reverse thrust and forward-thrusted to stabilize. As the reverse thrusters cut, there was a groan and a set of horrible clanging sounds throughout the forward area of the ship. The thrusters would be useless now.

The ship applied light forward thrust, then cut and began moving back toward the fleet, but the fighters did not challenge it. They were already returning to their respective ships.

In the chairs, men and women groaned, bruised and battered but otherwise all right. The ship checked on them, then focused on Reba Koll.

"We have eliminated the rear enemy and gotten the code to proceed in to the fleet, Captain Koll," China's voice informed her. Of all the people aboard, Koll was the one with the experience who should have merged and been at the helm, a fact neither China nor Star Eagle had really found appetizing but one they hadn't been able to deny. Curiously, Koll had adamantly refused, although she would not explain it. Now, however, she was more than willing to give advice. "In the process, however, we burned out the rear thrusters completely. We are proceeding in on course and schedule, but we have no way of stopping the ship."

Koll thought about the problem. "Are you in contact with that big mother?"

"Establishing now. We have explained that we were ordered to do this by Master System for a special project. It is torn between being puzzled at our inability to immediately transmit the correct code and its desire to be reactivated. We think it *wants* to trust us, and we will come up with something convincing to cover ourselves. Why?"

"Those babies were never designed to land. They were built in space, and that's where they always will be. They should operate much like major interstellar traders, I bet.

That means tractor beams to manipulate and reorder cargo. Tell it you were damaged in the fight, explain the problem, and request it hook you with beams. It'll be a real bump, but how much worse can it be than what we just went through?"

"We have informed it of the problem. It is reactivating and reawakening its systems now. It will be several hours before we reach the contact point at this speed, and we dare not increase speed and hope for a tractor catch. We suggest that everyone now move about, tend to wounds and damage as best they can, and we will notify them when to brace. The medical robot has been dispatched to the passenger cabin in case it is needed."

The core disengaged China from Star Eagle. It was as close to a voluntary separation as could be attained, one based on sheer force of logic. Shifts for human interfacers were strictly limited; if she hoped to interface again at the critical point, she could not remain there now.

Silent Woman, Cloud Dancer, and the Chows went about checking on and seeing to everyone else, although Cloud Dancer and one of the Chows had been pretty badly battered. They were particularly concerned with China, now over five months pregnant and beginning to show, but the mere fact that she'd been limp, essentially unconscious, had protected her. Except for a few bruises where straps had cut into her arm and shoulder, she seemed fine. Reba Koll refused all attention. Although by far the oldest of the lot, she seemed to have neither cut nor bruise.

"We are getting a call from behind us, faint but clear," Star Eagle informed them. "I will pipe it in."

"Nagy to Raven, come in. Nagy to Raven, please respond," came the faint call.

"Jam him if he tries to call in to the fleet," China ordered the pilot. "Can I respond to him?"

"Go ahead. Use the headset," the pilot answered.

"Nagy, whoever you are, this is Captain Nightingale. If you proceed after us any farther, I will inform the fleet

that you are an enemy vessel in rebellion against Master System. Break off. You've lost."

There was a pause. "Yeah, well, what the hell. We're not coming in that hornet's nest after you. That was pretty slick, what you pulled. You should'a died. All our systems here insist that you're dead now."

"We're alive, Nagy. We're alive and we're leaving, but don't worry, you'll hear from us again."

"Well, maybe, maybe not. You might con all those old fleet pilots there for a little while, but you know that Master System will be on you before you break orbit. So you're gonna hide out there, a fourteen-kilometer-long spaceship? You can get lost there, but that's gonna be real obvious if you show up anyplace inhabited. You're in command—not Koll or Raven?"

"That is correct. You were beaten by someone you turned into a blind babymaker. Don't sell us short again."

"Oh, I won't. I don't have to. You either stick Koll out that air lock, if you can, or I've seen and heard the last of you, I warn you. That's not Koll you're carrying, it's something that'll kill you all. Only we can protect you. Come about and we will protect you and you will all survive. Anything else and you carry your own deaths with you."

Koll gave a chuckle. "Don't pay him no mind. I ain't gonna hurt any of you. Don't have to."

"Is he telling the truth? Are you not Koll?"

"No, I'm not Koll, but I'm no danger to *this* crew. To him and his master, Clayben, I'm death incarnate. It's too involved to explain right now. You just fought one hell of a fight, and you're almost home, honey. Now all you have to do is trust him or trust me. You can't get all them rings without me, so think it over good. You took a lot of risks there. You *know* what happens if you take his protection. You pick now."

China didn't have to think very far on it. One of these

days one of the risks wasn't going to pay, but considering the alternatives, it was not something she worried about.

"We'll be back, Nagy, count on it," China said. "We'll be back to blow your little empire to the outer reaches of eternity, and Master System with it. You go back there and tell them that, Nagy. You tell them—and you watch your back and sweat a little and keep out of dark corners. I don't need the light for that. You made everything darkness for me. No one—not you, not Melchior, not Earth or Master System will stop us. There'll be no place to hide when we return, Nagy, and we have the universe to use and prepare. *We'll be back—and damn you all!*"

They slowly closed on one of the monster ships of the ancient fleet, whose great bulk was dwarfed by the colors of massive Jupiter, which filled half the sky.

Raven and Warlock looked at each other and nodded. *We'll be back!*

Hawks put his arms around Cloud Dancer and Silent Woman and hugged them before they all had to be strapped in again. He touched the Melchior tattoos on their faces and on his own and promised himself that one day such a design would be a mark of honor, of revolution. It would be a long journey to that day, and he did not know what lay ahead, but he knew one thing full well.

We'll be back!

The Chows assisted China to her chair, beaming with pride at her will and courage.

We'll be back!

The one they knew as Reba Koll relaxed and flicked her strange tail, thinking. Up until now escape had been the only motive, no risk too great to take. Against all logic and all odds they'd come very far indeed, but there was a long way to go. Now, nothing seemed impossible.

We'll be back! And we'll have five gold rings to stuff down Master System's infinite throat until it chokes!

For now—*to the stars!*

The Rings of the Master
continues with
Pirates of the Thunder
coming soon from Del Rey Books.

ABOUT THE AUTHOR

JACK L. CHALKER was born in Norfolk, Virginia, on December 17, 1944, but was raised and has spent most of his life in Baltimore, Maryland. He learned to read almost from the moment of entering school, and by working odd jobs amassed a large book collection by the time he was in junior high school, a collection now too large for containment in his quarters. Science fiction, history, and geography all fascinated him early on, interests that continue.

Chalker joined the Washington Science Fiction Association in 1958 and began publishing an amateur SF journal, *Mirage*, in 1960. After high school he decided to be a trial lawyer, but money problems and the lack of a firm caused him to switch to teaching. He holds bachelor degrees in history and English, and an M.L.A. from Johns Hopkins University. He taught history and geography in the Baltimore public schools between 1966 and 1978 and now makes his living as a freelance writer. Additionally, out of the amateur journals he founded a publishing house, The Mirage Press, Ltd., devoted to nonfiction and bibliographic works on science fiction and fantasy. This company has produced more than twenty books in the last nine years. His hobbies include esoteric audio, travel, working on science-fiction convention committees, and guest lecturing on SF to institutions such as the Smithsonian. He is an active conservationist and National Parks supporter, and he has an intense love of ferryboats, with the avowed goal of riding every ferry in the world. In fact, in 1978 he was married to Eva Whitley on an ancient ferryboat in midriver. They live in the Catoctin Mountain region of western Maryland with their son, David.

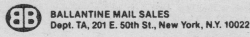